OUR UNSCRIPTED STORY

L. A. FIORE

L. A. FIORE

OUR
UNSCRIPTED
STORY

ISBN-13: 978-1984365187
ISBN-10: 1984365185

Cover Model: Miles Reza
Cover photo by Scott Hoover

Cover design by Melissa Stevens, The Illustrated Author
File creation, mobi and epub, by Melissa Stevens, The Illustrated Author
Typeset graphics, title page art and paperback and eBook formatting by Melissa Stevens, The Illustrated Author, www.theillustratedauthor.net

Editing by Editor in Heels, Trish Bacher

THE

PLAYLIST

SEPARATE LIVES...PHIL COLLINS

MAMA TOLD ME NOT TO COME...THREE DOG NIGHT

ANGELS...ROBBIE WILLIAMS

WAITING...ALICE BOMAN

HOLD ON...CHORD OVERSTREET

DANCING ON MY OWN...CALUM SCOTT

ONLY...RY X

WHEN SHE LOVED ME...SARAH MCLACHLAN

WHY CAN'T I BE YOU...THE CURE

WHAT ABOUT US...P!NK

PERFECT...ED SHEERAN

SAVE ME, SAN FRANCISCO...TRAIN

SEPARATE WAYS...JOURNEY

IT'S ALL COMING BACK TO ME NOW...CELINE DION

FOR NIKKI LEVY

PART ONE

THE

JOIN THE WRITING CLUB TO FIND OUT.

INSIDE

...X?

LOST

CAT

SEE ALEXIS OWENS IN WRITING CLUB TO CLAIM.

Love is just a word until someone comes along and gives it meaning.
– Paulo Coelho

PROLOGUE

1982

"Mama."

Sade smiled watching her daughter. She was only two, but sometimes she seemed older.

"Mama, mama." Alexis clapped, her little teeth appearing as she smiled.

"We're going to see Daddy."

"Daddy! Daddy!" Alexis' cheeks turned red, her brown eyes brightened with excitement. She was a total Daddy's girl. A lesser person might feel a pang of jealousy over the bond shared between her husband and daughter, but she loved it. Loved that their daughter brought her hard ass husband to his knees.

She swooped her daughter into her arms, setting off the giggles, and grabbed her purse. Rowdy was at the door, like he'd been for the last four months. They weren't allowed to go anywhere without an escort. She didn't know the details; it was safer for her and Alexis to be in the dark. It wasn't ideal, but she loved her husband, he was crazy about her, and they adored their daughter. They made it work.

She locked up; Rowdy walked them to the car.

"Let's strap you in, sweetie."

Alexis threw her arms over her head; it was her way of helping.

"You're Mommy's little helper."

Alexis gave her that toothy smile and her heart swelled. She could watch her daughter for hours, the wonder of her. How she worked things out, how she found interest in everything. She was a part of her, a part of her husband, the best parts.

"Mommy loves you."

She puckered her lips. Sade laughed before leaning in and pressing a kiss on that pucker.

Tires squealed around the corner. Sade's head snapped in the direction of the car, even as she shielded her baby with her body. Rowdy had already pulled his gun. Several pops rented the air, Rowdy went down, several more and Sade felt the bullets tearing through her. Adrenaline kept her from feeling the pain, her only thought was protecting her daughter. The car disappeared, neighbors ran out of their houses. Sade frantically ran her hands over Alexis, praying no bullets went through her into her baby girl. She wept in relief to find her unharmed. It was then that the pain came, a blinding pain that brought her to her knees. Blood pooled in her mouth.

"I love you, Alexis. Mommy loves you. Please remember that Mommy loves you."

The last sound she heard was her daughter screaming for her mama.

His legs went weak when they pulled the sheet down. His beautiful, funny, full of life wife was on a metal slab in the morgue. He curled his hands into fists even as he dropped to his knees and buried his face in her hair. The subtle scent of her favorite shampoo still clung to those brown strands. He remembered the first day he saw her, the hit of attraction that damn near knocked him off balance. A junior in high school, loaded down with books, her hair blowing in the breeze and the way her eyes warmed when she sought him out feeling the connection that bound two strangers. He loved her from the first moment he saw her. He had vowed to love her for the rest of their lives, but her life was cut short because of him.

He pressed a kiss on her mouth, her lips were cold and her taste was gone. His heart broke into pieces in his chest. As he said a final farewell to the love of his life, he knew what he had to do.

"She won't be anywhere near here, right?"

"No. I've requested special circumstances. Adoption is the only way to ensure a truly stable home though."

Everything in him rejected that idea. He had to give her up, but he wasn't going to cut that last tether he had to her. "No. I want her safe, but I won't sign away my rights. She is loved, so fucking much. Just put her in a home that will keep her safe, one that is nowhere near here."

"I'll do my best."

He held his daughter's little hand, her chubby fingers gripping his so tightly. She looked around with wide-eyed interest. She insisted on wearing her hot pink jacket because they were going out. She didn't understand she wouldn't be going home with him, didn't know her life was about to change. It'd been two months since Sade died, two months to get everything in order, two months to say goodbye to the last piece of his heart.

Tears burned his eyes, but he wouldn't let her see them. He knelt down next to her. He had a picture of the three of them; he zipped it into her jacket pocket. It was the only thing he would let her have, the only reminder of the life she had before the new one she was about to embark on.

"You look just like your mama. She loved you so much and you'll never know her. You'll never know how she would braid your hair in all those little braids, or how she would rub your back when you weren't feeling well. You won't remember that her hair always smelled like lilacs and when she smiled she brightened up a room. She sang when she baked, and talked to the flowers in the garden as she tended them. She liked to walk in the rain and dance in the streets. She was in labor for forty-three hours, but it only took ten minutes to push you into the world." He touched her round cheek, swiping his thumb over her soft skin. "When you were ready, there was no stopping you. You won't remember that you were the center of both of our worlds, but you are. You are loved, baby girl. My wish for you is to sing when you bake, to talk to the flowers, to walk in the rain, dance in the streets, to love until it hurts, and most of all to live every day like it's your last."

Alexis clapped, her smile lopsided when she grinned. "Daddy, Daddy."

He hugged her, inhaling her sweet baby scent and committed it to memory. He kissed her head, let his lips linger as he said goodbye and then he walked out of the office. The last sound he heard was his daughter screaming for her daddy.

ALEXIS 4 YEARS LATER

The board game was heavy, but I got it into the room. Ms. Evelyn and Mr. Howard were watching television. They weren't my parents. I had a picture of my mommy and daddy. I didn't know what happened to them. No one would tell me. I think they were in heaven. I wished I could go there too so I could see them again. I dropped down on the floor in front of the television.

"Wanna play?" They didn't look at me. "Wanna play?"

"Play in your room," Mr. Howard grumbled. He reminded me of Oscar the Grouch. He wasn't a bad person; he just didn't like people, especially children. I didn't want to be in my room. I wanted someone to play with.

"You can go first?"

"Not now," the woman said.

Not now, but later. That's what I heard. I carried my game back upstairs and set it up in my room. While I waited, I played with my dollies then I colored. I waited for the lady to come play with me, but she never did. I sat on my bed and tried not to cry but I was so lonely. The woman had bought me a journal. We were learning how to write sentences in school. I sat at my desk, scrunched up my nose thinking.

I didn't have a playmate, but I could make one up. Emily. She was my age, but her hair was blonde. She had parents that tucked her in at night and kissed her head, who played with her and baked cookies and sang songs. Emily had the life I wished I had.

SIX MONTHS LATER

I sat under the tree in the front yard with my journal. I liked writing because I had friends. Imaginary, but they were as real to me as the people I lived with.

Shouting turned my attention across the street. The twins were out. That girl was with them. The three of them played a lot. I wanted to play with them, but I was afraid to walk over there only for them to tell me to go away.

Loud voices came from the house. The foster monsters were fighting again. In my head, I imagined them looking like the creatures of The Muppets. I'd made them loveable in my imagination because in real life they weren't at all. I hated when they fought, but if they weren't watching TV they were yelling at each other. They weren't happy people.

"Hey, you." I looked over to see one of the twins crossing the street. I actually shook with excitement when he stopped in front of me. "Wanna play?"

My lower lip quivered hearing words I had wished so hard to hear.

"Do you?"

"Yes."

He held his hand out to me. "I'm Dylan."

"Alexis."

"The idiot over there is my brother Dominic and the girl is Debbie. Come on, we have a tree house."

I jumped up. I didn't tell the foster monsters where I was going. They wouldn't even know I was gone. Dominic and Debbie met us at the door.

17

The twins looked so much alike I wasn't sure I'd be able to tell them apart. Debbie looked a lot like them, but her eyes were blue not green, eyes that were staring at me long enough to make me uncomfortable. When she did smile, I didn't understand why her smile didn't bring one out in me.

The door opened on a woman. My tummy dropped. I took a step back, ready to go home.

"Hello, sweetheart."

I didn't know who she was talking to, maybe Debbie. I looked behind me but Debbie was next to Dominic. The woman looked sad when I turned back to her. "I'm Mrs. Cantenelli."

Nervousness had me twisting my fingers together. "Alexis."

"Would you like to stay for dinner?" A loud crash came from my house, loud enough we all looked over. Mrs. Cantenelli added, "I'll let your foster parents know."

Dinner at the house was usually in front of the TV, but with them fighting we probably wouldn't have dinner.

"Okay."

"We're going to play in the tree house," Dylan said and disappeared inside with the others.

I wasn't sure what to do. Mrs. Cantenelli smiled again, "Come in, sweetheart."

Their home was a happy one. Pictures of the twins were all over the walls and it smelled like cookies. Shoes were tossed near the door, their backpacks next to them. I was so busy looking around I didn't see Mrs. Cantenelli until she touched my shoulder.

"Come in, sweetie, make yourself at home. I have cookies. Would you like some?"

She was an angel. I looked really hard to see her wings, but she had them hidden.

"You are welcome here anytime. Whenever you want, just walk right in."

I didn't understand why she was being so nice to me, but it made my tummy hurt in a good way.

"Okay."

"Let's get those cookies. You can take some out for the others."

For the first time in a really long time, I was happy.

6 YEARS LATER

I ran inside after spending the day at the beach. Home was Mendocino in Northern California. I had never been to New England, but I was told our town was very reminiscent of New England's fishing towns. The quaint village was tucked up against the Pacific Ocean with dozens of little paths and lanes that stretched to the beaches and cliffs. I spent most days at the beach, observing and writing. Today I'd written a short story about a family of tourists. They were having so much fun chasing the waves, building sand castles, and picnicking on hot dogs. They probably got more sand in each bite than hot dog, but they didn't care. Even at twelve, I recognized the emotion. I was jealous.

I was feeling good; it had been a good day so when I entered the house and saw my foster parents watching television, I tried to spark conversation.

"Hi."

Evelyn looked over at me. That was the extent of her greeting, but it was better than Howard's. He didn't even bother looking. This was why I rarely acknowledged them.

Still riding the high I asked, "I wrote a short story. Would you like to read it?"

"Not now. The game is on," Howard barked, but his eyes never left the set.

Evelyn didn't respond.

Typical. When I was younger, I handled gaining their attention—I wasn't even looking for affection—like a tactical military operation. I had done all kinds of crazy things to get them to notice me; wearing my shoes on the wrong feet for a whole week, speaking in gibberish, standing like a statue in the living room while they watched television. Hanging upside down in the tree out front when they came home from work, talking openly with the neighbor's dog. None of it worked. I was invisible. Their indifference hurt a lot and I couldn't help wonder if there was something wrong with me because my birth parents gave me up and my foster parents wanted to.

I headed to my room. I wasn't going to cry. They were consistent, I had to give them that. I dropped my backpack on my bed and put my journal back in the bookcase then ran my fingers over the twenty other journals that shared the space. I didn't need them for company. I created my own company.

My eyes drifted to my nightstand. I didn't pull it out now, I wasn't sure I'd be able to keep my emotions in if I did. This wasn't supposed to be my life. I had parents who loved me. I had proof. How I ended up here, I didn't know despite the countless times I had asked. Crying wouldn't bring them back. For whatever reason, this was my life now.

The foster monsters were still glued to the television when I came back down. They didn't ask where I was going. They already knew, the Cantenellis. I spent more time with them than I did at home. Dylan answered the door. I heard his mom call, "Is that Alexis? She's just in time. We're having dinner in a few minutes."

Dylan grinned at me. "You can set the table."

I followed him into the house and closed the door behind me. I'd set the table...happily.

The diner made the best hot fudge sundaes. I was on my way to get one. I didn't see Debbie until it was too late. She didn't hang out with us anymore. I suspected the reason for that was she had started to mature and boys were noticing; the twins and I stopped being cool. What I didn't get was her open hostility, but she was nasty every time I saw her. Today was no exception.

"If it isn't Alexis. All alone today?"

I ignored her; she wasn't done. "No twins? Did they get tired of you too? No one seems to linger long, do they?"

My hands curled into fists even as the tears threatened.

"Are you going to cry?"

The diner door opened and the one girl who worked there walked out. She was older than me by several years, but she and I talked when I came in for ice cream, nothing more than *hi, how are you, nice weather.* She was pretty and nice. The nice stuck because she always had a smile and a kind word, unlike Debbie.

"I'm buying ice cream. You interested?" she called over. I thought she was talking to someone behind me and actually looked to see who it might be, but no, she was talking to me.

"Ah, yeah okay."

"How cute. Charity," Debbie purred.

"You're one to talk about charity. I'm pretty sure those jeans you're wearing were once mine," the girl shouted back.

Debbie paled then blushed and on a huff turned and walked away. I stood motionless, fighting back laughter.

"I was serious about the ice cream," she called to me.

After what she'd done, I should be buying her ice cream. I joined her; she offered her hand. "I'm Paige."

"Alexis." I glanced in Debbie's direction. "That was awesome."

"She's a bitch."

Truer words. "Let me treat for the ice cream, my way of saying thank you."

"Hot fudge?" she asked.

"You read my mind."

She flashed me a smile and held the door. That day was the start of a beautiful friendship.

1

ALEXIS 1996

My second-hand bike was baby blue with white daisy decals, most of which had turned pee-yellow with age. There was rust covering the fenders, the spokes of the tires had seen better days and the brown leather seat had a large tear being held together with duct tape. It was too small for me, but I absolutely loved riding it around.

I didn't have any particular routes, all of them had awesome hills, but I did like riding through the heart of town because of the endless whirl of activity. Sometimes I was lucky enough to see the fishermen unloading their catches of the day. The shipmaker was always hammering and sanding, crafting some wonderful creation from wood, the smell of sawdust mingling with the salty tang of the sea. And of course there were always tourists with cameras in hand to capture the quintessential small town shot. I had filled journals with stories about them; loved writing because in my imagination nothing was off limits.

It was cooler now that summer was coming to an end. In just a few days I'd be starting my junior year in high school. My hope was to get accepted to NYU for creative writing. I wasn't sure why New York, but from as far back as I could remember it was my dream to live there. Perhaps it was the iconic buildings, or the romance that seemed to weave through the lure of the city, or maybe it was just location... something completely different from what I knew.

Town was fairly empty; tourist season was winding down. I had some time before work so I headed to the jetty—it ran about a quarter of a mile into the Pacific Ocean but there was a particular cluster of rocks that was the perfect place to sit and think or write or just look out at the horizon. It was my favorite place.

I reached my destination and was climbing from my bike when I noticed my favorite spot was taken. The sun was setting, which made it harder to see the intruder, but what I could make out of him he was a sight worthy of seeing. Dark brown hair, shot through with red, and long enough that the breeze had it teasing his shoulders. He was wearing faded jeans, a black tee and his feet were bare. I thought he was reading then I saw the pencil and sketchpad. I wondered who he was, more than likely a tourist on vacation with his family. If I had a bit more nerve, I'd join him on the jetty, but I couldn't get my feet to move.

No one approached him. None of the families on the beach resembled him. He was alone. Not that being alone seemed to bother him. I wondered what he was sketching, the horizon, the ocean, the jetty or something else entirely? What surprised me was how much I wanted the answer to that. I wanted to see his face and hear his voice. I didn't know why he intrigued me so much, maybe it was just that he was the first person I'd ever seen sitting in my favorite spot. Or maybe it was because I saw a little bit of myself in him.

He rubbed the back of his neck, like he was rubbing an itch away, then turned his head and looked right at me like he knew I was there. I'd read books and heard songs about that hit of attraction, the kind that steals your breath and makes your knees weak, but this was the first time I'd felt it. I'm sure it wasn't more than a few seconds that we stared across the beach at each other, but it felt longer. Disappointment followed because I wasn't going to see him again. The first boy to literally make my knees weak and he was just passing through. I should march down there and introduce myself; at the very least get his name and hear his voice so I could recall it when I was eighty, rocking in my chair sharing stories of my youth with my grandkids. I didn't move though, because you couldn't miss what you didn't know. I wanted to connect with him, it was irrational but I needed some connection to him, so I lifted my hand in a sort of wave. He returned it and I felt ridiculously happy and surprisingly sad. I'd remember him just like that, branded the sight onto my brain, the perfect moment with a total stranger.

The diner was packed. My tray was loaded with the house specialty, the best damn cheeseburger around. Mel and Dee Baker opened the diner in the fifties and though the building had recently received a few face-lifts, the menu was the same as it had been when the doors opened all those years ago. It was simple fare, but it was delicious and cheap.

I had been working here for two years, so I could do it with my eyes closed, which was a good thing this morning because I was distracted thinking about the boy from the beach. Just thinking about him had me feeling all funny. That was one of the drawbacks of living in a tourist town; we had lots of visitors all of whom were just passing through. I wished I had talked to him, wished I could rewrite that scene, because I had a feeling whatever it was about him that intrigued me was special.

"You've had a weird look on your face since you got here. What's going on?" Paige cornered me in the kitchen as I dropped off empties. Since that day with Debbie four years earlier, we had become as thick as thieves.

The woman always looked like she'd stepped from the pages of a fashion magazine. It was damn frustrating. "How do you do it? After three hours, my hair looks a bit like Medusa's, my clothes are covered in food and my face is flushed. You look like you're heading to a modeling shoot. I swear you and that husband of yours have made a pact with the devil."

She grinned.

It was true though. Twenty-three and a mother of two, she was a modern day Snow White with her raven black hair and bright blue eyes. She had a figure like those pinup models of the forties, but she didn't work out and she ate whatever she wanted. Even the burgers Dee and

Mel sold. She didn't have to worry about men gawking or touching because her husband was a modern day Thor—a six foot five Norse god. And the man built custom motorcycles. I had a crush on Grant, our nine year age gap made no difference to me. The first time I met Grant my eyes popped out of my head and my tongue hit the floor. In the years that followed, my crush mellowed as we grew into family.

"What weird look?" I asked.

"Like gooey-eyed."

That was possible. I had been thinking about the hot kid on the beach. "There was a guy on my jetty."

She cocked her hip and narrowed her eyes. "I'm guessing he was cute."

"Yeah, well from what I could see."

"You didn't talk to him?"

"I didn't even climb off my bike."

"Why?"

"I felt something."

"Indigestion?"

"You're an idiot."

She smiled like the Cheshire cat before she guessed again. "Attraction."

"More than attraction. I've been attracted to guys, but I've never felt anything so visceral. He's literally a stranger off the street, but it was like a punch to the gut when he looked at me."

"The sweet burn."

"The what?"

"When your body burns in awareness, that sweet visceral reaction to someone. That doesn't happen every day."

"With my luck he's probably a tourist who's already heading home."

"Maybe, but it's pretty late in the season. He could be new to town."

"I think we would have heard if there were new folks in town."

"You're probably right. Well, lesson learned," she said as she started for the door.

"What lesson?"

She reached it and looked back at me. "Next time get off your damn bike."

The foster monsters were ripping into each other, so I grabbed my notebook and sweatshirt and climbed onto the roof outside my bedroom window. The moon was full; its pale glow illuminated the yard. I could hear the sound of the waves crashing against the cliffs in the distance.

My thoughts drifted to the boy from the beach. It had been two days and still he lingered in my thoughts. That was unusual. He had made quite the picture though. Sitting on the rocks, the waves crashing around him. Solitary, but not alone. I'd like to know his story. Who was he? Where did he come from? Where was he going? I'd asked those questions countless times over the years, made up the answers, created characters from the people I'd observed, but I didn't want to make up his answers. I wanted to know him. I never would, he was likely already gone, and that reality caused regret to twist in my gut. I should have talked to him.

I couldn't help scripting a bit of a story around him, he was too fascinating not to. How it could have been had we talked. He'd have smiled when I started down the beach toward him, moving to meet me halfway. It wouldn't have been awkward; we'd have chatted like friends catching up and not strangers meeting for the first time. Maybe one day I'd write a book based on those few minutes, fill in with my imagination what real life only hinted at.

I stood in the bathroom attempting to do something with my hair, but it was too thick to do anything fun. I contemplated cutting it, but with my figure that wasn't a good idea. I turned in the mirror this way and that, but the image didn't change. Long brown hair, the same color as my eyes, and a body that looked like that of an eight-year-old boy. I was still the ugly duckling. The swan was taking her time appearing.

I glanced at the clock. I was going to miss the bus. I grabbed my shoes and backpack and ran down the stairs. The foster monsters weren't around. There would be no Norman Rockwell scene of the parents sending their child off for their first day of school. Whatever. Slipping on my sneakers, I jogged out the front door and down the street to the bus stop. The Cantenelli twins were already there. They had always been skinny and scrawny, but this past summer they worked construction. Manual labor buffed them up. They were so identical that their own parents often had trouble telling them apart. Tall now, at least six feet, muscled with green eyes and messy blond hair, they were going to turn more than a few heads at school.

"Hey, Alexis. Looking good," Dylan greeted with a wink.

"I was thinking the same about you two."

He flexed his arm. "You like what you see?"

"You're a dope, but you're going to be beating the chicks away this year."

Dominic draped his arm over my shoulders. "What about you?"

"I remember the snot eating years. No, thanks."

He chuckled, "I was nine."

"Still too old to be eating your boogies."

"There was a study that people who eat their boogies are actually smarter than those who don't."

"I'd like to see that study. Probably done by someone who still eats his."

"We're working on Sophia after school if you want to join."

Sophia was their robot. They were inventors, became so out of laziness. If their mom wanted them to fold the laundry, they'd figure out a way to automate laundry folding. Mowing the lawn? Their lawn mower was wired and rigged to work itself with just a press of a button. Sophia was taking their laziness to a whole new level. Doing their chores, probably even their homework, she was going to be the answer to all of that. What was scarier? They were smart enough to pull it off. They were also boys, so Sophia had a seductive voice and large breasts from metal molds they made specifically for her boobs. They were goofs.

"I have work."

"We need to see you walk so we can program her code."

"I don't think I want to know what that means."

Dylan grinned, "Probably not. We also need to hear you say, oh baby, harder, yes, yes, yes."

A shudder went through me. "Too much information."

Dylan tossed his head back and laughed, "Just teasing."

But I suspected he really wasn't. Luckily the bus came and ended that conversation.

I stood at my locker listening to the buzz about the new kid—the high school attendance topped out at one hundred and eighty kids so whenever there was a 'new kid', it caused a flurry of excitement. I gave a passing thought to the new kid being the boy from the jetty, but I didn't have that kind of luck.

On the cusp of that thought, I felt a stirring at my nape—the sweet burn Paige mentioned. Twisting my neck, I couldn't believe my eyes. I was hallucinating; reality and my imagination were overlapping. I closed my eyes and opened them again. I even pinched myself, but no he was real. The boy who had consumed my thoughts, the guy from the jetty, was walking down the hall of my school. *He* was the new kid. Holy shit. He was every bit as beautiful as I remembered, and tall. He had been sitting that day on the beach, but he was at least a few inches over six feet. My heart was hammering so hard it should have beat right out of my chest, cracked my ribs and bounced onto the tile floor. Anticipation joined the other emotions as I waited for him to see me, sense me like he had that day on the beach. Would he walk over? Would I? What would our first words be? I actually felt tongue tied, speechless. That never happened to me. I followed him as he walked down the hall; every step that took him farther from me had disappointment replacing anticipation. He never looked over. I then noticed the other girls in the hall, all of them looking at him like I was, interested and awed.

My fairy tale took another hit when a girl called to him. I'd seen her around; she was a senior. I didn't know her name because she was in a social circle I didn't belong to. She was pretty if you were into petite, athletic chicks with bright blue eyes and big smiles. There was the slightest grin curving his mouth. He pushed his hands into the pockets of his jeans and leaned a shoulder against the lockers as they chatted. I was jealous, completely ridiculous because I held no claim on him, and yet seeing him with her had my stomach twisting into a knot.

The chick laughed, it was a melodious sound, as she tucked her hair behind her ear and looked at him through her lashes. I'd say it was orchestrated to perfection, but I had a feeling she was being genuine. I shouldn't be surprised by the interest. He wasn't just the new kid; he was the hot new kid.

Our moment on the beach, or rather how I remembered it, changed. Those few minutes we had shared had been special because of the 'what if'. What if he stayed? What if we spoke? My whole life I could have wondered 'what if' and there was magic in the wondering. But the reality was I had about as much chance with him as I did at becoming the next Nora Roberts. He wasn't the boy of my imagination—the one I had built a story around even knowing it was all a fairy tale—he was here and real and out of my league. I would have a front row seat to him doing with someone else all the things my imagination had us doing. It was my own fault, popping that happy bubble, because I had wished for a second chance, but I forgot the old adage…be careful what you wish for.

In the cafeteria, I pushed my stew around my plate. I wasn't hungry. All anyone could talk about was the new kid.

Greyson Ratcliffe. He even had a sexy name, a hero in a novel worthy name.

In the locker room, the girls were all daring and betting each other to be the first to get him into the eraser room, the worst kept secret in the school. The eraser room saw a lot of action. The staff had to know and yet it was never busted, probably because it wasn't just the students that took advantage of it.

I'm not sure why I looked up when I did, but I was treated to the sight of Greyson entering the cafeteria. I unapologetically checked him out. I might not have a chance in hell with him, but my eyes worked just fine. He moved in long sure strides. He didn't rush, it was deliberate how he walked and though I wouldn't call it a stroll, he wasn't in a hurry. He moved like a person very comfortable in his own skin. Why did he come here now? It seemed unusual that he'd switch schools in his senior year. And how many broken hearts did he leave behind?

He didn't get in line, but headed to one of the tables by the windows in the back of the cafeteria. He pulled out an apple and his spiral ring and started to sketch. I wondered what he was sketching, wondered if I would ever know him well enough to get a look at that notebook. I had a suspicion I would learn a great deal about Greyson by viewing his drawings.

My attention was pulled from Greyson when Debbie Demato arrived. And it was an arrival; she had a way of entering a room. She was very different from the girl I had once played with, homecoming queen and lead cheerleader. Mike Devane was her boyfriend, the quarterback, homecoming king, blah, blah. They were Malibu Barbie and Ken come to life. She was wearing the outfit that had bolstered her popularity, a miniskirt that showed off her very long legs and a sweater that was so tight it accentuated the two unnaturally large mounds of her breasts. You couldn't help but look at them because they stood out all perky and perfect. I wanted to gag. Glancing down at my own flat chest, I thought bitterly that some people just walked in the light.

She eyed the cafeteria, deciding whom she would grace with her presence, and spotted Greyson. She sauntered toward him like a super model on the catwalk. One would think he was being bestowed a great honor, but Debbie was all about Debbie. She was making it clear to the new kid that she was the queen bee and he needed to get in line with that. Most people did and the few of us that didn't, she went out of her way to be nasty. I usually ignored her, but sometimes her cruelty got under my skin.

Debbie leaned so far over Greyson's table her abnormally large chest was right in his face. I couldn't hear what she said, if anything, but it was Greyson's reaction to her that earned my admiration. He ignored her, never lifting his eyes, as he continued to eat his apple and sketch seemingly oblivious. Debbie was getting angry, a lovely blush colored her cheeks, but to look at Greyson his expression and body language gave nothing away. I had never seen anyone treat Debbie that way. Greyson then handed her his eaten apple, winked, packed up his shit and walked out. Debbie had no reaction at first, holding his

31

apple core, her mouth moving but no words coming out. I laughed and loud enough she'd hear. I'd pay for that later, but damn. As if I wasn't fascinated enough with the hot new kid, he goes and gives Debbie a taste of her own medicine. Despite knowing better, Greyson became my first real crush and I didn't even know him.

Advanced biology. I must have been on drugs when I filled out my course schedule last year. I was a junior who was voluntarily taking a senior's science class. Why? I wanted to be a writer. I didn't need advanced science for that. Luckily, I could drop the class; I just needed the teacher's signature. Distracted with how I was going to explain why I wanted to drop a course before the first day overview, I didn't immediately see Greyson until I was halfway to the teacher's desk. My feet just stopped. Greyson was in my biology class. I glanced behind me, convinced I'd see my fairy godmother because luck like I was experiencing today was rare for me, what with the boy from the jetty being the new kid and having lunch and biology with him. The old girl was earning her wings today.

I then noticed the seat next to him was empty and immediately the story unfolded in my mind. Our eyes would meet across the room. He'd give me that secret little smile I saw earlier. I'd stroll over to him; maybe I'd flip my hair behind my shoulder.

He'd say, "Please sit here."

And I'd say, "Really? You don't mind?

And he'd counter, "I think I'll die if you don't."

I'd giggle and bat my lashes before saying, "We don't want that to happen."

It would become our favorite class and at the end of the year, we'd be inseparable. Linked forever, bound together over dissections and anatomy. Ours would be a romance to rival the greatest romances in history, the start of the beginning of the rest of our lives.

"Young lady."

That voice didn't belong in my story. Following the voice, it was the teacher. It was then I realized I had been daydreaming; long enough that everyone was seated. The chair next to Greyson now occupied.

"The seat next to Gertrude is open," Mr. Price suggested.

My eyes drifted to Gertrude. She had her headgear on today. She was sweet, talked to herself a lot, and she always smelled like Doritos; she was nice, but she wasn't Greyson.

I felt his eyes on me. I didn't even want to know what he was thinking. Paige had shared often that I looked possessed when I slipped into my imagination. What a great visual. The girl who looked more like a boy, standing in the front of class spaced out while I planned our entire lives in the three minutes before the bell rang. It was so clear to visualize, my social life taking a nosedive, the crashing and burning so vivid I could almost smell the smoke.

I had to walk past Greyson; he had the prettiest pale green eyes. I knew this because he was staring at me, and even feeling ridiculous I stared back. My body felt funny, my legs were weak and I was lightheaded. It couldn't be said he was smiling at me, not even grinning, but his expression was intense. My guess, he was trying to figure out if I was dangerous or just a harmless crackpot.

I settled next to Gertrude. Even she was looking at me like I was nuts. I pulled my notebook out and a pencil while wishing the floor would open and swallow me whole. Mr. Price went over what to expect for the year and I was grateful when I no longer had the attention of most of the class. I tried to focus on his lecture, not because I was interested, but because I didn't want to think about my dismal entrance, however listening to him my performance took a back seat to horror. We were dissecting frogs again. We had already dissected frogs in the ninth grade. I understood the importance of knowing about your body, those of other animals, but to dissect perfectly healthy frogs seemed cruel. Looking around the room, no one else seemed to have a problem with putting the little fellows in jars filled with chloroform and waiting for them to pass out before performing live organ donations on them. Mr. Price wanted us to have a refresher before we got into advanced anatomy and the little frogs were the ones to pay the price. I wondered if the Giant from *Jack and the Beanstalk* had biology class, and if so, what did he dissect? Humans? The visual popped into my head of naked humans in huge ball jars with enormous chloroform-soaked cotton balls.

"Miss Owens! Miss Owens!"

"Sorry." Mr. Price and I were not getting off on the right foot. He was a little man with a balding head and the biggest comb over I had ever seen. He had no hair on the top of his head, but he brushed his hair from the back forward in an attempt to cover his baldness. His hair in the back had to reach past his shoulders to cover all the way to his forehead. Who did he think he was kidding? He drew more attention to his state of baldness with his comical attempt to cover it. Someone should tell him he looked ridiculous. I wondered if he was married, and if so, was his wife cruel or was she blind…blinded in a lab accident he conducted in their basement.

"Miss Owens, for the fifth time!"

"Sorry."

"Would you like to share with everyone whatever it is you are finding so amusing?"

Share? How funny would it be if I really did share? I might get some laughs, but then I'd feel guilty for being intentionally cruel.

"Alexis Owens!"

"No, I don't wish to share."

"I'm guessing you haven't heard a thing I've said."

Sheepishly I replied, "No, sir."

"Pay attention, Alexis. Mr. Ramsey you answer the question."

I stared at my desk so no one would see the blush that burned my face. I heard the deep chuckle and looked over to find Greyson grinning at me. Was he grinning at me or with me? Was I clown funny? Likely. I pulled my eyes from the hot boy. He might think I was a dope, but he was in my biology class. No surprise, I not only didn't drop biology, it became my very favorite class.

"Hey, you. Tell me about your first day?" Paige called as soon as I showed up for my shift at the diner.

I walked behind the counter and poured myself a cup of coffee. "The kid from the jetty wasn't a tourist." I should be jumping up and down, but sadly reality didn't quite live up to my imagination.

Paige didn't pick up on my somber tone, her own going up at least an octave from excitement. "No way. Seriously? That's awesome. Did you talk to him?"

"No."

My blunt answer turned her head, then she cocked her hip. She was getting ready to mother. I'd seen her take that stance with the girls a few times. She only said one word and yet there was so much behind that word. "Why?"

"Let's just say reality was a little different than my imagination."

"Your imagination is pretty wild, but it couldn't have been that bad."

"We're in the same biology class."

"That's great."

"Not so great. Advanced biology, a senior's class, and I'm staying in it because of him. That is dedication to the cause."

"Are we getting to the not so great part? Because so far this all sounds good to me."

"I had a moment."

She knew exactly what I meant by a moment. "Oh…how bad?"

"I had our entire lives planned in the three minutes before the bell rang. I was so engrossed in how it would be between us, I lost the chance to be his lab partner. Instead, I'm teamed up with Gertrude."

"Isn't she the girl who smells like Doritos?"

"The very one. I think I'm better off keeping my relationships to those in my head. I lack social skills in real life."

"Imaginary boyfriends don't hold your hand, or make your stomach jump or keep you warm at night."

"Yes, but they don't disappoint either."

"What's that mean?"

"I thought our moment that day on the beach was special, but I think I may have filled in the blanks to make it more than it was."

Her expression softened. "I'm sorry."

"Yeah, me too. He has a cool name though. I might have to steal it for a book. Greyson Ratcliffe."

"That is a cool name." Paige touched my arm. "It's only the first day. Something about him stirred you. Something had him looking back. Maybe it wasn't your imagination."

She was a 'glass half full' kind of gal. I was a 'usually didn't even have a glass' kind of gal, but I smiled before I headed to the kitchen to punch in. I wasn't a pessimist and I was happy. I had Paige and family, the Cantenellis, Dee and Mel, but I could admit deep down I was lonely. My birth parents abandoned me and my foster parents didn't see me. I lived in my head so much because I was happier there. That wasn't a bad thing for someone who wanted to be a writer. I may never have what Grant and Paige had, but I could create that so others could live vicariously through my stories…so I could live vicariously through them too.

I liked the bus. It was the only place that you could see the menagerie of people who made up the school. All cliques were forced to conform when it came to transportation to and from school.

Dylan and Dominic sat across the aisle from me devouring a box of Pop-Tarts. They loved them. Disgusting.

When we drove past the student parking lot, I didn't press my face to the window but it was close. Greyson was parking his motorcycle. He had a motorcycle. I adored motorcycles, always had even before my maiden voyage on the back of Grant's a few years back. It was like Greyson was custom made for me. Too bad he wasn't in the loop on that fact.

We exited the bus and as hard as I tried not to look in the direction of the parking lot, I did and saw that the chick from yesterday was detaining him. And I say detaining because in my imagination he didn't want to be there. Where the hell had she come from anyway? I sounded jealous because I was.

"Why are you walking so slowly?" Dylan demanded.

"I'm not." I so was.

"My grandmother walks faster and she needs a walker. Are you waiting for someone, like maybe the new kid?"

I twisted my head so fast I almost snapped my neck. He was grinning like an idiot. He hadn't seen my ridiculousness whenever Greyson was around. Unless word traveled, my stupidity turning to legend to forever haunt these hallowed halls. That thought was mortifying.

He leaned closer. "Don't worry. You aren't obvious, I just know you. Have you talked to him?"

"No."

"Why?"

"My brain and my mouth can't get on the same page."

"Why do I have the feeling there is more to the story?"

"I may have seen him during the summer and we had a moment, but it was only a moment in my head."

Dylan dropped his arm around my shoulders. "That imagination of yours is going to keep me in the lifestyle to which I've always wanted to be accustomed."

Dylan liked finding the silver lining and I liked this one, but if anyone was going to be crazy successful it was him and Dominic. I knocked my hip into his. "Sophia is going to do that and I will happily ride on your and Dominic's coattails."

He chuckled then released me. "See ya later, Alexis."

"Later."

My locker was in a prime spot, line of sight to the doors, so I saw Greyson come through them. He was wearing all black from the hoodie to his boots. Even his hair looked darker, those long strands that I found ridiculously sexy. I planned to talk to him today. I would locate my spine and walk over and say hi. What's the worst that could happen?

He stopped at a locker not far from mine, the magic of my fairy godmother at work again. I watched him swap out his books as my imagination scripted out the scene—a mental dress rehearsal. I'd saunter over to him, swaying my hips gently; his pale eyes would turn to me, the smile appearing in them first before reaching his lips. He'd pull me close and kiss me, tasting me with his tongue, before taking my books and reaching for my hand. Okay, I may have taken some creative license. He didn't have to hold my books. I grinned to myself and was so lost in the scene I didn't realize I wasn't alone until the smell hit me. I knew it was Debbie before I saw her; she bathed in her perfume. Her posse appeared, their attempt to intimidate me. They were high school students, but I swear they all looked like seasoned hookers.

"If it isn't little Alexis."

She'd started with the little last year even though I had three inches on her. Her visit was in response to me laughing yesterday at Greyson's diss. She couldn't let that go, had to maintain the order and that order was her on the top of the pile and me under it.

I didn't respond to her, just stared because I knew it would piss her off. She tried hard to fit into her crowd, but she wasn't in their crowd. They were the rich kids and she was from the other side of the tracks as it were. Her parents were hard workers, but they were dirt poor. Her mom did hair in the basement of their house and her dad worked at the service station. And even with money being tight, her mom came to the diner every holiday season with fresh baked cookies for the staff. How they afforded to dress Debbie, knowing the clothes she sported cost some coin, I didn't know. And shame on her for putting that on her parents.

I tried for my best bored voice when I asked, "What do you want, Debbie?"

"Just thought I do my act of kindness for the day by saying hello to…" She eyed me like I was roadkill. "You."

"Your kindness is in such limited supply you should bestow it on someone who gives a shit."

It was always a joy to see her face flush with temper.

"They've already got the sign up sheets outside the office for back-to-school night. Too bad there's no one who wants to come for you."

Pain sliced through me, her words hitting their mark with astounding accuracy. Once we shared our secrets and our pain, now she knew exactly where to stick the knife.

"Poor Alexis, not even your parents wanted you."

My eyes stung, but I refused to let her see how much her words hurt.

"Well, if it isn't queen bitch."

The twins. It was hard to believe they'd ever been friends with the animosity that radiated off the twins. Still, I lowered my eyes and bit my lip so I didn't make the situation worse by laughing at Dominic's greeting.

She had the nerve to act offended even though she relished the title. She turned from me, like she was finished with her minion.

"What? Not so easy to bully someone when you don't outnumber them seven to one," Dylan snarled.

Her brow rose; she pulled off haughty better than anyone I knew. "Someone?" She looked me right in the eyes. "I don't see anyone."

She walked away, her posse following after her.

"It's wrong to strike a girl, but I fucking want to strike her," Dylan growled.

I was of the same mindset about striking her, but I chose words when I called after her. "You're not as popular as you think."

Her head whipped around; she played regal like she'd been born with a silver spoon in her mouth.

"You're in their crowd, but you'll never be part of their crowd. And when they all ride off into the sunset, you'll be the one left behind. Enjoy it now, Debbie, your glory years, because this is as good as it's going to get for you." I had a twinge of guilt sinking to her level. I shook it off. "And a word of warning, we know all your secrets too."

Her face paled. Direct hit. I dismissed her, my focus shifting back to the twins when my gaze collided with Greyson. He was close, just a few lockers down from me. I assumed he was heading to homeroom, but his expression had the hair on my arms standing on end. He was pissed, but when his eyes shifted to me he smiled slightly before he turned and strolled away. Had he been coming to my rescue?

"The new kid seems like a decent dude." Dylan's comment turned my head. Greyson had been coming to my rescue. I felt all tingly inside. "Debbie on the other hand. She's a bitch, don't listen to her."

She was a bitch, but her words hit their mark just as she intended.

2

ALEXIS

That night, Debbie's words still haunted me. Despite being a bitch, she wasn't wrong about the lack of parental interest when it came to me. I did something I hadn't done in a long time. I tried to talk to the foster monsters. It wasn't hard to string words together, even small children could manage the task, but it was like the monsters believed you could run out of words so they were saving theirs. For what, I didn't know. I had asked about my parents many times and I'd always hit their wall of silence. I tried again.

They were in the living room, big surprise there. The amount of time they logged in front of the television had to be a world record. I waited for a commercial, because attempting conversation when their shows were on was pointless. "Do you know anything about my parents?"

They both looked over. Evelyn answered, "No."

"Nothing? Where they're from, their names?" Crickets. No reply at all. It was like I was talking to potted plants.

"How did I come to live with you?"

"A social worker."

Hallelujah, an answer. I tried my luck when I asked, "What social worker? From where?"

"I don't know. I have her papers somewhere, but I'm not looking for them now."

She wasn't going to look for them now? That was hilarious. She wasn't ever going to look for them.

"Why are you asking about this now?" Evelyn sounded genuinely surprised by my interest.

"I've asked this same question since I was a little kid. I want to know where I come from?"

Howard managed to string his next words together and with brutal accuracy. "Why? They didn't want you."

My chest got tight and tears burned the back of my eyes hearing out loud the same words I repeated often to myself.

I walked out and went to my room, wishing I had kept my mouth shut. I pulled the picture from my nightstand. I used to look at it all the time, but less so as I grew older because it hurt too much.

It was a picture of my parents and me. Mom was dressed in a sundress the color of watermelons and her brown hair was pulled back into a knot. It looked haphazardly done…an attempt to get it out of her face. Freckles sprinkled her nose and her dark eyes were bright and smiling. She wore a gold locket in the shape of a heart around her neck. Dad was in a white tee and faded jeans. He looked like he'd just pulled his fingers through his black spiky hair. His eyes were blue, dark like a sapphire, and they were looking at Mom with love. His arm was slung over her slender shoulders, his fingers holding my hand as I was pressed close to Mom's chest. We were all smiling. I loved that the most. I was very young in the picture; so young I didn't remember them, not how they talked, or walked, what their favorite colors were or quirky habits they may have had. We had been happy, so why did they abandon me?

There was a part of me that wanted to know, needed to understand how I had lost them. Sometimes I let myself imagine what life would have been like with them, the people we were in that photograph. My life was good. I had friends who loved me, but the little girl in me wished for the parents who would have tucked me in at night. Played catch with me and taught me to ride a bike. Shopping, I didn't even

41

like shopping, but I'd go every day if it meant I could do so with my mom. Looking at this picture gutted me—the promise of a lifetime filled not just with milestones, but all the little moments that made up a life—because they walked away from that. One day I'd find out what happened to break my family apart.

I studied myself in the mirror. One had to dress for success. Today was the day I talked to Greyson. I wore my overalls and my favorite flannel shirt. My chunky brown shoes I had gotten from the twins for Christmas. It was my most favorite outfit…comfortable and familiar.

I left my hair down, but brushed it until it shined. I even added a touch of mascara and lip gloss. I grabbed my bag and headed for the bus. The twins were already there.

"Hey, Alexis…are you wearing makeup?" Why did Dominic choose today to be observant? "She's wearing makeup. What's that all about?"

Dylan moved in, his expression neutral but I saw the wheels turning. "The new kid?"

"No."

"You're all dolled up and the only variable that has changed is the new kid." Dylan was smug because he knew he was right. "Do you need a wing man?"

He would too. One of the many reasons I loved the twins. "I think I've got this."

"Good luck."

I didn't need luck. I had destiny on my side. This was going to be easy peasy.

I almost hurled in my locker. I was a bundle of nerves. I wasn't plotting world domination; I just wanted to talk to the hot boy who made me feel all kinds of good things. I tried to calm down as I loitered, waiting for Greyson. I almost gave up, when the door at the end of the hall opened and in he walked. I got chills and went numb at the same time. My imagination embellished the scene as he strolled down the hall in slow motion in his sexy stride. The wind that stirred teased his hair as The Cure's "Lovesong" played softly in the background. I had enough brain cells functioning to turn from him so he didn't catch me gaping. When he reached his locker, I took a few deep breaths and gave myself a little pep talk. I was just saying hi. It was really no big deal. He was just a person, only a person—a beautiful, sexy, intriguing person whose mere presence knocked my world off its axis. Before I lost my nerve, I shut my locker and headed in his direction. The closer I grew, the more difficult it was to put one foot in front of the other. My heart was beating so hard and fast I was sure I'd be dropping dead of a heart attack before I ever reached him. He must have sensed me, because he turned and I was hit straight on with the power of his pale green eyes. Holy shit, they were beautiful. I'd never seen eyes quite that color before. Pale green, like a peridot, with speckles of gold. My focus shifted from his eyes to his mouth when he grinned. Just the slightest curving of his lips, but the impact on his face was heart stopping. What would his lips feel like on mine? What did he taste like? I realized I was fantasizing about kissing him while staring right at him. He was leaning against the lockers now, patient…waiting. Every thought left my head. I had nothing, couldn't form a word if my life depended on it. My moment and I was blowing it. *Say something, Alexis!* But my brain had closed up shop, boarded the windows and left town. Mortified, I turned from him and walked away. My face was on fire; I wanted to crawl into a locker and die. Instead, I slipped into the bathroom and pondered drowning myself in the toilet.

I settled at my desk in biology, opened my book and hid behind it. I had avoided Greyson at lunch by hiding in the corner. I was a coward, absolutely, but knowing was half of the battle.

I sensed his arrival, even with my book blocking my view. My body felt him. What must he think of me? I couldn't even allow my overactive imagination to take that thought and run with it because I'd be tossing myself out the window.

"Miss Owens."

Reluctantly, I lowered my book. Mr. Price was looking at me expectantly and though his mouth was moving, I didn't hear a word he said. All systems in my brain were working together to keep my eyes from drifting to Greyson. It was exhausting.

Gertrude whispered, "He wants you to join him at the front of the class."

It was like the cosmos was plotting against me. Mr. Price was getting me back for thinking poorly of his comb over. I felt like a dead man walking as I dragged my feet to join him.

"We don't have all day, Miss Owens."

Reaching Mr. Price's desk, I noticed the fetal pig. Horrified, I jerked my eyes from the pig to my teacher. He didn't want me to dissect this in front of the class, did he? This was worse than the frogs.

"Miss Owens, why do we dissect fetal pigs?"

Up close his comb over seemed to defy gravity. How much hairspray did he use? He cleared his throat, I quickly replied, "Because of the similarities to humans."

"Yes. Now, before we cut we study the specimen. What can you tell me about this pig, Miss Owens?"

What could I tell him about the pig? Seriously? He was little, pink and soon to be removed of all his organs. It was a dismal fate, so I created a better one. "He was the smallest in his litter. His brothers and sisters climbed over him to get to their mama's milk. They called him piglet five, but he thought of himself as Peter. He had dreams to father hundreds of piglets, to live his life slopping around in the mud and to die fat and happy. Life had other plans. They came at night..."

"Miss Owens!"

And the story was just getting good.

"It's a fetal pig. It was never born."

"I know, but it seems wrong to dissect him without at least giving him a story. I mean we could raise a glass for his sacrifice, but you're not allowed to serve alcohol to minors." I leaned closer and added, "But I won't tell if you won't."

What the hell was wrong with me? Did one slip slowly into madness or did it happen fast?

I could have been imaging it, since I was fairly certain I was losing my mind, but I swear Mr. Price chuckled. "You may take your seat."

He was probably going to kick me from his class. I couldn't say I blamed him. I had everyone's attention as I made my way back to my seat. *Don't look, don't look, don't look.* I looked, stared right into those pale green eyes as I passed Greyson's desk. Those butterflies started up again. I'd have sold Dylan's soul to know what Greyson was thinking because he looked charmed. Maybe I hadn't blown it. Feeling bold I reached his side and said, "Hi."

He smiled, showing white teeth, the front one overlapping the other just slightly. He wasn't perfect and somehow that just made him more perfect. My knees went weak. I reached my table and dropped into my chair. That smile should come with a warning.

After the final bell, I was at my locker and noticed Greyson at his. Some of my courage from biology had fled, but I made a bet with myself. If he looked my way, I was walking over and saying hi. Part of me hoped he'd look and part of me hoped he wouldn't because I couldn't be sure how I'd react. Around him all bets were off. I stared though, did so from behind my hair so he wouldn't know I was staring. I wasn't sure what it was about him, but I could watch him all day. Yes, he was hot, but there were other hot guys in school. There was something about him that drew me in like a moth to a flame. Oh to get burned by him. I'd die a very happy girl.

"Alexis!"

I jumped; my head hit my locker as my heart moved into my throat. "What the…?" I turned and bit my lip when I saw Mrs. Leer, my guidance counselor.

"I'm so glad I caught you."

So much for being subtle, the loud bang when my skull hit the locker echoed down the hall. Why didn't my power of invisibility work on everyone? Why was it just a select few? It was damn frustrating.

"Are you continuing the writing club this year?"

I had started the club last year at her encouragement. She wanted me to get more involved, said it would look good on my college applications. She had a point. I tended to stay to myself. I wasn't a football fan; I didn't want to be a cheerleader, not with Debbie Demato at the helm. I wasn't in a music group because I was tone deaf. I tried the debate club, but they wanted to debate real life issues. I was more interested in who would win in a war between the Klingons and the Empire. I rarely went to school dances because I couldn't dance. The twins once described my dancing like a little kid throwing a tantrum. So, I created the club, but I told no one. I got away with it all of last year. Just me during sixth period and the occasional visit from Mr. Dobbs, the teacher who had drawn the short straw and had to pop into all the clubs to keep us honest. It was only a matter of time before my luck ran out.

"Yes, I'm continuing the club."

"You need to recruit new members."

I'd get the twins to join.

"And not the twins."

Damn it.

"Create flyers and post them on the bulletin boards. I'd like to see several new members, but I'll be happy with just one."

I didn't want members in my club. She read my mind.

"One person doesn't make a club."

I didn't agree. My one-person club was awesome. To her I said, "Okay."

"Excellent. Have a good evening."

She hurried away, her heels clicking on the tile floor. Greyson was gone, but I didn't think for a second he hadn't seen me banging my head on my locker. Hell, he probably knew I was staring at him. All in all, this day sucked.

While watching television that night, I created my flyers for writing club. It took all of thirty seconds. On one flyer I drew a box in the center of the page and on the top I scribbled. *What's inside the box? Join the writing club to find out.* The second one was even better. It just said *LOST CAT. See Alexis Owens in writing club to claim.*

"What's with the sunglasses?" Dylan asked at the bus stop the following morning.

I wasn't just wearing sunglasses. I had a cap pulled low over my eyes and I was dressed in all black. If my power of invisibility refused to work when I needed it, I'd improvise.

"I'm guessing it didn't go well with the new kid?"

"I'm not generally awkward, am I?"

Dylan took a long minute to reply. I hit him in the arm. He laughed. "No."

"I am with him. I make a fool of myself every time he's near. I tried to talk to him, but I froze. I had no words. No words, Dylan."

"You've got it bad."

I yanked off my sunglasses. "How can I have it bad when I don't even know him?"

"You tell me."

"I have no idea. All I know is my body and brain freak out when he's near. He's likely getting a restraining order against me."

"So you're going incognito."

"I'm going to move in the shadows."

He chuckled, "Good luck with that."

As soon as the bus arrived, I detoured to the office to make copies of my flyers. The plan was to hang them under the other flyers on the boards. I had done as asked, I'd made the flyers. I couldn't help it if people didn't read them. I reached the first board and my plan went out the window. The cheerleaders' flyer was plastered all over the board. Sure, someone had spent a lot of time drawing a cheerleader in the center of the page; those horns they use were drawn in each corner. And like their cheers, it was a very upbeat message about being a winner and joining the squad. It wasn't a bad flyer, but I just knew it was Debbie who covered up everyone else's messages with her own. It was such a Debbie thing to do. I hung my flyers; I covered every inch of that board. Not to stir interest, to stick it to Debbie. I felt surprisingly good as I made my way to class.

Mr. Price was very animated today, his comb over taking flight a few times. His arms flapping at his side like a bird. He was at risk of taking off. He'd make a fun character in a book, so I jotted down his mannerisms, impressions of him so I could recall and embellish at a later date.

My focus shifted to Greyson. When he entered class earlier, I was looking at my textbook like I would find the secret to the fountain of youth in it. I felt him look my way, but I was too chicken to look back. I really needed to locate my spine. Studying him now, he tended to wear baggy clothes, but with the way he was leaning on his elbows the cotton of his shirt was snug across the muscles of his back. I wanted to run my hands over those muscles, wanted to feel them respond to my touch. His lab partner was of course a girl and pretty. That first day of school, and the luck I had marveled over, had been a fluke or maybe my fairy godmother was a tease. She should have her wings ripped off. The girl flipped her hair so many times I wanted to cut it off. I mean seriously, talk about overdoing it. Her hair probably smelled like strawberries, or peaches, or some shit like that. She had also mastered looking at him from the corner of her eye; you know that sexy look beneath her lashes. I couldn't see his expression, didn't know if he was eating it up. Likely yes, but in my head he was stoic and unfazed. And yes I was jealous.

Class was almost over, thankfully. Right before the bell rang a girl entered the classroom, the same chick that had cornered Greyson in the hall that first day. She hadn't really, but I rewrote that scene to one I liked better. Mr. Price had already retired to his desk. He looked exhausted.

"Alexis Owens?" I was focused on the pink paper in her hand. My flyer. This couldn't be good.

"Yes."

She turned the paper over. It was the LOST CAT flyer. I chuckled then realized the chick looked about ready to cry. Didn't she know you couldn't believe everything you read on a bulletin board?

"Did anyone claim him?"

Before I could answer her, her focus shifted to Greyson. My jaw might have dropped, but this chick did not walk into our class with a bogus flyer just to get a look at Greyson? By the way she was licking her lips, yes she had. I had to give it to her; she was bold.

I glanced over at the object of her obsession only to find he was looking at me. That sweet burn moved down my spine in the most pleasant way. Maybe she wasn't so crazy walking in here to get a look at him. If I wasn't such a coward, I'd take the opportunity to talk to him but I was glued to my seat.

I watched every move he made. I wasn't much better than the chick. He headed for the door, but as he passed the girl he said, "I claimed him. Cat is a delicacy in Ireland."

Those pale eyes glanced back at me and he winked before he walked from class. Two things hit me in that moment. One, Greyson had a cadence to his voice, a distinct Irish accent. And two, he had a sense of humor. The chick looked horrified, but I was biting my lip to keep from laughing out loud. Damn, he just got better and better.

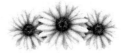

After school, as I waited for the big yellow chariot, I chuckled every time I heard Greyson saying cat was a delicacy. There was nothing sexier than a guy with a sense of humor.

My attention shifted when I saw Debbie and Mike leaving the building. They were heading for the parking lot, Mike's car being the newest and flashiest. Mike was a dick. He was the male version of Debbie. He was also insanely rich and a snob. His father built those cheesy strip malls. He hadn't set his sights on our town yet, but other towns in the area weren't so lucky. Why his parents allowed him to date Debbie I didn't know, but I knew she was setting herself up for a serious fall. She insisted on wearing blinders. Not my problem.

I saw the malicious gleam. It was like watching a car wreck. Even knowing it was coming, I couldn't move because I didn't believe it was happening. A few of the ninth graders didn't take a wide enough berth and Mike needed to prove he was so much bigger and tougher than the kids who were four years younger than him. The littlest of the group was the one Mike targeted. His glasses were skewed, his hair disheveled, his pants were just a tad too short and his skinny arms were struggling to hold all of his books. As the kid passed him, Mike stuck out his foot. The fall happened in slow motion. For a second, I thought he might not kiss the ground, but he wasn't so lucky. He dropped his books to break his fall. Mike and Debbie laughed, loud enough to gain the attention of others.

I walked over to the kid. I didn't hurry, so he wouldn't feel even more uncomfortable. Debbie and Mike were halfway to his car, their interests had moved on. Dropping down next to him, I noticed the silent tears running down his face. I fumbled in my school bag for a pack of tissues. Peeling several off, I handed them to him.

"Don't take it personally. They're jerks to everyone."

A pair of feet appeared seconds before a set of knees came into view. I looked up to see Greyson. His focus was on the kid. He held the kid's books. "Are you hurt?"

His voice was very deep and sexy and that accent was divine.

"No, I'm all right." The kid wiped his face again. "Thanks."

"I'm Greyson and this is Alexis."

He knew my name. Of course he did, it was shouted often enough in biology class.

"I'm Carl. Thanks, really."

We helped Carl with his belongings. He politely refused our offer to walk him home.

Greyson turned those pale eyes on me. How I stayed upright was a scientific wonder. "You missed your bus."

He was pretty. I really could stare at him all day and since I'd already hit rock bottom with him and started digging—it couldn't possibly get worse—I stared now. There was a second or two of awkward silence before I said, "I'll walk."

"Lost cat?"

It took a second to switch gears; a chuckle bubbled up my throat. "It was a joke. I didn't really think anyone would read it."

"You plastered them all over the bulletin board."

He saw that? "I didn't realize people actually read shit on the bulletin boards." I wasn't going to say anything, it wasn't my business, but my mouth opened anyway. "She wasn't there for my lost cat."

Some emotion moved across his face, but I wasn't sure what. He changed the subject. "You were the one at the beach the other day."

He *did* remember. I was mentally doing a little victory dance. "Yes, you were in my spot."

His eyebrow arched very slightly in response. "The rocks, great spot. We'll have to share it, Alexis."

Hearing my name from his mouth, speaking became difficult but I managed, "I'm sure the lawyers can draw up a satisfactory schedule."

He grinned. I didn't know a grin could be so sexy.

"Can I give you a ride?"

Give me a ride? I had to be hallucinating now. Like he had to ask. As if there was a chance I'd say no. Maybe I should say no. Keep up the mystery. Play a little hard to get. I wanted to ride on his bike though. I'd have an excuse to touch him.

"Alexis?" There was humor in his tone.

"Yes, that would be great." I looked over to the parking lot and his black motorcycle.

"Are you okay riding on my bike?"

As previously mentioned, I loved motorcycles and riding on the back of his was going to be close to perfection. "Absolutely."

We reached his bike and Greyson handed me a helmet, but I must have taken too long for the hand-off because he placed it on my head himself. His knuckles brushed my chin creating the most incredible tingles to sizzle just under my skin. He winked and I might have moaned audibly. He looked back at me to get my address after I settled behind him. His lashes were ridiculously long.

"Hold on."

Oh I was. I wrapped my arms around his waist like I'd been doing it since birth. That sounded better in my head. We sped out of the parking lot. I fell in love with the bike and the boy.

We reached my house and I didn't want to get off. I might have smelled him a few times during the ride because he had the most incredible scent. Not cologne, like the sea and paint. I loved the smell of paint and gasoline. I had to resist giving him a squeeze before I climbed from his bike and handed him the helmet.

"Thanks for the ride."

"Anytime."

I had a thousand questions. I wanted to go to the jetty and ask them, wanted to pry into this boy's life so I knew every detail of it. Instead, I bit my tongue. Based on the reactions to him, even mine, he probably had half the girls at school fawning over him. He didn't need another groupie even though I would happily be his groupie. Happily.

I walked up the path, but I couldn't help glancing over my shoulder at him. He hadn't moved. Those butterflies could have lifted me right off the ground. "Welcome to Mendocino, Greyson."

He waited for me to go inside before he pulled away. I managed to make it to my room before I freaked out. Greyson Ratcliffe had given me a ride home. I had touched him, smelled him; rode on the back of his bike. I dropped back on my bed and squealed like a girl at a Backstreet Boys concert. Maybe physical contact was a bad idea because my crush just amped up. Holy crap, but the guy was perfection. It was also Friday and I wouldn't see him again until Monday. It was tempting to hunt him down, but that was straddling the line of stalking. I jumped from bed and settled at my desk. I needed to write our first conversation down, every word of it.

3

GREYSON

I didn't drive off right away. I wanted her back on my bike, pressed to me like she had been, her thighs cradling mine and her arms wrapped tightly around my waist. It had been an uncomfortable ride and one I wanted to repeat. I was pretty sure she smelled me a few times too. She was unlike anyone I'd ever met.

I pulled from the curb and headed home. I couldn't explain my reaction to Alexis Owens. That first day on the beach I'd felt her, a persistent tingling at my nape, strong enough I tried to rub it away. Turning and seeing her holding the handles of that ugly ass bike, her hair blowing in the breeze. I wasn't good with words, I spoke through my art, but had I been standing I would have been brought to my knees. She was pretty, but it was the hit of attraction that took me by surprise, one so strong it reached across the distance between us. I wanted to chase her down to hear her voice, to get her name. Instead, I drew her. I wanted to remember how she looked, holding onto her bike, looking at me like I was her—curious, interested and slightly confused by the unseen connection that somehow linked two strangers.

She came across quiet and yet there was so much more going on under the surface. Every thought in her head was easy to read from her expressive eyes. That first day in biology, I'd have sold my soul to know what she was thinking. It was about me, but what specifically. One day I'd ask her.

I knew she worked at the diner. I'd seen her a few times in the window chatting with customers when I'd been in town. I think I needed to start making the diner a regular hangout.

Pulling into the drive of the house we were renting, I shut down my bike but I didn't climb off. The house rested on a cliff and the view was a forever changing canvas. Even a lifetime spent here and that view would always have something new.

Mom and Dad would have loved this house. It had been three years since they died and still sometimes I was blindsided with the pain of their loss. A car accident took them both. Mom was a force of nature. I smiled to myself realizing that Alexis reminded me of her. Dad loved poetry, always writing little sonnets for my mom. He'd been the one to teach me to shave and drive, had sat me down to give me the talk on the birds and the bees. Like Mom, his wish was for me to pursue my art.

We'd moved to Mendocino because Grandfather had a friend who wanted to manage me, believed he could make me a household name. As soon as I turned eighteen, Colin wanted me in the States. It had been the plan since I was in primary school. I didn't need to be a household name, but I did want a career doing what I loved, and that was art. My parents died and a part of me didn't want to leave home, but they had been my loudest cheerleaders. I would honor them more by going after my dreams. Grandfather was of the same mindset. I hadn't wanted to finish high school. I wanted to hit the ground running, and up until recently it was a sore point between us, but after meeting Alexis…a school year to get to know the girl who after just one glance I couldn't get out of my head. Yeah, I was good being right where I was.

On Monday, I took one of Alexis' flyers. Writing club. I couldn't write to save my life, but getting to spend the period with her, I'd fake it. I was at my locker when I saw Alexis coming down the hall. She was with the twins, one of them said something, but it was Alexis' response that had a grin pulling at my mouth. She scrunched up her nose before she playfully punched him in the arm. Part of the reason I hadn't made a move was because of the affection I'd seen between them. Their connection seemed familial, but I wasn't a hundred percent certain of that. I'd push a little and see what happened.

I knew the moment she knew I was watching. Her back straightened, as awareness tightened her muscles. She looked over and I smiled. Pink colored her cheeks as she absently tucked a lock of hair behind her ear. Her smile was hesitant, but it reached her eyes before it curved her lips. Whatever was happening between us, she felt it too.

"Hi, Greyson! I have that list of fun things to do. Maybe we could do some together."

I tried not to roll my eyes. Alexis' smile faded seeing Stephanie. With the amount of times the girl hunted me down, it would seem like there was something going on. I'd been grateful to her that first day, feeling like I was in a fish bowl, everyone staring and talking behind their hands. She called to me and I grabbed onto her like a lifeline. Since that day, well, I had to give it to her for being persistent. I hadn't asked for whatever list it was she had, certainly hadn't suggested we do things together off that list. I wasn't sure if it was a cultural thing and Americans were just more aggressive than I was used to, but the last straw for me was her showing up at my house with brownies. How the hell did she know where I lived? Grandfather thought it was charming, but he wasn't the one on the receiving end of her unwanted attention.

Turning to her, she looked expectant because I hadn't answered her. I didn't want to hurt her feelings, but I also didn't want to encourage her. Lucky for me, I was literally saved by the bell. "We've got to get to homeroom."

I didn't give a fuck about being late for homeroom, but I moved like I was on fire.

It was sixth period and I was down the hall from where the writing club met. As I approached, I heard The Cure playing softly. Reaching the room, I had to bite down on a laugh because Alexis was dancing. She looked more like a child throwing a tantrum, but the way her ass moved to the beat had my jeans growing snug. She had no idea I was there, completely lost in the music. I cleared my throat. She jerked around. I didn't miss the pleasure in her eyes before her face went as red as an apple. Her focus moved to the flyer I held.

"A Cure fan?"

The reminder that I'd just witnessed her dancing had her cheeks turning pink again. She lowered her arms and replied, "How can you tell?" Suspicion replaced embarrassment when she narrowed her eyes and asked, "Why are you here?"

I moved into the room and held up her flyer. "I came to find out what was in the box." Then I noticed there was no one else in the room. "Where is everyone?"

"It's just me."

I'd get her all to myself. Fuck yeah.

She was nervous, twisting her fingers together. "I'm the President and sole member, hence the need for the flyers. Mrs. Leer doesn't think being the only member of a club is helping with my social skills." Silence followed that comment, but she was definitely thinking something before she added, "She might have a point there."

Her gaze moved to my lips. She was so easy to read. She wanted to kiss me and I so wanted to kiss her, actually pondered backing her up to the wall, pressing in close and putting us both out of our misery.

I think she read my mind when she jerked her eyes from my face and blurted out, "Being the sole member helps to keep the disagreements to a minimum."

"But you still have some?" I actually bit my cheek to keep from laughing.

"The voices in my head are unruly. Why are you really here?"

"You're looking at your newest member."

Her eyes went wide and her lips formed an O. It was like I just told her she'd won a million dollars. I swear she was about to jump up and down. My head swelled a bit. Despite her excitement, she asked, "You want to join the writing club? Why?"

"Why not?"

Her eyes narrowed again. "Who put you up to this? It was Mrs. Leer wasn't it? You drew the short straw. New kid and all."

"I don't know who Mrs. Leer is."

"Guidance counselor."

"Don't know her." I lifted the flyer. "It was your flyers. Riveting. And the artwork is without equal."

She flared her nostrils. "You're an artist, aren't you? That day on the beach you were sketching."

She noticed that? "Yes."

"My box is dreadful, but in fairness I created that flyer in under thirty seconds."

I deadpanned. "I never would have guessed that." I moved closer and saw the pulse point at her neck jump. "What I want to know is what's in the box? Maybe it's the cat."

"You're not charming," But her expression suggested otherwise. "Whatever you want is in the box. It's called imagination."

"Really? So what's in your box?"

Her eyes burned hot. Fucking hell, she had no idea how easy she was to read. She practically shouted, "Pop-Tarts."

Pop-Tarts? Bullshit. "I've never had them."

"They're delicious and convenient." She was lying through her teeth.

"That's a glowing endorsement. I'll have to try them."

"Yum." That was all she had.

I moved to a desk because in another minute she was going to see what this conversation was doing to me. She was still watching, seemingly unconcerned that I knew she was undressing me with her eyes. I saw the light bulb go on over her head before she asked, "How's your eyesight?"

I bit my tongue so hard I drew blood, but Alexis was fucking hilarious and being sexy as sin…a dangerous combination. I eyed her from head to toe and back again to let her know I knew exactly what she was thinking.

"Twenty/twenty."

Her expression gave her away. She already knew the answer before she asked it. She took her seat. "I usually just do homework."

I surprised her when I asked, "What do you write?"

She mumbled it, but I still heard her. "My last will and testament because after this exchange my social life is definitely on life support." I lowered my head and grinned. She added, "Short stories mostly, but I'd like to write a novel, maybe a screenplay. How about you? What do you draw?"

"Anything and everything." I was purposely vague because I had some really great ideas for drawings that included her. I shifted in my seat. She turned back to her book, probably because I had been sort of dismissive. I pulled out my spiral ring. I needed to draw her, because I wanted to touch her. We weren't there yet, but we'd get there and I couldn't fucking wait.

That night, I had trouble focusing on my homework because my thoughts kept circling back to Alexis. It had been attraction that caught my attention at first, but now I couldn't stop smiling. She was so much more than a pretty face. I wasn't getting any work done, so I left it for now and went to the painting I had setup on an easel in the living room. It was Alexis from that first day. My heart took a jolt every time I looked at her, even my body was telling me to pay attention that something special was happening.

Grandfather returned from the market, his greeting pulling me back to the kitchen.

"Are there more bags?" I asked.

"No. There was a girl outside."

My heart pounded thinking it was Alexis.

"It was the one who brought the brownies. Stephanie, I believe." He stopped unpacking the groceries. "You're not interested."

"No."

"Have you told her?"

"I'm still working on a way to do that and not hurt her feelings."

Seeing the Pop-Tarts, I couldn't help the grin. Pop-Tarts were not what was in Alexis' box, but she really tried to sell the Pop-Tarts. I was bringing the Pop-Tarts to sixth period to see how far she was willing to take her deception. Knew she'd choke them down before she'd confess. I was looking forward to watching her.

I grabbed the milk from the fridge, and drank right out of the carton. Grandfather gave me the look. It didn't matter how many times he told me, I liked drinking the milk from the carton. He didn't drink milk, probably why he didn't push too hard to change my bad habit.

"So, talk to me about the painting in the living room. Who is that?"

"Alexis."

"You don't usually paint people." He studied me for a minute before he added, "She's the reason you're not interested in Stephanie."

I wasn't interested in Stephanie because she was a few cards shy of a deck, but I was very interested in Alexis. "Yeah."

"She's beautiful."

In more ways than one. I wanted to see her; she might be working tonight. I grabbed the Pop-Tarts.

Grandfather grinned. "Drive safely."

4

ALEXIS

I asked for a salad, dressing on the side." Debbie dropped her elbows on the table and tilted her head to me like I was slow. "It really isn't that hard, Alexis."

My hands curled into fists. How much fun it would be to plant one of them in the middle of her face. She had poured the dressing on herself. I had watched her.

Paige didn't miss a beat, sweeping in with a new salad, sans dressing. I enjoyed this part because as often as Debbie taunted us, she had zero learning curve. Paige was exquisite and every boy at Debbie's table thought so, including Mike. The green-eyed monster appeared on Debbie's shoulder as Mike flirted outrageously with Paige.

I turned for the kitchen when the bell over the door jingled. Glancing over, my heart skipped a beat when Greyson walked into the diner heading to a booth in my section.

Paige joined me. "Who's that?"

"That's the guy from the jetty."

"Ah. He *is* cute."

He was so much more than cute and so distracted at the sight of him, I didn't move. Frozen in place happily watching the boy who made me feel all kinds of crazy in the best possible way.

"You're staring," Paige whispered.

"Shit."

She chuckled, "You've got it bad."

I did and I hardly knew him. I took the opportunity, as I approached, to appreciate the muscles of his chest and arms accentuated by the black tee he wore. My body grew warm. I then saw the box of Pop-Tarts. My eyes narrowed. He was grinning.

"I brought dessert. Thought maybe you'd like to join me being such a lover of the Pop-Tart."

His sense of humor made him even sexier. Still, I wasn't confessing, no way in hell. I'd eat that whole damn box before I admitted he was what I wanted in my box.

"Do you know what you want?" He didn't answer. I had pencil to paper waiting, but the pause was so pronounced I glanced up to find him staring at me. How I stayed upright when my bones turned to liquid I couldn't say, but what a look. My voice was an octave too high when I asked, "Did you want something to eat or do you just want the toaster?"

His eyes warmed and my tummy quivered. "Cheeseburger, fries and a coke...please."

Maybe I should mention I was on the menu. Then I remembered he could read minds so I quickly asked, "How do you want your burger cooked?"

"Medium."

I loved his voice. I could listen to him talk all night, anything would do, even the instruction manual for the new gaming system Paige bought this past weekend.

I wrote his order down and turned to go, adding from over my shoulder, "Let me know when you want the toaster."

"What time do you get off work?"

Looking back at him, I couldn't read his expression but I liked it. "Nine."

"There's a full moon tonight. I was going to take a walk to the jetty later. Do you want to come?"

61

In my head I screamed yes while jumping up and down. To him, I said, "That sounds like fun."

He responded with a smile that was slow to form, but magnificent when done.

Giant spiders could attack the diner or The Cure could walk through the door, but I'd be oblivious because that smile just made it to the top of my favorite things list. I wondered if he'd sketch that for me? I almost asked. I needed a chaperone around this boy because he did funny things to my body and my head. Time to abort before I did something stupid, like lick him like a lollipop. "I'll go place this. It shouldn't be longer than ten minutes."

"Thank you, Alexis."

The way my name rolled off his tongue, inflected with that sexy accent, caused goosebumps. Forming words was simply out of the question. I fled like I was on fire. In the kitchen, I gave thought to dunking my head in the cold dishwater.

Paige followed me. "The fireworks going off between the two of you, it was definitely not your imagination that first day."

"I don't know what it is about him, but he makes me crazy."

She rested her hip against the counter. "In a good way?"

"Yes."

"Nice."

"Not nice. I can't control my thoughts when I'm around him. I'm…" I lowered my voice so Mel wouldn't overhear, "Thinking about him naked, Paige."

"What's wrong with that?"

"It's objectifying."

"So."

"And embarrassing."

"He's hot and you're a teenager. I think about Grant naked all the time. Even right now." A wicked look swept her face. She really was thinking about Grant naked. I couldn't help the laugh.

"Stop it."

She chuckled, "Relax, Alexis. You're human."

"And horny."

"You're a teenager, that's a perpetual state. Welcome to the club."

I tried for cool when I left the kitchen, but I kept looking over at Greyson's table. I hoped I was being subtle, but I couldn't help looking. He was here; he was waiting for me. My insides felt like a bottle of bubbly that had been shaken. He was sketching. I wondered what he was sketching because he hadn't lifted his head from the paper.

At closing time, Paige offered to finish up for me. I pulled off my apron, washed my hands and went to join Greyson. Approaching his table, my heart pounded and I had chills of excitement racing down my arms because he had stayed for me. Had I been a cartoon there would be colored hearts drifting over my head. Reaching his table, I kind of stumbled a bit seeing what he'd been diligently working on. It was me. Studying the lines of my face, how he saw me, I was beautiful to him.

Speechless, I could only nod when he said, "Shall we?"

His bike was out front. Like we'd been doing it for years, he handed me the helmet. The bike roared to life. I held him like I had that first ride, as close as possible.

The moon was full providing enough light to see our way to the jetty. The ocean was calm tonight. We settled on the rocks.

"This is a great spot," Greyson offered.

It was and even more so now with him. I wasn't going to pry, but we were here. "Can I ask you something?"

"Sure."

"Where did you come from?"

He chuckled, "Did my accent give it away?"

"Sorry, it's just you're a senior and you're here. I'm curious."

"Home is Ireland, a little place outside of Kerry. My grandfather has an artist friend who retired in San Francisco. We moved to the States so he could start managing me. He thinks I should be touring, has already contacted a few of his connections to sponsor shows for me at their galleries, but Grandfather wants me to finish my schooling. That's why we settled here, far enough from San Francisco to keep me focused on school but close enough to make my agent's work easier."

Was it fate that put people in each other's paths? Or was my fairy godmother trying to tell me something? They could have settled in any number of small towns along the West Coast and yet by chance he was dropped right into the middle of my world.

63

"It must feel good to not only know what you want to do with your life, but to know you're good enough to do it."

His expression softened in reply before he asked, "What about you? Is writing what you want to do?"

"Yes. I've been writing short stories for as long as I can remember, but I'd like to start a full-length novel."

"Do you have a subject?"

Him. I didn't say that though. "I'm working on it. My hope is to study creative writing at NYU."

Surprised, he said, "That's quite a hike."

I shifted my focus to the horizon. "I like it here, but I've always felt drawn to New York City. I don't know why, maybe because it is so far from home, something different."

"I've never been to New York."

"If your art ever takes you to the East Coast, look me up. I'll give you a tour." I was teasing, but not really. One day he'd been gone. Maybe we could give fate a little hand and get our paths to cross again.

"I'm going to take you up on that, Alexis."

"I hope you do."

I wished I knew what he was thinking; his expression was intense.

"I should probably get you home." I didn't want to go home. I wanted to stay right here with him, but we did have school in the morning.

He stood and reached for my hand. I didn't know what it was about that moment, but it was one I knew I would remember always. The way he looked in the moonlight. His wide palm held out to me, the look of interest on his face that matched my own. I slipped my hand into his and knew with certainty that my life would never be the same.

"I don't agree. McDonalds is infinitely better than Burger King."

"Flame broiled, babe, all the way," Greyson countered.

It was sixth period and we weren't writing. We were learning about each other in the silliest way. "Let me guess, you're a Pepsi fan too."

Humor danced in his eyes. "You're not?"

"No."

"Star Wars or Star Trek?"

"Star Wars, hands down," I said a little too emphatically.

"That we agree on."

I sighed loudly. "Lucky, because I can't be friends with someone who likes Captain Kirk over Luke Skywalker."

Greyson was working in his spiral ring again. He'd been vague the last time I asked, it didn't discourage me from asking again. "Is your portfolio mostly sketches or do you have paintings as well?"

His gaze lifted. "Mostly paintings. The sketches are for fun."

"Do you have a preference…people, landscapes?"

"Usually landscapes in oil. I rarely paint people."

He had sketched me. I wanted to preen like a peacock at the honor. "You mentioned your grandfather's friend was lining up galleries to showcase your work. Do you have any idea what to expect?"

"Lots of touring. Living out of my suitcase, meeting more people than I'll ever remember, trying to squeeze in painting while networking."

"Will you come back here?"

"I'll likely get an apartment in San Francisco and Grandfather will go home. He misses it."

I didn't know him; I liked who I was getting to know, but he really was just passing through.

"I have no illusions. It's going to suck in the beginning, lots of hard work and socializing, something I'm not really good at, but it is necessary. You'll have to do the same. Writing the book is only part of it, marketing and promoting, carving out a niche for yourself is just as important."

He was right, but I didn't want to talk about me. I wanted to know more about him. "Are your parents here too?"

His shoulders tensed and he stopped sketching. "No. They died a few years ago, a car accident."

My heart broke. He had lost his parents too.

"Why do I have a feeling you can relate?" he asked.

"I was abandoned very young. I have foster parents and well, they aren't really parents."

"What do you mean?"

"They aren't interested in parenting; they just want the check."

His expression turned dark. "Seriously?"

"Yeah, but I have family. I'm good. I'm sorry about your parents." He was old enough to remember them. That was a double-edged sword. He had memories of his parents, but he also knew them well enough to feel the loss of them.

"I try to remember the good times. Like my mom, she loved horses. Whenever she had free time, she was riding the moors. She taught me to ride when I was very little."

I could see him on horseback. He'd be magnificent. "Do you still?"

"I haven't since we arrived in the States, but back home I'd go out a few times a month."

I wanted to see that; him on horseback, riding over his land, and was surprised at the sadness that washed over me knowing I never would.

He studied me for a second before a grin pulled at his mouth. "Ding Dongs or Twinkies?"

I was grateful for the subject change because I knew I was going to miss him when he was gone; how much was what worried me. "Twinkies."

5

ALEXIS

"Seriously, what is up with the gooey eyes?" Dominic asked as we sat at the table in front of Grant's garage.

"I don't have gooey eyes."

"You do. You look kind of dopey."

"Dopey? If I was closer, I'd smack you in the head." I'm sure I did look dopey because I had Greyson on the brain.

Grant walked from one of the bays, a giggling Tara on his shoulders and a squealing Amanda on his foot. They were four and three respectively. Paige and Grant's children were cherubs; that's what I called them. And Grant. It wasn't a wonder that I crushed on him for so long. He was awesome with his tattoos and long hair. Badass and yet he doted over his girls. He was totally swoon worthy.

"The garage has rodents. I need to call an exterminator," he teased.

"Serious rodents. Look at the size of them," Dominic said as he swept Mandy into the air. "Good eating right here."

She squealed louder.

"Where's Paige?" I asked as Grant dropped Tara to her feet; she immediately climbed into my lap.

"The salon."

"I'll watch these two if you have to get back to work."

"Would you mind? I might be able to leave on time if I get this bike done."

"No problem. I'll fill them with sugar and wind them up; that's what aunts are for."

Grant laughed and pressed a kiss on my head. "Thanks, Alexis."

I sighed softly because he really was the perfect man.

A motorcycle pulled into the lot. I followed Grant's gaze and sighed again. Greyson.

"Can I help you?" Grant asked as he approached Greyson whose pale eyes were on me. A grin tugged at his mouth before his focus turned to Grant. He offered his hand.

"Who's that?" Tara asked.

"His name is Greyson."

Her wide eyes looked up into mine. "Do you know him?"

"Yes."

"He is pretty."

"Yes, he is."

"The new kid. I wonder what's brought him here," Dylan teased when he returned with the sundaes.

"Your guess is as good as mine," Dominic added. They were dorks. He dropped Mandy at the table. The girls helped themselves to the twin's ice cream.

I rested my head on my hand and watched Greyson and Grant. I loved Grant, but it was Greyson who gave me butterflies and made my palms sweaty.

"I'll take a look at it. Give me a few minutes." Grant headed back into his shop. Greyson strolled over to me.

"Hey, Alexis."

"Hi. Something wrong with your bike?"

"Nothing major, I hope."

Tara was pulling on my arm. "I want to meet him." She thought she was whispering but she wasn't.

Greyson hunched down next to her as I offered the introductions. "Greyson, Tara, Tara, Greyson."

He lifted Tara's hand and pressed a kiss on it. You could see it in her eyes, her little heart was lost, her first crush. I understood completely.

"My hand, my hand," Mandy called. "Kissy my hand too." She thrust her hand out at Greyson. He was a sport because he did kiss her hand, like she was the only girl whose hand he had ever kissed. Mandy fell in love too.

"These two are Dominic and Dylan."

"You don't need to kiss my hand." Dylan was such a dork. "Nice to meet you."

"And you."

"Irish?" Dominic asked.

"Aye."

"I'm getting more ice cream since the rodents ate ours," Dylan pointed out. "Do you want anything?"

"No thanks, mate."

I think I fell in love too.

"Alexis, if you can pry your eyes from Greyson. Do you want some ice cream?"

Dylan was completely unfazed by my death rays. "No, thank you."

"Dom, come with me. Don't say anything important until we get back."

I gave Dylan a face then turned to Greyson to find he was gone. Tara had one hand, Mandy had the other, and they were leading him to their hopscotch board. I watched completely charmed as Greyson made two little girls' day...hell, their year.

I didn't hear Paige until she knocked her shoulder into mine. "Looks like my girls are giving you some competition."

"How sweet is that?"

"Very."

I turned to her then took a double take. "You cut your hair."

"It was getting to be too much."

"I love it." Instead of falling to mid-back, her black locks brushed her shoulders.

"Does Grant know you were doing that?"

"No."

"He loves your hair."

"I know."

"So we might get some unexpected fireworks."

Dylan and Dominic had a huge crush on Paige. Always competing for her attention. Today was no exception when they returned and immediately pushed me out of the way so they could each have a side.

"We got ice cream. Would you like some?" I understood the dopey look Dylan mentioned earlier because he was sporting it now.

"I got chocolate," Dominic said.

"So did I."

"But mine has sprinkles," Dominic lifted his spoon to Paige's mouth. She was trying hard not to laugh.

"Maybe she doesn't like sprinkles," Dylan hissed.

"Maybe she does."

Before they started taking swings at each other, Grant walked from the garage, saw Paige and froze. I wanted to be on the receiving end of a look like that. It wasn't just love, it was lust, it was familiarity…it was like they shared a secret. I envied them.

Grant changed direction and I took a step back because I knew what was coming. He grabbed his wife and knocked her socks off with a kiss so passionate I felt it.

The girls immediately started making gagging sounds. I looked back. Greyson was watching me, a look that I could get used to seeing. I joined him.

"Paige," I offered.

"His wife," he guessed.

"Yep."

Paige was breathless when Grant released her. She called, "Pizza for dinner. Who's coming with me to get it?"

The twins offered instantly, both looking a little heartbroken witnessing the obvious love between Paige and Grant. Poor guys.

Grant headed to Greyson's bike.

"Stay for pizza." The invite was out of my mouth before I realized I was going to offer it.

"Are you sure?"

"Absolutely." I called to Grant, "Greyson's joining us for pizza."

"Cool," he called back.

"See. Easy peasy."

"Greyson, it's your turn," Tara called.

He flashed me a smile that stilled my heart before he returned to the girls.

"Do you have to go home now?" Greyson asked after we'd said goodnight to the gang. I liked him hanging with us, liked that he fit.

"No."

"Do you want to get dessert?"

"The diner makes the best hot fudge sundae."

"Sold. I'll bring some food home for Grandfather and Nigel."

"Nigel?"

"His estate manager. He flew in earlier to go over the books and pending business matters. I decided to make myself scarce because the two of them can get quite rowdy."

I was still stuck on the estate part. "An estate?"

"Yeah, my family's home is one of the oldest castles in Ireland."

My jaw dropped. He grinned and touched my chin to close it.

"You live in a castle?"

"Yeah."

"Like staff and housekeeper and gardener?"

"Yes. It's been in my family since the fourteenth century."

What must that feel like to have ancestry like that, to walk the same halls as family had centuries earlier. I didn't even know my parents and he had generations of family. I was a little envious.

We reached the diner, Greyson held the door for me. We lucked out to get a booth. Once we settled, Meg took our order. After she left I asked, "What's your castle like?"

There was a faraway look about him, like he was traveling in his mind to his home. "It's magnificent, hundreds of acres of land, a forest, rolling hills, a lake."

I wanted to see it, wanted it to be him that showed me. "How can you stand to be away from it?"

"Since my parents died, it's hard to be there and not see them."

71

The faraway look wasn't for his home; it was for his parents. My eyes burned. "I'm sorry."

"They wanted me to come to the States, had been encouraging me to pursue art since I was a kid. Gave me my first paint set; set up my first lessons. Hung up everything I ever made, even the stick figures that were hardly recognizable. Part of my wish to succeed is for them."

Tears welled, but I couldn't stop them hearing both love and pain in his words. I tried to imagine his parents and knew they had been incredible because they had an incredible son.

I doubted very much anything he drew, even at the age of three, was unrecognizable. I loved his passion, it reminded me of how I felt about writing, and I was happy he was going to pursue it, had people ready to help him turn his dreams into reality.

Our sundae arrived, one sundae, two spoons. He dipped in, spooned up some whipped cream and offered it to me. My heart fluttered, my mouth closing around his spoon as he watched with heat in his gaze. It was a look similar to the one I saw Grant giving Paige, a look I really, really liked. I must have had some on my face because he reached across the table and wiped it away with his thumb then brought that thumb to his mouth. It was both erotic and unbearably sweet.

We devoured the sundae. Conversation with him was so natural. I had a huge crush on him. You'd think I'd be stumbling over my words, but we really were like old friends catching up. Toward the end of the evening, he held my gaze and said softly, "Maybe one day you'll see my home."

It was very unlikely that day would ever come. In less than a year he'd be gone. In two, I would be across the country. We had plans that sent us down two different paths, but to him I spoke from my heart. "I'd really like that."

I never liked dressing for gym, hated it even more when gym was swimming. We were only allowed to wear a one-piece bathing suit otherwise some of the chicks in my class would be in their string bikinis, mortifying when you had a body like a board. Another reason I hated swimming, it was coed. I pulled my hair into a knot, grabbed my towel and headed to the pool.

"There was a mess up, so we're sharing the pool with a senior's class. Instead of trying to run two classes, we're going to work together."

Great. Seniors. Oh well, I could handle that for one class. Debbie entered with her chick gang...on second thought. Even I stared at her. It was like she inflated her breasts. She had the uncanny ability of sniffing me out like a bloodhound. I was self-conscious enough, but standing next to her in our bathing suits only reinforced just how flat I was. It was a nightmare.

Her mouth opened and I had no doubt she intended to be cruel, but her words died on her tongue when something behind me caught her attention. Curious as to what shut her up mid-scathing comment, I followed her gaze.

Greyson.

In.

A.

Bathing suit.

Holy shit.

His hair was knotted on his head. Wide shoulders, muscled arms, a chiseled chest and a six-pack. He had a six-pack at eighteen. I had to roll my tongue back into my mouth. It then dawned that he'd see my boy body, made even more pronounced with Debbie prancing around. Fantastic.

"I want a taste of that," one of Debbie's friends said. I almost pushed her into the pool. Her hips swayed as she sauntered to Greyson. She tossed her hair over her shoulder, stealing my move though I doubt I would have done it so well. She wet her lips. That was a good one. I hadn't thought of that. They glistened like she'd just been kissed. She was sexy; I couldn't argue that point. I was almost seventeen. Had puberty passed me by?

I didn't want to look, but I couldn't tear my gaze away. Would he offer her one of those grins, or a wink? Would he look at her like he did me, focused and intense like he was trying to figure me out? Were our interactions unique, or was he like that with everyone? I didn't want to burst my bubble so I turned from the scene, surely to be the talk of the lunch hour, and walked to the other side of the pool to work on my power of invisibility.

"Pick partners," one of the teachers called.

Pick partners? It just went from bad to worse.

"Hey, partner."

My heart slammed into my ribs so hard I was sure I heard them crack. Turning around, I was eye level with Greyson's chest. His very beautiful, chiseled chest. If I leaned forward my lips would be on him. What would he taste like?

I didn't realize I licked my lips in anticipation until Greyson growled, "Keep doing that and I'm not accountable for what happens."

My eyes jerked to his face then my breath caught because he looked hungry.

"What happened to...?" I waved my hand in the chick's direction.

He shrugged. "Don't know, don't care. So, partners?"

"Yes!" At least I didn't jump up and down and clap.

"You're going to practice an in water rescue. I'll demonstrate and then you'll work with your partner."

Was I dreaming? I got to touch his bare body and had a school-approved reason for doing so. My fairy godmother had sprinkled fairy dust on me. It was the only explanation that made any sense.

The teacher demonstrated, then we were called into the pool. I didn't think Greyson in swim trunks could be topped. I was wrong. A wet Greyson in swim trunks was even better.

"Do you want to save me first?"

I was a good swimmer, but I didn't know if I'd be able to manage rescuing him.

"How about you rescue me first?" I countered.

"All right, damsel. Get in distress."

As I have previously mentioned, I had a wonderful imagination. Flailing my arms, going under. I'm sure I looked like a deranged lunatic, but I played the part to perfection. His arm wrapped around me like we were instructed and I stopped flailing. I forgot everything but the feel of his strong arm around me, the heat from his skin, feeling his muscled chest against my back. Effortlessly he swam me to the side. My nipples were hard and I felt more than pool water between my legs. I was embarrassed, but so turned on. I didn't understand the effect this boy had on me. I hardly knew him, but my body liked him just fine.

I managed to pull myself together and turned to him. His eyes looked darker and there was that hunger again. Lust tap-danced down my spine.

"Your turn," I said.

Like I had done, he flailed his arms. He looked like a deranged lunatic. It was awesome. I wrapped my arm around him. I felt his muscles tense under my touch. His heart pounded hard under my hand. I swam him to the side, but I didn't let him go right away. He made no move to get away. I even wrapped my other hand around his stomach, touched his thighs with my feet. He turned so fast and pressed me back against the side of the pool. A hummingbird's wings, that's how fast my heart was pounding. He dipped his chin, his face getting right into mine. I thought he was going to kiss me.

Instead, he whispered, "You saved my life. How can I ever repay you?"

What a ridiculous thing to say. It was so unexpected and totally charming. He purred the next part, "I'll do anything."

Tingles of anticipation exploded inside me as my focus shifted to his mouth. I wanted to know how it felt against mine, wanted his taste on my tongue. He touched my cheek, a delicate swipe of his thumb. "You have to say it, sweetheart."

I was rocked by the lust burning in his gaze. I almost said it. I almost told him to kiss me, but the teacher called end of class. He didn't move, kept me pinned to the side of the pool.

"We're not done with this conversation."

I couldn't speak; it was like someone scrambled my brains so I nodded my head. He chuckled then released me. "See you later, Alexis."

He swam to the other end of the pool, in long sure strokes. He pulled himself from the water; it sheeted off him. His trunks hugged his ass and what an ass. Electric was how I felt. I should have been electrocuted feeling as I did in water. I dunked my head, hoping to cool the heat raging through me. When I surfaced, Greyson was still standing there, watching me. A knowing grin curved his lips before he headed to the locker room. My legs were wobbly when I climbed from the pool. I didn't know what upset me more, that I almost kissed Greyson in the school pool or that I hadn't kissed Greyson in the school pool.

My nerves were frayed. It was sixth period, writing club. I couldn't get our moment out of my head. I had to though because Greyson would be showing up any minute and he had the uncanny ability of reading my mind, which was filled with thoughts of him naked. I put on The Cure; they never failed to distract me.

I was jamming at my desk when Greyson entered. "You really like them."

My head jerked up, every second of our encounter earlier flashed through my head. I almost moaned. He was staring at me expectantly. What had he said? Oh right, The Cure. "They follow their own path."

"Trailblazers, yeah I can see that. You're one too, you know."

I had been writing, but my pencil slipped. It was one of the nicest things anyone had ever said to me. "Thank you."

He dropped his backpack on the floor then dropped down on the desk in front of me. "About the pool."

I lowered my gaze. He had gotten carried away, wanted to set my expectations that we were friends and not to read into it. I expected the one eighty, but it still hurt.

"I was a little forward; I'm sorry. I just…" He stood. I looked then as he paced away from me, pulling a hand through his hair. He turned back and my breath caught. He didn't look disinterested, not at all. "I want to kiss you. It's all I think about, but coming on that strong in class was wrong. I'm sorry."

We needed to stop, rewind so I could record this conversation. He was apologizing for wanting to kiss me? Did I fall asleep? I had to have fallen asleep, but it seemed so real.

A smile curved his lips. "You have the most expressive face. Every thought is so easy to read."

What? No, that wasn't true.

"Right now, you're dubious. Wondering if this is really happening."

Shit.

"The day at the beach, you felt it too. That hit of attraction."

Holy crap, he did have the power to read minds.

"Biology that first day…" He moved closer to me. "I don't know exactly what you were thinking, but I'd really like to. Your box is not filled with Pop-Tarts. You detest them." He pushed his hands into his pockets. His voice dropped to a sexy purr. "In the pool, you wanted me to kiss you. You want me to kiss you now, almost as badly as I want to. All you have to do is close the distance, Alexis, and I'll put us both out of our misery."

I was dreaming.

"You're not dreaming."

"How do you know I'm thinking that?"

"You said *that* out loud."

"I do hate Pop-Tarts."

"They're pretty dreadful."

I didn't tell my body to move, but it had a mind of its own. I stood. His eyes went dark. How I put one foot in front of the other amazed me. I felt so many things all at once. What I felt the strongest? I wanted to kiss him, my first real kiss. The air crackled between us. My breath hitched when his fingers threaded through my hair. He stepped closer, our bodies touching from chest to thigh. Tingles swept through me, my heart pounding so hard he had to feel it. I inhaled his scent as my mouth watered. I had only a second to see what I was feeling in his gaze before he kissed me. It was barely a kiss; his lips brushing mine lightly, and yet I felt that kiss down to my bones. He traced my lower lip with his tongue before he slid it into my mouth, leaving his taste on my tongue. He growled deep in his throat and took the kiss deeper, drinking me in like a thirsty man finally finding water. My eyes closed as I reached for him, partly to feel him and partly to stay upright.

I was breathless when he ended it. He touched his forehead to mine and curled his fingers around my neck. "One taste isn't enough."

"Why stop at one?" Bold for me, but I was already hooked after only a taste.

He rubbed my lower lip with his thumb, his eyes following the motion. "Good question."

My arms went around his neck and I pressed myself against him. It was me who tasted him, sweeping his mouth, hungry for the taste of him.

He broke the kiss and stepped back. "Too easy to forget where we are."

School. Right. Mr. Dobbs could pop in at any minute.

His focus was on my mouth; my blood felt like liquid fire.

"We're picking this up later."

We had three more periods in the day, but, oh hell yeah, we were picking this up later.

Finally, it was last period. I hadn't paid attention in my last few classes. I'd never kissed a boy before, well not like that. Just thinking about it…I understood now the appeal of the eraser room. What I didn't understand was why people didn't kiss all day long. Knowing something felt that good, people should be attacking each other. I worried I would. My lips were still tingling from his kiss, the pressure of his mouth on mine, the way his tongue stroke out more pleasure, the complete shutdown of my body as all systems focused on the magic of his kiss.

The bell rang; yet another class I hadn't heard a damn thing in. I headed to my locker, turned the corner and stopped dead at the sight of Greyson leaning against my locker talking to some kid. On cue, my body grew warm. I felt a bit like a car revving at the starting line, so eager for the flag to drop so I could rush to Greyson, push the kid out of the way and kiss him senseless. He laughed and I felt that in the center of my chest. I might not have ever known him, the reality of that was not something I wanted to think too much on; he could have picked another town to wait out his senior year; we could have been like those two ships passing in the night. Now that would have been a tragedy.

His focus shifted, a smile touched his lips when he saw me. Even riding the high of kissing him, I felt sad too because our time had an expiration date. He met me halfway, moving so close we were touching. His focus was on my mouth before he lifted that hot gaze.

"Do you have work?"

"No."

"Come with me?"

Anywhere. "Yes."

It was with superhuman speed that I swapped out the books in my locker, eager to get on the back of his bike. More eager to get somewhere private so I could kiss him again. He took my backpack and reached for my hand. I grinned at the memory of scripting a scene very similar to this when I was working up the nerve to talk to him. Maybe I should script out a few more scenes and see what happened.

We made it to his bike, before he dropped my backpack and pulled his hands through my hair in one seamless move. He kissed me, this time with a bit of familiarity, and way more hunger. He feasted; it was the only word that came to mind to describe the way his mouth, teeth and tongue worked together to draw out so much pleasure. Though, in fairness, my brain wasn't thinking vocabulary at the moment. I explored every inch of his mouth, curling my hands into his shirt to pull him closer. Chills moved from my head to my toes in the most delicious way. I wanted the world to stop so we could live in this moment forever. We were both breathing heavy; I even forgot where we were for a minute.

"I want to show you something," he said against my mouth.

I wanted to see it, but I didn't think we were talking about the same thing. He growled, reading my thoughts perfectly. He strapped my backpack onto his bike and handed me the helmet. I didn't care where we were going just as long as there would be more kissing.

We reached the bluffs and though I had lived most of my life here I had never seen this particular spot. It was a little piece of heaven. Patches of sea grass and wildflowers still in bloom softened the rocky cliff. Seagulls flew low and the salty sea scented the air. The ocean spread out before us, reaching to the horizon, with the only sound being the crashing of the waves against the surf.

"I've lived here my whole life and I never knew about this place. It's magnificent."

"I want to paint it."

"I can see why."

His focus turned to me. "I want to paint you too."

79

My blood ignited. "Okay."

"I'm going to hold you to that."

I held his gaze. "I hope you do."

He yanked me close, his eyes on my mouth again. "Now that I've had a taste it's all I can think about."

"You and me both."

Then he kissed me. Yep, I could so totally spend the rest of my life kissing this boy.

6

GREYSON

I had Alexis on the brain. I was hooked, fucking addicted. I was leaving at the end of the school year. My agent had the next few years all planned out. Getting involved with her when I knew I was leaving was stupid, but I couldn't stay away. I'd never been so drawn to someone, wanted someone as badly as I wanted her and I hardly knew her.

I then made matters worse by kissing her. Holy shit, that kiss. I found myself daydreaming about it and I didn't daydream. It wasn't just because it was the best fucking kiss, it was the familiarity that hooked into me and refused to let go. I knew her and yet we'd never met before this. I was going mad, but there was comfort knowing Alexis was right there with me.

Arriving at school, I headed to Alexis' locker. She was already there, unloading her bag. I swear she looked to be talking to herself. I wouldn't be surprised if she were. She had her hair up, her neck exposed and I wanted to kiss her right where her neck met her shoulder. So I did. She knew I was there, her body tensed before I reached her. She moaned and my balls tightened.

"Is that you, Greyson?" she teased.

I bit her.

"Ouch."

Taking her backpack, I dropped my arm around her shoulders and pressed my lips to her ear. "Maybe the eraser room is empty."

By the way her body responded, she liked that idea.

I was so fucking hard, but I couldn't taste her enough. I wanted to consume her, wanted to pull her into me and keep her there.

"I never understood the eraser room," she said between kisses. "I so love the eraser room."

I chuckled, but I never stopped kissing her. In the very back of my mind a warning sounded. I needed to stop this, needed to put on the brakes, because Alexis wasn't just any girl. If anyone had the power to change my plans, it was her. I ignored the warning, but I did pull from her because another minute and I wouldn't have control.

"Are you okay?"

"I will be."

I couldn't see her face, but I knew she blushed. "Sorry."

"I'm not."

I needed distance to get my cock to calm down, but I couldn't help touching her face, running my finger along her jaw. It wasn't just lust I felt, it was the stronger emotion that caused concern. I was leaving, but I was beginning to understand I wouldn't be doing so whole. This girl had claimed a piece of me.

"My grandfather's birthday is this weekend. I'm cooking him dinner. Come." What the hell was I doing? We should be slowing things down, not integrating her more into my life. Clearly, when it came to the idea of stepping away from her I lacked conviction.

"You can cook?"

"Why do you sound so surprised?"

"Not surprised just...okay I'm surprised. You're only eighteen. That's cool. I can't even boil water."

"Have you tried to cook?"

"No."

"So how do you know you can't?"

"Because if I say I can't then I don't have guilt mooching a meal from the Cantenellis as often as I do."

"What's up with that? You guys act more like brothers and sister than friends."

"They live across the street from me. Their family took me in when I was young, became a sort of surrogate family. I do think of those knuckleheads as brothers."

I suspected that, but I did like hearing it confirmed. "Will you come? It's Saturday."

"I'd love too; I'll make the cake."

"I thought you couldn't cook."

"I haven't tried to cook, but I think I can manage a cake."

"Maybe I should get a back up cake, just in case."

"Fiend."

"We should probably get to class."

"I guess, but I want it noted that I don't want to go to class."

"Noted."

I checked if the coast was clear, but the eraser room had been chosen well, located in a section of the school that saw very little foot traffic. We headed for her homeroom; passing her locker I remembered the scene with that bitch Debbie, which had me asking, "What's up with Debbie? Why is she such a bitch to you?"

"I don't really know. I met her through the twins and for several years we were close, but in middle school she started to mature, boys noticed. By the eighth grade she had morphed into the Debbie you see now. She stopped hanging out with us and started going out of her way to be a bitch."

I had no doubt Debbie was jealous. She didn't compare to Alexis and never would. She grinned then added, "It's possible she's pissed that you are spending time with me not her."

I couldn't help the shudder, but what a thought. My balls shriveled up.

Alexis stopped walking; I glanced back at her. "You don't find her attractive? I mean, sure she's a bitch, but look at her."

"She looks like a plastic surgeon got carried away."

83

Her jaw actually dropped. She was fucking adorable. "But she's got those…" She gestured with her hands.

"They're ridiculous."

Disbelief swept her expression. "Are you serious? I thought for guys the bigger the better."

"Maybe some guys, but me, I prefer long and lean."

Her eyes narrowed. "You're kidding."

I moved right into her, lowered my head and whispered, "I like long legs that end in the gentle swell of hips, the curve of a woman's back…" I ran my hand over the small of her back. "Drives me nuts. As far as…" Our eyes meet and held. "Bigger is not better. Enough to fill my palm, pale pink, tight…"

She slammed her hand over my mouth. "Please stop or I'm not responsible for what happens."

Her cheeks were flush with arousal. She wasn't the only one. Grabbing her hand, I pulled her down the hall before we backtracked to the eraser room. Feeling smug, I said, "Glad we cleared that up."

ALEXIS

"It's crooked." It was more than crooked. It was an abomination and I had such high hopes. I picked up a few magazines at the market when I bought the ingredients. I had thought to create a tiered wonder. How hard could it be? Famous last words. Instead of a white-tiered confection, it looked more like what became of a cake at a one-year-old's birthday party. We were in Greyson's granddad's car.

"Tastes good though."

"I can't understand how you could have seen this and thought oh, I wonder what that tastes like? Some things are best staying a mystery."

He glanced over at me. "But you're bringing it."

"I know. I couldn't leave it at home. It's not the cake's fault that I'm Dr. Frankenstein. The poor unsuspecting flour and sugar, those eggs and butter, they deserved a better fate than this, but I want your granddad to know I tried, even if my attempt looks like roadkill with icing."

He laughed, a raucous laugh, but his eyes warmed when he looked over again. "It's the thought that counts."

I pointed at him. "Yes, that's exactly what I'm trying to say in the most round about way."

He pulled up a long drive. "So this is where you live. I almost hunted you down after the first time you drove me home." Why did I tell him that?

He parked and shut off the engine. "Why didn't you?"

The cat was out of the bag now about my latent stalker tendencies. "It felt stalkerish."

He had a reaction to that, but I couldn't for the life of me read him. "What?"

"I wouldn't have thought you were being stalkerish."

"We'll get back to that. What was that look for? Did someone hunt you down?"

"Stephanie. She brought me brownies."

I almost dropped the cake, which might have improved its appearance. "Are you serious?"

"Yeah, she's been here at least one other time but didn't knock. Granddad saw her."

"Was she in a tree across the street with binoculars?"

He grinned. "I hope not."

"I get it. I mean had things gone differently with us, I might have driven by your house a few times hoping to catch a glimpse of you."

He shifted so he was facing me. "Really?"

"You have to know you're ridiculously handsome, that face and hair, your eyes and body." *Shut up, Alexis.*

Now he was grinning and why not? I had verbal diarrhea. "You don't say."

I couldn't believe I was being so bold, but my mouth opened and more came out. "What Stephanie doesn't know is there is more to you than pretty packaging."

"Are you purposely trying to drive me crazy?" he asked.

"Yes, payback for sneaking a taste of the cake."

He muttered before he climbed from the car, "If that's payback, I'm going to eat the whole fucking thing."

He took the cake, and even humming with sexual tension, my attention was on his house. It was a beautiful Victorian, painted in a dove gray with lots of creamy white gingerbread trim and palladium windows. The back of the house overlooked the Pacific Ocean.

"What a wonderful place."

"Yeah, I love that view. It's forever changing."

The artist in him would see that.

"I would love a house like this," I confessed.

"I thought you wanted the hustle and bustle of the city."

"Yeah, but when I settle down with a family I'd love a place just like this one."

He seemed to have a thought on that, but offered nothing. He walked me to the door that opened to an incredible smell. His grandfather was behind the island chopping vegetables, and damn but talk about family resemblance. He was older, obviously, but he had the same bone structure, same eyes, same build. I was looking at Greyson in forty years. He'd still be hot.

"Alexis, this is my grandfather, Callum."

He walked around the kitchen island and took my hand. I blurted out, "I can't believe how much Greyson looks like you."

He smiled and brought my hand to his lips, just like his grandson had done to Tara and Mandy. "It's very nice to meet you." He glanced over at the cake. "Is that for me?"

"It doesn't look great, but Greyson assures me it tastes good."

"A homemade cake. I haven't had one of those in far too long. Thank you."

"My pleasure."

"Greyson made shepherd's pie. I hope that's okay."

"Smells amazing."

"I'll finish the salad. Why don't you two go wash up."

Greyson grabbed my hand and pulled me down the hall. We didn't go to the bathroom; he pulled me into his bedroom. My back hit the door as soon as he closed it. He kissed my neck. I tilted my head to give him better access. "You taste so good." His tongue moved down my neck and along my shoulder.

My blood ignited. "Kiss me, Greyson."

He did, his lips brushing back and forth before his tongue pushed into my mouth, tasting me with a thoroughness that left me weak. I wanted him. I wanted him to be my first. I wanted that so badly. I didn't understand all the emotions he pulled from me, how hot he made me, how my body ached in so many ways, but I knew I wanted him to be my first.

"I can't get enough of you," he said as he dragged his lips to my ear, tracing it with his tongue before taking a little bite.

I fisted his shirt and drew him closer.

He pulled his hand through my hair. "I want you, Alexis."

My eyes went wide. "Not now."

He didn't react at first and then he laughed out loud. "No, not now."

"Because I could be tempted."

His smile died as the sexiest look swept his face. "Don't say that or I'm locking this door."

"Your granddad?"

"Will be celebrating his birthday alone."

At least he'd have cake.

He kissed me hard on the mouth. "You go first. I need to…"

My gaze drifted down to his hard-on and I felt powerful being able to bring this boy to that. "Sorry."

"I'm not."

"I'll see you out there."

"A little less of me, aye." He sounded adorably disgruntled.

I giggled then slipped out of his room.

Dinner had been delicious. Greyson wasn't kidding when he said he knew how to cook. Throughout dinner, I marveled at how much alike Greyson and his grandfather were and not just their physical appearance, but their personalities, humor and mannerisms. And their accents, that beautiful lilt had images of Ireland rolling through my mind, at least the Ireland I knew from pictures. I understood Greyson's passion that brought him to the States, the loss of his parents, and still I couldn't imagine staying away from what I saw as paradise.

"Greyson mentioned you live in a castle."

Callum leaned back in his chair, his expression turning a bit faraway. "Taisce Manor." He looked nostalgic before he added, "It's one of the oldest castles in Ireland."

I loved hearing the pride they had in their home, was a little envious too. "Greyson mentioned that. It sounds wonderful."

"One day you'll have to come for a visit. The landscape is like nothing you've ever seen."

An ache formed. The invitation was sincere, but it was also a fairy tale.

"Greyson tells me you are a writer. Is that what you hope to do, write professionally?"

"First step is to study creative writing at NYU and then yes, I'd love to write for a living, novels, plays, and screenplays. I'd like to try my hand at all of them."

"Ireland is a land filled with stories just waiting to be written. In fact, our family has its own legend."

My elbows dropped on the table. Bad manners, but how fascinating. "Really?"

"Aye. 'Tis believed that a goddess disguised as a mortal woman visited the very first Ratcliffe, Aenfinn himself. They loved as man and woman but she was not of his world and was forced to return to her own. She couldn't leave without giving him something to remember her by and so it is told that she conjured a diamond through magic, binding it with love. The stone is called Mo Chuisle, My Pulse. Years later, Aenfinn eventually married to continue his bloodline, but he never parted with the stone. He had it embedded into his great sword, a sword he was never without."

What a beautiful and sad story. "Do you believe the legend?"

Callum didn't hesitate to answer. "His goddess' sacred place is believed to be in our backyard. In the portrait gallery, Aenfinn's portrait depicts the stone in his sword. It appears later in a broach worn by a couple of Ratcliffe women."

It was a fascinating story, more so because Callum believed it. A reasonable and educated man believed it. I did too. "Where's the stone now?"

"It was lost several generations back, after a fire. Some of the household books were lost too, so trying to piece together what became of it has been very difficult. I've often thought I'd like to write it down, but I don't have skill to do the story justice." His eyes met mine before he offered, "Would you be interested in writing the story? Documenting it for future generations so the story isn't lost. "

I wasn't sure I heard him correctly, offering something so significant to me. He hardly knew me. And yet I wanted to write the story because it would be a link to Greyson, to his family, his heritage. When he left, I'd still have a part of him.

"Are you sure you wouldn't rather an established writer doing it?"

Callum's focus shifted to Greyson, I followed his gaze. Tenderness looked back at me.

"I think you're the right person for the job. Don't you, Greyson?"

"Absolutely."

"I can have copies of what records remain shipped here."

"Thank you. I would love to, but seriously are you sure you wouldn't rather someone with more experience?"

"Why don't you review the files and you tell me if you'd be interested?" Callum suggested.

"I'd like that."

Greyson brought me home. We stood at my front door, unwilling to say good night. He tasted so good, my fingers tangling into his hair to pull him closer. "I had a really good time tonight," I said in between kisses.

"I'm glad you came. Grandfather likes you."

"Yeah?"

He nipped on my bottom lip. "Definitely."

"I am very flattered with Callum's offer to write the book for your family, but I'll understand totally if you get someone else to do it. That's a big deal and it should be done right."

"You don't think you could write the story?"

"I do, but..."

"You know us. Anyone we hired wouldn't. Besides, the story is for the family. We're not looking to make a coffee table book, we just don't want the story to be lost." He pulled me closer. "One day you'll have works in the Library of Congress, but you'll also have a work handed down to future Ratcliffes. Some child in 2800 will read your words."

It was a humbling thought. "It'll take a while. Years if not longer with school and college."

"It's waited almost seven hundred years, it can wait a few more."

"That was incredible. Thank you." It was Friday night dinner at the Atzers. I liked seeing Greyson at Paige's table, liked that he was part of us now.

"We're glad you could join us, Greyson," Paige said.

Tara and Mandy had been itchy all through dinner. The expression ants in your pants fit them perfectly. As soon as Grant started clearing the table, Tara jumped up from her chair.

"I have to show you my room." Tara didn't wait for a reply, grabbing Greyson's hand and dragging him down the hall.

"My room next," Mandy called and ran after them.

"You cooked. I'll clean," Grant offered.

"You don't have to twist my arm," Paige teased. Grant kissed her temple. "You two go relax outside. I'll be out in a minute."

We settled on the deck. It was cooler; maybe Grant would light the fire pit.

"I like Greyson," Paige said.

"Me too."

"I see the way you look at each other. It reminds me of Grant and me."

"I really like him, Paige. A part of me worries about how much I like him. He is leaving at the end of the school year and he won't be staying any place long enough to settle."

"June is quite a while away, but I understand. If you feel how you do now, what happens then?"

"Exactly."

"From what I've seen, I think it will be worth the heartache later."

Our eyes met. "Me too." I dropped my voice. "I want to have sex with him."

"I wondered. Do we need to have the talk?"

She was being serious. I loved that she cared. "No."

"I have condoms. Take some before you leave."

"I don't feel uncomfortable having this conversation. I thought I would."

"It means you're ready. It may not be the moment you're expecting the first time, but believe me it does get better."

"Just being with him will make it the moment I'm expecting."

Paige smiled. "I felt that way too."

Greyson brought me home. Having said out loud what I'd been thinking, and with the weight of the condoms in my pocket, the words just tumbled from my mouth. "Come to my house on Sunday. The foster monsters won't be home."

I felt his muscles tense. His head dipped so we were almost eye-to-eye. "Are you saying what I think you are?"

My gaze dropped as some of my bravado fled. I was talking about having sex with Greyson, to Greyson.

He touched my chin. "Alexis."

"Paige gave me condoms."

"So that's what you two were talking about." He trailed his finger along my jaw. "Are you a virgin?"

"Yes. Are you?"

I saw it in his eyes. He wasn't. "No, but I wish I were for you."

I didn't know her, didn't know him when he'd had sex with her and still I hated whoever came before me. I didn't realize I said that out loud until he said, "I was sixteen. She was willing. If I knew I'd meet you, I would have waited." He studied me a minute before he added, "We don't have to."

"I want to."

His voice got all gravelly. "So do I." I thought he was going to kiss me, but instead he laced his fingers through my hair and just stared, studying me like he had a tendency of doing. "Sunday."

I waited to hear his bike drive off, and still I didn't move. The foster monsters were in bed; I heard the television. I leaned back against the door and dreamily thought about sex with Greyson. My back went rod straight. I was having sex with Greyson on Sunday. I had to shower and shave and lotion. I ran upstairs and stripped, but I didn't head to the shower. I stood in front of the full-length mirror. My breasts were very small, but my stomach was flat and my legs were long. Remembering that day at school and his seductively spoken words had goosebumps breaking out over my body. He was going to see me, all of me. I felt a bit nervous about that, despite his declarations, but I was going to see all of him too. I'd imagined his body countless times, but I'd be touching and tasting him. I knew the mechanics of sex, but actually doing it...maybe I should have talked to Paige.

I reached for my robe to cover myself. My thoughts shifted. This was a conversation I would have had with my mom. Sitting in my room, heads together as she gave me the talk. She'd be reluctant, her baby girl wasn't a baby anymore, but it was a right of passage when a girl became a woman. Dad would greet Greyson at the door, looking stern. He wouldn't know, but he'd suspect. He'd make small talk then warn Greyson if he broke my heart he'd kill him. And if I did have my heart broken, they'd be there to hold me...to heal me. The tears fell as yet another milestone came and went. They'd missed so much of my life, but I didn't care where they were or why they left me. If they showed up on my doorstep tomorrow, I would welcome them with open arms.

"I love you, wherever you are."

Collecting my toiletries, I headed to the shower.

I was going to throw up. I'd been up for hours. The foster monsters left, the house was empty, Greyson was due any minute. I wanted to

have sex, wanted it to be with Greyson, but now that we were here I wasn't sure I knew what to do. I wasn't sure if I was pretty enough, sexy enough.

A knock at the door had my stomach dropping. Maybe I wasn't ready for this. Pulling it open, I was surprised to see he looked how I felt. His eyes moved over my face then he smiled. "You've been up for hours too."

Relieved that I wasn't the only one, my shoulders unknotted. "Yeah." Glancing behind him, I didn't see his bike. "Where's your bike?"

Sheepishly he confessed, "I parked on another street."

It took a second, but if the twins saw it, they'd be over. That would be awkward.

He stepped inside; I locked the door. We didn't move from the foyer. Grasping at anything to buy me a bit more time I blurted out, "Would you like something to drink?"

He shoved his hands into his pockets. "Water would be good."

My stomach was jumping around; those butterflies were freaking out. My hands shook as I reached for a glass and filled it with water. I hadn't heard Greyson follow me, so I almost dropped the glass when I turned to find him leaning against the doorjamb.

"We don't have to do this, Alexis. We could go to the beach or take a ride."

"I want to, I'm just afraid you'll be disappointed."

His expression turned fierce. "Disappointed? How the hell could I be disappointed?"

"I'm not curvy."

Silenced followed and I grew more insecure.

"There's a little beauty mark where your neck meets your shoulder. Do you know how often I find myself wanting to lick that spot?"

I might have been looking at him in wonder, but what a thing to say.

"Your hair is a palette of colors, chocolate to blonde and every color in between. It feels like silk. I love burying my hands in it, love it even more when I'm pulling you to me to kiss that mouth. Those lips, your taste. I'm fucking addicted to them."

Now I was growing hot. I drank his water, the whole glass, to ease the burning.

"And your eyes." He stepped closer, took the glass from me and put it on the counter. He didn't touch me, but he moved so close that I could feel the heat from his body. "There's sadness buried in them. It's not as pronounced at times, but it's always there. And still you find it in you to make up stories about a fetal pig, to dance during sixth period, to act the part of a drowning victim, to bake my grandfather a birthday cake." His gaze moved over my face. "You could never disappoint me."

The feeling the first day, the one that nearly knocked me over, I knew now what it was. Love. I never believed in love at first sight, but I was willing to admit when I was wrong. I got up on my tiptoes and touched my lips to his, the lightest of kisses. We weren't touching, only our mouths, and it was so damn sweet.

I kissed him again, but this time I traced his lips with my tongue. His arms moved around me and pulled me tight against his body, one hand moved up my back to get lost in my hair; he tilted my head and kissed me deeper. The nerves fled, my tongue warring with his, eager for his taste, as addicted to him as he was to me. Edgy and needy I broke the kiss, reached for his hand and started for the stairs.

"Are you sure?"

That he even asked. "Yes."

In my room, Greyson looked around at the books and journals; I had a lot. His focus lingered on the picture of *Alice in Wonderland*. I agreed with the Cat, we were all mad here.

"It suits you."

My gaze drifted around my room. I never really thought about it, but it did. He closed the distance and wrapped my face in his hands. This time, *he* traced my lips. My mouth opened for his tongue. Goosebumps rose even as little fires sizzled under my skin. His palm closed over my breast, but I didn't feel inadequate, I felt desired. He brushed his thumb over my nipple and my clit pulsed. Feeling bold, I fisted his shirt, yanked my mouth from his, and pulled it over his head. He was exquisite. Flattening my palms on his chest, I ran them down his body to his six-pack. His sharp inhale turned the pulsing between my legs into an ache.

"You're beautiful," I whispered.

"My turn." My shirt followed his. He palmed my breasts and even with the cotton between us, that ache between my legs turned to a throbbing. He ran his tongue along my collarbone, kissed the swells of my breasts. With a twist of his fingers, my breasts spilled free. Nervousness pushed at the pleasure until his mouth replaced his hand, pulling my nipple between his teeth, touching the tip with his tongue. I had never felt anything so incredible until he sucked me into his mouth.

"Please don't stop."

He squeezed my breast, rolling my nipple between his fingers while he sucked on the other. The throbbing became painful. His hand drifted down my stomach before finding the part of me aching for him. He touched my clit and pleasure shot down my spine. One finger slipped into me, pulling a moan.

He withdrew his finger, his eyes worried. "Did I hurt you?"

"No." I covered his hand with my own and guided him back. "Please."

He played with my clit, my hips responding to his touch. He slid one finger in, circling me on the inside. I bit my lip at the sensation that was like nothing I'd ever felt. He watched me; seeming to enjoy the pleasure he was giving. Another finger joined the first, curling inside me. My head dropped as the knot in my gut loosened; climbing to a climax I wanted so badly to reach. He pressed his thumb to my clit and I came apart. Chills raced down my arms and light exploded behind my closed lids. Greyson wrapped his arm around my waist, holding me up, as he drew out the pleasure.

"That was fucking hot," he whispered in my ear.

He brought the fingers that had been inside me to his mouth and licked my taste off.

That was fucking hot.

He dropped to his knees and pulled my sweats and panties off. Pressing a kiss between my legs, his tongue running through my folds. My fingers dug into his shoulders because holy shit that felt good.

"Maybe you should get on the bed for this part." He looked up at me with the hottest eyes. He walked me backwards until the bed hit my legs. I sat. He curled his hand around my nape and he kissed me as he

95

lowered me onto the bed. Kissing down my body, spending some time on my breasts, he spread my legs wider, got on his knees and buried his face between them.

I practically came off the mattress. He tongued my clit, sucked on it, moved his head from side to side before thrusting his tongue inside me. I fisted the sheets as my hips jerked into his mouth, moving with him. He sucked on my clit and pushed two fingers into me and I was a goner. Every part of me felt that orgasm. I was exhausted when it finally subsided, but he was just getting started. Greyson dropped his jeans and briefs and that ache was back. I'd never seen a cock in real life, never thought they were particularly attractive, but I was wrong. His was long, thick and bent slight at the top. I wanted to touch it, taste it. I wasn't sure why I was so bold, but after what he'd just done to me, I wanted to give a little of that back. I sat up, ran a finger along the vein that was popping up. My eyes lifted to his, but they were closed. I closed my hand around the base and he moaned. It was silky smooth and hard as a rock. I traced the veins with my finger again then I did it with my tongue.

"I'll come if you do that."

I wanted to taste him like he had me. I wanted to pull him into my mouth and make him lose control.

He read my mind when he said, "First time I come, I want to be inside you."

Inside me. Yes, I liked this idea.

He rolled on a condom then settled between my legs. "It's going to hurt."

I pulled his mouth to mine. Kissing him was like a drug. Every part of my body went loose. He rubbed himself over me, lifted my hips and surged forward filling me in one long stroke. Holy shit it hurt. My body tensed. He froze.

"I'm sorry."

I reached for him, though I wasn't sure if I wanted to pull him close or push him away. He sucked on my lower lip. That felt nice. His mouth settled over mine for a kiss that slowly turned the pain into pleasure. I raised my hips and he sank deeper; we both moaned. Deliberately he created the friction that had lust curling in my gut. I ran my hands down his body to his ass, drawing him closer as I sought more of him. The pleasure built, my body tingled and my breath stilled right before the most incredible sensation exploded inside me, like I was floating and shattering apart all at once. His muscles went taut right before he drove in deep and closed his eyes. My name rolled off his tongue in a sexy whisper.

He dropped his head on my shoulder. We were both breathing heavy. "Is it always like that?"

He brushed his thumb across my cheek. "No."

I wanted to protest when he pulled out; I missed the connection to him. I assumed he went to clean up, disappearing into the bathroom. I loved having a naked Greyson walking around my room. He was beautiful. I stared my fill when he returned.

"Like what you see?"

"Very much."

Remembering his mouth on me, I wanted to taste him.

"You don't have to ask."

My eyes jerked to his face. He was smiling.

"How do you know what I'm thinking?"

"You're looking at my cock like a lollipop."

I shifted to my knees. "I've never…"

"Feel free to practice on me."

I didn't chuckle at his comment because I was distracted. I touched his stomach, running my fingers down his abs. His muscles moved under my touch. I traced the tip of his cock with my finger. He moaned. I traced it again with my tongue.

"Fuck, Alexis."

I closed my mouth around him. His body tensed, his fingers twisted into my hair, like he was holding himself up. I ran my tongue along the length of him, sucked, swirled it over the tip. His thigh muscles were like granite, as he held himself still while I explored him. The throbbing between my legs made me even bolder. I tongued the tip, fisted the base and stroked him up and down his shaft. He grew hard, his hips started to move. I felt him lose control before he thrust into my mouth. My eyes watered as he pushed into the back of my throat, but I held on because feeling this boy lose control was incredible.

"I'm going to come. If you don't—"

I sucked harder. His salty taste filled my mouth, a strange sensation, but I'd brought him to that. I'd made him lose control. I swallowed.

He yanked me up his body, his eyes on fire, before he kissed me.

GREYSON

Alexis moved around the kitchen in pajamas that had ice cream cones all over them. They were almost as ugly as her bike, so why was I having a problem keeping from getting hard. She'd pulled her hair up into a knot, exposing that beauty mark that drove me nuts. I'd just spent the last two hours worshipping her body and I wanted more.

She was making peanut butter and jelly sandwiches. We'd worked up an appetite.

"Can you get the plates? They're in the cabinet over the dishwasher."

I padded across the linoleum floor. I tried not to think about her home because it pissed me off. There was nothing warm about it because there was nothing of her in it. Her asshole foster parents didn't even have her picture on the wall.

I turned to find her watching me, her focus on my chest. I'd only tugged on my jeans. She was so easy to read and since I was feeling the same, I moved into her and caught her bottom lip between my teeth, sinking in enough to make it hurt. Her eyes glazed over and it was tempting to pull her onto the kitchen table. I controlled that.

I took the sandwiches, she got us water, and we went back to the only room in the house I liked. Alexis was stamped all over it, from the books piled in the corners, the posters of The Cure, *Alice in Wonderland* and the cat in a precarious position that stated *Hang in There*, to her bookcase stuffed with journals that I knew were filled with her stories. She was in every inch of this room. I fucking loved this room.

We settled on the bed across from each other sitting cross-legged. She took a bite from her sandwich, but her focus was still on my chest. "Do you work out?" Her expressive face changed realizing she'd asked that out loud. She then shrugged and added, "You have a six pack. How did you get that?"

She was making me hard with nothing more than a look, but what a fucking look. "I'm ready to go again whenever you are."

Her eyes flew to my face then she smiled. I'd lost interest in my sandwich. There was something so much sweeter within reach. I put my plate on the table then moved toward her. Her eyes went wide, then heated.

"I swim."

She was thinking about what was coming, so she didn't acknowledge me. She put her plate on her bedside table then settled back on her bed. I crawled over her, covering her body with my own. She was beautiful, so fucking beautiful, but those sad eyes tore at my heart.

"Why the sadness behind your eyes?"

Surprise shifted to pain when her eyes brightened. I felt like a dick. "I'm sorry."

"No, I wasn't expecting the conversation to go there." She reached into her nightstand and pulled out a picture. I settled next to her, taking it when she offered it. Her parents, she looked just like her mom. Alexis was only a toddler, adorable, happy, no sadness in her eyes. There was a hard edge to her dad, the man had seen and done things, but there was no denying the love for his girls. I'd had countless pictures like this with my parents; even losing them, I had albums of memories. This was Alexis' only memory.

Her voice was distant, like she was lost in that memory. "I don't know what happened to them. I don't know why they gave me up. There's love in that picture. They loved me, but they didn't keep me. I don't understand that. And even being angry and hurt, I miss them and I don't even remember them."

I wiped away her tears. She took the picture and put it back in the drawer. It broke my heart that she kept it close and for how worn it was, she looked at it often.

"Are you going to look for them?"

"Yes."

"You look just like your mom."

Her smile was shaky. I moved over her again, closed the distance and kissed her. For the next few hours I tried really hard to take that sadness from her gaze.

Alexis was working until closing; Paige was driving her home. I had the whole night, so I pulled out the canvas I'd been working on and my paints. That first day when I felt her on the beach, I knew she was special but I hadn't appreciated how special. These last few months getting to know her, I wasn't ready to let her go. We rang in the New Year. Our time was coming to an end. I was leaving, there was no changing that, and she wanted NYU. We had plans that didn't include the other and yet for the first time in my life I wanted something more than I wanted my art. I owed it to my grandfather, to my parents, to myself to pursue my dream, but that didn't mean I wasn't going to miss her like hell.

Nigel surprised us with a visit; it was where Grandfather was now, the two of them were hitting the town. He brought with him the files for Alexis. I loved that she wanted to look into our family. It was a link we'd always have, whatever happened between us.

I wondered about her parents. She was right. There was love in the picture, so what happened? I understood better now the sadness in her eyes. I came from an ancestry that spanned centuries and she didn't even know who her parents were. That had to make her feel very small in a great big world. It didn't help that she was living with the world's biggest assholes. They needed to answer for their treatment of her. I'd make sure one day they did.

I studied the painting coming to life on the canvas. It was Alexis that first day, clutching that ugly ass bike. I'd always remember her just like that, the image already burned onto my brain. The day was coming when I would have to let her go, but I'd always have this…my girl who claimed my heart with no more than a look.

ALEXIS

I swear I spent the day in a daze. I'd seen Greyson more today than I ever had at school. He was at my locker between classes, waiting for me outside of homeroom. I loved that he wanted to see me as much I wanted to see him.

The day was almost over. I reached my locker and was disappointed that he wasn't there. As soon as I opened it, a note fell out. Excitement swept through me because I had never before gotten a note in my locker. Unfolding it revealed a strong masculine script.

Hey, beautiful. Meet me at my bike after school.
G

My heart started pounding, my hands got sweaty, and the damn butterflies started again. I wouldn't be paying a lick of attention for the rest of the day. At least the rest of the day was only two more periods. I folded up the note and tucked it into my pocket. I would keep it forever, pressed in between the pages of a favorite book.

After the final bell, I headed outside. A strong arm wrapped around my waist and pulled me back against a familiar muscled chest…so much for meeting at his bike.

"Come with me."

"Anywhere."

He took me to the bluff, the place he wanted to paint. As soon as he climbed off his bike he had me in his arms. The kiss was hot and sweet. "Hi."

I really liked this new way he had for saying hi.

He reached for my hand. We walked along the bluff. Neither of us needed words, the silence was comforting. We found a spot and sat down. It really was beautiful here. The year was moving so quickly and as much as I was going to miss him, I was excited for him and what came next. He was looking out at the horizon, the wind teasing his hair. He looked a lot like how he had that day on my jetty. I'd remember him like this, had already tucked the sight away with my other memories.

"Have you thought about where you'll be in twenty years?" He glanced over. "I know you know what to expect, and I'm not looking for you to say with me because we both had dreams before we met, but where do you hope to end up?"

He had thought about it because he didn't need time to answer. "I'd like to be known. Not necessarily a household name like my agent is hoping, but enough that galleries are bidding to show my work. Ideally, the dream would be to get an exhibit at The Met and have a small paragraph in the history books as an artist of mention. But I'd be happy to make a living off my art, one where I can pick and chose commissions. I'd like a house on the water, a wife I can't get enough of…" He grinned and my heart flipped. "Kids. What about you?"

"The ultimate dream is to win an Academy Award for best adapted screenplay based on my international best seller."

Humor danced in his eyes. "Are you sure? Do you need time to think about it?"

"I want to rub his bald, golden head, put it in a case that is on a motion sensor so every time someone walks into the room, the case lights up and the Academy music starts to play."

He was laughing, but not at me. "You've really thought about this."

"Yeah, since I was a kid. But I'd be happy with being successful enough I could support myself with my writing, having a fan base. I'd like to do a play that is shown Off-Off-Broadway, but if I'm being really ambitious, Off-Broadway."

"Not on Broadway."

"I'd love that, but I need to be somewhat realistic."

He chuckled before he asked, "Do you see yourself married?"

To him, I could see that so clearly. "Yes, and kids."

He touched my cheek. "It's you I see with me. I know there's a lot that can happen between then and now, but right now I see us, older, more gray, but I'm still as crazy about you as I am now."

I rested my head on his shoulder. "I see that too."

"I've never felt this way before."

Tears prickled my eyes. "Me either."

"When it is time for me to go, I have to just go or I won't be able to."

Thinking about the day that was coming too soon, my chest grew tight. I wasn't sure how I'd survive him walking out of my life. "Like a Band-Aid. Just rip it off. Maybe our paths will cross again."

He lifted my chin to look me in the eyes. "Our paths will definitely cross again. This thing between us is just getting started."

The moment was bittersweet because your first boyfriend was rarely your forever boyfriend, but in that perfect moment I let myself believe.

7

ALEXIS

January and February flew by and we were halfway through March. I tried not to think about May, about graduation and Greyson leaving, but it followed me like a dark cloud. We were in the library. He was working on a sketch and I was researching his family. The papers Callum had given me were the copies of household journals, dating back to the fourteenth century. Handwriting from people who had died centuries earlier, proof they had lived. It was incredible. There were pictures too, portraits from the gallery of the Ratcliffe ancestors. And like Callum had said, the diamond was in several of them.

"The fire Callum mentioned, it was pretty substantial."

Greyson looked up from his sketch. "They did an incredible job with the rebuild because you can't tell."

"Do you have a sketch of home?"

He flipped through his spiral ring then pushed it across the table to me. It really was a castle, a medieval one with circular towers and battlements, archways and hundreds of glazed windows. Ivy grew over the weathered stone and garden beds wrapped around it. It was old, massive and beautiful.

"I can't believe you live there. When will you go back?"

"I don't know." His eyes met mine. "I meant it, Alexis, I want you to see my home."

I wanted that too. Maybe one day I would.

He grew playful when he teased, "Did you know Stephanie asked me to prom?"

Stephanie. She really was persistent. "When?"

"Last week."

"Doesn't she know you and I are together?"

"Yeah, but she doesn't want to believe it."

An unpleasant sensation moved down my spine. I understood the enticement, I really did, but we were together, a fact that had circulated through the school. For her to continue her pursuit of him was a little disturbing.

He leaned back in his chair, stretching his legs out in front of him. "Don't you want to know what I said to her?"

"Hell no, I hope."

"I told her it was up to my girl if we went."

I dropped my head on my hand. I had no doubt my eyes went all dreamy before I asked, "Who's your girl?"

He looked wicked when he said, "If you have to ask, I'm not doing it right."

"You're doing it right."

He tugged on my hair. "I know. We can go to prom if you want, but I was thinking of doing something different."

Where my thoughts went in response, yeah I think doing something different was a really good idea.

He moved so fast, pulling my mouth to his. "That wasn't what I was thinking, but I'm all for that." He bit my lower lip. "So?" he asked.

"What were we talking about?"

He grinned. "Prom."

"I'm not really into prom."

105

"Good answer." He stood, grabbed my hand and pulled me into the stacks. He pressed me up against the wall, his body crowding me. "My girl," he whispered then he kissed me.

"What are you doing up there?" Dylan called from the base of the tree house. When we were younger, we had practically lived here.

"Just thinking."

Dylan's head appeared in the cutout of the floor. "About what?" He answered his own question. "Greyson?"

"I'm in love with him."

"I know."

"How do you know?"

"I've known you since you were six." He settled in the beanbag next to mine. "How are you handling him leaving?"

"I'm not at the moment."

"Denial."

"Yeah."

"When is he leaving?"

"I don't know. That's not entirely true." I pulled a hand through my hair and clarified, "I don't want to know."

"You guys work. Too bad your timing sucks."

"Big understatement. Do you and Dom still want Berkley?"

"Yep."

"It's a good thing, all of us going off to pursue our dreams, but it kind of sucks too. I'm going to miss you knuckleheads."

His eyes were surprisingly bright when he knocked me in the shoulder with his own. "We're not leaving for another year, so cut that shit out."

He was right, but that year was going to fly. This one certainly had.

I was working when Greyson entered. He strolled to the booth he always sat in when here; he caught my eye on the way and smiled. I loved him. I loved the way he walked and how he didn't assess a room when he entered. I loved those long locks that framed his beautiful face and how he was always carrying that spiral ring. I loved the way he looked at me, like I was his favorite sight and how even when we were just talking he touched my cheek or my jaw, playing with my hair like he was making sure I was there. I loved how I felt around him and the person I was around him. I was almost seventeen and yet I had found the love of my life and in a few weeks he was leaving. Just the thought caused a wicked pain that stole my breath.

I joined him, resting my hip on the booth.

"I heard you have a birthday coming up," he said in way of greeting.

"Was it Paige or her girls?"

"Her girls. I saw them the other day at the market. Weren't you going tell me?"

I shrugged; I didn't really get into the whole birthday thing. "It's just a birthday."

"I guess you don't want your present then."

I liked presents. "I'll take the present, you know, since you went to the trouble of getting me one and all."

"It's what I thought we could do instead of prom."

"I'm intrigued."

He reached into his pocket and pulled out an envelope.

"Is that it?"

"Yep."

He offered it, but when I reached for it he pulled it away.

"Tease."

He laughed then handed it to me. I opened the envelope and my smile dropped from my face.

Tickets to The Cure.

It was a dream to see them, but none of my friends liked them. I never thought I would. Seeing them with Greyson, my eyes stung at the greatest gift I had ever been given.

"Alexis?"

I was crazy out of my head in love with him. My heart was so full and yet it hurt. We were running out of time. I kissed him, leaned over and right there in the diner I kissed him like it was my job. He wasn't shy about kissing me back.

"Is that a yes?" he asked against my lips.

"It's a hell yes."

The bus was relatively empty. Greyson and I took seats toward the back. I had brought my journal and he his sketchpad to whittle some of the time because it was a four-hour bus ride to San Francisco.

"When did you know you wanted to be an artist?"

"Sounds crazy, but the first time I picked up a crayon. I love the entire process of creating something from nothing. Thinking it in your head and bringing it to life with your hands." Our eyes met. "You have to know what that feels like with your writing."

I did.

"When did you know you wanted to be a writer?"

"In the beginning, my stories kept me company. My foster parents wouldn't play with me, so I created friends. In my stories, I could go anywhere and do anything. My characters kept me company."

He unclenched his jaw. He didn't like my foster parents. "And now?"

"I love getting lost in my imagination, creating worlds and characters that are real to me. And if even just one person finds an escape when they need it, or a lonely child finds a companion in the pages, I will consider myself a success."

He reached into his bag and pulled out a pack of Pop-Tarts. "Because I know how much you love them."

I scrunched up my face. He handed me one, took the other for himself, then lit a match from a box he had in his bag. "Happy birthday, Alexis."

Tears hit my eyes.

"Make a wish."

I wished for him.

I blew out his version of a candle and we ate our Pop-Tarts. I hated Pop-Tarts, but I loved that one.

I rested my head on his shoulder. "I don't know what the future holds for us, but I'm so glad your art brought you to Mendocino."

The concert was awesome. By the end of the show I had no voice left from screaming and singing along. Catching a glimpse of Greyson, I saw that he was watching me not the concert.

When "Just like Heaven" started, I reached for his hand. He had other plans. He yanked me against him and kissed me long and hard. "Just like Heaven" became, and would remain always, my favorite song.

After the concert we found a late night diner, one that catered to truckers, and ate pancakes at midnight. By the time the bus rolled in we were exhausted. A few minutes after we took our seats, we were both sound asleep.

The bus pulled into the depot, but I didn't want our time to end. Greyson wasn't ready either. We reached his bike that was parked at the depot when he said, "There's somewhere else I want to go."

We went to the bluffs. We walked, but spoke very little. We seemed more content to just be in the other's company. The day had been the best of my life and even when I was old and gray it would still rank at the very top.

Greyson broke the silence when he said, "I want to ask you to come with me."

"And I want to say yes, but I still have a year left of school."

"With how I'm feeling, I believe we can make it work, that you and I are only at the beginning, but life often has other plans."

My throat went tight hearing him voice my greatest fear.

His expression was intense. "Promise me if we lose touch, you'll look me up. A year, two, ten."

I couldn't stand the thought of life continuing on with us apart, that this past year was all we'd ever have. "I promise."

"I love you, Alexis."

My eyes burned and my throat went tight. He loved me. I knew he did, but we had never said the words. "I love you."

Silence followed as we marked the moment, then he kissed me, hungrily, greedily, his tongue tasting, exploring, memorizing. Desire pooled in my belly. He curled his arm around my waist, lowered me to the ground and settled in the cradle of my body. I dragged my hands through his hair, wanting more of him. He rubbed himself against me, hitting my clit and sending pleasure shooting down my legs. I hooked my heels around his thighs and moved with him. My body grew tight with the pending orgasm.

Then he was gone, sitting back on his legs looking guilty. "I'm sorry. We shouldn't do this here."

"Why not?"

His head jerked to me; love and lust burned in those pale eyes. "You deserve better."

"No one's here and it's our special spot. I can't think of a better place to make love."

His mouth came back down on mine. There was an urgency about him, like he was trying to get his fill. My heart cracked because we had run out of time. I touched every part of him, memorizing his body, his taste, the feel of those long locks between my fingers, the weight of him over me.

"No condom," I whispered.

"But you could get pregnant."

Maybe, but I didn't care. I touched his face. "No condom. I need to feel all of you."

I'll never forget how he looked just then. Love, pure and simple. He was deliberate when he joined us and so achingly sweet. He made my body sing, but it was my heart he was touching, branding and claiming even as it was breaking. He stayed buried inside me for a while after, both of us unwilling to let the other go. He kissed me; saying goodbye without words and though I was dying inside, that kiss would go down as the most beautiful kiss of my life.

We dressed slowly, prolonging the inevitable. He pulled me into his arms, and buried his face in my hair. "You've changed my life."

I lost the battle with my tears. "And you've changed mine."

He drove me home and walked me to the door. "Remember your promise."

"I'll remember."

He touched his lips to mine and let them linger before he whispered, "Goodbye."

My heart shattered as I watched the one person I wanted most in the world walking out of my life. I wanted to beg him to stay, but instead I watched him climb onto his bike. His eyes found mine and we shared a moment. Unspoken words that were understood…one day we would pick up where we left off because we weren't at the end. We were only at the beginning.

The following morning, Greyson left Mendocino and he took my heart with him.

1998 GREYSON

"The saturation is outstanding and the flow is organic, but you could make better use of your negative space and even in landscapes there should be a focal point to pull the eye, to entice. It's also imperative you keep your brushes in good condition. Your detail work is a little off here. You should have used a new round brush. Do you see your lines are not precise? That small distortion distracts from the image." Philippe Rainier, a brilliant artist and also my tutor, studied me like he had my painting. "It is the little mistakes that separate a master from an apprentice."

He dismissed me and turned to Colin, my agent. "You were right to bring him to me. We have work, but he has it."

The man was a genius when it came to art, social skills on the other hand.

"Let's work on negative space," he announced and pulled a blank canvas from the pile stacked against the wall.

"We're up at five tomorrow morning. Our flight to London is at nine. After London, we have Paris and I've just confirmed a show in Amsterdam. I know you're exhausted, but we need the exposure."

I could seriously sleep for a month.

He grinned; the man read my thoughts as easily as I could read Alexis'. "I told you going in, the first five years were going to be nonstop. There's no time for anything but learning, promoting and working. You put the time in now, once you're established you'll be able to set your own schedule. Get some sleep." Looks were deceiving when it came to my grandfather's friend. The man never slowed down. He was determined to make me a household name, I appreciated all of his efforts, but damn there was only one speed and that was fast.

"I'm already packed." I had never unpacked.

"See you in the morning."

"Night."

The door closed behind him. Pulling a hand through my hair, fuck I was tired. When I wasn't with Rainier, I was doing interviews or working on my art. I'd started dabbling in clay, loved the process of sculpting. My days were scheduled, right down to eating and sleeping. I kept my eyes on the prize, was grateful I had people helping me, but it was exhausting.

I should go to sleep. Morning would be here in only a few short hours, but I had something more important to do. I pulled the painting from my leather portfolio. So many memories flooded my mind; it was just a year in my life, and yet that one year changed me. I missed her so fucking much. We tried to keep in touch, but with my crazy ass schedule and hers, it wasn't easy. I thought about her all the time. Every new experience was one I wanted to share with her. Maybe what we had was just young love and in time it would fade to a really great memory, but it had been a year since I left and I was still just as captivated by her as I'd been that first day on the beach. I loved her even then. Wherever our lives led us, I vowed to find her, to give us a chance to pick up where we left off. In the meantime, my memories would keep me going.

I added my signature then pulled out a piece of paper. I'd have the concierge mail it tomorrow. It should arrive in time.

ALEXIS

Paige and Grant threw a graduation party for me. I couldn't believe I was leaving for New York in a few days. I was both terrified and excited. The twins drove me home. We were spending the night in our tree house. Hurrying up the drive, I saw the package. My hands were shaking when I brought it inside and unwrapped it, tears followed. It was my jetty, so beautifully captured, as if he'd read my mind and captured the image I had there. I smiled to myself. He'd always been able to read me so well. I brushed my fingers over his signature. There was a note.

Congratulations, Alexis. Good luck in New York City.
Here's a little piece of home to take with you. I miss you.
Love, Greyson

My tears dripped onto his note, the words whispered softly but felt so deeply. "I love you." One day we'd find a way back to each other.

PART
TWO

Love, to be real, must cost, it must hurt, it must empty us of self.
– *Mother Teresa*

8

ALEXIS 2000

"Alexis!" Mrs. Cantenelli screamed and pulled me in for a hug. Her familiar scent brought back so many happy memories. "It's so good to see you." She stepped back, eyeing me. "New York definitely agrees with you."

I was home for a few weeks before I headed back to New York for my junior year at NYU. I loved New York City, the sights and sounds of the city and how there was always something going on. I had been apprehensive leaving home and going so far away, but I was so happy I took the chance.

"I heard you and Mr. Cantenelli visited Paris."

"Oh, Alexis, it was magical. We're going back. In fact, I don't know if the boys told you but we've decided to move there."

No, they hadn't told me that.

She laughed. "Based on your expression, you haven't heard. The boys are happy in Berkeley, rarely coming home, you're in New York and Mr. Cantenelli and I are both retired. We've always wanted to see Paris and now we have a chance to live there."

I loved that I was a part of their consideration. "It sounds like a dream come true."

"It really is. And who knows, maybe in two years we'll be ready to come home."

We shared a look and said at the same time, "Not likely."

She touched my shoulder, leading me into the kitchen. I remembered the little girl I had been and how it had felt the first time she had done that, welcomed me into their hearts and home.

"I love you, Mrs. Cantenelli."

She missed a step and her eyes grew bright. "I love you, Alexis."

I settled at the counter like I had done countless times as a kid. She walked to the refrigerator to get us a drink. The front door slammed open.

"Is she here?" Dylan called.

I jumped from the stool. They saw me when I saw them. We plowed into each other, limbs were everywhere, too many for only three people. I had always thought of them as siblings and they were. These two knuckleheads were my brothers and I had missed them.

"It's been too fucking long," Dylan said.

"Language!" Mrs. Cantenelli called from the kitchen.

"You look good, Alexis. Hot." Dominic hadn't changed.

"You're an idiot." Dylan said what I was thinking.

"How's Berkeley?"

"Awesome. We're like the kings of the school. We're beating the girls away." Dominic was a goof, but I bet they were.

"And NYU?" Dylan asked.

"I'm working on a play."

"Nice."

Mrs. Cantenelli put iced tea and cookies out for us. We were older, but something so familiar felt good. It felt like home.

"Are you going to see Paige?"

The look of love on Dylan's face was pitiful. "You're still smitten?"

"With Paige, oh hell yeah."

"She is very happily married."

"I know," he said through clenched teeth. Poor Dylan. Unrequited love sucked.

"She asked that I invite you two clowns to dinner."

"What are we waiting for?" Dylan was halfway to the door.

"Thanks for the snack, Mrs. Cantenelli."

"Anytime. Come to dinner tomorrow night."

"I will, thank you."

"Alexis, get the lead out," they both called from the door.

It was nice that even older, the twins were still the adorable dopes I loved.

"It's because he's family that I'm not ripping his arm from its socket," Grant announced as we sat on the deck watching Paige, the girls and the twins playing volleyball in the yard. There was a new cherub, Heather. She had just turned one and was the spitting image of her mom.

"He can't help himself. He's in love. Poor guy." Dylan kept touching Paige, in encouragement, or when she fell he was there to help her up. It was harmless, but clear he still had his crush.

Grant glanced over at me; humor and irritation twisted his features. "Yeah, poor guy," he offered sarcastically, then asked, "You ready to head back to school?"

"Yes, but I have missed home."

"You're missed."

For years, I had thought my life wasn't the one I was supposed to have, not without my parents. But had I not lived this life, I never would have met Grant and Paige, the Cantenellis, Dee and Mel. Greyson. Things happened for a reason.

"Have you given thought to when you graduate?"

"I'm staying in New York, at least for a little while. I want to write and there are so many playhouses, agencies, papers and opportunities I would be foolish to not take advantage."

"I would have persuaded you to do that, had you been thinking about coming home."

"This is home. I will be coming back."

"And until then there's email and those mobile phones. Technology is making the world smaller."

He was right about that.

He glanced out at the others then stood and offered his hand. "Shall we show them how it's done?"

"Absolutely."

Paige and I were outside. The girls were in bed and Grant and the twins were watching a movie. I missed this.

"Do you want to talk about Greyson?"

My body still reacted to his name as my heart did a long slow roll in my chest. There wasn't much to say. We had lost touch after I moved to New York between my classes and work and his schedule. I thought about him often though. He claimed a piece of my heart that would always belong to him.

"You haven't spoken to him."

"No. He's a rising star."

"I've got to tell you it's weird seeing his mug staring back at me from the magazines at the checkout counter."

The first time I saw Greyson on the cover of a magazine, I'd been hurrying to class. I didn't make that class. I bought up every copy from the newsstand, went back to my room and stared at his image for the longest time, marveling how his face had matured in the few years since I'd last seen him. I read the article so many times I had it memorized. It was the magazines that came later that I didn't much care for—the tabloids with Greyson and some beautiful woman on his arm, never the same woman. He was among the beautiful people now. He certainly belonged there, but it was hard seeing him living a life I had no part in. It was only a year, not even, but he forever changed me.

"Of course the nonsense with that fan, that was scary."

"Terrifying is a better word. The ugly side to stardom." I still got a chill thinking about the incident that had made the World News several months back. Greyson had returned from a show to find a woman in his room. I had thought Stephanie from high school had been a bit stalkerish, but I was wrong. This woman had been the real-life Annie from *Misery*. She was convinced she and Greyson were soul mates. She refused to leave when asked, even when hotel security got involved. The police had to come. It turned out she had bribed a hotel employee to let her in. His agent filed charges, as he should have. It wasn't just trespassing; it was deeply disturbing that Greyson was the outlet for the woman's crazy. I didn't want to think about the ugly, so I moved the conversation on.

"I miss him, Paige. I don't regret the time I spent with him, I'd do it again even knowing how it would end, but there's this hole in me that I can't seem to fill."

"You're young, Alexis. There's still time for you and Greyson to find each other again or for you to find someone else."

Greyson and I weren't the same people and we definitely did not move in the same social circles. It seemed unlikely we would cross paths. I didn't forget the promise I'd made, but that promise wasn't as easy to keep as I had once thought. And finding someone new, there had been no one significant since him. I was busy with school, but in truth no one I'd met after him came close to making me feel what he did. I wasn't interested in second best, but that didn't mean I wasn't looking.

I changed the subject. "I'm going to hire an investigator to find my parents."

Paige turned in her chair. "You are?"

"I need to know. I've been saving money and with not having to pay tuition..." I glared at her. I got a full ride to NYU. I didn't know how that happened, was convinced Paige and Grant or Dee and Mel or the Cantenellis were behind it. They all denied it emphatically. "I have a nice sum put away."

"We weren't behind your tuition, Alexis. As much as I wish we were, Grant and I can't afford it. I am glad you're looking for your parents. If nothing else comes out of it, maybe you'll find closure."

I rested my head on the seat back and looked up at the sky. The stars were out tonight. My fairy godmother had been oddly quiet for the last few years. One particular star twinkled down at us. I wished on that star, the same wish I made every time I took a moment to look up at them. Maybe one day it would come true.

THREE MONTHS LATER

I stopped at the market after class because my pantry was bare, my fridge too. Moving up and down the aisle, I dropped stuff in my cart. I finally tried my hand at cooking and I wasn't much of a cook, but I was able to boil pasta, grill up some chicken breasts and scramble a few eggs. I was also slightly addicted to Toaster Strudels. Unlike their competitors, I couldn't get enough of them. Every time I made one, I thought of Greyson.

I got in line and saw him. It was just a tabloid and still my heart fluttered. He had some leggy blonde draped around him, but I couldn't get past *his* image because he'd cut his hair. His once long locks were cut close to his head, the top longer, spiky yet wispy. Gone were the baggy clothes. He was in a tailored suit. He looked amazing, elegant, but he didn't look like my Greyson. I had it bad when I hurt thinking about those mahogany strands left abandoned on the salon floor, swept up and tossed in the trash.

I bought a copy; okay I bought six copies. Back at my off-campus studio apartment—it was really just a hovel, but it was my hovel—I locked up, put the groceries away and turned on The Cure. I needed a little Rob. I toasted up two strudels, made a pot of tea and curled up on my futon with the magazine.

"She's not even pretty. Her lips are too full and her eyes. Who has lavender eyes? And her legs look like stilts." I stuffed half of the Toaster Strudel in my mouth. Who was I kidding? She was exquisite. It was Greyson's expression that had me wanting to eat the whole box of strudels. I knew that look, the slight grin and the warm twinkle in his eyes. Whoever she was to him, he knew her and liked her. She wasn't just arm candy.

I was glad he'd changed his look. It made it easier to see him with these women because the sophisticated man staring back at me wasn't the Greyson of my youth. He had been a caterpillar in Mendocino who had morphed into a butterfly—beautiful, polished and refined, but I missed the caterpillar. I loved the caterpillar. My eyes drifted to his painting and immediately I was transported back to sixteen, standing on the pier, clutching my bike, staring at the boy who I knew, even then, was going to forever change me. We'd always have that, our beautiful moment that had been far too fleeting.

ONE YEAR LATER

It was hard to believe I was midway through my senior year. Finals were in a few weeks and then I was flying home for Christmas. I couldn't wait to see Paige and family. The twins would be home too, on winter break from Berkley. I hadn't seen them since the summer before junior year. I missed them, though we did talk all the time. Email was a wonderful invention.

I'd started a weekly column, my adventures in the city. It was only published in the school's paper, but it was a fun project and with technology, people could post comments on the articles. Sure there were assholes, haters were going to hate, but the majority of comments were sharing with me other places and scenes I had to check out. In addition to the column, I was working on another play for one of my classes—I really liked the format of plays and how it wasn't just dialogue but stage direction and scene setup. There was also the novel I started freshman year, one about Greyson and me. Our story was too beautiful not to write down.

I checked the posts for my latest article. There was a German festival happening over the weekend. That sounded like fun. It was while I scrolled through the other suggestions that a name caught my attention. It had been four and a half years and still my blood rushed through my veins.

Greyson Ratcliffe.

He was in town, had a show in a gallery off Fifth Avenue. I purposely didn't follow his career, unless it was blatantly staring at me from a magazine. Especially with the Internet on the rise, one could get preoccupied. He had moved on, found love again, if the tabloids were to be believed, but we were both in the same city. My promise had become a weight on my shoulders, nagging me to follow through. If I ever planned on keeping it, now was the time. It was a long shot, those events were usually by invitation only, but I'd call the gallery and see what I could do.

"Heather, stop climbing your sister's leg. She's not a tree," Paige hollered.

I held the phone from my ear. "A warning would be nice."

"Sorry. Heather's taken to climbing things."

I could see her doing that too. Tara and Mandy were little ladies; Heather was a hellion. I adored her.

"Grant encourages her." She was feigning annoyance, but all I heard was love.

"How is Grant?"

"Wonderful." Her voice went soft like it had a habit of doing when thinking of her husband. "He misses you. We were cleaning out the garage and we found a box of your short stories. We spent the night reading them. He cried."

I missed them too, sometimes so much I wanted to pack it up and come home. Those bouts of homesickness didn't last long even with how frequently I had them.

"Did you ever hire that investigator?" Paige asked.

"No. I got sidetracked. I've an appointment with one after the holidays."

"Good. You need to do this, Alexis."

"I know. I want to. Guess who's in town?"

Dead silence followed my announcement.

"Paige?"

"Have you seen him?"

"No, but I'm going to his show."

"Does he know?"

A few days after inquiring about the show, an invitation appeared in my mailbox. I was certain I was sent one because I'd be representing the university. It was highly unlikely Greyson even knew I was coming. "I don't think so. I reached out to the gallery, said I was writing a story for my university's paper."

"It's been what, four and a half years? You must be crawling out of your skin in anticipation."

"Yes, and I'm scared too."

She understood. "You're afraid it won't be like you remember."

"Yeah."

"That's not a bad thing. You're still carrying a torch for him and I get that because I saw you together, but if it is different you can let him go. Move on with your life, find love again."

She was right and yet instinct was to argue against her words.

"Call me. I want to know everything."

"I miss you, Paige."

"I miss you."

Greyson's show was in two days and I had nothing to wear. Walking down Fifth Avenue, the bite of cold felt good. The Christmas season was in full swing; the streets were crowded with tourists, the hustle and bustle of the city slowed as crowds clogged the flow, stopping to snap photos and memories.

I slipped into Bergdorfs. It was pricey for me, but then this was a very special occasion. An associate offered me assistance, but I didn't want to feel obligated to talk to her. The truth was my imagination had been scripting Greyson and my reunion since I received the invitation. Despite knowing we were over, it had been years since we'd seen each other and we'd been more than sweethearts. I missed him.

I had a fluttering in my chest; anticipation at the thought of being in the same room with him again, but there was another emotion twisting around in me too. What if he didn't remember me? I wasn't sure how I'd handle that, him seeing through me instead of into me like he used to. My hand shook a bit as I touched the silky fabric of a gown. What if everything I was clinging to he wasn't? What if I was nothing more to him than just an old girlfriend? Then I'd do what Paige suggested. I'd leave him in the past, a memory that I could pull out from time to time. I would move on.

I looked in the mirror this way then that, the image staring back was quite a bit different than the one at sixteen. I'd never be a Debbie, but I had curves now. I loved the dress I'd picked out, the embroidered top with a deep V neckline and tulle skirt. I felt pretty, a bit like Cinderella heading to the ball. I was nervous, my heart beating in a staccato rhythm and hard enough it hurt. I had to calm down. I probably wouldn't even see him and if I did, it was doubtful I'd get a chance to talk to him. He was the featured artist; he'd be swamped with critics and collectors and groupies. He had groupies; the tabloids weren't shy about posting those pictures. Before I could talk myself out of it, I grabbed my coat and clutch and headed downstairs for a cab.

Limos pulled up along the curb in front of the gallery. Old iron gas lanterns lit the front door as the beautiful people made their way inside. My legs felt wooden as I walked over the threshold. It was a good thing I hadn't eaten because I wouldn't have been able to keep it down. I checked my coat before walking into the main room of the gallery. Crystal chandeliers hung from the ceiling, their ambient light perfect for viewing art. My breath stilled as my eyes roamed around the room. Nerves fled as I soaked in Greyson's creations—oil and pastel landscapes, sculptures created in copper, iron and clay. There was no distinct style; each piece was unique and exquisite. One landscape beautifully captured the whimsy of Ireland with its rolling hills of green and majestic cliffs as they were battered by the violent surf, the spray so life-like I believed if I reached out and touched it, my fingers would come back wet. His home. I made my way through the exhibit studying his pieces and wishing I had been with him, the man he became to create such beauty. One painting had my heart moving into my throat. I stepped closer. It was me on the day I met Greyson. He didn't paint portraits and yet here I was among his works. Love washed over me. I studied the painting, how he saw me. I was beautiful in his eyes. Then I saw the caption next to the painting and both my heart and eyes filled. It wasn't for sale, a part of the artist's private collection.

I listened to those around me discussing his technique and compositions. Theorizing on his motivation and inspiration and I nearly burst with pride. This room was filled to capacity and every single one of them had come to see Greyson. He'd done it; he had made his dream a reality.

Heat sizzled down my spine; nostalgia swept through me. It had been too long since I felt that sweet burn. Turning, my breath caught when I saw him. Melancholy replaced nostalgia at the reminder that he wasn't *my* Greyson anymore. His hair was still short and spiky. He was taller, wider in the shoulders and dressed in a beautiful tux. It was his eyes though that had changed the most. I wouldn't say he was cynical, but he was shrewd—a man who'd learned through experiences that life wasn't fair. I saw very little of the boy I fell in love with, the boy who was my first kiss, my first love and my first heartbreak. And still I willed him to see me, to feel me like he had in our youth. He didn't. He laughed; the sound carried across the room and settled happily in my chest. Cameras flashed, voices called out his name; papers were thrust in front of him to sign. He posed with a few people, that easy smile I hadn't seen in far too long curving his lips. He looked good in this new life; he belonged there. I then saw the leggy blonde walking with him—the same one from the magazine, the one with lavender eyes—her adoration as she stared up at him, his when he looked down at her. I knew we were over, had been for years, but seeing in the flesh the evidence that he had moved on was painful. Suddenly I felt out of place. I wasn't part of this world. I really was Cinderella playing dress up for the night, but the clock was getting ready to strike midnight and my outer coverings would disappear exposing the real me. The one who was an outsider in his new life.

I shouldn't have come. Even wishing to keep my promise, I shouldn't have come. Sometimes it was best to keep the past in the past because you couldn't go back, and second chances rarely lived up to the memories you were clinging to. Greyson didn't belong to me anymore;

he belonged to them. I really did have to let him go. It was with a heavy heart that I turned from him and walked out.

My chest ached; my lungs struggled to pull in breath. The lights of the city blurred as tears filled my eyes. I was happy for him, I truly was. The tears were for me because I'd lost another person in my life and I didn't even have a picture of us to keep in my bedside table.

I didn't go right home. I wandered around for a while. One day the memories wouldn't bring pain. It had only been nine months, but we had jammed a lot into those months. I wondered how his grandfather was, wondered if his new girl had seen their home in Ireland? Had he painted her? Did he call her his girl? That caused an ache in my chest. I wasn't his girl anymore, but that endearment was mine.

I stopped on my way back to my apartment for some ice cream therapy. The sundae at the local diner where I worked wasn't as good as the one from Dee and Mel's, but then nothing was ever as good as home. A few people stared, dressed as I was eating a sundae in a diner in the middle of the night. I'd go home, curl up in bed, have a good cry and do the whole moving on thing in the morning. Reaching my apartment, I was digging into my purse for my keys—in my misery I didn't have them in my hand like I usually did. I didn't see the figure in the shadows until I was almost on top of him. The scream caught in my throat when Greyson stepped into the light. There was a part of me that thought he was a hallucination; then he spoke.

"Hello, Alexis."

My breath caught, he literally took my breath away. My eyes that hadn't stopped burning started to tear again. It all came back; the onslaught of memories was overwhelming.

"You kept your promise."

I stared, not quite believing he was there; so close I could touch him.

"Why did you leave?"

For a hallucination, he sure was inquisitive. When he didn't vanish and continued to stare expectantly, I questioned if he *was* a hallucination. "You knew I was there?"

"Who do you think sent you the invitation?"

A smile pulled at my mouth because that sounded like the Greyson I knew.

"Why did you leave, Alexis?"

He really was here; he'd left his show to follow me. That felt really good. Wait. He left his show. "Why did *you* leave your show?"

He smiled and my heart stopped. I'd missed that smile. "They've had me for every second of the last four and a half years. They'll deal."

And your girlfriend? I couldn't seem to ask that.

"It's been a long time. Can we go somewhere and catch up?"

There was nowhere else I'd rather be. "I would really like that."

He hailed a cab and once we were settled he gave the cabbie the name of an upscale speakeasy that I didn't think we had a chance in hell of getting into. Like in our youth, he could read my mind.

"The owner bought a painting, extended an open invitation." He settled back on the seat, taking a moment to study me. "Is New York everything you hoped it would be?"

Even with all the emotions I'd felt over the last few hours, being with him felt natural. The nerves that had plagued me all night were gone. "I love it here. There is so much going on, the culture and the people. I can't tell you how many journals I've filled. I miss home, Paige and the family, the twins, but I do love New York."

"How is the gang?"

"Paige and Grant had another daughter, Heather. She's two. Tara and Mandy are eight and seven, third and second grade respectively."

"Wow, that's a little scary. And the twins?"

"They're at Berkley. One day I fear they will take over the world. They're too smart for their own good."

The cab pulled over, Greyson paid and helped me from it. Holding his hand brought on a wave of memories. His was bigger, more callused, and still my hand fit perfectly. The hostess greeted him with a huge smile before she walked us to a small sitting area near a roaring fire. She took my coat and his before she disappeared.

Greyson waited for me to sit before settling next to me on the sofa. The service was phenomenal, a waitress appearing seconds later to take Greyson's order for champagne. She disappeared as soundlessly as she appeared. Those pale eyes returned to me. They were different, wiser, and yet I was happy to see a bit of the boy I knew in them.

"You painted me," I hadn't meant to blurt that out, but I was still in awe.

His eyes warmed. "It's my favorite painting."

"It's beautiful."

"You're beautiful."

I looked down as my heart moved into my throat. I tried to move the conversation along before I did something he might not welcome. "When did you start sculpting?"

He didn't answer right away and I wondered what he was thinking. There was a time I would have asked him, but we weren't those people anymore.

"About a year after I left."

"Is that your preference, sculpting?"

"No. Whatever strikes me is the medium I use."

"Is it everything you thought it would be?"

"It's a lot of work. I spend more time promoting myself than I do creating. I get it, I need to carve out a niche, but I can't wait for a time when I can focus solely on my art."

"How close are you to that?"

"Next year I should be able to call the shots, not the other way around."

I'd be out of school then. Maybe fate would be kind and we'd meet again. I didn't dwell on that, though I could have. Instead I asked, "How's your grandfather?"

His expression softened. "He's great, happy to be home. I try to see him as often as my schedule will allow. He's come to visit me in San Francisco a few times."

"Please tell him I said hello the next time you speak to him."

"I will. He's asked about you."

That both surprised and pleased me. "He has?"

"He took a fancy to you."

My cheeks warm, but I liked hearing that. "The feeling is mutual. I'm working on the book of your family."

It was his turn to be surprised. "You are?"

"I don't get to spend as much time on it as I would like, but your family is fascinating. There are a few mysteries buried in your ancestry."

"That sounds intriguing."

"When I graduate, I intend to dedicate more time on it. I want to solve those mysteries."

His expression softened as tenderness stared back at me. "I made plans to visit Mendocino a few times, New York too, but my damn schedule fucked it up."

Pleasure washed over me hearing he had tried to keep in touch. "I love that you tried."

"I should have done more than try. Despite my schedule being insane, I should have done more than try."

"You're not alone in that. I should have made the effort too."

Silence followed before he added, "I can't believe it's been almost five years." An act born of familiarity, he ran his thumb along my jaw. "Why did you leave the show?"

I didn't mean to be so blunt; I blamed it on the emotional rollercoaster I'd been riding all night. "Seeing you with your girlfriend hit me harder than I expected."

"Girlfriend?"

"The woman you were with earlier. She's quite beautiful. She could pass for a model."

"She is."

Of course she was. She probably walked on water too.

"She's not my girlfriend."

This was where my imagination started inserting lines because there was no way he just said that.

He grinned at me, the same look I got often when we were kids, the look that said he was reading my mind.

"My agent thought it would be good for publicity. She's just a friend."

"You're serious? She's not your girlfriend."

"No."

"Friends with benefits?"

He looked sexy as sin when he grinned. "No."

I was suddenly very thirsty. Where was that champagne?

He leaned closer. "You thought she was? How did that make you feel?"

How did it make me feel? How did he think it made me feel? Homicidal and terribly sad. I didn't say that though. "It's been a long time since I held a claim on you."

"That's not answering my question."

What was he after, an emotional cleansing? Seemed stupid to open that Pandora's box here, so I lied through my teeth. "Happy you were happy."

"That's bullshit."

"What do you want me to say, that I hated seeing you with her, and the countless tabloid shots with you and women each more beautiful than the last. I hate that once upon a time your smile and laugh and words were only for me and now..." I bit my lip and looked away as I struggled to put my emotions back in the box. It was all water under the bridge now.

Softly and with conviction he confessed, "There's been no one since you."

I turned my head so fast I think I sprained it. No one since me, I had to be tripping, but I saw the truth of his words in those pale eyes. Maybe it was foolish to feel hope, his confession changed nothing, but I did. "For me either."

He leaned in and dropped his voice to a sexy purr, "Have you missed me, Alexis?"

"Every damn day."

His eyes warmed and his focus moved to my mouth. I felt very warm. Maybe they could turn off the fireplace. "I'm glad to hear I'm not the only one holding on."

Happiness filled me, the kind I realized I hadn't felt since he left. I reached for his hand, his fingers curled around mine. "You're not the only one holding on."

The waitress returned, Greyson offered to pour the champagne. He handed me a glass. "So, tell me about the last four and a half years. Leave nothing out."

It was very late when he saw me to my door. "When are you leaving?" I asked.

"We're off to Boston in the morning."

I wished time would stop. I wasn't ready to say goodbye again.

"Call, email. I will respond," Greyson urged.

"That goes both ways."

He stared at my mouth for the longest time, but he didn't kiss me. I don't know that I would have survived him leaving again if he had. Instead, he hugged me and it felt so good to be in his arms again. His heart was beating as hard as my own. I buried my face in his chest and breathed him in.

"It was so fucking good to see you, Alexis."

"It was so fucking good to be seen, Greyson. Enjoy Boston."

He let me go, but he touched my hair, rubbing the strands between his fingers. "Call me."

We'd exchanged phone numbers and email. You had to love mobile phones. "I will."

It hurt watching him go, but not as much as the last time because I made my own vow. I wasn't letting him slip through my fingers again. I locked up my apartment then called Paige.

"So?" She answered on the first ring.

"He looks so good, happy, living his dream. I left his show, he followed me out."

"He did not."

"He left his show to spend the evening with me. Paige, I'm still in love with him."

"Alexis, honey, it sounds like he's still in love with you too."

Dear Alexis,

It is driving Colin crazy wondering who the woman is I keep sketching. I don't even realize I'm doing it. You were always beautiful, but maturity has turned beautiful into exquisite, the curve of your cheekbones, the smooth line of your jaw, the arc of your brows and the fullness of your lips. I'd like to really sketch you, have you sit for me. As well as I

*knew every inch of your face, it's different now and I want
to learn it all over again.*

*Boston was beautiful. There were a few places you would
have liked. I took pictures and once I figure out how to
attach them in this software, I'll send them.*

*I shouldn't have let us lose touch. I know you feel responsible
too, but it was me traveling, me with the crazy schedule, me
who was in a different location every week. You were always
in my thoughts. I still feel it, Alexis, even stronger than I
did then. I'm coming for you.*

*Until then, know there's a semi-famous artist who'd give it
all up for a walk along the bluff with the woman who stole
his heart that first day, despite her unfortunate means of
transportation.*

Love always,

Greyson

I laughed through my tears. I wondered if it was possible to print this. I needed to save it, look back on it in fifty years. There was so much I wanted to say, but I couldn't get my thoughts together, so my reply was simple but heartfelt.

Greyson,

134 E 13th Street, Apt. C, New York NY

I'll be waiting.

Love, Alexis

9

ALEXIS 2002

I stared at the wooden sign hanging over the old Brownstone, muted gold lettering against a hunter green backdrop, charming, old world in a time when people were into neon and metal.

Nathaniel Breen, the private investigator I had settled on, the man who would share with me what became of my parents. I wanted to know and I feared knowing. Feared they were alive and well, living in their suburban house with three kids and two dogs, but the alternative of them being dead, I'd be happy knowing *they* were happy once I got over the visceral pain of being left behind.

I wiped my hands on my pants, took a deep breath then took the first step in discovering my parentage.

Inside was charming with muted gray walls and old wooden floors that had long ago lost their patina, but the marks and signs of age added character. Two wingback chairs were tucked under the front window, and a fire was burning in the small stone fireplace. A door leading into a bigger room was open and an elderly gentleman, with white hair and a three-piece suit, sat behind the massive desk. He glanced up.

"Miss Owens."

"Yes."

Walking around his desk, he offered me his hand. "Nathaniel Breen. Nice to meet you." He gestured to one of the two leather chairs before settling back behind his desk.

"You want to find your parents."

"Yes."

"What do you know about them?"

I reached into my purse for the picture. I hated to part with it, but it was the only thing I had of them and if it helped him find them...

He reached for his glasses and slipped them on so he could study the picture. Compassion looked back at me when he saw how worn it was. "This is all you have?"

"I'm afraid so. My foster parents wouldn't tell me anything. I contacted social services in my hometown of Mendocino, but they had no record of me. They said that would happen if I was placed with my foster parents in another state and special circumstances allowed them to move me out of state."

"And your foster parents wouldn't share the details?"

"No. They shared nothing with me."

He thought as I did on that. What the hell? "What are the names of your foster parents?"

"Evelyn and Howard Rafferty."

"And you're Alexis Owens. Your father's name perhaps?"

"I've always thought so."

"How old were you when you were placed with the Raffertys?"

"Two."

"And you remember living only in Mendocino and here when you moved for school."

"Yes. Will you be able to find them?"

He pulled off his glasses and leaned back in his chair. "It may not seem like much, but I have more than enough to get the ball rolling. As soon as I have something, I'll call you. Do you have a mobile phone?"

"No, but I have an answering machine on my home phone and I have an email account."

"I'll take both."

He scribbled them down then stood. "Do you have any questions for me?"

"No, just eager to know what happened to them."

We walked into his waiting room. "As soon as I have something, I will call. I hesitate to set an expectation and not be able to keep it."

"I understand."

"Thank you for trusting me with this," he said with a smile.

"Thank you for seeing me so quickly."

"It was nice to meet you, Alexis."

"And you, Mr. Breen."

"Nat, please. We'll talk soon."

I really hoped that was true.

Glancing at the clock, it was two in the morning. I couldn't sleep, had been restless since returning from Mr. Breen's office. Had he started searching? Did he know even now who my parents were? Where they were? What if I was wrong about them? What if they didn't love me or want me? Could I bear to hear that, to know for certain that it wasn't them, it was me? Had I once again scripted a story that was more fantasy than reality? I wanted to talk to Greyson but he was in Europe and it was too late to call Paige with the girls sleeping. I wondered if the twins were still awake. It'd be after eleven for them. I reached for my phone.

"Yo."

I couldn't help the smile hearing Dylan's voice. For as identical as they were, their voices were different. Dylan's was a bit deeper than Dominic's.

"Hey, you."

"Alexis! Everyone shut up, I can't hear."

"I'm interrupting. I can call back."

"No!"

"Hey, lady," Dominic picked up another line.

"Hi, knucklehead."

"What's up? It's two where you are. What's going on?" Dylan missed nothing.

"I visited the PI today."

One of them hung up, the background noise disappeared as Dylan moved to another room. He put his phone on speaker so Dominic could hear too. "Your parents," he asked.

"Yeah."

"This is a good thing. You've wanted to find them since we were kids," Dominic said.

"I know."

"You're worried they don't want to be found," Dylan voiced my fear.

"Yes."

"The people in that picture would not have given you up, not unless something forced their hand."

I wanted so much to agree with Dylan, but now that I was doing it, looking for them, I wasn't so sure. It had been almost two decades and they never once reached out.

"Alexis, don't overthink it and don't worry until you have cause to worry. If nothing else, you'll know about your parents one way or the other. You can let it go and move on," Dominic was often a goof, but he had it in him to be very wise.

I curled up on my sofa. "Thank you. I needed this. So what are you two doing?"

"Celebrating. Sophia made it into the finals of the Rembrandt Awards for excellence in robotics."

"You didn't tell me about this. Guys, that's incredible. You must be on the moon."

"Understatement," they said together.

"How is Sophia?"

"It's better for you to see with your own eyes."

I was scared. She probably had four breasts and...no I didn't even want to go there.

"I'll let you go, back to your celebrating."

"We'd rather chill with you," Dylan said then added, "What movies have you seen lately?"

Winter in the city was brutal. It was early February and the temperatures were dipping to below freezing often. I was ready for summer. I thought of the bluff at home and my jetty, which had Greyson drifting into my thoughts. It had been two months since his show, but as promised we stayed in touch through email. I LOVED email.

After class, I stopped for my mail before heading up to my apartment. A neighborhood paper had picked up my weekly column, the one about my adventures in the city. The pay was pennies, but I had my own byline. That was super cool. I dropped everything on the counter; one envelope in particular caught my attention seeing the familiar handwriting.

Greyson.

Like when we were younger, those butterflies took off in my stomach. I ripped open the envelope to find a plane ticket, a ticket for a black-tie affair and a note.

I have a show in Chicago. Please come.

Like he had to ask. Even with my column, class and assignments due, I would make it work.

I hopped onto my computer and sent him an email.

See you in Chicago.

His reply was almost instant.

I'll be waiting at the airport.

As soon as I stepped off the plane, a fluttering started under my ribs seeing him, damn he was a nice sight dressed in jeans, a tee and leather

139

jacket. I'd never seen him wearing a ball cap, but he was wearing one now, drawn low over his eyes. He looked sexy as hell. Our eyes connected and I was that damn moth being drawn in by him.

He reached for my bag and pressed a kiss on my cheek. "How was your flight?"

"Decadent. I've never flown first-class. I hate to admit that not only am I spoiled now, but I turned into a bit of a snob."

His eyes were laughing. "What do you mean?"

"We got to board before everyone else, served champagne while the peasants herded onto the plane. And that was how I thought of them, peasants. I am one of them, coach rider all the way, but not today, not while sitting in first-class. That makes me a terrible person."

He chuckled, "It makes you human."

I wasn't so sure about that. Glancing up at him, I really liked the cap. "I've never seen you wear a hat before. It's a good look."

He kept his head lowered, but he glanced at me from the corner of his eyes. A little grin curved his mouth. "It's for function not fashion."

It took me a second to understand his meaning. A smile split my face. "People recognize you, even here?"

"Yes."

"And that's a bad thing?"

"Usually it's not, but I encountered a few overzealous fans when I arrived earlier in the week. They've been following me."

I wasn't sure if I should laugh or be concerned. I couldn't say I was surprised he had crazy fans remembering high school and Stephanie's reaction to him. Hell, even mine. "Overzealous?"

He flashed me a smile. "It's nothing for you to worry about."

But was he?

He led me to the visitor parking lot and a sleek black sports car. After loading my bag into the trunk and holding the passenger door for me, he settled behind the wheel and started the car. Only then did he take off his cap. Those pale eyes met mine. It was like coming home.

"Why did you cut your hair?" *Nice smooth transition, Alexis.*

"You don't like it?"

"I do, but I like it better long."

He didn't answer and instead said, "I have a suite at the hotel. I thought we could share, unless you want your own room."

A shiver moved down my body thinking about us in the same room. I wasn't so sure that was a great idea. The man was too tempting and I couldn't guard against my feelings twenty-four seven. It was exhausting. On the other hand, there was no way in hell I was staying in any other room than the one he was in.

"It's nice that some things stay the same." Shit, I forgot he could read my mind. Confirmed when he said, "Same room."

Maybe I should make one of those tinfoil helmets to block my brain waves. I wondered if that would work?

"What would you like to see while here?"

Him...naked. Damn it. I glanced over and by the wicked look in his eyes he'd read my thoughts again.

"We've been here before."

I didn't think we had ever left.

"I guess we need to find some Pop-Tarts," he teased as he pulled from the parking lot. "That was what you wanted to fill your box with if I recall." But it was the glance; the one that silently called bullshit that had my cheeks burning even as my nipples went hard. Yep, he could read me so easily.

"How about you surprise me?" I answered his original question, but purposely added the innuendo because I wasn't opposed to him taking me back to the hotel and us getting naked. In fact, I voted for that.

He caught on immediately when he replied, "As you wish."

After dropping my stuff at the room, so I could hang my gown, we toured the city. It was February and cold and still we bundled up and acted like tourists. He took me to the Navy Pier and Wrigley Field. We walked the shopping district and were on our way to see the observation deck that had a three sixty degree view of the city when Greyson asked, "Are you hungry?"

"Yes."

"Do you trust me?"

Trust him? What was he up to? "I do, but you asking makes me wary."

Grabbing my hand, he pulled me to a street vendor. "Two dogs with everything."

"You got it," the man said before he began to build two hot dogs and I did mean build—chili, onions, cheese, jalapenos and sour cream. We were given a plastic knife and fork because there was no way a person could wrap their mouths around the toppings resting precariously on top of the poor hot dog. We settled on a bench, our hot dogs sitting between us. I stood corrected when Greyson brought the dog to his mouth and took a huge bite.

"How the hell did you do that?"

He grinned around his food. "It's a gift."

I didn't try. Not only wouldn't I get it all in my mouth, most of it would end up on my shirt. Even eating it with a fork and knife was difficult but I managed a forkful with all the toppings. I hesitated, because talk about instant indigestion.

"Chicken?" Greyson taunted. Unbelievably he'd finished his hot dog.

As soon as the flavors exploded on my tongue, I moaned because damn that was good.

"Amazing, isn't it?"

"So good. I wasn't sure all the toppings would work, but they do and that hot dog. There's garlic in that hot dog."

"Best fucking hot dog I've ever tasted," he said then twisted the cap from his water and took a long drink. I forgot about my hot dog, watching him, the long stretch of his throat, the muscles, his Adam's apple. Who would have thought watching someone drinking would be so sexy?

He knew exactly what I was thinking. I wasn't trying to hide it. Those pales eyes heated. I wanted to touch him, wanted to relearn his body that was different from the one I knew. I wanted him to kiss me. Even with hot dog breath, I wanted to feel those lips on mine again.

He swiped his thumb over my cheek; I smiled at the familiar gesture. There was a promise buried in his expression; he wanted to pick up where we'd left off too. For now we'd eat hot dogs and play tourists.

He dropped our trash in a can then held out his hand to me. "Ready?"

"Lead the way."

Chicago was a beautiful city. After a day of exploring, we returned to the room to get ready for his show. The door closed behind him as I stepped farther into the room. Greyson didn't move from the door, leaning against it, his hands shoved into his pockets. Needing something to do with my own hands, I twisted my fingers together. We had never been uncomfortable around each other and it wasn't discomfort now. It was want that sizzled the air between us. I wanted him so badly I was dizzy with it. He felt it too by the way his jaw clenched and his eyes roamed over me. I had already caused him to miss one show; I didn't want to be responsible for another.

He was thinking the same when he offered, "Why don't you take the shower first. I'll grab my stuff and change out here. You can have the bedroom."

I wanted him in the shower with me, but once we got naked we wouldn't be going anywhere. I nodded my agreement and headed for the bedroom, but stopped to look back at him. "Thank you for inviting me this weekend. I had a lot of fun today."

The look he gave me was one I'd seen Grant giving Paige, the one born from familiarity and history. "Me too."

We never did prom, I liked what we did so much more, but dressing for his show I felt a bit like I was dressing for prom. I took time twisting my hair into a knot. I didn't generally wear makeup, but tonight I added mascara and liner, a touch of shadow and blush and tinted my lips pink. My gown was a black sheath that hugged my figure. I loved it, simple and elegant. After I slipped on my black heels, I grabbed my clutch and wrap and joined Greyson. He stood on the balcony, his back to me. His muscled frame looked elegant in the tux. He turned when he heard me. His expression I was sure matched my own. His eyes moved down my body in a slow appreciative perusal. I was guilty of doing the same to him.

"You look beautiful," he whispered.

"So do you."

He held out his hand. "Are you ready?"

I linked our fingers and felt the familiar heat burning up my arm. "Yes."

His show was being held at a private museum. Floor to ceiling windows graced the front of the modern building, showing glimpses of the large brightly colored artisan chandeliers that hung from the high ceilings. His agent had a limo pick us up and when we pulled in front of the museum, I felt like I was at the Oscars. There was a red carpet and pylons with red velvet ropes cordoning off the curious passerbys from the entrance. And there were a lot of them, shoulder to shoulder. It was pretty spectacular. The driver opened the door, Greyson climbed out then reached for my hand, holding it tightly. It was only then that I realized all the fanfare made him uncomfortable.

As soon as we entered, a waiter carrying a tray of champagne walked over; Greyson handed me glass. "I have to do an interview. Will you be okay on your own?"

"Yes, of course." My focus was on his art that filled the space, a few of which I hadn't seen at his show in New York. "There are several new pieces."

"How I found the time to work with the grueling schedule Colin demands is nothing short of amazing." He tried for irritated, but I only heard affection.

I squeezed his hand. "Have fun. I'll be fine."

He seemed hesitant to leave, but he did, his long strides carrying him away from me. Like in our youth, he had that same deliberate way of walking, not hurried and not a stroll. And like then, it was sexy as hell. I took a sip of champagne; the fruity effervesce quenched my suddenly parched throat, before I turned my focus on Greyson's art. A painting of a lighthouse in turbulent seas felt alive; the beam of golden light shining through the gray, the churning white caps, the rocks. It was magnificent.

One of his new pieces was of the view from the house where Greyson stayed when in Mendocino. One of my dreams, one I'd never put a voice to, was to live in that house with Greyson and our family. I could see it so clearly, dogs running around the yard, children playing, Greyson in front of an easel. I loved New York, but one day I wanted to go home, wanted to start a family with Greyson in that house and not just because it was incredible and the location was without equal, but because it was a piece of our story.

It had been over an hour since we arrived and Greyson had been unable to break free of the crowd. I watched him from my place across the room. The last time I'd seen him in his element, I hadn't noticed the little things. Under the polish, he was exhausted. That didn't stop him from posing for pictures or signing the countless programs. Every person who approached him, he took a moment to talk to. He appreciated the attention, was grateful for it, but he was fried and after five years of this I understood.

Most took him to a specific work to discuss, but there were a few women who were there for the man not the artist. A few even bold enough to tuck something in his pocket, likely their phone numbers. I couldn't help think of that woman who had gone so far as to invade his privacy by sneaking into his hotel room. Groupies even for artists, a chill moved down my spine. Who would have thought? But then when the artist looked like Greyson, I guess I wasn't really that surprised.

"Good evening." My gaze shifted to the older man who appeared at my side. "You must be Alexis Owens. I'm Colin Rogers, Greyson's agent."

Stately came to mind, refined, elegant. He didn't have the Irish cadence, but his voice was cultured. This was Callum's friend. I smiled to myself because I could see them being friends. "Hello. It's very nice to meet you."

"And you. Are you enjoying the evening?"

"Very much. His work is beautiful. I thought he was amazing as kids, but his newer work is exceptional."

"And he hasn't even come close to hitting his stride." Colin turned his attention to Greyson. "I'm going to break him free in a minute. Perhaps you should make your way to the door. I've called for the limo."

"Does that happen often?" I asked, gesturing toward the crowd around Greyson.

"Only when the events are open to the public. Collectors are more subtle." He turned to me. "I feel I know you with the number of times I've caught Greyson sketching…" He lowered his eyes and pink spread over his cheekbones. "I suppose I shouldn't have said that."

Greyson sketched me? My own cheeks burned but not from embarrassment. "I'm glad you told me."

"He has worked very hard, sacrificed a lot, you both have, but he can see the light at the end of the tunnel."

Did Greyson discuss me with his agent? I wish I had been a fly on the wall for those conversations. "We both had paths to follow, but I'm seeing the light at the end of the tunnel too."

"I'm happy to hear that." He took my hand and like Callum had done, kissed the back of it. "Maybe I'll see you before you go. We could do lunch."

"I'd like that."

"Wonderful. All right, I'm going in. You best make your way to the door for the getaway."

10

ALEXIS

Unlike his normal gait, Greyson moved like he was on fire after Colin freed him from the masses. He took my hand as he walked past, and pulled me outside to the waiting limo. The driver was already holding the door. As soon as we climbed in, Greyson dropped his head on the seat back and closed his eyes.

"I'm exhausted."

"What's it feel like?"

He rolled his head to me.

"They were all there to see you. They dressed up, made their way to that museum, bought tickets, waited in line to talk to you about your art."

His expression shifted to one of awe. "For as long as I've been doing this, it still boggles my mind when I see the crowds. It's humbling and awesome and terrifying."

"Your painting of the house in Mendocino is exquisite."

He teased, "Your favorite?"

"No, the painting you sent me, the one of the jetty, that's my favorite. You captured it, what made the spot so perfect, what lured me in as a little kid, what kept me coming back year after year...you recreated it. I have it hanging in my living room and every time I look at it I think of you. I think of the most perfect time in my life and how one day I want to get back to us, want to live the life our youth gave us a glimpse of."

Love and longing looked back at me. He shifted into me, his big hand cradling my cheek as he pulled my mouth to his. As soon as our lips touched, every moment from that perfect year came back. There was a reason there had been no one since him, because he was all I wanted.

He didn't take the kiss deep; he tasted me like one would a fine wine or a favorite dessert. I moved closer, curled my fingers around the hand that held my cheek and drank him in. His free arm wrapped around my waist, pressing me tight against him as his tongue traced my lips, teasing but not penetrating. I appreciated his restraint because it had been a long time and feeling what I did for this man I wasn't feeling as disciplined.

He broke the kiss when the limo stopped. He didn't wait for the driver, climbing out and pulling me with him. I was running to keep up, but that only meant we'd get to the room faster. The elevator was empty; as soon as the doors closed, he had me up against the wall, pulling his hands through my hair before he kissed me, sweeping my mouth with his tongue. I moaned as his taste filled me, my tongue as eager as his. So lost in the kiss, we didn't realize the elevator had stopped until someone cleared his throat. Greyson managed a smile and a greeting. I wasn't feeling as charitable. We reached the room and my body gave a delicious shudder at the idea of ripping each other's cloths off, so I was confused when he released my hand and walked farther into the room.

"Greyson?"

I had never seen him looking unsure when it came to us, but he was now as he rubbed a hand over his head, the muscles of his arm straining the silk blend of his tux. "I'm sorry."

Sorry? "For what?"

"I'm acting like a fucking wild animal. It's been too long and tasting you again...that doesn't make it right."

He looked adorably contrite and for no reason. He could have taken me in the limo, with the driver looking on, and I wouldn't have protested. I didn't move from my spot across the room, but I did smile as the memory teased me. The words he once spoke to me I offered back to him. "All you have to do is close the distance, Greyson, and I'll put us both out of our misery."

His head snapped to me, those pale eyes several shades darker. The smile he offered stole my breath as he remembered too. My blood was rushing through my veins when he closed the distance. He moved right into me, curled his spine and kissed me like he'd die if he didn't. Passion turned hotter when he reached for the zipper of my dress. We moved toward the bedroom; I yanked his jacket down his arms and started on the buttons of his shirt. We tore at each other clothes but we never broke the kiss. My dress slid down my body and only then did Greyson pull his mouth from mine, his hot eyes devouring the sight of me in my black lace bra and panties.

"You are fucking beautiful. I want to paint you, just like that."

My tummy quivered at the hunger in his eyes. "Not right now."

He grinned and reached for me. "No, not right now."

Feeling his hands on me again set off those little fires under my skin. In the bedroom I worked on his pants, but I was taking too long. He stepped back, yanked his shirt off, kicked off his shoes, pulled his socks off and dropped his trousers and briefs. I just stared because gone was the long, lean body of the boy I knew. He was wider and thicker; his was the body of a man. That realization brought a wave of sadness over the years we'd missed.

"Alexis?"

"I hate that we lost all those years. That I didn't get to witness you become the success you are." I walked to him, traced his pec muscles. "That I didn't get to see you change from a boy to a man." My gaze met his. "I want those five years back."

He palmed my neck, lifting my chin with his thumb to bring my mouth to his. He took his time, his lips, tongue and teeth as he drew out the pleasure. Drugging, consuming, my body coming to life like a spring bulb under the heat of the sun. We weren't frenzied or rushed. It had been years, both of us hungry for the other, but we took our time.

Savoring the other. I touched him, the expanse of muscles along his back, the deep ridges of his abs, the V that cut his hips. He twisted the clasp of my bra and pulled the straps down my arms. Without breaking our kiss, he cupped my breasts. I moaned into his mouth when he swiped my nipples with his thumbs. He dropped to his knees, tonguing my nipple as he tugged on the lace of my panties and dragged them slowly down my legs. He kissed the valley between my breasts, down my stomach, over my hip.

"Step out of them," he whispered.

He traced a finger up my leg; his focus was on the triangle of curls between them. Fingering my clit, he lifted his gaze to my face to see what his touch was doing. I drew my lower lip between my teeth as my hips moved into his touch. How I had missed this. His thumb replaced his finger working that nub of nerves as he slipped his middle finger into me. My legs went weak, my hands grabbing his shoulders to hold myself up. Another finger joined the first; my hips were pumping, as pleasure uncurled in my gut. He sucked my breast into his mouth and I lost it. The scream tore from my throat as waves of pleasure crashed over on me. He stood, lifted my leg and thrust into me. Sparks danced behind my eyes feeling him inside me again. My back hit the mattress; he came down on top of me, lifted my hips and slammed into me again. Over and over he pulled out, only to sink in deeper. Tears ran down my cheeks from the beauty. Another orgasm followed the first before he sank in deeper; his body went still as he found his own release.

It was several minutes later when Greyson said, "I didn't use a condom."

"I'm on the pill."

He liked that when his eyes grew dark. He kissed me, sweetly at first but it had been a long time. Sweet turned passionate as we started the climb all over again.

We sat on the floor of the suite, the television on in the background, a feast from room service spread out before us. Greyson had the bed sheet wrapped around his waist; I wore his dress shirt.

The deep-dish pizza was good, but I preferred a New York slice any day. Greyson reached for his beer and took a long drink. My body warmed watching him. He'd already gifted me with four orgasms and still I wanted him. The beauty of us, even being wild for the other, it was like it had always been. Easy and comfortable.

"Do you remember the first time we made love?"

He gave me a look. "Do I remember?"

"Okay, stupid question. This is kind of like that, though we never did finish those sandwiches I made."

"Not when something so much sweeter was in reach."

I actually felt my bones turn to liquid.

"I'm ready to go again if you are." The same words he spoke then.

"I need fuel."

He chuckled, but helped himself to the steak sandwich with melted cheese, peppers and onions oozing from it. Sex, when done right, really worked up an appetite.

I studied him, taking note of the small differences in his face, the new laugh lines around his mouth and at the corners of his eyes. We were the same but different. The last time we'd been here he was still a dreamer and now he was Greyson Ratcliffe, a rising star. "When you thought about your future as a kid, did you see yourself being as successful as you are?"

"No, and honestly I still scratch my head from time to time. It's amazing, don't get me wrong, but it's more visible than I thought. And I know that is in part because of who buys my stuff, actors and rock stars encouraged by their brokers to buy art as an investment. Their celebrity rubs off."

"Sure, that may be part of it, but you are as hot and sexy as any actor out there. And you're more attainable."

His bottle stopped midway to his mouth. A mischievous look entered his expression. "You don't say." He took a drink then asked, "What about you? You're graduating soon. Have you written your novel, submitted it?"

"I am working on a novel. It's a labor of love."

"What's it about?"

Us, but I didn't want to share that yet. "Just something of interest to me. I have written a few plays over the years. The one I'm working on now for a class, my professor loves. He's got some feelers out to some companies Off-Broadway.

His joy for me was seen first in his expression. "That's amazing, Alexis."

"I don't want to jinx it."

"What's it about?"

"The foster monsters."

I'd never seen an expression shift so fast. He didn't like them, but that look said more. He hated them. "Why would you write about those assholes?"

"Because the best stories are the ones that mean something to the writer. I lived it. I survived it and I took that and made a parody that draws on all the emotions of my childhood while shining a light on a problem that isn't a new one."

I couldn't read his thoughts and wondered what he was thinking. I didn't have to wait long. "I wasn't kidding. I want a life with you."

It was my pizza that stopped midway to my mouth. Loved washed through me. "I want that too."

He separated the cotton of the shirt I wore, his hand slipping inside to cup my breast. "When do you graduate?"

I had trouble focusing on the conversation as he played with my nipple. "June."

"It's February. I have commitments through August." He rolled my nipple then pulled. My eyes glazed over. "We have to get in our fill to last us until September."

I dropped my pizza on the plate and climbed into his lap. "We better get started then."

Focus was a problem for me since I returned from Chicago. I wished for September, the month I had circled in red on my calendar. The month where Greyson and I would be at a place to pick up where we left off.

Five months and hopefully we would both be on the same coast, in the same city and the same apartment. My email chimed.

I had Pop-Tarts for breakfast. They're as nasty as I remembered.

I laughed out loud at his email.

Try Toaster Strudels. They're delicious. I worked it out and am coming home for spring break. Please say you'll be around the week of April 16th

My phone rang. I grinned and answered on the first ring. Greyson didn't even let me say hello. "Damn it. I'll be in Europe."

I was disappointed, but I knew it was a long shot.

"Maybe I can cancel—"

I cut him off. "Colin would have a stroke."

"Likely."

Despite the humor in his tone, he sounded tired. "How are you?" I asked.

"I'm ready to slow down, to see you every fucking day."

"I was just thinking about that. How we only have five more months before we are hopefully on the same coast."

"Five months too long."

He wasn't wrong.

"There is a magazine that wants to do an interview with me," he said out of the blue.

"And you're thinking about not doing it?"

"No, it's just..."

"Just what?"

"Don't laugh."

"I won't."

I heard his exhale over the line. "I can't stand the groupies, but if I do the interview I'm asking for it."

I had witnessed his fans. At first glance, it seemed flattering but I think a daily diet of it would get old fast. "You do seem to attract them. Did even in high school."

153

Silence followed before Greyson said, "Oh, Stephanie. I forgot about her."

I hadn't.

"I saw some ladies tucking their numbers in your pocket at your show."

"Not just their numbers, but photographs, resumes on why they are my perfect match." He exhaled before adding, "I've had sixteen marriage proposals."

I laughed at how irritated he sounded.

"You're laughing."

"So it's not your favorite part of the business."

He didn't answer. He didn't need to.

"You should do the interview. I understand your thinking, that if you don't put yourself out there you won't attract groupies, but you already put yourself out there through your art."

"That's what Colin keeps saying."

"You should do it. I'll definitely buy it."

"So, tell me, Alexis, what are you wearing?"

I glanced down at my sweats. "A NYU tee and black sweatpants. Oh shit, some of the filling from my strudel dripped on my shirt. Damn it, this is my last clean shirt. Now I have to do laundry. I hate doing laundry."

He chuckled.

"What? It's not funny. I loathe laundry."

I was grateful phones had not advanced to videophones so he wouldn't see me licking the filling off my shirt. It was strawberry and delicious. It was while I behaved with absolutely no manners that the true meaning of his question dawned. I felt like such a dope. It must be how Dominic felt all the time. I snickered to myself.

"You weren't really asking me what I was wearing."

"No."

"Can I change my answer?"

"I was hoping you would, though the filling stain added a nice touch to the visual."

"Okay, ask me again."

"What are you wearing, Alexis?"

"A leather bustier and thong. Wait, no a thong is dental floss for your ass and leather doesn't breathe so how is that sexy? Getting to the prize and she's all sweaty and gross. And I sweat. I don't perspire."

He was chuckling again.

Ah shit. I sucked at this. "Let me try again."

He deadpanned, "Maybe we should order dinner. I have a feeling we're going to be here awhile."

I almost peed myself from laughing so hard.

The flight home for spring break had been long, but as soon as I passed the security checkpoint I saw five familiar smiling faces. Paige screamed and ran to me. I dropped my bags and met her halfway. "It is so good to see you." She hugged me so hard it hurt.

She grabbed my arms and looked me up and down. "You're all grown up."

Grant chuckled, "It hasn't been that long, Paige." He nudged his wife out of the way to hug me. "Looking good, darling." It was still there, my crush, probably always would be. I pressed my face in his chest and hugged him back.

The girls attacked, talking all at once that I only got snippets of what they said. Someone had a new bike; someone wanted to show me their soccer moves. Grant lifted Heather to his shoulders.

"Let her breathe," he chided softly. "She'll see everything once we get home."

Seeing their beautiful, smiling faces, yep, I was home.

On my first night, as Paige helped me unpack she filled me in on all the town gossip.

"The foster monsters moved away last year. No one knows exactly what happened, it was all very strange. One day there was a sold sign on their front lawn. Apparently, their landlord sold the house right out from under them."

"Weird."

"The Bakers are thinking about selling the diner."

I stopped unpacking. "No, really?"

"They are getting up there in years."

I could certainly understand their wish to retire. "I'd hate to see the diner sold or worse changed into something else."

"That's why the Bakers told me first, to give Grant and I the chance to buy it. If we can swing it, we're going to do it."

"That would be so awesome."

"It'll be fun to be on the other side of the swing doors. Speaking of swing doors, Debbie is back."

I jerked my head to Paige. "She left?"

"She went to Hollywood to find herself, was convinced she would make it big."

"As a runner chasing down lattes and meatless tacos maybe."

Paige chuckled, "Not even that. She returned with her tail between her legs. She's working with her mom doing hair in the basement of their home."

I felt a pang of sympathy for her, but you reap what you sow. "Karma."

Paige touched her nose. "Amen to that."

The diner looked exactly as I remembered. As soon as I entered, Mel and Dee came running out of the kitchen to greet me.

"Welcome home, Alexis," Mel kissed my cheek. "You look like a New Yorker, very fashionable." I couldn't afford the latest trends, but I raided consignment and discount shops. They were last year or later fashions, but I loved my wardrobe.

"Looks like you've lost some weight. I'll go fix you a burger, on the house," Dee said. She kissed my cheek before reaching for my hand and squeezing. "It really is so good to have you home."

"It's really nice to be home."

Paige and I took a table by the windows and as soon as we settled she asked, "Are you going to see Greyson while you're home?"

"No, he's in Europe."

"How are things with you two?"

"Like the last five years never happened. Everything I felt as a kid, I still do, but deeper. He's it for me."

She smiled. "You know what they say. Absence makes the heart grow fonder."

It certainly had in our case.

LAX was a massive airport. I was worried I might not find the twins, but when I reached the baggage claim there they were. Dominic and Dylan looked older, their faces had matured, but they still exuded that confidence they'd had when we were younger. They were dressed in jeans and polo shirts, their hair longer and streaked with even more blond and their green eyes were lit with love. We were spending spring break in LA, the twins' idea.

Dominic pulled me to him and planted a sloppy kiss on my mouth, "New York definitely agrees with you. You look hot."

"You're still a dope."

Dylan pushed him out of the way, lifted me off the floor and spun me around. "It's so good to see you." He dropped me on my feet. "All right, let's check out LA."

For two days we went everywhere, from the Hollywood sign to Rodeo drive and the Hollywood Bowl. I was exhausted. We got back to the hotel and I was ready to crash.

"We have dinner reservations tonight. Dylan and I have an interview, so we'll meet you at the restaurant."

"An interview?"

It's partly why we suggested LA. Two birds. "There's a company interested in Sophia."

"Winning that award has really put you two in the spotlight."

"Sophia in the spotlight, but it's cool," Dylan added.

It was more than cool. It was incredible. "I'm afraid to ask what she's capable of doing now."

There was a twinkle in Dylan's eyes. "I've grown tired of paying bills, so I'm automating."

"You two are scary."

"Reservations are at seven. I'll write down the address," Dominic offered.

"Hopefully we'll have something to celebrate."

At seven, I stepped into the restaurant. The hostess looked up in greeting.

"I'm meeting my friends. The reservation is under Dylan Cantenelli."

"The rest of your party is here."

We reached the table, but it wasn't Dylan and Dominic waiting. It was Greyson. He stood as I approached. He looked stunning in his suit, but it was his hair. He was growing it out. I didn't even care about the scene I made when I moved around the hostess and threw myself into his arms.

"Surprise," he whispered in my ear.

I was surprised, the best fucking surprise ever. I touched his longer locks. "You're growing out your hair."

"My girl likes it long."

His girl. My heart swelled.

He held my chair before taking his own. "How are you enjoying LA?"

"The twins aren't on an interview, are they?"

"No. I had a show, so they brought you to me."

"Sneaky." But so awesome. "So Europe was a lie?"

He grinned. "Yep."

He was here. We were here. "I don't want dinner."

"You read my mind."

He stood like his seat was on fire, grabbed my hand and dragged me to the door. The memory of him doing similarly the last time I saw him had my heart hammering in my chest knowing where this was leading. A cab appeared; he pulled me into it. My butt hit the seat and his mouth was on me. I tried to touch as much of him as I could as our tongues warred. I wanted him, hard and fast. Wanted him so badly I didn't have a problem with doing it in the back of a cab. Greyson had more restraint. "We're almost there," he whispered against my lips.

The cab stopped, I had no idea where we were. Greyson paid the man then whisked me inside to the elevator. The doors closed and he had my breast out of my dress and in his mouth. Heat pooled between my legs and my eyes rolled into the back of my head.

"I smell you, beautiful." I was so wet. He kissed my breast then pulled my dress back up. The doors opened and he looked completely calm. I looked like I'd just gotten fucked in the elevator. We reached his room; my back hit the door as soon as it closed. He wasn't as cool as he appeared because he ripped my panties off and buried his cock deep inside me.

We both moaned. I hooked my feet around his waist. He grinned then rolled his hips. My arms went around his neck as my mouth found his. The kiss was hungry and hot as we moved together, wild with need and longing. We came together.

He caught his breath before declaring, "All night, Alexis. I've got you all night."

I squeezed him tight as he started for the bedroom. "Less talk."

He laughed then tossed me on the bed.

Three weeks after returning from LA, Greyson sent me an email to check out the newsstand. He'd done it, taken the interview. On my way to class, I stopped at a stand. He didn't just give an interview; he was on the cover. I bought several copies then found a bench. It was an older picture because his hair was short, an artistic photograph done in black and white, all but his eyes that were in color. Women around the world were going to fall in love with him because those pale green eyes looked like he could see right into you.

The article was about Greyson's art, his background, but the journalist was a woman. I'd have known that even without the byline because there was a thread throughout the article about Greyson's dating. As I reached the end of it, she finally gave in to her curiosity and asked him outright what she had been hinting at throughout the article. Butterflies took off in my belly as I read on.

> *"Tell me, Greyson, I know you are a very private person, but is there someone special?"*
> *"Yes."*
> *"Care to expand on that?"*
> *He pulled a hand through his hair at my question and leaned back in his chair, but it was the look on his face when he thought of this woman that was the most telling. I'm afraid to report that Greyson Ratcliffe is most definitely taken. When he finally answered me, it was with an explanation that meant very little to me, but I imagined meant everything to the woman of whom he spoke.*
> *"She entered my life on a beat-up second-hand bike and from the moment I saw her, she was it. She's my heart." A smile spread over his face before he added, "She's my muse."*
> *"A lucky woman."*
> *"No, Teresa, I'm the lucky one."*

I hadn't realized I was crying until I felt a tear roll down my cheek. Later, and after much effort, I was able to speak to the journalist who wrote the article. In the next issue an addendum to Greyson's article was printed.

> *I'm happy to report that I have a final note to add to our story on Greyson Ratcliffe. After reading the article, Greyson's muse contacted me and gave me a statement, and readers if only we were all lucky enough to find what they have.*
> *"Greyson, from the moment I saw him, has been like that favorite tune you can't stop humming; he's a part of me, the very best part."*

11

GREYSON

EXCLUSIVE INTERVIEW! GREYSON RATCLIFFE EXCLUSIVE INTERVIEW!

I stared at the addendum Teresa forwarded to me, my chest growing tight thinking about Alexis. Who would have thought at eighteen I'd meet the girl I wanted to spend the rest of my life with.

I set out to make a name for myself and I had. Spending the last five years being a performing monkey hadn't been exactly what I was expecting, but I'd done it. People knew my name; they knew my work. I had made my one dream a reality. And it was realizing that dream that brought into focus the simple truth. I wanted Alexis more. I wasn't sorry for the years that separated us. We each grew as people, we learned we could function separately; I could now support her while she worked to make her own dream a reality. But more, the separation only solidified what we suspected as kids. We belonged together.

I had a graduation present for her. It was one that benefited me as much as her. I couldn't wait to see her face when she saw it.

I was supposed to be working. Colin handled the bills and contracts; I took care of the correspondence. There was a pile on my desk, a purple envelope stood out. Thinking it might be from Alexis, I ripped it open. I was not new to fan letters, I still received dozens of them weekly, but this was different. Alarm and unease moved through me reading the words of a clearly disturbed person detailing what she'd like to do to me.

I wished it were as simple as tossing the letter to remove the images she'd put in my head. After the last incident with the woman in my hotel room, the police profiled the personality so I knew this had nothing to do with me. I was just the outlet for their sickness. Didn't change the fact that it was unsettling to say the least. I was about to toss the letter when a flustered Colin hurried into the room. "It's your grandfather. He took a tumble down the stairs. He's okay but he's in the hospital."

I didn't immediately react because I couldn't even remember a time when he was sick. "You're sure he's okay?"

"Yes, but you can see for yourself. I've already booked the flight," Colin added.

I wasn't going to make Alexis' graduation. "I'll be ready in ten minutes."

Eight hours after learning of his fall, I rushed into grandfather's hospital room not sure what I'd find, but I hadn't expected to see him looking so irritated. Eyes I shared skewered me as soon as I entered. "This is bullshit."

I'd been so worried, wondering if there was an underlying illness that had caused the fall, but seeing how annoyed he was it really had just been a fall. I bit my lip to keep from laughing. He rarely cursed, only when he was really pissed.

"I fell down the stairs. I didn't break a hip."

He could have. "How did you fall?"

A blush colored his cheeks. He was embarrassed. I had definitely never seen that look on his face. "Since giving the household files to Alexis, I've been curious about the diamond so I've started exploring the castle. I was in the lower levels when I slipped on the stone steps."

Fear bloomed because he could have done far more damage than scrapes and bruises. "You're lucky you were only roughed up."

He said nothing, but he knew that too.

It then dawned where he'd been. "Who found you? I can't imagine the staff goes down there."

"William happened by, thankfully."

A chill moved through me because he could have been down in that dark, damp place for a hell of a lot longer before his absence was noticed.

He fiddled with his blanket. "I'm sorry. I know Alexis is graduating. You should be there."

"No. She'd want me here. I'll see her soon enough. If I have my way, we'll be under the same roof come September."

ALEXIS

Graduation day. I played with my tassels as I thought about my years at NYU. My writing had really taken off with a few of my short stories being published in some of the local magazines. I was still writing my adventure column, which had been picked up by Leisure magazine. My play about the foster monsters, the parody that my professor was pulling some strings for, was opening Off-Broadway next year. It still hadn't sunk in that a marquee was going to light up my play. I understood better Greyson's comment about how humbling and terrifying it was when he reached *his* dream.

My phone rang. Speaking of the devil.

"Hey. Are you on your way? I can't wait to see you."

"I'm sorry, but I'm not going to make it. I'm in Ireland. Grandfather took a fall down the stairs. He's okay, he didn't break anything miraculously, but moving around will be a little difficult for a few weeks. I'm going to stay and help out."

I had to sit. Thinking about Callum in any other way than the robust man I'd known was difficult and scary. "There wasn't any medical reason for the fall?"

"My thought too, but no. It was just a fall. He actually cursed at the nurse."

"Really? That doesn't sound like him."

"That's how annoyed he is with himself."

"That's a relief to hear. Please give him my love."

"I will. I do have a present for you."

He was all I wanted.

"As soon as I finish the last of my commitments, I'm moving to New York. I'm hoping you'll agree to be my roommate."

It didn't feel real. A part of me thought I was dreaming. "Alexis?"

"We're really doing this."

His voice was like a soft caress. "There's no reason why I can't move my studio to New York. I'll move it anywhere you are, if that's still what you want."

"Absolutely it's what I want."

He chuckled, "I found a place. If you like it, my lawyers can handle the details. You can move in at your leisure. I should be on your door step the first week of September."

"I can't believe we're finally here."

"Believe it. I don't want to keep you. Enjoy your day and tell the gang I said hi."

Everyone was already at the stadium. Even Mr. and Mrs. C. flew in for the ceremony. "I will."

"My girl, a college grad. Congratulations, beautiful."

I placed the phone back and couldn't help the smile. Greyson and I were moving in together. Excitement bubbled up and I may have even done a little dance.

I had to get to the stadium. I grabbed my purse and yanked the door opened and almost stepped on a little gift bag. I looked up and down the hall, but it was empty. I stared at it like it was going to break out into song. I brought the bag inside and placed it on the kitchen counter then stared at it a little longer. Who sent it to me? Why not knock and hand it to me? There was no tag, no card. It seemed like something Greyson would do, especially now that he couldn't make the ceremony. Logistically, I didn't know how he would have pulled that off, but I didn't care because I was too excited. I pulled the tissue paper from the bag to reveal a small black box. My hands were actually shaking when I opened it. Another emotion filled me staring down at the gold locket in the shape of a heart. My eyes stung as I lifted the locket. The gold was worn from age and that only made it more beautiful. Flipping it over, it simply said *Love Always.* I opened it. There were two pictures, one of my dad and one of me. The tears started then. My mom's locket. Wherever they were, they were finally part of one of my milestones. I fastened it around my neck and palmed the locket. "Thank you, Mom and Dad."

A few days after graduation, Grant and the kids returned to Mendocino, the twins to Berkley and their parents to France. Paige delayed her return after learning of Greyson's graduation present and my mom's locket. I was feeling a little tender so for two days we ate ice cream, watched movies and had girl time. Today we were heading to the apartment Greyson had found. The directions took us to a high rise just off Central Park.

"Are you sure this is the place?" Paige asked.

I double-checked the address. "Yes."

Paige's expression matched my own, surprise.

A doorman greeted us. He was dressed in an emerald green uniform.

"Fancy," Paige whispered.

The entrance hall was done in Italian marble from floor to ceiling. Crystal chandeliers that burned like fire and ice hung in a row from front to back pulling your eyes to the large, marble desk where two men in the same emerald green uniform sat.

As we approached, they both stood. "Welcome Ms. Owens and Mrs. Atzer. Benny will show you the apartment."

Paige and I shared a look. We were getting a taste of what Greyson's celebrity life was like. I noticed a man and a woman sitting in the small reception area drinking coffee. It looked very cozy. We walked right past the elevators to a smaller one concealed discreetly on the back wall; it made only one stop. The penthouse. Paige saw it when I did because her mouth fell open. We exited on the top floor into a circular foyer with walnut floors that were so clean you could eat off them. In the center of the foyer was an octagonal mahogany table that held a large vase of fresh flowers.

"This is beautiful," Paige whispered.

I whispered back, "How can Greyson and I afford this?"

Glancing at her, she'd been thinking the same thing. I still wanted to see the apartment. How often did one get to see a place like this?

Benny walked to the carved walnut door with a security pad just to the right of it. He entered the code and pushed the door open. "I'll wait for you outside," he offered.

As soon as I crossed over the threshold, I was in love. The floors were the same walnut as the foyer; the walls were a combination of brick and painted plaster in pale yellow. Ionic columns were scattered throughout the open floor plan adding a touch of charm and warmth to what could have been an overwhelming space. The kitchen sat against the inner wall, black granite counter tops, stainless steel appliances and an island that spanned the length of the kitchen. The cabinets that lined the entire wall were a beautiful cherry wood with paned glass. It was the most beautiful kitchen, almost too beautiful to use.

"I could live in the kitchen," Paige whispered at my side.

"I think I need to be pinched."

"No, I'm seeing it too," she offered with a chuckle before she took my hand and led me to the opposite wall which framed floor to ceiling windows that overlooked Central Park. A balcony wrapped around the entire floor.

The bathroom was almost as big as my studio apartment, and the only other room on the first level was flooded with light from the floor to ceiling windows. A room that was perfect for a studio.

The upstairs had three bedrooms and two baths. The walnut floors continued throughout the second floor and each bedroom was spacious and had its own balcony. The baths were natural stone with steam showers, jet tubs and double vanities. There was even an elevator. When I entered the master bedroom, I fell in love. The entire outer wall was windows. A button on the wall operated the blinds that fed up into the ceiling. On the far wall was a fireplace, trimmed in creamy white wood. The walls were painted Wedgwood blue so it felt like we were walking among the clouds. I turned to Paige.

"It's perfect, but there is no way we can afford this."

"Greyson doesn't seem the type to pussyfoot."

I knew he'd been very busy over the last five years, but did he really make the kind of money needed to afford a place like this? We headed back downstairs as I battled disappointment. Now that I'd seen the apartment, I wanted it. Anywhere else would just be runner up, but I didn't want us to be house poor either.

"Miss Owens?" The woman and man who had been in the receiving area were walking toward us.

"Yes."

She handed me a phone.

"What do you think?"

"Greyson." I stepped away. "Can we afford this?"

"Yes. My art has done very well, but I also have family money."

Family money? I hadn't thought of that but he did live in a castle. Maybe it was stupid, but I didn't like not being able to contribute particularly when the place had the price tag this one did.

"Stop overthinking it, Alexis. You're just getting started."

How did he do that? "How do you know what I'm thinking?"

"Because I know you."

Even feeling apprehensive, I couldn't help the smile at how well we fit.

"Do you like it?"

"I love it. One room is perfect for your studio."

"I thought so too. Tell my lawyers we'll take it."

"How did you see the apartment?"

"A virtual tour."

"A what?"

"The realtor sent me a tour of the apartment through the computer."

"You can do that?"

"Yep."

Scary. "How did you know I was coming today?"

"Benny called me."

Of course he did.

"Give the phone back to Patricia and tell her yes."

"Are you sure you don't need to see it in person?"

"My only requirement is anywhere you are."

"I wish you were here right now."

167

He growled deep in his throat, his voice gruff when he added, "Get the apartment and tell Paige I said hi."

I almost stuck my tongue out at him. Know it all.

I walked to Patricia and handed her the phone. "We'll take it."

"Excellent." She reached in her briefcase for an envelope that she handed to me. "Enjoy your new home." Then she put the phone to her ear and walked out, her companion following after her.

I recognized the stationery. Inside was a platinum American Express card and a note.

Have fun shopping with Paige.
Love, Greyson

GREYSON

I pocketed my cell and wished I had been there to see Alexis' face as she walked through the apartment. Hell, when she stood outside the building. It was an expense, but it was also an investment and one both my business manager and my grandfather urged me to make. I had the money and would happily part with it to ensure a safe and welcoming home for my girl.

"Based on your expression, she said yes."

Grandfather guessed when he joined me in the study. We'd only just gotten home from the hospital and instead of taking it easy, he was trying to catch up on his to-do list. He looked good though.

His gaze caught mine. "Congratulations."

"Shouldn't you be resting?"

"I'll rest when I'm dead."

"Too soon for talk like that."

Contrition shifted his expression. "I'm sorry."

"Just take it easy. You don't have to be on the move all the time. You do have people."

As if my words conjured him, Nigel entered the study. Grandfather and he went back a long time; their father's shared the same relationship, as did their grandfathers. That was how it worked in these old homes; the families that supported the estates did so generation after generation. It was a point of pride and honor on both sides. Grandfather and Nigel could bicker like siblings, but they were family. "I've been saying the same thing. He listens to you as well as he listens to me."

Grandfather took a seat. I grinned. He did listen, just begrudgingly.

"Greyson and his girl are moving in together."

Nigel turned to me and though he didn't smile, not his style, he dipped his head before he offered, "Congratulations."

He joined grandfather on the sofa. "Is this the same young woman working on the family history? The one the photocopies were for?"

Nigel had an incredible memory. "She's been researching our family. Says there are a few mysteries buried in our ancestry that she wants to solve."

Grandfather's face lit up. "I look forward to talking with her about it."

"About what with who?" Maggie, the housekeeper, asked as she entered pushing the tea cart. She didn't typically serve us tea, we weren't that formal, but she was worried about Grandfather too. She knew he wouldn't slow down unless he was made to slow down, even if that was just for a cup of tea and a scone. Her red hair had faded over the years, but her green eyes were as bright and lively as they were when I was younger and she'd sneak me biscuits before dinner. She had been a rock when we lost my parents. Had a spine of steel and an overflowing heart. She wasn't staff. Like Nigel and William, she was family.

"The Ratcliffe mysteries with Alexis."

She turned to me, her smile blinding. "Finally on the Alexis front."

My thoughts too.

"With as long as Ratcliffes have been around, I'm not surprised to hear they stirred up a scandal or two," she continued then winked.

William entered, dressed in the black three-piece suit he insisted on wearing despite Grandfather's encouragement to dress down. He was old school and took his role of butler very seriously. He scanned the room, taking in the occupants before he asked, "After tea, would you still like me to have Lady saddled for a ride?"

Lady was my mother's horse. She'd just been a filly then, but even at ten she was magnificent.

"I'm going to pass on tea, so you can have her saddled now. Thank you, William."

He nodded before he turned and walked out.

"The man needs to loosen up," Nigel teased.

"Let's have tea," Maggie didn't wait for an answer and started pouring.

I headed for the door. I hadn't ridden in far too long. I was eager to see the estate as only you could on horseback. "Enjoy your tea. Grandfather, taking a nap doesn't make you an old man."

"So noted."

"I'll see you later."

"I'd like to send Alexis a graduation gift. Perhaps we can discuss it later this evening," Grandfather's offer halted my exit.

"Me too. It could be from all of us," Maggie added.

I could see Alexis' face, the surprise and tears over a gesture and from people she didn't know. "She'd love that."

It was thinking about Alexis that had me detouring to my parents' rooms. They had been gone for eight years and still their rooms were maintained as if they were still with us. When I was younger, I didn't come in here. The housemaids were always talking amongst themselves about ghosts that haunted the halls and hills. I'd never seen one, but the idea of seeing my parents as apparitions, that they'd come back to hover at the foot of my bed terrified me.

"You can take anything in here." I turned at the sound of my grandfather's voice. He stood just in the doorway. "I knew you'd come here."

It shouldn't surprise me he knew me so well and still it did.

"Anything you want."

I touched the shade of the lamp on the bedside table before reaching for the framed photo of my mother, father and me. It reminded me of the photo Alexis had of her parents; the one not framed but kept in a drawer, the picture that was well loved.

"You never came in here after they died."

I traced the lines of my mom's face. "I feared seeing their ghosts."

"Some of the younger women on the staff do have quite the imaginations."

I picked up their wedding picture. "They loved each other."

"It is one thing I will say about the Ratcliffe men. If we choose love, we love forever. Your grandmother was the love of my life, not just my wife, but part of me. Your father had that with your mother, you have it with Alexis. That's special, but it can also be a curse. Losing a love like that, you don't ever get over it. You learn to move on, to get out of bed every morning, to function, but a part of you never comes back. Losing your father and your mother will always hurt, but there is a part of me grateful they died together. To be the one left behind is very difficult."

A chill moved through me thinking about Alexis.

Grandfather was thinking about Alexis too. "They would have loved her."

My eyes burned. "I know."

"Anything you want, Greyson. Your parents would want you to have whatever you want."

He walked from the room, I moved to Mom's desk. Everything had a place, the pretty floral pattern of her blotter and pencil holder. I sat down and remembered as a kid sitting on her lap, talking and laughing. The memory was so vivid as I reached under her desk and felt around for the secret compartment she'd showed me. Pushing in the right sequence, a drawer popped open on the side of her desk. Her diary. That was something I would take. I closed up the secret drawer, stood and pushed in the chair being sure to leave the room as it was when I entered.

"You really would have loved her. She would have loved you too."

I reached the door and took another look around as I remembered. "I'll give Lady your love, Mom." I pulled the door closed behind me, leaving those memories in that room with them.

12

ALEXIS

I was finding my rhythm in the weeks since I graduated. The mornings I spent at the playhouse and my afternoons I worked on my column and new material. I still took shifts at the diner because I had to contribute to our apartment, even if my offerings were meager. My hope was once the play released I could quit, provided it didn't tank.

My new home was still a bit surreal. The building and the location were amazing. I hadn't purchased anything for the apartment with the exception of a bed and bedding for the master bedroom and some things for the kitchen. I wanted to wait until Greyson and I could do it together.

I did bring my living room furniture from my apartment so I had something to use until we furnished our home. Our home. I really liked the sound of that. I had an idea for our bedroom and hoped Greyson could fit it into his schedule. As a graduation present, Paige and Grant bought me a laptop, so while watching television I worked on my novel—the one about Greyson and me. The one I wasn't sure I'd ever show anyone, but loved working on.

The phone pulled me from the scene and I almost didn't answer it, but it could be Greyson calling so I hurried to the kitchen.

"Hello."

"Miss Owens, it's Nathaniel Breen."

It was funny how the human body responded to stimuli, like right now chills moved down my body from both excitement and fear. I even had trouble speaking, my voice no louder than a whisper when I replied, "Hello, Mr. Breen, how are you?"

"Nat, please. I'm well, thank you. I have some information regarding your parents. I wondered if you had time today to meet."

"Yes," I answered a little too quickly.

He chuckled before he suggested, "Could we meet here? Say in an hour?"

"I'll be there."

I tried really hard to calm down on the way to his office, but as I stood on the sidewalk just outside of it I wanted to throw up. I had theories on what happened to them, but if I stepped inside I wouldn't get to pretend anymore, wouldn't get to fill in the gaps with what I wanted the story to be. I needed to know; I had to move on one way or the other, so I took a deep breath and pulled open the door. Mr. Breen was waiting for me.

"It's so good to see you, Alexis. It's okay that I call you Alexis?"

"Yes, of course."

He gestured to his office; I took a seat, he settled behind his desk. He opened a file and slid my picture across the table to me.

My hand shook when I reached for it. He saw when he said, "I won't keep you waiting. I'm afraid I have some..." He removed his glasses and pinched the bridge of his nose. I knew what was coming before he said it. "I'm sorry to tell you that your mother died in a drive-by shooting when you were two."

My hand moved to my locket, but I didn't immediately acknowledge his words, because doing so would mean all the dreams I'd clung to—her coming for me, us sitting on my jetty for hours at a time talking, of her

173

fixing my veil on my wedding day and holding my hand as I delivered my babies, those dreams would shatter. I looked at the picture, her smiling face and how tightly she held me. I knew, had always known, she was gone. The woman holding me, there was nothing that would have kept her from her child, nothing but death. Slowly, reality penetrated, I would never know her. I would never hear her voice or see her smile. All I had of her was this picture and her locket. The tears filled my eyes and rolled down my cheeks. Mr. Breen handed me a tissue, I curled my hand around it, but I kept my focus on her as I silently said goodbye.

"You were there."

My head snapped up. "I was there?"

"From all the accounts I've read she shielded you."

I traced her image. She died protecting me. She hadn't abandoned me; she had given the ultimate sacrifice. I bit down on the sob. "What was her name?"

"Sade Ann Owens."

I met Mr. Breen's compassionate gaze. "Owens is my father's name?"

"No, her maiden name."

I liked that. It was fitting I should take her name. "And my father? Is he alive?"

"Yes, but I hesitate to give you his name. His lifestyle is dangerous to say the least."

"Please."

He leaned back in his chair and rubbed his neck before he relented. "Finn Levy."

"He lives here, doesn't he?"

A pregnant pause before he replied, "Yes."

"Did I live here with them?"

"Yes. As you suspected, you were placed with the Raffertys here before you moved to California."

Tears welled again as I lowered my head and studied my parents. I'd been drawn to New York because it was calling me home.

"Your foster parents were reluctant to tell you about your parents because they were encouraged strongly not to."

"Encouraged by whom?"

"Your father."

That insight made them marginally better, but not much. "Where does he live?"

"It's not that easy."

"Why not?"

"Your father is not…" He rubbed his neck again. How bad was it? "He is in the business of skirting the law."

"What does that mean?"

Thwarted in his attempt to keep my dad's information from me, he answered reluctantly, "He's a member of Lucifer's Warriors."

A chill moved down my spine. "What's that?"

"Only the most cutthroat motorcycle club on the east coast." He announced then added, "Your father is the president."

He knew something else. "What aren't you telling me?"

He stopped fidgeting and met my gaze. "Your mom's death was linked to his club. It's why he gave you up, to get you out of his world."

Curled up on my sofa, I studied the picture of my parents. Mom was so happy in it, so full of life, so young and to know she died not long after the photo was taken. The promise of a life we could have had, snatched away. My father believed he was responsible. His wife was killed because of him, so he pushed me as far from him as possible. Cut me from his life as efficiently as those bullets had cut her from ours. I wanted to rage, to scream and throw things, but I understood. As hard as it was to say, I understood why he acted as he had. He loved my mom, and she died because of him. How did someone come back from that? To know the one you loved most in the world was gone and they were only gone because of you. I stared into her eyes and accepted the truth. She was gone. The sob ripped from my throat as I let it out, everything I'd held in at Mr. Breen's. My mom was dead.

It took a while for the tears to slow, but there was a large hole in my chest. I reached for my phone and called Greyson. I needed him. If anyone could get me through this he could, but the call went to voice mail. I wouldn't leave him my news in a message. "Hey. Just wanted to say hi. I miss you. This apartment is way too big for one person. I'm counting the days."

I hung up and called Paige.

"Hey you. Grant and I were just talking about you."

"I met with Mr. Breen today." My voice broke.

"Grant, grab the other line."

"Alexis?" Grant's worried voice came over the line.

"My mom was gunned down likely from shit related to the MC where my father is president. And he lives here in New York."

"Oh Alexis."

"I always hoped we'd find each other. I know they gave me up, but I really believed one day we'd be a family again; we'd be the people we were in that picture, just older. But she's gone. She's really gone. How can you miss someone you hardly knew?"

"We're on the first plane out," Grant said.

"No. I'm okay. You have the diner and the girls. I'm okay. I'll be okay. Thank you for taking me in, for giving me a family. I don't know that I've ever thanked you for that."

Paige was crying. "Oh Alexis. You are family, never, ever forget that."

"I love you."

Even Grant's voice broke. "We love you."

Later that night the phone woke me.

"Alexis, what's wrong?"

Greyson. Of course he would know something was wrong.

I was exhausted, had cried myself to sleep. I could have been more tactful when I answered him, but this was Greyson. "My mom is dead. My dad belongs to a ruthless MC, and he lives here in New York."

"I'm on my way."

I wanted to argue, but I didn't.

"I have to tie up a few things, but I'll be home by the end of the week. What can I do?"

"Just talk to me. I'm numb and exhausted and empty but hearing your voice makes it better."

A slight pause before he said, "Ask me what I'm wearing."

I grinned at the memory. "What are you wearing?"

"A speedo and I've shaved, hairless like one of those cats. And I'm oiled but I can't sit down or I'll stain the furniture and we're only leasing it."

I felt miserable and yet he made me laugh. "I love you."

His voice warmed. "I know."

"What color is this speedo?"

"What color do you want it to be?"

For the next hour, he took away the sadness by making me laugh.

I stood backstage in the small theater where my play, *Monsters,* was opening in the spring. The marquee was already up; the first time I saw it I lost track of time. I stood gaping and still I didn't quite believe my eyes. Today, I didn't stop to look. It had been two days since learning about my parents. I was dealing, but it was hard knowing the person who created me, the one I had so many questions for, was gone. I'd missed knowing her. That left a hole.

The lead actors who played the foster monsters didn't have their costumes yet, and what costumes they were. The characters were actually depicted as monsters—they looked how my younger self had seen them. Howard had always reminded me of Oscar the Grouch. Exquisitely crafted costumes using bright fur from head to toe, but for their faces, which were painted so their expressions and mannerisms could be seen. I didn't use actual examples of my foster monsters' neglect but drew parallels from my own experiences and then twisted them with a comedic edge. Even knowing why they kept my parents from me, neglect was still neglect.

As I stood back stage, I watched the scene where the mommy and daddy monster were sitting in front of the television with their tray tables eating dinner while baby monster tried to get their attention. She ran through the house with scissors, played with matches, jumped around on the furniture but all of her antics went completely unnoticed. The scene ends with mommy and daddy monster shutting down the television, turning off the lights and going to bed while baby monster still stood in the middle of the room dressed like the Statue of Liberty, using the living room curtains and a Coleman lantern. I could find humor in it now, but when I was that little kid it hurt a lot.

I felt that sweet burn tickle my spine and turned to see Greyson. The hole in my heart grew smaller. We moved at the same time, crashing into each other, his arms coming around me to hold me tight.

"I'm sorry it took so long to get here."

"You're here now."

He cradled my face and studied me. I saw his concern shining out of those wonderful eyes. "You're hurting."

"I am, but it hurts less with you here."

"Let's go somewhere and talk."

"No."

He arched his brow. "No?"

"Take me home, Greyson." I pressed my mouth to his, "Make love to me."

He didn't have to be told twice. He took my hand and pulled me off the stage. We reached the lobby of the playhouse before he turned and pushed me against the wall. I had a moment to see the hungry look in his eyes before his mouth slammed down on mine. My purse dropped, my hands moved over him as I sought to touch as much of him as I could. As fast as he yanked me to him, he pulled away, retrieved my purse and continued to drag me from the building. He led me to a sexy black sports car, one very similar to the one we drove in Chicago. He practically closed the door on me before sliding across the hood and climbing in. His hand snaked around my neck, pulling my mouth to his for another searing kiss. We peeled from the curb.

Somehow we made it back to the apartment in one piece. He parked the car illegally. Rounded it, took my hand and tossed the keys to the doorman.

"Take care of that."

He didn't wait for an answer. His strides were so long I was practically running to keep up with him. Once the elevator doors closed, he crushed his mouth on mine as he worked to get my blouse off. My fingers fumbled as I tried to yank his shirt over his head, his mouth pulling from me only long enough so I could discard it. The elevator opened and we stumbled into the foyer.

"Your shoes," I breathlessly whispered that complaint before finding the crook of his neck and sinking my teeth in. He growled and lifted me into his arms. He managed to keep kissing me while he punched in the code for the door. He shut the door with his foot.

"Tell me you bought a bed," he demanded.

"King-size."

He growled again, low in his throat, before taking the steps two at a time.

"Don't you want the tour?" I teased.

"After."

GREYSON

We left a trail of clothes to the bedroom. I tossed her on the bed and landed on top of her. I saw the chain around her neck and followed it until I found the locket. My eyes moved from the locket to her face.

"My mother's."

"From your dad."

"A graduation present."

That sadness was back. I could take that away, at least for a little while, so I kissed her, devoured her; her taste was my drug and I'd been without it for too long. She spread her legs in invitation and I didn't make her wait, filling her in one powerful thrust. My mouth closed over her breast, her hands moved over my body, squeezing my ass. Our hips moved together, the sound of our skin slapping together and the scent of our arousal filled the room. I grabbed her thighs, lifted her hips and pounded into her.

I was home.

She came on a moan. I came right after her.

I dropped my head on her shoulder. I fucking missed this.

"Welcome home, Greyson."

My head lifted, her bright eyes made my heart ache in a good way. As soon as possible, I wanted my ring on her finger.

"What are you thinking," she asked, brushing my hair from my face.

"I love you."

She moved her hips. "I know."

Wrapping my arm around her waist, I flipped us so she straddled me. Sliding my hands over her body, I cupped her breasts. They were perfect, just like the rest of her. She closed her eyes and drew her lower lip between her teeth. I jerked my hips and she moaned. She took her time riding my cock. I was so hard it hurt, but I let her play until I couldn't take anymore and rolled her to her back. Her legs wrapped around my waist and I hammered into her until we both came.

We were in the living room, sitting on the floor. Alexis was wearing my tee. I had pulled on my jeans.

"My stuff is arriving tomorrow."

"We need furniture."

"Yeah." I looked around at the space. As soon as I saw it, I knew this was home. "I think we should be sparse though."

"I agree. I like all the open space. And that room in the back is perfect for you."

"Yeah."

I brushed the hair from her face, ran my thumb along her cheek. She was trying, but the sadness behind her eyes was killing me. "Talk to me."

"I don't understand how I can miss her so much when I don't even remember her."

"She was your mom. She loved you, you lost her."

"I always hoped we'd be a family again and it hurts to know we never will be." Her voice broke. I pulled her close, pressing her face to my chest. I ached for her, wished I could take her pain, but all I could do was hold her, love her, show her she wasn't alone and never would be again.

"I want to visit her grave. Mr. Breen shared where she was buried. He doesn't think I should visit, but I need to."

"I'll take you."

"I want to visit my father."

"Okay."

She glanced up at me. "No objections?"

"No, but we'll need to proceed carefully with him. I'd like to look into his MC, get a feel for what we're getting into."

"Okay."

I grinned. "No objections?"

"No."

Even with the smile, there was pain burning brightly in her dark eyes. Cradling her face in my hand, I kissed her and filled it with everything she made me feel. Lowering her to her back, I spent the next hour doing all I could to remove that sadness.

ALEXIS

I woke in the morning; stretched and ached in places I hadn't ached in a long time.

Greyson.

I reached for him, but his side of the bed was empty. Yesterday, he didn't push when it came to my dad and he didn't go all cavemen when I said I wanted to meet him despite the danger. He had been exactly what I needed him to be. My heart still hurt, but it hurt less.

Reaching for his pillow, I inhaled his scent. He was here. His scent was on the sheets. I only needed to walk from my room to find him. The memory came back so clearly, biology that first day and my scripted story of our romance rivaling the greatest romances of history and how our meeting was the beginning of the rest of our lives. We were there, at the start of something beautiful.

Climbing from bed, I pulled on his tee and went in search of him. He was in the kitchen making coffee. He had pulled on his jeans, his bare back to me. I leaned against the counter and couldn't control the smile. Every morning I would get to wake up next to him, I'd get to see him just like that making coffee. It was very surreal when a dream came true.

"Are you just going to stare," he teased.

"It doesn't feel real."

He turned and pushed his hands into his pockets. "I woke and spent the first hour just watching you sleep."

A person shouldn't be so happy. "Next time wake me up."

"How are you?"

"It hurts less today than it did yesterday. That's thanks to you."

Tenderness swept his face, but turned wicked when he eyed me from head to toe. "What are you wearing under my tee?"

I lifted it a little. "Nothing."

He moved so fast, lifting me over his shoulder. His hand moved to my bare ass where he squeezed. I laughed the whole way to our bedroom.

Greyson and I set up his studio. He had crates and crates filled with paintings that were each one more beautiful than the next. He was also working on a sculpture. The ones I had seen at his shows were amazing, how he twisted metal and molded clay and carved stone, so I was more than a little surprised, and disappointed, that I couldn't see this one. In fact, I wasn't even allowed to touch it. It stood in the far corner of the studio, covered by a large sheet.

While he worked on setting up his paints, I sat on the floor going through his paintings. Most were landscapes in the cities he had visited during his touring years—a street in Paris, a gondola in Venice, a vineyard in Tuscany.

"These are beautiful. Why aren't these in the shows?"

When he didn't answer I looked over to find him watching me. "I painted those for you. You couldn't be with me, so I brought the places to you."

Just when I thought I couldn't love him more. "I love you."

His smile stilled my heart. "I know."

"Is there a place in your travels you really want to see again? I am ready and willing to travel."

"If you are willing to travel, let's go to Ireland. You can see Grandfather, the estate."

I was teasing about traveling. I only wanted to be where he was, but seeing his home, seeing Callum again. I really wanted to do that. "Are you serious?"

"Yeah. Once we get settled, I'll call Grandfather and arrange it."

"I'd love that. Speaking of places, I have a request."

"Anything."

"Would you recreate the bluffs on our bedroom wall?"

His expression softened as he remembered too. "Yeah, I can do that."

"I don't want to take you from your commissions, so whenever you can fit it in."

"I'll start it today."

GREYSON

I moved the mattress to another room. I didn't want Alexis seeing this until it was done. I stood back and studied the scene coming to life on the wall. It was so easy to go back, to remember her at sixteen and how my heart raced in my chest and my palms itched to touch her.

My cell rang. I wasn't going to answer it until I saw Colin's name. He stayed in San Francisco. Unlike when we first started, he didn't need to follow me. Technology made it very easy to continue to work together even being on opposite coasts.

"Hey, Colin."

"Hello, Greyson. How are you settling in?"

I woke with her hair on my pillow and her scent on me. I was fucking settling in just fine.

"We're great. A long time coming."

"I'm happy to hear that. I do have some opportunities for you. I'll send you an email."

"Sounds great."

"Your fan mail is piling up. I'm sending it to you, but that's actually why I'm calling."

There was an odd note in his voice. "Is something wrong?"

"There was one letter that was, well unpleasant to put it nicely. I found a letter on similar stationery in your desk when I packed it up."

I'd forgotten all about that disturbing letter. "I'd gotten that right before Grandfather's accident. Did you read it?"

"I did. I hope that is okay."

"Yeah, is this other the same?"

"I'm afraid so."

Concern twisted in my gut. "Was there a postmark?"

"No and no return address."

"So whoever is delivering them is doing it by hand." That was a good thing. They were in San Francisco and I was clear across the country. Alexis was clear across the country. "Can you send them to me?"

"Yes. May I ask what you intend?"

"I want to have them in case I need to go to the cops."

"It's part of the package, the unwanted attention, the unsettling letters, but I have to say these bother me more than any I've read. I think caution is wise."

I didn't like it, not with Alexis coming back into my life. I wasn't giving her up, no fucking way. I waited too long to be with her, but I didn't like the thought of her in harm's way because of me. If needed, I'd hire someone to look into it, but my hope was it wouldn't get that far.

"I'll be cautious."

"Excellent. I will get these in the post immediately. Please send my regards to Alexis. And check your email for the upcoming events and let me know if you are interested in any of them."

"Thanks, Colin."

"Talk soon."

I dropped my phone on the floor. I wasn't really worried about the letters and I sure as hell wasn't going to think about them now. Life was too sweet to think about the sour.

ALEXIS

Greyson worked on the mural for two weeks. We took another bedroom because I wasn't allowed to see it until it was done. Day and night, he was in our room. I was in the living room working one night when he joined me. He wore a bandana when he painted so his hair stayed out of his face. I loved that he had grown his hair out. I had missed those long locks. The boxes from Callum were spread around the room as I organized while reading.

"Are these my family's files?"

"Yes." I patted the sofa next to me. "The legend Callum shared with us about the green diamond, do you believe it's real?"

He settled next to me and I handed him the photograph of one of his ancestors, an image he likely was very familiar with since the original was life-size and hung in the portrait gallery of his home.

"I don't know, but my ancestors believed in it."

"The diamond is here in his sword and in these..." I pulled out two photographs of Ratcliffe women who were wearing the diamond, which had been crafted into a brooch. "Why only two of your ancestors and not every Ratcliffe woman?"

"I don't know."

"I do."

His eyes found mine as a grin curved his lips. "You are enjoying this."

"I am. I've always loved a good story, and Greyson, you have an incredible story in your ancestry. The diamond became a sort of testament to love. If a Ratcliffe man was marrying for love and not duty, on their wedding day he gave his betrothed the diamond."

"Seriously?"

"Yeah. It's kind of sad. All the generations of Ratcliffes and only two unions were love matches. Duty bound to continue the bloodline the rest of your ancestors chose the continuation of family over love. I get it. I mean, it's incredible to have a lineage that dates back to the thirteen hundreds, but I guess I never realized to maintain a lineage like that there has to be sacrifices."

Greyson studied the images of his ancestors. "What happened to the diamond? Have you read anything in those papers?"

"No. After the fire, the diamond went missing. I could just be filling in reality with fantasy as I have a habit of doing, but what if the fire was started as a diversion so someone could steal the diamond?"

"Sounds feasible."

"I believe it's real. I believe all of it. Had I not met you, I might not have been inclined to believe in a love like that, but I'm living it."

He touched my cheek. "The bedroom is done."

"What?" I jumped from the sofa. "It's done and you let me rattle on. Come on." I grabbed his hand.

He stood, but instead of heading to our bedroom, he yanked me close and kissed me hard on the mouth. And only after my legs turned to noodles and my insides to mush did he lead me upstairs. As soon as I saw our walls, I was transported back. Not just to Mendocino, but to the past...our past. It was the bluff; every detail lovingly recreated—the crashing surf, the rock cliffs, the sea grass blowing in the breeze, the spray of the water. Even the gulls.

The swell of love had my voice a little rough when I said, "It's exactly how I remember it."

"Not exactly," he whispered.

He pulled me down to the floor and covered my body with his. "Now, it's exactly how *I* remember it."

"We need furniture. I love my futon, but it doesn't work in here." Greyson and I were lying on said futon, my back to his chest, watching television. We hadn't left the apartment since he arrived. It had been two weeks of nothing but loving, eating and sleeping. The best two weeks ever.

"You told me once you'd show me your city, do you remember that?"

"Yes." And I loved that he did too.

He glanced down and grinned. "So show me your city."

We'd been to the Statue of Liberty, The Met and The New York Library. I offered to take him to the American Girl store, but he declined. Instead, he wanted to see Coney Island, but first we stopped for lunch.

"Do you trust me?"

He grinned at the memory. "Yes."

I ordered two Nathan's hot dogs and two lemonades. "No toppings needed. Trust me."

We ate while we walked. "You're right. These are fucking delicious."

"What do you want to do first?" I asked. He didn't answer, just took my hand and pulled me along.

"I'm going to be sick," I held my stomach. Going on a rollercoaster after eating a hot dog was not smart.

Greyson was like a kid in a candy store. The dude was an adrenaline junky. "We have to go again. Are you really feeling sick?"

I hadn't seen this side of him even when we were kids. I loved it, totally worth the upset stomach. "No, I'm good."

"Are you sure?"

"Yep. I didn't know you liked amusement parks so much."

"I've never been to one."

"So this is a first."

"Yeah, and it's fucking awesome."

It was, more so watching how much he was enjoying it. To think we had a lifetime of firsts. The need to pinch myself was back. "I look forward to sharing more firsts with you, Mr. Ratcliffe."

He jerked his head to me, then pulled me close to kiss me senseless and I *was* fairly brain dead when he finished.

"Rollercoaster," he said against my lips.

He could have led me anywhere and I would have gone happily.

We rode the rollercoaster three more times before we decided to head to the Empire State Building. On our way Greyson said cryptically, "We need to make a stop."

A tattoo parlor was our stop. Inside, the guy behind the counter called Greyson by name. "Perfect timing, Greyson. We're all set up."

"Set up for what?"

"I'm getting a tattoo."

That was news to me. "You are?"

The artist, Tiggs, took a transparency and pressed it to Greyson's left arm, the inside near his heart. It was a seagull in flight holding sea grass and the sea grass spelled my name. Us forever inked on his skin.

My bright eyes met his. "I love it."

He brushed my lips with his thumb then settled back in the chair. "All right, let's do this."

For the next hour I watched as Greyson branded himself for me.

"Harder, please Greyson, harder." We never made it to the Empire State Building. We hadn't even made it into our apartment. In the foyer off the elevator, I attacked him. I wanted to kiss his tattoo, that had to wait, but being pressed up against the wall as Greyson drilled his cock into me was fucking fantastic.

I grabbed his hair and yanked his head to mine, my tongue pushed into his mouth, my hips following his lead as he drove us both wild.

I came on a scream, muffled by Greyson's tongue in my mouth. He came right after me. His powerful body went still as a moan burned up his throat.

He dropped his head on my shoulder. "I need to catch my breath."

"We need to do that again," I countered.

Pale eyes lifted to me. "I'm taking you like the tattoo."

"I love the tattoo."

His big hand covered my breast. I pressed into his touch and bit my lip as pleasure coiled in my gut. He looked wicked when he said, "I'm ready for round two."

"Are you sure you want to do this?" Greyson asked while we waited at a stoplight. We were on the way to see my mother. I was born in the Bronx, lived on Earley Street for the first two years of my life. On the way to the cemetery we were driving by my old house. The place where I believe I had been happy, loved, the place where my mother had died protecting me.

"Yes."

He reached for my hand and though I knew he had his reservations, he didn't push his will on me.

"Thank you." He glanced over. "For being here, for letting me see this through, for having your opinions but not forcing them on me."

"Don't thank me just yet. I know what else is going on in that head of yours. Seeing your house, your mom, I get. Poking a fucking tiger, I'm not going to be as accommodating."

I wanted to see my father's clubhouse or whatever it was called. Hoped I'd get a glimpse of the man in my photo.

"We won't get out of the car."

"From what I've read about your father's gang or club or whatever, they're criminals. I'm not talking stealing cars and shit, I'm talking trafficking in drugs, murder. If the rumors are to be believed, they are not people you want to know."

I couldn't believe that of the man in my picture, but after losing everything he loved I supposed it was possible he chose to live recklessly if he believed he had nothing left to live for.

"If we believe he left you to keep you safe, you showing up right in the middle of his fucked up world is not going to win you any points with him."

"He doesn't need to know we're there."

"People living in his world, they have to know everything as a means of survival. Hell, he probably already knows you're living in New York."

The idea my dad had kept tabs on me over the years had my heart hammering. Despite what he had become, a man would only do that if he cared. "You think he's been watching?"

"I shouldn't have said that."

"But you think he's kept me on his radar."

"Yes, if for no other reason than to keep you away."

My focus shifted outside. Greyson's words were meant to discourage me, but I wasn't at all. I was going to know my dad, whether my dad liked it or not.

My house was a little brick house with a covered porch sitting on a postage-stamp sized lawn. It was a happy looking house on a happy street, marred by violence that changed at least three lives irrevocably.

I stood on the street in front of the house and tried to picture my parents walking over the threshold after they married, sitting on the porch, Mom ripe with me as Dad touched her belly talking to me. I was using my imagination but somehow I knew it had been like that. Love, between them, for me. And then I thought of the bullets that ripped through her as she stood protecting me. All that love, all that promise over in a blink of an eye.

Greyson wiped the tears from my cheeks then pulled me close, silently offering his strength.

"I'm ready," I offered after a while. This wasn't my house; it was a memory, one that I could tuck away and recall when I wanted to remember.

He pressed a kiss on my head then led me to the car. We drove in silence to the graveyard. I was mentally preparing myself. Seeing our house had been hard, but I was going to my mom's grave. She was there, physically, but maybe her spirit roamed the graveyard, restless because she had unfinished business. Maybe this reunion would put her at ease, allow her to move on. I knew it was what I was hoping to get out of it.

For the city, the cemetery was quiet. Big oak trees and hills of green spread out before us as we drove along the curving road to the caretaker's office. Greyson kept the car idling while running in to get her plot location. My focus was out the window, my fingers twisting together. There was a weight in my chest that grew heavier the closer we got. It would make it real, seeing her name etched on the stone. Her final resting place.

Greyson pulled the car to the side of the road and shut it off. I reached into my purse and pulled out the very first journal I ever wrote, the one that told the tale of my imaginary friend Emily. I wanted to leave my mom something of me. I thought it fitting to give her the very first stories I ever wrote.

Greyson insisted on photocopying the journal; he took the book to the library and photocopied it himself. It was the little things, the small acts of love that left me breathless.

I climbed from the car, Greyson reached for my hand as I came around it. Silently we walked to her stone. I held his hand tighter when we reached a stone of an angel resting over the top of a heart. The inscription was the last straw, my legs crumbled under me as I sank down next to her grave and silently wept.

Sade Owens-Levy
1962-1982
Beloved Wife and Devoted Mother
You were an angel among us
but now you're home

Greyson's strong arms came around me. My fingers twisted his shirt as a lifetime of heartache broke free. She loved me. I didn't appreciate the gravity of that until seeing her grave. She was so young when she died, younger than I was now. She had only been at the beginning. I don't know how long I wept at her graveside. Greyson never let me go, held me until I cried myself dry. I pulled from the safety of his arms, glanced up into his compassion filled eyes then turned to my mom's stone.

I ran my fingers over her name. "I'm here, Mom. I found you. I love you. I've loved you my whole life. I kept you close and I always will." I placed the journal on her grave. "A piece of me." I wiped at my cheeks. "One day we'll meet again. I love you, Mom."

GREYSON

My fucking heart was breaking. Alexis' focus was out the side window. She'd been quiet since leaving the cemetery, but seeing her weeping at her mother's grave, holding her body as it shook with sobs, was so damn hard knowing there was nothing I could do to ease that pain.

She wanted to meet her dad, but I wasn't on the same page. He lived through the loss of his wife; he cut his daughter from his life to keep her out of his world. He knew the dangers and as much as it hurt Alexis to lose her parents, I respected the man for having the balls to give her up. I hoped I would have the strength to do the very same if ever my lifestyle put the ones I loved in danger.

"I want to see him."

I could hear the tears in her voice.

"We won't get out of the car. I just want to see a part of his world."

I didn't like it, but I acquiesced.

Lucifer's Warriors clubhouse wasn't much to look at, a brick, single story building. There was a detached four-car garage at the back of the lot and a fence that enclosed the entire property. Motorcycles were parked in the front and muscle cars and newer model pickups in the parking lot that spanned the side. Two flags hung from the pole, the American flag and just under that their club's flag.

She didn't pull her gaze from the window, hoping for a glimpse of her father.

"Are you a bad person if you do bad things?" she asked.

"Depends."

"Do you think my dad is a bad person?"

"He gave you up to protect you, he loved your mother, honored her even in death. No, I don't think he's a bad person."

"But he's dangerous."

"Yes, as is the world he lives in."

She reached for my hand and linked our fingers. The sadness in her eyes was so prominent but she tried for a smile. "I'm ready to go home."

I brought her hand to my lips and pressed a kiss in her palm. She held that hand in her other, curled her fingers around my kiss. I couldn't give her back her parents, but I could give her a family. One that stemmed from the kind of love her dad had for her and her mom, a selfless and powerful love. Now wasn't the time, her heart was broken; I would do everything in my power to mend it and then I'd put my ring on her finger.

ALEXIS

"You seriously aren't buying furniture? You're keeping this sea of bean bags?"

The twins moved to New York after their graduation. Their apartment was a loft in Soho. It was a great location and a great building, but they insisted on decorating like they were still in college. I loved they were here. Having family close helped ease the pain of losing my mom that still lingered and I suspected always would.

"Why spend money on furniture. I'd rather use it for gaming systems or computers," Dylan stated as if it were obvious. Spoken like the geeks they were. "Besides your place is so fancy, we'll just hang with you."

Greyson made a sound in the back of his throat. He liked the twins, but he didn't want them popping over whenever they wanted. We were still christening the apartment.

"I haven't seen your face at the checkout counter lately. What's up with that? Did you get tired of the spotlight already?" Dominic asked.

"Bugger off," Greyson grumbled. "My agent wanted me to do those shoots, wanted the press. I'm done with that now."

"So you don't like having beautiful women stuffing their numbers in your pocket."

"The only beautiful woman I want is right here."

I grinned. Good answer.

"Yeah, yeah, we get that, but proximity my friend. You don't want them, Dylan and I are willing to take one for the team."

"You'd want a woman that forward?" To me, the women seemed a bit desperate.

"Not to marry, but to roll around in the sheets, hell yeah."

I stood and started for the kitchen. I was hungry. They had to have something and hopefully not shelves of Pop-Tarts. "I'm happy you have such high standards."

Dominic called after me, "We can't all land a hot celebrity."

"Bullocks," Greyson swore but it was drowned out by Dylan's laughter.

13

ALEXIS 2003

G reyson and I were heading to Ireland. I was going to see Callum
and his home, the portrait gallery and the paintings I had studied
the copies of, but first we were heading home. I hadn't seen Paige and
Grant since I graduated. They were worried about me after my call
to them when I first learned about my parents. I was dealing. It had
been five months and each day it hurt less. They wanted to visit, I had
encouraged them to, but Grant insisted Greyson and I needed the time.
We'd been apart for so long, the first few months should be just us. I
was glad he insisted because those months had been the happiest of my
life.

Greyson sat next to me on the plane sketching. I had yet to see
that spiral ring from all those years ago, though I knew he still had it
because I had seen it amongst his things when we unpacked his studio.

"Are you ever going to let me look at the spiral ring?"

Greyson looked up, but his mind was still on his sketch. His
concentration shifted gears. "Which spiral ring?"

"The one you were constantly working in your senior year."

He smiled then, a secret little smile. "Oh, that spiral ring."

I waited for him to say more, but instead he grinned like a fool. "Well?"

"I don't know. That is my earlier work and there are many who would love to get their hands on it."

What nonsense was that? "I'm not just anyone, pal."

"True, but still. I've been instructed by my very competent legal team that I really shouldn't let anyone outside of the family see it."

I glared at him. "Really?"

He then stretched his long legs out in front of him—lucky for him we were in first class—and pulled his hands behind his head. "Yup."

I just wanted to look at the damn book; you'd think he'd be a bit more accommodating.

"There is a way, though, Alexis." He turned serious. "Marry me."

I wasn't sure I heard him correctly. Maybe the plane just nose-dived and the lack of oxygen was causing a hallucination.

"Alexis." A grin pulled at his mouth. "You're thinking you're having an hallucination, aren't you?"

"Are you serious?"

He reached into his pocket and pulled out a small leather black box. He opened it to reveal an emerald-cut diamond, a huge emerald cut diamond. "Marry me."

Some could argue we were rushing, but we weren't. We'd been working toward this since that very first day. I wanted to remember every part of this moment so I could tell it to our kids and grandkids.

"Alexis?"

"You just asked me to marry you."

"Yes, and you didn't answer."

Despite his words, he didn't look overly worried, as sure of us as I was, so I teased him. "Do I get to look at the spiral ring?"

His expression went blank for a second before he howled with laughter. Love shined in his eyes. "Yes."

I grabbed his face and kissed him. "Yes, I'll marry you."

For a second or two we silently acknowledged the beauty of the moment before he slipped his ring onto my finger.

GREYSON

Alexis was sleeping, her hand in mine. I played with the ring on her finger. If she only knew how long I had been holding on to it. My first commission was used to buy it. I'd carried it around for six years knowing one day it would sit on her finger.

I wanted to paint her. Naked, looking at me like she had earlier when she said yes. I wasn't sure how she'd feel having her body on display on our walls, but maybe for our bedroom she'd be okay with it.

I was looking forward to seeing Paige, Grant and the girls, was itching to see Ireland again and my grandfather. Wanted to share my home with Alexis, my past. I had my mother's diary. Having watched Alexis at her own mother's grave, I decided to give Mom's diary to her. For a woman like Alexis, words had the most meaning. I wanted her to know my mom and how better than from her own writings. I'd find the right moment to give it to her.

I ran a finger over the stone. She'd said yes. I didn't doubt it for a second. Pressing a kiss on her ring, I let myself follow her into sleep.

ALEXIS

Paige and Grant met us at the airport. The girls were spending the day with the Bakers. Now that Mel and Dee were retired they often watched the girls because they just adored them, and having no children of their own, they loved the opportunity to act like grandparents.

As soon as I saw Paige, I pulled from Greyson and ran to her. We hugged; tears fell freely. I heard Grant and Greyson saying hello but we were talking at once and though we understood everything the other said, the men were left scratching their heads. I didn't even get to show off my ring. Paige's eyes narrowed in on the sparkling rock on my finger. She stared at it a moment before she said, "Ah, what, oh, wow." And then we were hugging again.

It wasn't until we were settled at the diner, in the booth Greyson always sat in, that Paige took my hands from across the table and asked, "Talk to me about your parents?"

They say time heals all wounds, and I was healing, though I wasn't sure if it was time or Greyson. I suspected the latter. "First, I have to say I've been very fortunate. I have you, Grant and the girls, the Cantenellis, Mel and Dee..." I glanced to my side. "Greyson." Love looked back. Turning to Paige I added, "I had a very full and happy childhood, but I'm still struggling with my mom's death." Just talking about it caused a lump in my throat. "But I hurt less knowing they loved me."

"Of course they loved you. How could they not?" Paige wiped at her eyes.

"You're biased." And I loved that she was.

"Maybe, but she isn't wrong," Grant added.

I was so lucky I found them, but I needed to change the subject before I started crying. "How does it feel being diner owners?"

Paige squeezed my hands before releasing them and settled back in the booth. "Amazing because I don't have to wait tables anymore."

"You still do though, don't you?"

She flashed me a grin. Yeah, she did.

"How's the motorcycle business?"

"It's thriving; there's been a resurgence of interest in owning motorcycles. What about you, Greyson? I have to say it's a little weird sitting across from the kid I knew now a man who has appeared on the cover of magazines. Did Mark Hamill really buy one of your paintings?"

"Wait! What? Why didn't I know that?" I turned in my seat to face Greyson. "Luke Skywalker bought one of your paintings?"

"Yes. I'm surprised that story is out already. I just signed the deal a few days ago and he only confirmed last night. I was waiting for it to be a done deal before I mentioned it." Greyson turned back to Grant. "How did you hear about it?"

"We have a resident Greyson groupie. Stephanie Peck. Do you remember her?" Paige asked.

Greyson and I both had the same reaction as we mouthed an O. Stephanie was his first groupie.

"What's she doing now?"

"Besides tracking Greyson's every move? She runs the florist."

"Is she married?"

"No, I think she's holding out for Greyson," Paige teased as her gaze lowered to my ring. "She's going to be very disappointed when word of that gets around."

That was mildly unnerving that Stephanie had held a torch for Greyson for so long, but then so had I. I was just lucky enough to be the one he held a torch for too.

The door to the diner opened as three young ladies came barreling through. I had seen them not even a year ago and still they had grown. Tara was now eleven, Mandy ten and little Heather was four. They raced toward our table until they saw Greyson. It was like a comic strip, how Tara stopped, causing Mandy and Heather to slam into her back.

"Why'd you stop?" Heather demanded.

I climbed from the booth and held out my arms. Greyson was temporarily forgotten as I was wrapped with six limbs. Tara was almost as tall as me. She totally took after Grant. Heather on the other hand was all Paige, and Mandy was a happy blend.

When we detangled, I gestured to Greyson. "You remember Greyson."

He had moved from the booth and like he had done all those years ago, he kissed each of their hands. Tara was at an age that her face went red, her eyes grew wide with puppy love. Mandy too, shifted on her feet, embarrassed yet in love, looking up at Greyson through her lashes. Heather on the other hand, climbed him like a tree; took his face into her little hands and stared for so long it got awkward. She then said with the authority of a four year old, "You're pretty."

It was late; Paige and family were asleep when Greyson and I snuck out.

"Where do you want to go first?"

"Let's go see your house."

"You really like that house."

"I always saw us there, married, kids, you painting the view."

He yanked me close. "I always saw that too."

After spying on the house, we headed to our bluff. It was late, dark and secluded so when Greyson lifted my shirt to cup my breasts, I moved into his touch. I worked on his zipper; he undid my bra and sucked my breast into his mouth. I stroked him from base to tip. He responded by biting my nipple, then sucking me deeper into his mouth. I wanted him inside me. He was thinking the same when he dragged me to the ground and yanked off my jeans and panties. He lifted my hips and sank in deep. I watched him as he watched me. The gentle shifting of his hips, in and out, creating the friction that turned gentle to frenzied. He swallowed my scream when I came with a kiss and I returned the favor.

He curled into me and kissed my neck. "Life coming full circle. I wanted you to be mine then, now you are."

Wrapping my legs around his waist, I drew him closer. "I always was."

Ireland. We landed in Dublin then took a smaller aircraft to the Kerry Airport. Greyson's car was waiting at the airport. We drove along curving roads surrounded by green hills. Before long we were pulling through the gates of Greyson's ancestral home: Taisce Manor.

I knew he lived in a castle, I saw the drawing of it, but seeing it was an experience. It was beautiful, huge and very old. The tower, the keep at one time, dated back to medieval times. Medieval times, it boggled the mind that this structure had been around for so long. The gardens were sleeping, but I bet they were gorgeous in full bloom.

"It's beautiful, Greyson. All of this land belongs to your family?"

"Yes."

"It's wonderful to see it so preserved. I'm sure it has modern updates like plumbing and electricity..." I stopped talking because I didn't actually know if the place did have modern conveniences. "It does have electricity and plumbing, right?"

Greyson spared me a look, despite the fact that he was driving, and smiled, "Yes."

No electricity I could handle. No plumbing, no way. Call me a hothouse flower, but peeing in a hole in the ground. Nope. I looked around at the grounds; the vast open landscape seemingly untouched by humans. It was incredible. "You can forget that we're in the twenty-first century, it's almost as if we stepped back in time. It doesn't seem right for there to be cars, it spoils the illusion. I'm thinking brawny men, with long hair, wearing kilts and riding warhorses is more appropriate." I glanced over at Greyson. "You know, you could—"

I didn't get to finish that statement before Greyson said, and quite emphatically, "No kilt, I'm Irish not a bloody Scot."

I looked away to hide my smile. "Pity, I bet you'd be sexy as hell in a kilt."

We drove through an archway to find Callum waiting, but it was the line of people behind him that had my jaw dropping. Twenty women in pale gray dresses and at least the same number of men in black suits.

Greyson answered my unasked question. "It's tradition for the household staff to greet a returning member of the family."

It was the first time since knowing Greyson that I felt inadequate, and not physically like I had when we were younger, but socially. I didn't mind his celebrity because I had known him before he became a rising star, but what I hadn't appreciated was where Greyson came from. I knew he lived in a castle in Ireland and that his ancestry dated back centuries, but I didn't really get what that meant until seeing the massive staff standing in front of a magnificent castle waiting for their young master to return. Talk about different social circles.

I didn't get to fret on the staggering differences in Greyson and my backgrounds because as soon as the car stopped, my door opened and I was pulled into a hard hug.

"What a joy to see you again, Alexis. I want to know everything you've been up to but that can wait. You must be exhausted." Callum saw the ring. His eyes lifted. "Greyson told me. Congratulations."

I could only smile in reply because I still got emotional thinking about Greyson and me being engaged. I studied Callum. It had been six years and he looked just the same. Remembering his fall, I asked, "How are you? You look wonderful."

"I'm doing very well. As healthy as a horse."

"I'm happy to hear that."

"Would you like to nap, eat or take a tour?"

"A tour sounds great."

"Food sounds better." Greyson winked before he added, "Let's give the lady the tour, Grandfather, and then we can eat."

Before we started the tour we stopped in front of the staff. I thought he was giving them a chance to say hello to Greyson. I was wrong. "I'd like to introduce you to the future lady of the manor, Greyson's fiancée, Alexis Owens."

My eyes flew to him, then the clapping started, a thunderous applause for someone they knew nothing about. That hole in my heart filled in more.

"Alexis, this is William, Nigel and Maggie."

I got a little emotional remembering the beautiful Mont Blanc pen they had sent me for my graduation gift. I'd christened the pen writing their thank you notes. I was never without it. "It is so nice to meet you." I wasn't sure of the protocol, at home I would have hugged Maggie, but it was all so formal here. I offered her my hand instead; she ignored my hand and yanked me into her arms.

William was more reserved, his handshake a bit stiff. Nigel, on the other hand, was quite affable when he covered our joined hands with his free one. "Lovely to meet you, Miss Owens."

"All right, let me show you around," Callum said.

We walked over the threshold and that feeling of going back in time washed over me again. The foyer was massive, the ceilings at least twenty feet high, but it was the age and history of the place that held me captive. Greyson's ancestors had walked these halls; it had survived plagues, famine and wars. It was the link that tied Greyson, the last of the Ratcliffes, to the Aenfinn, the very first of them. And more extraordinary, everyone in between had walked these halls.

The walls were painted an aged cream and the floors were a beautiful dark mahogany. There was a large round pedestal table in the center of the foyer; the sight brought a smile. A vase of fresh cut flowers rested atop it. I wondered if that was the selling point for the apartment when Greyson saw a touch of home. This vase was an antique Waterford…an heirloom. Hanging over the table, from the high ceiling, was a crystal chandelier that looked to be raining diamonds. Callum led me from the foyer into a drawing room that was filled with old paintings and several pieces I recognized as Greyson's. I wanted to study his earlier work and would be coming back to do just that. The furniture was done in rich, deep-toned fabrics, and there was a concert grand piano sitting in the corner, but the room was so large that the massive instrument actually looked small. The fireplace was like nothing I'd ever seen. It was huge, walk in and cook yourself huge.

The dining room looked more like a ballroom in size. The table sat thirty, but it was lost in the space. Dark green walls showcased large oil paintings that were old from the look of them. Two fireplaces on opposite walls would compete to keep the room warm. Above the table were what I thought were brass chandeliers, but as I studied them I realized I was mistaken. A gold chandelier was extraordinary in and of itself, but when it came in a set of four it was mind blowing.

Each room in the castle was more beautiful than the previous, the history within the walls was overwhelming, and the more I saw the more insecure I felt.

"This was Greyson's room." Even feeling as I was I couldn't deny the excitement at seeing Greyson's childhood room. A large walnut sleigh bed took up most of the space and flanking it were matching nightstands. The floors were wood, aged and worn but beautiful. The walls were a soothing mossy green, but it was the paintings on the walls that I studied. He didn't have posters of bands or movies. Greyson's walls were covered in his drawings and later paintings. One was of stick people, but they were the nicest looking stick people I'd ever seen. Another was of a horse in a field, the date was when he was five and yet his drawing was better than anything I could do now. There were framed photos of his parents, of the three of them, and one of all three Ratcliffe men. It was scary how much they looked alike.

"I know you must be tired so I can have your dinners brought up to you."

I glanced over at Greyson before I replied, "We'd like to have dinner with you."

Callum answered with a smile. "See you soon."

The door closed and as was his way Greyson knew exactly what was going through my mind. He crossed the room to me. "I love you and you me. That's what you measure us by, nothing else."

I had trouble meeting his gaze. In theory he was right, but I was already having a hard time accepting that I wasn't able to contribute more toward our apartment. Sure, he'd been working all these years and I was going to school, but I wanted to be on equal footing when we started our life together. I had to accept for the time being we wouldn't be, but seeing where he came from, we would never be on equal footing. Even if I was lucky enough to become crazy successful, he had a family rich in history, hell, he was probably some kind of Irish nobility, and my father chose to break the law for a living.

Greyson touched my chin to gain my attention. "Understand?"

I avoided answering. "I love your room."

He wouldn't let me. "Alexis."

The words were out before I could stop them. "Why me?"

My words were like a slap with the way his head reared back in shock. "Why, because you like Luke Skywalker over Captain Kirk and Toaster Strudels over Pop-Tarts. You have that beauty mark on your neck that still drives me crazy. You can make up a story about anything on a whim and you have appalling taste in bicycles." He pulled me into his arms. "But you have excellent taste in fiancés." He lowered his head. "Are we good?"

This is why we worked because despite where we came from we fit. "Yes, we're good." But I wasn't able to shake off my insecurity so easily because I feared one day he might discover he needed more than I could give.

That night, I couldn't sleep. I wanted to say it was jet lag, but insecurity played a part too. He would be upset knowing I was still thinking that, but staring at my surroundings it was hard not to. I grabbed my robe and slipped from the room. We hadn't toured the portrait gallery, we planned to in the morning, but I wanted to see in person the paintings I had studied so closely.

I was prepared for massive, the entire castle was massive, but when light flooded the room my breath caught. The gallery was the size of a football field; the ceilings were at least twenty feet high, which made the space seem even more immense and every inch of wall space was covered in paintings. Plaques on the bottom of each gilded frame identified the subject. Every Ratcliffe from the first was represented.

I started at the very beginning, to the man who had started it all. Aenfinn Ratcliffe. He was a giant of a man and he had those eyes that had trickled down the DNA line all the way to Greyson. He carried a sword, a large deadly looking weapon, but it was the stone centered on the hilt that held my attention. It looked like an emerald, but the clarity was perfect. It had to be at least a hundred carats. Even though it was only paint, the stone seemed to pulse with life. The diamond. Standing in that room, looking at that painting, I so believed the legend.

I moved down the line from Aenfinn. There was no denying the impact of DNA because every generation had the same bone structure, but more they all had those wonderful eyes.

I spent a little more time studying the portraits of the only two women to wear the diamond, the only love matches in the Ratcliffe's long history. Celeste Ratcliffe wore it in the fifteenth century and though the stone was magnificent, the artist who captured it during this century had not as successfully brought the heat of the stone to life like the first portrait. Caitlin Ratcliffe was the second woman in the nineteenth century. Had the diamond not been lost, it would have appeared on at least two more women, Callum's wife and Greyson's mom. It would have appeared on my portrait. That thought made me a little weak in the knees, the idea that I would be a part of this extraordinary family. Still, five love matches in a family that spanned seven centuries was sad that so many chose duty over love. But had they not, I wouldn't be standing in this room.

I stopped in front of Callum's portrait. His was done when he was much younger, late twenties I would guess. He looked so much like

Greyson it was a bit startling. His wife, Colleen, her feistiness came through the painting, a red head with laughing blue eyes. After Callum was Ardan Ratcliffe, Greyson's father. It was shocking how much father and son looked alike and I thought the resemblance to Callum was startling. Honestly the three of them could be triplets. And next to Ardan was his wife, Greyson's mom, Cara. Sultry was the word that came to mind. She was exotic, exquisite, smiling a secret little smile. It was heartbreaking to know their lives were cut short leaving behind their son who would have only memories of them, but at least he had those memories.

I reached Greyson's portrait and looked into those beloved eyes. He was younger, far younger than the others in his portrait; I would guess it was done right before he moved to Mendocino. He looked just like he had that first day on the beach, the boy who had taken my spot on the jetty and had claimed my heart without having to do a thing. It was overwhelming what being a Ratcliffe entailed and their staggering wealth, but despite my doubts I wanted so much to be one. I wanted my portrait in this hall, next to Greyson's so some young woman hundreds of years from now would know we had lived and loved. The hour and jet lag hit me. I turned to leave and saw Greyson strolling into the room in that sexy way he had. Dressed in only his pajama pants, he looked like Zeus just leaving his lover's bed.

"Couldn't sleep?" he asked when he was close enough.

"No, and I really wanted to see this."

His focus shifted behind me. "There are a lot of them, aren't there?"

I reached for his hand and walked him to his portrait. "When was this done?"

"About six months before we left for the States."

"I thought you looked just like Callum, but you and your dad could be twins."

"Yeah, Mom always said that." He studied her portrait for a few minutes before he said, "She didn't come from money; her dad owned the local pub. Dad fell for her on first sight." His gaze turned on me. "She was overwhelmed by all of this too, but she loved my father, he loved her, the rest she knew would fall into place."

"I'm being given a lesson, aren't I?"

His next words were so easily given, words that came right from his heart. "I would give all of this up for you, every painting, every cornerstone, every acre. That's how much you mean to me."

Being in this room, I understood exactly what he was willing to give up. *His* love was humbling.

"If the roles were reversed, would you want me any less because I didn't come from all of this?"

Was he smoking crack? "Of course not."

"It really is that simple, please don't complicate it."

For the first week, Greyson and Callum showed me around County Kerry. I fell in love with the place. It was as if the entire area was pulled from the pages of a storybook. There were vast open spaces of rolling emerald-colored hills and stone cliffs that cradled lakes of brilliant sapphire water. In contrast, there were sections of the greenest lushest forests with the only interruption to the green being trickling streams of cool, clear water tumbling over rock beds. In the midst of all this was a charming village. I realized that the house in Mendocino, where Callum and Greyson had lived, had a view very similar to Kerry's and was probably why Callum had picked the place.

The second week of our visit Greyson spent a great deal of time working; he couldn't resist the enticement around him. I watched him sometimes, loved to see how he completely lost himself in his work. It was almost as if when he touched his brush to the canvas that some higher being took over.

One day I found myself outside with Callum and Nigel having tea. Nigel was the estate manager, but it was the dynamic between Callum and Nigel that was fun to watch because it reminded me of the relationship I had with the twins. The weather was unseasonably warm.

"It's beautiful here. I find myself wondering how Greyson could have left here and stayed away."

Callum looked thoughtful before he answered, "Greyson loves it here, but even as a child he felt a calling...a pull. I always thought it was because of his gift that he wanted to see the world, see it and paint it."

"And now?"

"Seeing him with you and you with him, I wonder now if it was the world that called to him or you."

I swear I needed to start carrying tissues because honestly the waterworks were getting to be a bit much, but no one had ever said anything so wonderful to me.

He glanced at Nigel, who was graciously staring into his tea. "I don't mean to embarrass you, but it's very special what you two share. I can't tell you how happy I am that you have found your way back to each other."

"That is a sentiment we agree on." I looked behind him to the castle that sat majestically on its little piece of the world and the family who had owned it since the beginning. "I've been working on your family's book and you were right, it's fascinating."

Callum leaned back in his chair and smiled knowingly.

My attention turned to Nigel. "I imagine you must know about the legend of the diamond."

"I do indeed."

"I personally believe it was conjured as the legend states."

"Another hopeless romantic," Nigel teased.

"You don't believe the story?"

"I believe in what I can see and touch."

"Nigel is a very practical man," Callum said in a way that was clear they'd had the discussion before.

"Playing devil's advocate. What if it wasn't conjured? What if it was created the old fashion way?" I theorized.

"I'm listening," Callum encouraged.

"A stone that unique, there would have to be records. Someone mined it and someone cut it. I had originally thought the diamond was stolen, that the fire was set as a diversion, but there's been no sighting of it. And if we assume the thief kept it hidden for a generation or two so the story of its origins could die out, surely someone would have worn it by now, an insurance company would have insured it, a jeweler inspected it." I looked at Nigel. "As the estate manager, you would have found records of its existence."

"Agreed."

"And yet there has been nothing," Callum added.

"Exactly. If the stone is just a myth, then why does it show up in two additional paintings as a brooch? Why the story about the stone passing down to love matches?"

"You have been busy," Callum offered with a smile.

"I love a good mystery. I think the diamond is real, but I don't think it was stolen."

"So where is it?" Nigel asked.

I leaned back in my chair and blew out a breath because that was one part of the story I couldn't figure out. "I don't know."

"The argument could be made there is nothing of the diamond because it is just a lovely bedtime story," Nigel countered.

"You're right, but the romantic in me refuses to believe that."

"Here, here," Callum agreed.

"It's sad that there were so few love matches in your family's history."

Callum reached for his tea, his expression thoughtful. "That was the way of it. These large estates were maintained through marriage. It was very unbecoming for the Lord of the manor to work. His life was one of leisure and privilege but you can't sustain an estate on balls and tea parties. There was definitely a separation of class and yet without the families that supported these estates through the generations, there wouldn't be an estate." Callum glanced at Nigel, clearly that generational continuation he mentioned applied to him. "For all the pomp and frill of the nobility, they were dependent on the ones they believed themselves to be superior to, not very different from today's social dynamic. And as much as it pains me to say it, the period in our history when the lord had married for love were the hardest, the Ratcliffes really struggled with staying afloat."

"Somewhere along the line that changed."

He smiled. "Yes. My great, great grandfather was a renaissance man and knew the estates would die off unless those responsible for them started taking responsibility for them. I'm happy to say we no longer depend on the dowry of wealthy, eligible women." He winked at me. "We can marry for love not duty."

I played with my ring. It was a bit surreal that I was directly affected by this conversation, mind boggling actually.

After the talk with Callum and Nigel, I went in search of Greyson. He had an easel set up on the south lawn, his focus toward the forest. Many of the trees were bare, their naked branches curling up toward the sun, but there were evergreens tucked in here and there. Hills rose up to meet that patch of trees, stone walls stretched out to the horizon. Living in New York City where every inch was developed, the crowds and the noise, this was paradise.

As I approached, I wasn't expecting Greyson's attention because when he worked his focus was singular so I was surprised when he turned to me. His gaze moved down my body before settling on my face. He set his palette down and strolled over to me.

"Hey, beautiful."

I glanced at his painting, the brushstrokes of color, the composition. He really was gifted. "That's beautiful."

He glanced back. "I thought we'd hang it in the apartment."

We had hung his other paintings, the ones he had done for me. The walls in our apartment looked much like the portrait gallery with every inch covered. I loved it. Greyson was all around me.

He glanced behind me to the footman. There was always someone close by. It was fascinating. "Could you take that in for me? The parlor is fine." He took my hand. "I want to show you something."

We walked to a part of the castle I hadn't seen yet. He opened the door to a bedroom with a large mahogany bed, windows trimmed in dark blue silk, a massive fireplace that had doors flanking it—his and her dressing rooms. His parents' room.

"I don't know if it's wise to keep the room like this, but it was one concession my grandfather agreed to."

There were photos of Greyson as a boy and I found myself drawn to those, seeing him as a child. A few had his parents in them; there were photos of horses.

Greyson broke the silence when he said, "I found her diary. I haven't read it. I want you to have it. My dad wrote poetry. I've found a few of his notebooks. I want you to have them too."

"Me?"

"They would have loved you and words are your medium. What better way for you to know them than through their words."

210

I was without words then; his gesture overwhelmed me. I wanted to kiss him, but we were in his parents' room. Instead I asked, "Are you sure?"

"Yes." *He* kissed me and it was then I realized he had just declared his intentions to the memory of his parents.

Opening night of my play and I wanted to throw up. In the two months since we returned from Ireland, every day had been filled with set and costume checks, last minute tweaks on the script, lighting issues and dress rehearsals. Those two months flew.

I checked myself in the mirror for the sixth time. The box office was sold out. Part of that was due to Greyson's presence, but I was okay with that. More importantly, Paige, Grant and the girls were downstairs, as were the twins and their parents, and Callum.

I felt Greyson approach before his arms wrapped around me. "You look beautiful and nervous."

I turned into him so I could enjoy the sight of him in a tux. "My stomach won't stop jumping."

"It's going to be amazing."

There were so many things that could go wrong, lighting, sets. This was going to be a very long night.

"Try to enjoy yourself. You've worked so hard to get here."

I loved that he was here, that I got to share this first with him. I reached for his hand. "Stay at my side."

"Always."

We joined the others. Paige looked beautiful in her blush-colored gown. As soon as she saw me, she hugged me. "I'm so proud of you. It is going to be amazing. Try to enjoy it."

"Easier said than done, but do try to soak in the significance of tonight. Your words, your thoughts will be on display for a sold out audience. That's incredible. Enjoy the ride," Grant added before he kissed my head.

Mrs. Cantenelli pressed a lace handkerchief in my hand. "You're going to need that." Then she hugged me. "We're so happy to be here for this."

"Thank you for making the trip. It is such a long flight."

She waved that off. "Nonsense. We wouldn't have missed it."

Paige and Grant were talking to Callum, too impatient for the introductions. Like the Cantenellis, he had come a long way for this. I reached for his hands. "Thank you for coming."

"Your debut play, you couldn't keep me away." He squeezed my hand. "Try to savor the evening and…" He grinned before he added, "Break a leg."

The twins crowded me. "How you holding up?" Dylan asked.

"I'm numb from excitement."

Dominic draped his arm over my shoulders and started for the door. "Don't worry. We got you."

In the theater, we sat in the front so I couldn't see the reactions of the crowd, though the laughs were loud and often. Greyson held my hand throughout, leaned over a few times to kiss my temple. I had the strangest sensation someone was watching me, but considering the circumstances many probably were. When the curtain lifted for the final time, a roar of applause broke out. It went on for so long, they turned up the house lights and the cast gestured for me to join them. I will never forget walking up on that stage and looking out into the audience who were on their feet applauding. It was one of the most amazing moments of my life.

My eyes drifted to Greyson, clapping and whistling louder than anyone. I don't know why my focus shifted to the rear of the theater, maybe it was the flutter that tickled the nape of my neck, but standing at the back was a man. Spiky black hair framed a face, although older, was one I knew well because I had memorized every line and curve. Everything else faded for me, it was just he and I. Despite the distance between us, the moment was meaningful, as words not spoken were understood. He'd come; he had not only known about this momentous moment, he had come. He touched his fingers to his lips then he was gone. I stood trapped in that moment, unable to move or speak because my dad had found me.

"He was there." Greyson pulled a hand through his hair as he paced our bedroom. I waited until we were home to tell him about my father.

I didn't want to mention it to the others only because of the potential danger to them. He stopped pacing and looked back at me. "I'm happy for you that he was there."

"But you're nervous."

"He did rip you from his life, so showing up at your play…yeah, I'm nervous." He joined me on the bed, taking my hand into his. "Are you okay?"

"I saw my dad, Greyson. Just in passing, but I saw those eyes that I've spent countless hours staring into. He was there. For one of the biggest moments of my life, he was there. I feel wonderful."

He tucked some hair behind my ear. "There was so much of you in your play, your humor and compassion and there was also a vein of pain, the same pain I've seen in your eyes since we were kids. It was you up there; you opened up your heart, your life, and put it on display. Bravest fucking thing I've ever seen." I climbed into his lap, straddled him, and wrapped my arms around his neck. His hands moved up my back. "Your father saw it too."

"Maybe that's a good thing. What was the lesser of two evils, safe from harm or damaged from neglect?"

"Not anymore," Greyson snarled. "You'll never be alone again."

I rubbed myself against him and traced his lips with my tongue. He tugged on my zipper and slowly pulled it down. I had a surprise for him. He stood, dropped me on my feet, my gown followed.

"Fuck, Alexis."

I wasn't wearing anything under my gown. The front of his pants tented. I rubbed him, he growled and moved his hips into my touch.

"I'm glad I didn't know you had nothing on under that gown because we would have missed the play." He nipped at my lips as his hands roamed over my body. I worked his zipper; pulled his cock free and dropped to my knees. The sexiest sound rumbled in his chest. It broke free when I closed my lips around him and sucked him deep into my throat. His fingers curled into my hair as I tongued his cock, swirling around the tip while squeezing the base, the heel of my hand pressing into his balls. I was just getting a rhythm when I felt myself flying through the air. I landed on the bed; Greyson stripped in record time and pounced. Grabbing my ass he lifted my hips and slammed into me. My legs wrapped around his waist as my hips moved into his thrusts. His fingers threaded into my hair before he kissed me, mirroring with his tongue what his cock was doing. When we came, it was together. It was the perfect ending to a perfect day.

14

I watched her sleep, though what I wanted to do was wake her up and taste every inch of her. She was exhausted. Her play ran for two years, the box office consistently busy and the reviews shining. It was hailed a success. She went every week for two years to show her support; she had started a novel, not the one I caught her working on from time to time, this was something new, trying her hand at a psychological thriller. She was also working on a script for a cable television show. And on top of all of this she was planning our wedding. We weren't in a rush to get married; she'd been busy with her play. My ring was on her finger and she was in my bed, but she wanted the dress and flowers and cake. I just wanted her. Paige was helping with the planning. I offered to help, but Alexis knew all I cared about were the words so she graciously spared me discussions on fabric and colors. She was on her stomach, that beauty mark on her neck staring up at me. I didn't kiss it like I wanted to, because that would lead to more than kissing. I brushed my finger over it then headed to the shower.

Colin scheduled a meeting for later, a possible commission piece. It had been a long time since I'd done one. I was eager to take it. The hot water felt good, pressing my hand against the wall, I lowered my head and let it pour down on me. I felt her a second before her hands moved around my waist.

"Good morning," she said then kissed my back.

"It is now."

I turned, pulled her close and kissed her, taking a minute to suck on that fucking beauty mark I loved. Her hands roaming over me went right to my balls. Digging my fingers into her thigh, I lifted her leg and slid into her. Her head dropped back, exposing her neck, I licked the long, delicate line of her throat. Her heel pressed into my ass as we found our rhythm, one arm wrapped around my neck, pulling my mouth to hers. When we came it wasn't hard or fast, it was so fucking sweet.

She didn't unwrap herself from me, I wouldn't have let her. Our eyes met. "Good morning," I whispered.

"It is now." I grinned hearing her use my words back at me. "What are your plans for today?"

"I have a meeting with Colin and a client for a commission."

"Nice. You've been itchy."

I had been. I liked that she knew it. "What about you?"

"My agent sent me a script for a television series that's writing is getting a little tired. They asked me to have a go at it. It's a prime time show."

"Holy shit. That's incredible. Why didn't you tell me?"

She looked down, but I didn't let her get out of it. Touching her chin, I asked again. "Why?"

"I wasn't sure I was going to do it."

"Why not?"

"I'm not sure I'm good enough."

"That's bullshit, but *you'll* never know until you try."

She brushed her fingers down my neck, my body humming in response. I could watch her for hours when she was working. She talked to herself but that was part of her process. How easily it all came to her, the concepts, the characters and the story. She truly was an artist and words were her medium.

"When's your meeting?" she asked, looking up at me through her lashes.

216

I pressed into her then rocked my hips. She moaned. "I have some time."

Breathlessly she said, "I was hoping you'd say that."

Colin and I lingered on the phone after the client hung up.

"I'm guessing you're going to take it."

Mrs. Ellis was looking for an original Greyson Ratcliffe oil painting for her husband's sixtieth birthday. She gave me a year and half notice, free reign on design and a nice purse. Sold.

"Absolutely."

"I'll send them the contract."

Colin sounded off; he had for the whole call. "Is something wrong?"

He was rather abrupt when he asked, "Did you ever go to the cops?"

It took a minute for me to shift gears then a knot formed because I hadn't. "Shit. No. Did you get another one?"

"Yes. This one is even more disturbing than the last." A pause before he added, "She mentions Alexis by name."

Rage hit as fast as alarm. "What the fuck does she say about Alexis?"

Her exact words are, "You're mine. Leave that bitch."

I felt sick and numb and pissed as hell. Pulling a hand through my hair, I paced my studio. "Do you think it's the woman who broke into my hotel room?"

"I called the detective on the case after our last conversation. She's still locked up and the ward she's in doesn't allow correspondence with the outside. I can hire an investigator," Colin offered.

I tried to think about the situation rationally, hard given the link it had to Alexis. Statistically these things never amounted to anything. They were frustrating and hair-raising, but not an actual threat. I'd been here before, I'd be here again, but I did want to know who this person was. Liked being able to keep tabs, like we could with my uninvited hotel guest. "Yeah, let's do that. Send me the letter you have. I'll take the others to the cops now."

"I'll have it overnighted."

Samuel was in his fifties. Thinning brown hair and a pot belly likely the result of donuts, one sitting half eaten on his desk. A mug that was so stained from coffee it looked more tan than white was half filled. He studied the letters before he dropped them on his desk and leaned back in his chair. It made a painful sound like it was struggling to hold his weight.

"I understand your concern. These are definitely disturbing. Would you mind if I had the in-house psychologist look at them to give us an insight into the author?"

"Not at all."

"You said there was a third one?"

"Yes. My agent is overnighting it."

"Please bring it in when you have it. We don't have jurisdiction, you understand that, right?"

"Yes."

"Without a postmark they are likely a resident of San Francisco or somewhere close. I'll reach out to the local cops, see if they can get a hit on the stationery. I would recommend you talk with your fiancée; she needs to pay attention to her surroundings, to not go anywhere alone. That's just safe city living." He slid his business card across the table to me. "Anything happens, call me."

"Thank you."

"It's most likely that this person is across the country, their letters their only way of connecting with you. Try not to worry, though I know that's harder to do than say."

World's biggest fucking understatement.

ALEXIS

The expression, time flies when you are having fun, was so true. It was hard to believe we'd been engaged for two years. My play had run throughout that time as well. We had done well, not Broadway well, but for my first play I was thrilled. And now I had time to work on the screenplay for the prime time show I was dabbling with.

I hadn't seen my father since opening night. I didn't really think I would, but there was a part of me that hoped him showing up was a prelude to reconciliation. I should have known better.

I had a lot of work to keep me busy, but I had a wedding to plan. I found my dress, an exquisite lace and tulle fantailed gown that I fell in love with the second I saw it. Greyson had a suit custom-made, an exquisitely cut linen suit that he was pairing with a white linen shirt, no tie. Six months from now we would be saying I do. I couldn't wait, but we had to plan it. Greyson wasn't much help.

"Whatever colors you want works for me."

I opened my mouth, but he stopped me. "Same goes for the flowers."

I had a binder and a checklist. He was making it very easy.

"All right, what about food?"

"Cheeseburgers," he immediately suggested.

I loved cheeseburgers. "What else?"

Silence. I glanced up at him, he was grinning. "You're serious? You would be okay with cheeseburgers for the reception?"

"Why not. We're having it at the diner and they make a damn fine cheeseburger."

He leaned across the table and kissed me, stroking my lower lip with his tongue. As tempting as it was to drop what we were doing, we were running out of time.

"We have to finish this," I said between kisses.

"I know."

He settled back in his chair. "I imagine Paige has ideas for the food. I'm fine with whatever she picks."

"Me too. The cake?"

"I like chocolate."

"Chocolate chip?"

"That works. I'll take care of the topper," he offered cryptically.

I stopped writing and met his gaze. "You're going to make our cake topper?" I love this idea.

"Yes." He touched my cheek. "What else is on your list?" List? What list? He smiled, which only distracted me more. "Cake, food, flowers," he reminded me. Right the flowers.

"Are you okay with Stephanie Peck doing the flowers? You remember Stephanie from school?"

I was watching him so I saw the shadow that moved over his face. "Greyson?"

He looked unnerved. I didn't think I'd ever seen that look on his face before. "What's wrong?"

He stood and started to pace. "You're scaring me."

He stopped and turned. "I've been getting some disturbing letters."

Unease had a chill moving through me; it was chased with fear. "Are they coming here?"

"No. The office in San Francisco."

I exhaled on a sigh. "How disturbing?"

"Enough to cause concern. I've been to the cops. They've reached out to the San Francisco police."

"Wait. Are they threatening?"

He hesitated to answer, but reluctantly did. "The last one was. Colin has hired an investigator, the San Francisco cops are looking into it and the cops here have their psychologist giving them a profile."

Worried, I asked, "Do you think it's that woman who showed up in your hotel room?"

"You know about that?"

"It was on the news."

"No, Colin looked into her. She's still locked up with no contact to the outside."

I looked down at my notebook, to Stephanie's name marked in red. My head snapped up. "You don't think it's Stephanie?"

He pulled a hand through his hair and started pacing again. "I don't think it's Stephanie. I really don't, but the proximity of where she lives and where the letters are being sent, it's only smart to look into her. She was persistent when we were kids, showing up at my house, loitering outside of it. She's still watching me. It could be simple infatuation, most likely it is, but if there is more to it…" He didn't finish; he didn't need to. "Let's let the investigator look into her, so hold off on the flowers."

"Okay." I stood and crossed the room to him. His muscles were tense when I wrapped him in my arms. "You're worried."

His arms came around me. "My worry is for you. Please be careful when you're out, mindful of your surroundings."

"I am, but I will be doubly so."

His expression shifted, serious but beautiful. "I don't need the flowers or the food or the cake. I just need you saying I do." He touched my hair, focusing on those strands. There was a touch of wonder in his tone when he said, "We're getting married."

"In five months, two weeks and four days. But who is counting."

"I will be eternally grateful that my art led me to you."

"Not as grateful as me."

"Wanna bet," he challenged.

I kissed him then moved to the stairs, reaching for my shirt and yanking it off. His eyes went hot. "First one upstairs…"

GREYSON

I should be working, but I couldn't focus. Standing in my studio, I looked down on Manhattan, the people hurrying to get somewhere. I had been that person, hurrying to get somewhere; well, to get to someone. Now she was right outside the door, at her desk in the living room probably talking to herself as she brought the stories in her head to life through her words.

She hadn't seen herself writing for television, but I knew she loved it. Comedy she definitely had the talent for, but it was the drama scripts she let me read that showed a deeper depth to her writing, pain drawn from her own experiences.

Her father remained a ghost, but Alexis drew comfort from the knowledge that he lived in the same city and that even unseen, he was there on the periphery of her life, not part of it, but an observer.

I hadn't stopped thinking about those fucking letters. The likelihood anything would come of them was slim and still there was a sense of foreboding that slithered through me. I understood a bit about how

Finn felt. The situations weren't the same, there was no immediate threat on Alexis, but to know someone's unstable fixation on me had such animosity aimed at Alexis was really fucking with me. What Finn lived through, knowing he was the cause of his wife's death, knowing how much he loved her and Alexis and yet he had the strength to let her go. Feeling as I do for Alexis, letting her go…I don't know that I could do it. And I hoped like hell I was never put in a situation that found myself having to.

My cell pulled me from my thoughts.

"Colin, give me good news."

"Stephanie Peck is not the one writing the letters."

Relief hit hard and fast. I hadn't thought so, but I liked hearing it confirmed.

"He tested her handwriting and it doesn't match. He also learned she hasn't been on vacation since taking over the florist eight years ago. None of the shops in or around Mendocino sell the type of stationery the letters are written on. He is looking into the stationery to see where it's sold in San Francisco. That will help narrow down the search. He's on it, so don't worry about anything but your wedding."

A grin curved my lips because Alexis could get her flowers now. I was relieved but Mendocino was close to San Francisco and this fruit loop lived there. I wasn't taking any chances; nothing was going to fuck with our day. If I had to hire a fucking army to watch Alexis' back, I would. She was getting her day that's been a long time coming, we both were.

"That's great news. Thank you, Colin."

"Easier said than done, but try not to worry and enjoy this. You've waited a long time."

He wasn't wrong. "I'll see you in Mendocino."

I disconnected then called Grant. He needed to be in the loop.

"Greyson what's up?"

"We need to talk. Do you have time now?"

15

ALEXIS 2007

The car was waiting out front to take Greyson and I to the airport. The Cantenellis and Callum were already in Mendocino helping Paige and Grant with the last minute details. I couldn't believe that in two days Greyson and I were going to be husband and wife.

I was checking and double-checking that I had everything, tap dancing on the edge of crazy, but our wedding had been in the making for a long, long time. Greyson strolled into our room and looked as cool as a cucumber. He was even eating a Toaster Strudel. How the hell could he eat at a time like this? He leaned against the doorjamb, the heavenly scent of his little pastry treat wafted over to me. My stomach growled.

"The car is here."

"I know. Where's your stuff?"

"Already loaded."

I looked under the bed. I didn't even know why I did that. Like I said, I was tap dancing.

"What are you looking for?"

"Just making sure I didn't forget anything."

"Under the bed?"

"I looked in the toilet tank too." I really had. Maybe I wasn't tap dancing anymore.

"Alexis."

I glanced over at him; damn I was marrying that man in two days.

He moved in that way of his. "You need to relax."

"I can't."

He remedied that when he kissed me, the taste of his strudel still on his tongue. My bones liquefied. He spoke against my mouth. "All that matters is you say I do. The rest is just wrapping."

Calmer, I marveled that he could do that for me with so few words. He was right; I was getting lost in the details. "Promise you'll always be around to talk me off the ledge."

"I promise. You promise me you'll always be around for me to talk off the ledge."

Easiest promise ever. I kissed him and said against his lips, "I promise."

We arrived in Mendocino. Greyson left with the twins and Grant to take care of honeymoon details. I was with Paige and the girls and Mrs. Cantenelli. Dee and Mel were taking care of the last minute menu crisis that arose. They didn't work the diner anymore but they had a lot of friends in catering. Paige had said, and often, she wouldn't have gotten it all pulled together without them. I'd been thinking about asking Greyson to paint the diner for them. It had been their lives for so long, it would make the perfect thank you gift.

We were in Paige's bedroom. My wedding dress was hanging up next to her pale pink sheath and the girls' dresses.

Heather ran over to hers. "Don't you love my shoes?" Heather's dress was silk, straight lines, cap sleeves and paired with it, hot pink Doc Martens. It was so Heather. I loved it.

Mrs. C.'s eyes widen at Heather's choice of footwear. "They are certainly unique."

"Yeah. I can't wait to wear them. I wasn't allowed to until after the wedding then I'm never taking them off."

Tara and Mandy shared a look and giggled. Their dresses were similar, tea length, organza, a little lace work on the bodice and a princess skirt. Tara's sandals had a bit of a heel, Mandy's were flats but both were pale pink.

I caught Tara watching me. It wasn't the first time since I arrived. There was something on her mind, and as much as I wanted to find a quiet corner and talk with her, she was the kind of person who needed to come to you. And she would, when she was ready, so I smiled at her and knew she understood I was ready to listen whenever she was.

Mrs. C. touched my gown, the tulle and lace bodice with the cut out back, the fantail train. It hugged my figure. I adored it. My sandals were simple white ones. I wasn't wearing a veil, just a messy updo. In two days I'd be walking down the aisle, walking toward the one person I wanted to spend the rest of my life with. I was feeling the need to pinch myself again.

Mrs. C. had tears in her eyes. "You're going to make the most beautiful bride. I can't believe the little girl that came to my house that first day is getting married." She looked at me, a little smile curving her lips. "We love Greyson, Mr. C. and I. He's a good man."

"He's the best," Paige chimed in.

He was more than that, so much more than that and soon we would be bound by not just love but by vows spoken in front of everyone who mattered most…almost everyone.

"I have champagne downstairs." Paige looked at the girls. "And young lady champagne."

Sparkling grape juice.

"Cake too," Mandy chimed in.

Paige laughed. Mandy had an insatiable sweet tooth. "Yes, cake too. Let's go celebrate."

Dylan, Dominic and I walked along the beach. We'd done this a lot as kids, the scents bringing back so many memories.

"I can't believe you're getting married," Dylan announced then glanced at me. "Married."

A happy shiver moved right down my body. "I have trouble believing it too."

"I like him," he added.

"Me too. He's a good guy," Dominic seconded.

I loved that they thought so. "I'm glad because we're all family," I said.

"Yeah, we are."

"What about you two? Any thoughts about tying the knot?"

Dylan reached for a shell and tossed it in the ocean. "Not at the moment. Work keeps us plenty busy."

"Not that we don't have our share of the ladies..." Dominic was still a clown.

"You're happy though, right?" I asked.

"Absolutely," they said together.

Dylan took my hand. "Even married, you ever need us...anything, Alexis."

Tears burned my eyes. My arm went around him; I pulled Dominic close and hugged them both. "I love you. Thank you for walking across the street that day."

Dylan pressed a kiss on my head. "Smartest thing I ever did."

GREYSON

Alexis was sitting so close she was practically on top of me. It was late; the girls had gone to bed hours ago. We were at Grant's, the twins too. We were outside, sitting under the stars. The sky was so clear here, unlike in Manhattan. I'd forgotten how magnificent a sight it was.

"Not to bring the mood down, but I've been in touch with the sheriff," Grant offered out of the blue.

"For?" Alexis asked.

Grant turned his focus on me, Alexis followed. "Greyson?"

"Just being cautious."

It took her a minute before her face paled slightly. "The letters?"

Seeing her unease twisted in my gut, even as anger burned through me. That someone would put that look on her face fucking pissed me off.

"What letters?" Dylan asked, looking to me then Grant.

"Fan letters that are unsettling."

In all the years I'd known the twins, they were serious about five percent of the time. Now was one of those times.

"How unsettling?" Dylan demanded.

"Enough that I'm taking precautions."

"What kind of precautions?" Dominic asked.

"It is more than likely whoever is writing them lives in the San Francisco area. We aren't too far from there."

Alexis stiffened next to me. "You think she might crash our wedding?"

My gut said no, but I wasn't leaving it to chance. She didn't need to worry about the details. Nothing was going to fuck this up for her. Nothing. I touched her cheek and met her worried gaze. "No, but it can't hurt to be cautious."

Paige touched Alexis' leg and added, "He's right. It's likely nothing, just some lonely woman living in her parents' basement being creepy, but why risk it?"

"I've got a PI looking into it, the San Francisco cops are too. Whoever it is, they'll find her but in the meantime we just have to play it safe."

"Have you had to deal with this before?" I didn't like how her voice shook, the urge to curl my fist and snarl was so fucking strong.

"Not quite like this, but I'm not the first person in the public eye who has had to deal with a creepy fan and I won't be the last." I dipped my head, getting eye level with her; those beautiful brown eyes were clouded with concern. That twisted in my gut too. "Statistically, it never comes to anything. We're not going to let this ruin our day." I touched her chin. "Understood."

I watched her work it out, witnessed as she pushed worry back and let excitement replace it. There's my girl.

"Understood," she said then grinned. "A person in the public eye? Don't you mean celebrity? Can't you say the words?"

Her eyes went wide a second before I had her on her back, tickling her in all the right places. She cried uncle, and I relented, but it worked because there was only joy in those eyes now.

ALEXIS

The weather couldn't have been more perfect. The ceremony was being held on our bluff. Chairs and a white silk runner were set up on our spot. To reach the ceremony, the wedding party had to walk up the bluffs. I couldn't see Greyson, he had arrived earlier, but I knew he was already standing next to the mayor, a close friend of Dee's, who was officiating the ceremony.

"You look beautiful, Alexis. Are you ready?" Paige asked.

"I've been ready for this day for a long time."

She smiled. "I know."

"You look so pretty, Auntie Alexis. I like your hair up like that," Mandy said.

"And look at you. Beautiful. Thank you for being a part of today. I wouldn't want to have it without you."

She touched her gown, her eyes bright with excitement. "I feel so pretty."

"You are pretty, no dress needed." She smiled then ran to Grant, who looked amazing in his black suit, and like Greyson, he didn't wear a tie.

Heather was spinning in circles, but it was Tara who drew my attention. She was looking at me and I knew she was ready now. While Paige went to calm Heather down, I joined Tara. She was clasping her arrangement of pale pink peonies and white hydrangeas tightly in her hand.

"Are you okay?"

Her eyes lifted; she wasn't a little kid anymore. "You love him."

My heart broke a little when understanding dawned. "I do."

"And he loves you."

"Yes."

She straightened her shoulders. "Then I'll let him go."

Tears burned my eyes. She was fourteen, only two years younger than I was when I fell for Greyson. He was her first crush and she was letting go of him for me.

"He'll always be a part of your life, Tara, because you are a part of my life and always will be."

"I know." Her eyes were bright, but she tried for a smile. "He's too old for me anyway."

Understanding the significance of what she just offered, and how much it cost her, I replied sincerely, "Thank you."

We hugged then joined the others. Paige and Grant both eyed me, I mouthed that I'd tell them later.

The music changed, Paige called the girls together. "Are you ready?"

They were, even little Heather took her part seriously. Paige looked back at me. "See you on the other side."

We watched as they walked up the hill, disappearing on the rise.

"Thank you, Grant, for today and for making me a part of your family."

His eyes grew bright. He pressed a kiss on my cheek. "We are family. Never forget that." The music changed again. "Are you ready?" He linked my arm through his.

I was so ready.

My legs were shaking because Greyson and I were finally here. We were starting the beginning of our lives together. We reached the rise. I closed my eyes and took a deep breath then opened them to see my present and future staring back.

GREYSON

I was getting close to hunting Alexis down, throwing her over my shoulder and bringing her to the mayor myself. What the fuck was taking so long? Grandfather stood calmly next to me.

"You're going to rip up the grass if you don't stop fidgeting," he whispered.

Fuck the grass. I was minutes away from making Alexis mine... heart, body and soul. The fucking grass would grow back. My gaze drifted over our guests. It was a small crowd, but it was everyone we wanted to witness our union. My throat got tight, almost everyone. I knew Mom and Dad were looking down, and I knew how much Mom would have loved Alexis. Would have loved this day. My eyes stung, then the music changed. The girls and Paige appeared, the four of them pretty in pale pink. Grant was a lucky man. Even Heather was cooperating. There had been a fifty-fifty chance that she'd detour from the aisle to explore. Instead, her face was tense with focus, as serious as I'd ever seen her. The music changed again, my eyes trained on the spot as anticipation hummed through me. She appeared and everything else faded. My heart slammed into my ribs even as my body urged me forward to take, to claim. She was a fucking vision. Her gown hugged her willowy frame, her hands clasping a bouquet of pink peonies, a flower I didn't know until she picked it for the wedding. Her hair was up, soft and loose to frame her beautiful face. But it was her eyes, those gorgeous eyes, bright with love staring at me like I was the beginning, middle and end of her story. I couldn't wait for them to make the trip down the aisle, couldn't wait for her to come to me. I met them halfway.

ALEXIS

I only had eyes for Greyson and in his I saw what I was feeling. He didn't wait for us, meeting us halfway. Grant chuckled, then kissed my cheek. Our eyes connected and Grant was crying. Greyson took my hand, pulled me right up against him. His mouth touched my ear.

"You are exquisite."

He was shaking, not from fear or nerves, but anticipation and excitement.

I tried to listen to the ceremony, but it all passed in a blur. I remembered saying my vows. I remembered hearing Greyson say his. He slipped a platinum and diamond band on my finger and I slipped a platinum band on his. I had something engraved on his ring. He'd see it eventually.

The mayor declared us husband and wife. We didn't kiss right away. Greyson took my face in his hands and curled his spine to look in my eyes. In my whole life, I would remember that moment as the most perfect of my life. Then he smiled, a big beautiful smile.

"Kiss me, husband."

It wasn't soft; it wasn't fast. Like the moment, it was perfect. Lips touched, tongues tasted, a silent vow as strong and binding as the words we spoke. His lips lingered and he whispered, "Mrs. Ratcliffe."

His hand moved down my arm leaving chills in its wake. His fingers linked with mine, the beginning of the rest of our lives... finally.

I didn't recognize the diner. It looked amazing, flowers, white cloths, crystal stemware and china dishes. Waiters in black suits walked around with champagne and appetizers, but my eyes lingered on our cake, more specifically the cake topper that Greyson had made. It was us on the back of a motorcycle, fashioned from iron.

"My bike or yours," he teased. He really hated my bike. I still had it. It was in Paige's garage. Maybe I'd wrap it up and give it to him as a first anniversary gift.

I studied the topper. It was so us. "It's perfect."

And it was resting atop a four-tiered sugary confection with our wedding flowers, peonies and hydrangeas recreated in gum paste, cascading down the side.

We had a line of people waiting to give us their best, but Greyson maneuvered us through the masses to somewhere more private. "Before we get overwhelmed and are pulled this way and that, I need a moment with my wife."

His wife. I hoped hearing him say that always had me feeling what I did then. "I like hearing you say that."

"Not as much as I like saying it."

He kissed me long and hard. "That's going to have to hold us over for a bit." He touched my chin. "You've got to stop looking at me like that or we're leaving."

I really wouldn't have a problem with that, but Paige and Grant had gone to a lot of work for this. "Tara let me have you."

His expression went blank for a second.

I clarified, "She's had a crush on you from day one, but today she let you go for me."

Love moved over his face. "She's a good kid. They all are."

"Yeah, they are."

He glanced over at our guests. "Are you ready, Mrs. Ratcliffe."

I linked our fingers. "Absolutely."

We worked the line and ended with Paige and Grant. It was both a surprise and a joy to see Greyson and Grant hug. Paige said a few words to Greyson. He smiled then kissed her before his focus moved to the girls.

He greeted each of them, kissing their hands as he had a habit of doing. He greeted Tara last. He didn't release her hand and asked, "May I have this dance?"

She would always remember that moment and I loved Greyson all the more for giving that to her. She blushed, but nodded her head. Greyson turned to the dance floor but looked back at Mandy and Heather. "Save me a dance, ladies."

They hurried after them.

"What did she say to you before the ceremony?"

My heart was so full watching Greyson with the girls. "She gave him up for me."

Tears filled Paige's eyes. "She said that?"

"Yeah, and it cost her too. You've got three amazing daughters."

"Yeah, we'll keep them," Grant teased then pulled Paige close and pressed a kiss on her temple. She curled into him.

"When will we have little ones to play with?" Paige asked.

Grant rolled his eyes. "They just said I do. Give them some time."

"What he said," I teased.

"Well, when you do have kids I'm going to spoil them."

Tara squealed in delight turning our attention back on Greyson and the girls.

"He is going to be a wonderful father." Paige wasn't wrong.

We danced, we ate, we laughed. At one point, "Just Like Heaven" played. Greyson pulled me to the dance floor. "Our song," he whispered.

After the last guest left, and Paige and Grant took the girls home, Greyson and I headed to the house he had rented. Our honeymoon was chilling in Mendocino for two weeks. Like the wedding, it was perfect.

Memories teased me as we pulled up the drive to the house he and his grandfather had rented once upon a time. "We're staying here?"

"I thought you'd like it." He climbed from the car and came around for me. Hand in hand we walked to the door we'd entered countless times as kids. He unlocked it, but didn't let me in.

"What are you doing?"

He answered by lifting me into his arms. My heart rolled in my chest. He went right to the bedroom and dropped me to my feet.

"Mrs. Ratcliffe." He brushed his finger along my collarbone. "You're stunning."

Tingles started, shooting right down my arms.

He pulled on the zipper of my dress and my heart pounded. His dark head lowered, his tongue running over the swells of my breasts. The dress slipped from my body. Brushing my nipple with his thumb, he touched the other with his tongue.

Slowly, he moved his hands down my sides, then he dropped to his knees. He played with the edge of the lace panties I wore. "I love these," he murmured. Kissing me where the lace sat low on my belly. "I'll buy you a new pair."

He tore them from me. I wanted to laugh but then his face was between my legs, his tongue working magic. Instead, I grabbed his shoulders, spread my legs wider, closed my eyes and rode his face. He nipped and bit, sucked and savored. He thrust his tongue into me; the orgasm stole my breath.

He lingered, savoring my taste before he moved back up my body. His cock was tenting his trousers.

"You're wearing too many clothes."

Slowly, I unbuttoned his shirt, pulled it and his jacket down his arms. It landed on the floor with my dress. Unsnapping his trouser, I took my time dragging the fabric down his legs. His briefs went with them. I touched his cock with my tongue. Just the tip. He moaned.

"Later," he growled. "Right now I want inside you."

We tumbled on the bed. He moved between my legs. I closed my eyes because him joining us was one of my most favorite things.

"No. Eyes open. The first time as husband and wife I want you to watch as I make you mine."

Exquisitely slow, he filled me, stretching me to take him. I bit my lower lip and lifted my hips. His focus moved to my lip a second before he drew it between his teeth. I slid my hands down his back to his ass and squeezed.

He felt so good. I couldn't take any more, wanted him to move his hips to start that magnificent friction, but he stopped. Tenderness stared back. "My wife."

It wasn't frenzied. He moved slowly, deliberately working us both, building the pleasure so when it crashed over us, it took us both in the most exquisite orgasm.

GREYSON

I couldn't get enough of her, buried deep and still coming down from the best fucking orgasm and I was getting hard. It had always been like that, but it added another dimension fucking my wife. My wife. Her eyes were closed, her cheeks rosy from desire, her chest rising and falling as she pulled air into her lungs.

"That was incredible," she whispered dreamily. Her eyes opened, passion and love stared back. "Better, if possible."

She was so fucking beautiful. "I want to paint you."

Her entire body blushed. "Like this?"

My cock liked that idea. She felt it too when desire swept her face.

"I do want to paint you naked, would you consider that?"

"For you, yes, but it would have to stay in our bedroom. And when we have kids, perhaps your studio."

I shifted my hips in agreement; she closed her eyes on a moan.

My fingers brushed along her face, she should be captured in clay too. "Sit for me tomorrow. I want this face."

"Okay." Her eyes warmed. "We're married. It feels like a dream."

"Then we're dreaming it together, beautiful."

ALEXIS

We'd been married for three weeks and still I was floating. We spent our honeymoon in bed, on the beach and bluffs, or with Paige and family, but mostly in bed. He'd invited Teresa to the wedding, the journalist who had done the article on him. She was the only one he invited. The photograph that was featured on the cover of her magazine I liked so much I asked for the original; the photographer captured us right after we were announced husband and wife. It was my favorite photo of us. We'd been home for a week and even though we'd been living together for years, it felt different now that we were married. Better. Sometimes I just watched him doing something simple like brushing his teeth or washing the dishes and I felt incredibly lucky knowing I had a lifetime of this.

A lifetime with him.

It was hard getting back into work and today was no different, the morning flew by as I sat lost in thought and not ones circling the script I was working on. It was lunchtime, though my eagerness had less to do with food and more to do with convincing Greyson to join me. Not that he needed convincing.

His studio door was open, but the room was empty. I grinned, we even thought alike. Entering the kitchen, he had the fridge open while he chugged the milk from the carton. I'd suggested countless times over the years that he might want a glass, but he was pretty fixed in his ways. I didn't care. I wasn't a milk drinker but having his mouth on the carton, I saw nothing wrong with that. He glanced over, a twinkle in his eyes getting caught. He wasn't at all repentant.

"What are you in the mood for?" he asked while putting the milk back. He was in his painting outfit—faded jeans, a tee and his bandana. He didn't wear shoes or socks when he painted. That first day on the jetty he had been barefoot too. I had thought it was because he had been on the beach, but it was just part of his process. The man was sexy as sin.

"You."

It was one seamless move how he closed the fridge and moved into me, pressing me back against the counter. "I'm always up for that."

"You wanted to paint me."

His eyes went hot, his fingers already moving over my body studying his subject. "All of you?"

Desire, thousands of pinpoints of it, tingled my nerve endings from my head down to my toes. "Yes."

It wasn't just arousal or even love in his gaze; he was the artist now working the image and how he wanted it translated. "I'll get set up." But he didn't move; those pale green eyes looked directly into mine and then he kissed me, long and sweet. My body went liquid. He touched a few strands of my hair, rubbing them between his fingers. "Thank you."

I left Greyson in his studio and went to our room. I felt a little nervous as I undressed because this was permanent, my naked image forever captured in oil. It was definitely in part sexual, but it was about more than that. Trust, me giving it to him and him giving it back. I stood in front of the mirror, my robe hanging from my shoulders as I studied my body. I remembered doing similarly once upon a time. Greyson created beauty. Whatever he envisioned, whatever he brought to life, was going to be beautiful because it was us.

He was sharpening his pencils when I entered. He sketched first. The paint would come later; he first had to get the vision on the canvas. He stopped working when I entered, a smile curving his lips. One wall of his studio was all windows, but he had a white screen up and angled so any curious people in the buildings around us wouldn't see anything if they happened to be looking.

He crossed the room, took my hand and silently led me to the screen. He turned into me, our bodies so close we were practically touching. His fingers curled around the silk of my robe, his focus on me when he slowly moved it down one shoulder. It was his expression, love, lust and awe that had my nerves settling. His finger ran along the underside of my breast, his thumb brushed over my nipple. It was the lightest of touches, but he grinned as he moved his hand down my arm over the evidence of what he did to me.

"Hold it here." His voice was gruff as he curled my fingers of one hand around the silk at my hip. He kept my other shoulder covered.

"Sideways." He guided my body in the position he wanted. He had a painting on an easel at the other side of the studio, close to the windows. "I want you to look at that." He touched my chin to lower my head slightly and pulled a few tendrils of hair over my shoulder, to curl near my breast. I thought he wanted me completely naked, but this was Greyson. Only my breasts, shoulder and stomach were bare and with how he wanted me to stand, in profile, it was the simple beauty of the female form he was after.

"Just like that," he said and moved in long strides to his easel. I wanted to watch him work; instead, I looked where he asked but thought of him drawing the lines of my body, blending them with his fingers, his touch on my shoulder, my arms, over my stomach, across my nipple. Desire pooled in my gut and my nipples went hard.

"Fuck," he growled. "Don't you move."

He knew I was turned on, the scratching of his pencil over the canvas sped up and all the while I imagined him touching me, first with his hands, then his tongue. I imagined him backing me up against the wall, lifting my leg and driving his cock into me. My clit spasmed at the thought.

I didn't know how long I stood there, but I was a bundle of lust when I heard the pencil drop on the floor. In three strides, he had me in his arms. "I could smell you, beautiful," he said right before he kissed me, a kiss so hungry it left me weak. As I knew he would, he read my mind when he backed me against the wall. I worked his jeans, yanking them down enough to free his cock. He never broke the kiss. He curled his fingers into my thigh, lifted my leg and slammed into me. I threw my arms around his neck and moaned into his mouth because real life was so much better than my imaginings.

GREYSON

It was the fastest I'd ever completed a painting and it was without question the best fucking thing I'd ever done. If I put this up for sale, collectors would be banging down my door, a bidding war would ensue, it would sell for millions. I understood why too. It was Alexis, that innocence of hers that weaved through everything she did and yet she trusted me enough to pose naked. The combination of innocence and seduction was fucking magnificent, just like the woman it depicted. I painted her rings. She was mine, every part of her belonged to me. I was one lucky bastard.

She was working, her desk in the corner of the living room. I leaned against one of the columns and watched her. Her lips were moving, her fingers dancing over the keyboard. I didn't want to interrupt her, she was in the flow so I stood and watched the magic of her mind working. She realized I was there when her head lifted and her eyes warmed.

"Hey. What are you doing? Keeping the roof up," she snickered, and rolled back from her desk.

Fucking adorable.

She crossed the room to me, and I wasn't shy about watching her, the gentle sway of her hips and those long legs. She usually moved right into me, pressing in close, but she stopped a few feet from me and pushed her hands into the pockets of her jeans.

"Whatcha looking at?"

"My wife."

Her eyes warmed even as her lips turned up into a smile.

"It's done."

Excitement danced in her eyes now. She caught my hand as she headed for my studio. "Show me."

I grinned. If I didn't move, she wouldn't be going very far, but I wanted her to see the painting. I let her pull me into my studio, her feet coming to a stop when we entered. She approached the painting slowly, almost like she wasn't sure it was real. I walked to the side of the room to watch her experience it. Her expression was one of wonder; her hand lifted like she was going to touch it, but she curled her fingers into a fist at the last minute.

"That's me?" There was a bit of disbelief in her tone. "It looks almost ethereal…" She looked over. "Like I'm stepping out of a dream. I don't look like this."

"Yes, you do."

She didn't believe me, but her focus shifted back to the painting. "I knew whatever you created was going to be beautiful, but Greyson this is beyond beautiful."

I walked to her, wrapping her in my arms. "It's how I see you. Beautiful, innocent, sexy."

"I'm pretty amazing in your eyes."

"You're amazing period."

"We should hang it in the living room."

That surprised me, I glanced down as she looked up, "Are you serious?"

"I know I'm naked but it's art, really beautiful art."

I held her tighter. "I'd love that, but I'm selfish and don't want to share this part of you."

She leaned back into me, linking her fingers with mine. "Our bedroom then. You need to have a frame made."

"Yeah, I'll call my guy."

"We should eat," she said and pulled from my arms.

I grabbed her arm, tossed her over my shoulder and headed to our bedroom. "You read my mind."

16

ALEXIS 2009

It was fall, the weather beautiful in the city, so we were walking to the grocery store. Two years we'd been married and what an amazing two years they had been. I adored the painting he'd done of me. It hung over our bed and every time I studied it, how he saw me, that hole in my heart was just about gone.

He was wearing a hat I knitted. I wasn't very creative, outside of my writing. I still couldn't cook; my last attempt at a cake had not fared any better than my first attempt. My knitting skills were not much better than my baking skills. There were so many missed stitches that there were large holes marring the design. The color was pretty, brown and light green like his eyes, but it was a really ugly hat. Still, he was wearing it along with his leather and shearling jacket that cost a small fortune and his designer jeans, tee and sneakers. He was a walking advertisement for the *Sesame Street* game, 'One of these things is not like the others', but he wore that hat with pride.

"You don't have to wear the hat, you know?"

He glanced down at me. "Why wouldn't I?"

"It's hideous."

"You made it."

"Doesn't change the fact that it's an eye sore."

He dragged me closer and draped an arm over my shoulders. "I like my hat and it's warm."

We passed a pet store and there was the cutest little cat in the window. He was all gray with the biggest black eyes.

"Greyson, look at him."

I pulled him to the window then tapped on the glass. The little guy was scared, his body shook, but it didn't keep him from moving closer.

Glancing at Greyson to gauge his interest in a pet, he was watching me not the cat. "What?"

He touched my cheek, but said nothing.

"You want to lose the hat but don't have it in you."

He grinned, but I understood the look. It happened to me too, at the oddest times I was nearly overwhelmed with the reality that we were married. I smiled in understanding then I asked, "What are your thoughts on cats?"

His focus shifted to the cat. "He is cute."

"We have plenty of room at the apartment."

"We do."

We wanted children, but we were enjoying it just being us at the moment. There was time to start a family and getting a cat was a good first step.

"He has to stay out of the studio. Cat claws and canvas don't mix."

"Agreed."

"All right." He held the door. "Let's see about bringing the little guy home."

It wasn't just the cat we brought home. It was the carrier, the cat bed, food, toys, litter box, litter. The little fella was shy. He only left his carrier for a few minutes at a time, exploring a little farther than his last effort before he darted back into the safety of what was familiar. Greyson and I lay on the floor watching him for hours. He was the cutest little thing.

"Maybe we should leave him alone. He knows where his litter box is and his food. If we stop hovering, maybe he'll grow more bold," Greyson suggested.

That seemed logical. "Okay. Let's watch a scary movie."

Greyson stood then offered his hand to me. "You pick the movie, I'll get the popcorn."

"And the—"

"M&M's I know. You can't have popcorn without M&M's."

"It's brilliant and you know it. The heat from the popcorn melts the chocolate, but the candy coating keeps it from getting all over."

He chuckled and kissed my head. "Find a movie." He started for the kitchen, but glanced back at me and grinned. "Don't forget I double as a damn fine blanket."

My entire body throbbed. Understatement. He was the best fucking blanket ever.

It was several days after we brought the cat home that I learned the meaning of the expression curiosity killed the cat. It was also the same day we settled on his name.

He roamed the house now, was comfortable with us about a day after his homecoming. He didn't sleep in our room, but I was hopeful he would eventually. He did sit with us, usually curled up in his cat bed, but every once in a while he slept on our laps and we were pathetic because every time he did, we beamed like we'd just been bestowed a great honor. And there were people that said animals were dumb.

Greyson and I had a tradition of having pancakes for dinner at least once a week. These weren't any old pancakes though. Greyson created art from the pancake batter, anything from a cactus to the Eiffel Tower.

I was sitting at the counter. Greyson was working at the stove.

"Have you ever considered cooking in the nude?" I asked.

He glanced over his shoulder at me. "Have you?"

"As you know I can't cook, but I could be your sous chef."

"My naked sous chef?" His grin was sexy as sin. "We'd starve to death." He paused as he thought it through. "We'd never get anything done." He looked wicked when he added, "We'd fuck ourselves to death."

"What a way to go though."

Neither of us saw the cat walk into the kitchen. The flour was kept on the bottom shelf of one of the cabinets. It was usually sealed in a canister, but Greyson had yet to seal it. A puff of flour, that resembled a mushroom cloud, rose up next to Greyson. He looked down. "You bugger!"

Glancing over the counter, I was treated to the sight of our cat looking like an uncooked chicken cutlet. His eyes looked particularly dark against the white flour.

"He's going to track flour throughout the house. We need to give him a bath." Greyson reached for him. Startled, the cat took off trailing flour in his wake. I watched as he flew past me then turned to Greyson. He was pulling the pancakes from the heat.

"You're seriously going to chase the cat?"

"Aren't you?"

"No. We're not going to catch him."

"I'm like a ninja when I need to be," he boasted.

Oh, I was going to enjoy this.

I turned in my chair to watch my husband move like a ninja. I chuckled and wished I had some popcorn. There was no way he was outrunning a cat. He realized it too when the cursing started. The apartment filled with profanity, which was just sexy as hell because of his Irish accent. I listened to the footsteps upstairs, much like the dad from *A Christmas Story* when listening for Ralphie and Randy to get in bed before he and the Mrs. pulled out the Christmas presents. I walked to the stairs and timed it perfectly. The cat came darting down them. I swooped him up when he hit the bottom. Both the cat and I looked up when Greyson appeared at the top of the staircase. I didn't want to laugh, but I couldn't help it. He had more flour on him than the cat.

His eyes narrowed as he started down the steps. "What's so funny?"

"You. That was a spectacular demonstration of ninja moves. I've never seen such agility before. My mind is blown."

It was the look; I knew that look. "At least I tried, you just sat there."

"I was waiting for my pancakes." Though it wasn't pancakes I wanted now.

I slowly backed away, releasing the cat so he could flee to safety.

"I seem to be in need of a shower."

And though he was going for menacing, my body throbbed with anticipation. Still, I had to tease him because Greyson was many things, but a ninja was not one of them. "Your hair is white and there is a smear here," I pointed to my cheek for reference.

"Alexis."

"Yes, Greyson."

"Run."

It wasn't cursing that filled the house, but laughter.

GREYSON

"I'm hungry," Alexis was curled up against my side. We'd worked up an appetite, first in the shower and then out of it.

"Give me a minute to get feeling back in my legs and I'll go finish the pancakes."

"I know what we can call our cat."

I glanced down at her.

"Buggers."

I grinned because it was a very fitting name. "I like that."

She kissed my chest then climbed from bed. I loved the sight of her moving, loved that she was slipping on my tee, didn't like she was covering up her body because I wasn't even close to being done with her yet. She headed for the door, but looked back at me and smiled.

"Greyson."

"Yeah, beautiful."

"You're not much of a ninja."

I jumped from bed, she ran. I was going after her when my cell rang. I almost let it go, but it was Colin.

I answered, but called after her, "You can't hide, Alexis." Chuckling, I greeted Colin.

"I'm interrupting."

I pulled on my jeans. "It's good. What's up?"

"I have good news."

"Yeah? I like good news."

"They found the writer of those letters."

A chill moved through me, my legs even went a bit weak as I dropped down onto the edge of the bed. I'd forgotten about those letters, life had been so fucking sweet.

"She lives in San Francisco, still lives with her parents. She works in the fast food industry. By all accounts she's antisocial and a loner, but she doesn't have the means to travel. Her parents were shocked to learn of the letters and are taking her in for evaluation."

"How old is she?"

"Thirty-eight."

"And they didn't notice before now that she might need help?"

"My thoughts too. Pressure from the authorities I'm sure has helped open their eyes."

I hoped so, more for the woman's sake than mine. "This is great news." I'd forgotten about the letters and the woman, but closure was good.

"I'll let you get back to Alexis. Please give her my love."

"Will do."

In the kitchen, the coffee was brewing, Buggers was eating and Alexis was whipping up the batter for the pancakes. I walked up behind her and slipped my hands around her waist.

"That was Colin."

"Yeah. How is he?"

I didn't answer she waited then looked up.

"They found her."

It took her a second, but her expression said it all. Relief.

"She lives with her parents. They're getting her help."

She placed the bowl down and turned into me, linking her fingers behind my back. "I'm happy she's getting help and thrilled not to have to worry about her."

I lowered my head to look her in the eyes. "Were you worried?"

"Yeah, for you."

I kissed her. Words weren't needed. I whispered against her mouth, "Pancakes."

"Pancakes." She poured us each coffee, setting mine next to me before taking a seat at the counter. "You should make a ninja."

A smile she wouldn't see cracked over my face. I wasn't ever living that down.

ALEXIS

"How's wedded bliss?" Paige asked during our weekly phone conversation. I loved the hour we gave ourselves to get caught up. It made the distance between us seem not so long.

"Is it possible to be too happy?"

"No."

"I can't stop smiling, Paige. I feel a smile on my face during the oddest times. Walking down the aisle in the grocery store or filling Greyson's car with gas. It's ridiculous. It's been two years and I still feel like a newlywed."

"Don't question it, Alexis. Just enjoy the ride."

"Oh, and they found the woman."

"Letter lady?"

"Yeah, she's getting help."

"I'm glad to hear that. I'll let Grant know. How's work?"

"I'm officially lead writer for *Happenstance*. I've had to give up my adventure in the city column because I just don't have the time."

"You kept that column for far longer than you intended."

"True."

"I love *Happenstance*. More so now that you are writing for it."

"You're biased."

"True, I'm still right. Any more thoughts on writing another play?"

"I might, but I'm trying a screenplay first. My agent, Adele, has gotten me on a project."

"For a movie? I'm coming to the premiere."

I laughed because that was fast. "I haven't written it yet."

"When you do."

"The whole family will have to come. Speaking of the family, how are Grant and the girls?"

"Tara was selected for county orchestra. Mandy's painting of a clown was selected for the annual school district art show and little Heather is reading at a high school level and she's only in fifth grade. Grant's amazing. He's working on a new bike for himself. He's never made one for himself, which is bizarre. We are financially sound, so I told him to treat himself."

"I can't wait to see it. Please congratulate the girls for me. Now I want to come home so I can hear Tara play and see Mandy's painting and have Heather read me a bedtime story."

"The door is always open. I've got to feed the family. We'll talk soon."

"Please kiss everyone."

"Will do. You kiss that handsome husband of yours and the twins from me."

"That will make Dylan's day."

She chuckled, "Talk soon, Alexis."

"Bye."

I smiled as I dropped the phone on the sofa next to me. I'd finished work for the day so I planned on spending the rest of the afternoon reading Greyson's mom's diary. Greyson was in his studio working. I loved that even when we were working we were in the same place.

I curled up on the sofa with Cara's diary. She had beautiful handwriting. Page after page I read snapshots in time of Greyson's life. His mother had a sense of humor; she was also a wonderful writer. I laughed, teared up and smiled, seeing in my mind Greyson growing up through her words. There were also passages on her husband. One in particular had me turning the pages.

Stubborn, the man is so stubborn. I want to pull my hair out. Hell, I want to pull his hair out. The Ratcliffe men, I love them but damn when they get an idea in their head. I've continued it too. Some poor unsuspecting woman is going to have to deal with that impossible stubbornness. I'm sorry, whoever you are. Ratcliffe men are fiercely loyal, protective, loving, but when they get a bug up their ass they do not yield. Nothing will sway them. They will follow through, even when it makes no logical sense. It is so damn frustrating. The good news, they eventually realize their error, but until they do you have to be prepared to ride out the storm. I apologize now for the hunks of missing hair and dangerously high blood pressure you will no doubt experience with my son. But then you've got my son so... you're welcome.

Greyson dropped down onto the sofa next to me. I hadn't experienced that stubbornness. Not really. It must have skipped a generation.

"She's a wonderful writer."

"Yeah?"

"I was just reading about the stubbornness of the Ratcliffe men. Your mom even gave a warning to your future wife."

"She did not."

I handed him the diary. "I haven't experienced that stubbornness with you, but I'm glad I've been given the heads up."

He looked adorably offended. "I am the definition of accommodating."

"Really?"

He placed the diary on the table, leaned back and pulled his hands behind his head. "I go with the flow."

"So if I said get naked."

He yanked off his shirt.

I grew warm in the most delicious way. "That's not a true test. You want to get naked."

He grinned.

"Sing to me."

"No."

"Dance, shake that booty just for me."

"Hell, no."

"She was right. Stubborn."

"Because I won't sing or dance?"

"Yes. I'd sing for you."

I opened my mouth to do just that and he closed his hand over my face.

"I'd rather you didn't."

Yanking his arm away, I glared. "Why not?"

"I don't know how to tell you this, but…"

My eyes narrowed.

"When you sing it sounds like an animal dying."

My jaw dropped.

He laughed. He actually laughed at me. "And dancing…have you ever seen a plastic bag stuck on a branch of a tree when it's windy and it's flapping this way and that?"

Where was he going with this? "Yes."

"Those plastic bags have better control over themselves than you do when you dance."

I wanted to laugh; my chest was shaking from it. I managed a glare instead before I stood with as much dignity as I could muster after that insight.

"Since my form is so repugnant to you, you may have the sofa tonight."

I got about two feet before I was over his shoulder. He took the stairs two at a time.

"That's a hell fucking no."

"And you call yourself accommodating."

He ran his hand up my leg to my ass and squeezed. "I'll show you how accommodating I am."

Lust made my next words a little breathy. "I'll need several examples."

He dropped me on the bed and grinned. "My pleasure. See… accommodating."

17

ALEXIS 2010

Greyson and I escaped the heat of the city with a long weekend on the Jersey shore. It was different from the beaches at home, more congested and there were the casinos as backdrop. I loved it. We spent our days swimming and sunbathing and the nights eating, drinking and making love. Best vacation ever.

Greyson was swimming now, had gone past the waves and every once in a while I saw him cutting the water, a strong front stroke that would make our gym teacher proud. Remembering that day in the pool, the first time I saw him in board shorts. That was a really great memory.

I'd gotten us hot dogs, but I couldn't wait to eat mine. There was something about a hot dog on the beach that was just so freaking good. Greyson appeared, walking from the water, and I almost choked because my husband was hot. Those muscles he had at eighteen were bigger and more defined. He moved with that unhurried grace he had, his long hair pulled back from his face. As long as we'd been together and still I got those butterflies.

I wasn't the only one checking him out, but I was the only one *he* was checking out. He dropped down next to me, water from his body dripped on me. For a second, I almost forgot we were on the beach because I had ideas about touching that body, first with my hands then with my tongue.

"Stop looking at me like that or this is going to get really interesting."

I stuck my tongue out because honestly none of my thoughts were private.

I handed him a dog, he ate half of it in one mouthful.

"Do you remember that day in the pool?"

His eyes grew warm. "You saved my life. I never did thank you properly."

"It's been almost fourteen years since I first saw you on my jetty."

"Your jetty?" he teased.

"My jetty."

"Best fucking day of my life," he said with sincerity, then he teased, "Whatever happened to your bike?"

"Paige has it." I really was going to give it to him, a homecoming gift when we moved back to Mendocino.

"That thing was fucking ugly."

"It *is*, present tense, not ugly. It is just old."

"No, it *is* ugly."

"I loved that bike." I glanced at him and he looked bewildered. I added, "That bike brought me to you."

I couldn't read his expression, but he then said, "I fucking love that bike."

I had just lathered up and intended to soak up some rays. Greyson had other plans. My breath was knocked from me when he swept me up and over his shoulder. "What are you doing?"

"I have a damsel to rescue."

I couldn't help the laugh, because playful Greyson was charming. He didn't put me down until a wave came then he took us both under. He never let me go, pulled me up against him. I didn't know how long we played in the water like kids. At one point, he pressed me close and kissed me, a kiss that was both passionate and sweet. He let his lips linger when he whispered, "Here's to another seventy years as fucking amazing as the last fourteen.

251

It was me who kissed him until we were knocked over by a wave, but even as we tossed and turned, he never let go of my hand.

Quarter slots, I was rocking at them, up by a hundred dollars. I looked around; some people were using two or three machines, dropping the coins in, pressing the buttons. Most had a cigarette in one hand and a glass of something in the other. These were the diehards. Was it the quest for money, or the familiarity of the routine, I didn't know. It was fascinating. An idea for a book started to form, I pulled out the pad and pen I always carried around and wrote it down.

We'd been to dinner. Greyson had learned not to ask the concierge for the best places to eat, but the housekeeper or the bellhop. They always knew about the gems and dinner was no exception. The little Greek place we'd dined at was amazing. I didn't get out a lot, I liked being home, but I had fun dressing up for the evening. Greyson looking dapper in a black suit with a pale green shirt, and me, I was a firm believer in the little black dress, so versatile from simple and elegant to sexy when embellished with shoes, hair and jewelry. I was going simple tonight. My hair down and my only jewelry were my wedding and engagement rings that I never took off.

Greyson had left to get us drinks. Not the cheap stuff they gave for free, the good stuff. If my liver was taking a hit, it would do so with quality. He'd been gone a while though, almost a half an hour. The place was crowded but not that crowded. I hesitated leaving my spot. We could spend hours looking for one another because I still didn't have a cell phone. I knew they were all the rage. Everyone who was anyone had one. Not me. I didn't care for talking on the phone, so why would I carry one around with me so I never had an excuse not to answer it. No thanks.

I dropped a few more quarters in the machine, but I was just losing the nice little stash I'd made so I called it quits and waited near the closest pillar for Greyson. About ten minutes later I saw him moving through the crowd. He was easy to spot because he was taller than most people. I noticed two things, he looked irritated and he didn't have drinks. He reached me, caught my hand and kept on moving.

"Do you have to cash out?"

"Yes."

We detoured to one of the cashiers and while I collected my winnings, he looked around but not out of curiosity, more like a lookout. As soon as I put my money away, he took my hand again and beelined for the door leading out to the boardwalk.

"Do you want to tell me what's going on or should I guess?"

It was like walking into a wall of heat when we stepped outside, even with the sun down. I reached into my purse for an elastic and tied my hair back or I'd be a puddle. Like I so eloquently told Greyson once, I sweat I did not perspire.

"I was detained."

"Like by a cop?"

Greyson's expression was comical.

"You were arrested for looking too good. Right? Am I right?"

He tried not to smile but his lips moved anyway.

"Two women wanted an autograph, then a photograph. When they offered a home cooked meal I bailed."

"Those bastards." I threw my arms in the air in feigned outrage. "They offered to feed you a home cooked meal. Son of a bitch." I looked around the boardwalk. "Where are the cops? They need to be arrested."

He crossed his arms over his chest. "You're making fun of me."

I was going for innocent, but I had to bite my tongue to keep from laughing. "Me? No." I got it, some of the attention was irritating and some was disturbing, but this was just women taking advantage of an opportunity. If I saw Brad Pitt, I'd be asking for a photograph. Hell, I'd offer him dinner too.

"When you're on the other side of it we'll see if you find it so funny."

"That's not going to happen. I'm a hermit; people have no idea who I am except for your wife. I like it that way. Besides, one celebrity in the house is enough."

Greyson wasn't hunted down, he wasn't Hollywood star famous, but he still showed up on magazine covers occasionally. Sometimes I was even in those pictures with him. But there was a time when his face had been everywhere including on the side of buses. He was to the art world what Mikhail Baryshnikov was to ballet. It wasn't a bad thing, but when you couldn't order a drink for your wife and yourself, I could see that being irritating.

"Those pictures will no doubt show up on the website," he was muttering to himself.

What website? "What now?"

He actually blushed. It was the first time I'd ever seen Greyson blush. "There's a website?"

He had his own website for his work, but I was pretty sure he wasn't talking about that. "You have a fan website? You've really arrived."

It was the best 'duh' face I'd ever seen. "There's a website dedicated to a cat who can play the piano. It's not a big accomplishment."

I loved that cat.

"So there's a website where fans post pictures of you. Is that a bad thing?"

"When you have a woman like the one who wrote those letters, having a place you can track where I am. Yeah, it can be a bad thing."

I felt the blood drain from my face. He saw it too, he closed the distance and yanked me into his arms.

"I didn't think of that," I confessed.

"That's all I thought about."

I should have known there was more to his irritation. It wasn't like Greyson to be melodramatic.

He kissed my head. "Sorry for acting like an ass."

"Temperamental artist. Comes with the territory."

He chuckled, "I owe you a drink."

I looked up into those green eyes. "Let's have it back at the room."

He kissed me long and hard. "My thoughts exactly."

ALEXIS

Summer flew by and fall was approaching. We were at UCLA, dropping Tara off for her freshmen year. Tara, little Tara, was in college. I was trying not to cry, but I couldn't stop the tears from rolling down my cheeks. Greyson's arm was wrapped around me offering strength as well as taking some. Paige and Grant were all smiles, but I knew the tears were threatening. The twins were returning the grocery carts the kids were using to get their stuff inside.

Mandy didn't leave Tara's side. They had always been very close; I couldn't imagine how Mandy was feeling. Happy for her sister, absolutely, but her best friend no longer would be one room away. Heather being so much younger than her siblings, moved to the beat of her own drum. Like at the moment, she was hanging from a nearby tree.

Paige and Grant had gotten through the road trip that took two days, the family dinners that would signify the last time in a while, maybe ever, that they would all be under the same roof as a family. They endured the unloading of their baby's things and the setting up of those things in her room. We had gone to lunch and then dinner and now it was time for them to let her go.

Grant hugged her, spoke softly in her ear. Tara had been putting on a brave face too but whatever he said she broke down. Grant held her closer, yanked Paige to them who dragged Mandy into it. Heather, seeing the group hug, jumped from the tree and pressed herself against her dad's legs.

I turned my head into Greyson's chest. I was happy for Tara and wanted only the best for her. Growing up, leaving home, it was all a part of life, but that didn't mean it didn't hurt like hell. They were lucky though, coming from such a loving and close family. They'd always have that, no matter how much distance separated them; they'd always have each other.

Greyson kissed my head, his arm tightened around me. "Tara is walking over."

I wiped at my eyes and tried to hold it in, but seeing her beautiful face, a face I had watch mature from an infant to the young lady she was, I lost it. She hugged me, like she always did, as tightly as possible.

"Be safe, be smart and have fun," I whispered in her ear. "We are all only a phone call away."

Her face was wet with tears. "Thank you for coming, Auntie Alexis."

"I wouldn't have missed this."

She turned to Greyson. Her crush had mellowed over the years, as we all became family. The thought brought a smile, history repeating itself. Greyson wrapped her close and pressed a kiss on her head. He too whispered something in her ear. She nodded her head before he released her. Mandy walked with her to the door and my heart broke when they hugged, a hug only sisters could have. It was a hug Paige and I shared every time we left the other. Tara looked back at us and waved and then she was gone. Heather walked up to Mandy and took her hand, staring up at her big sister with a smile. Paige wrapped her arm around Mandy's shoulders as the three of them joined Grant. Greyson and I gave them some time and headed back to the hotel.

"Are you okay?" he asked taking my hand in his.

My focus was out the window, my heart hurt, but not in a bad way. It was beautiful the scene we'd just left. "They are lucky they have that."

"Yes they are."

I glanced over at him; he looked back. "One day we'll experience that."

He smiled. "Several times I'm hoping."

"Me too. I can't believe she's in college. Life goes so fast. You blink and it's over."

He brought my hand to his lips. "But it's a beautiful ride."

That night after the girls fell asleep, Paige, Grant, Greyson and I sat at the hotel bar. It had been an emotionally draining few days.

Paige's eyes were puffy and I knew she wasn't done crying. "I can't believe we're here already. I've been preparing for this day, but damn it came so fast."

I reached across the table for her hand. She held mine tightly. Her focus shifted to Greyson. "What did you say to her?"

"Distance doesn't make a difference when you're family."

Paige teared up.

"We'll be doing this next year for Mandy," Grant said then added, "At least we'll get a break before it's Heather's turn."

Trying to lighten the mood I said, "When Heather is ready, Tara and Mandy might be back home."

Paige smiled. "I hope so."

18

ALEXIS 2012

G reyson and I stood in the twin's apartment, his expression matched my own because everything was automated. We were picking them up to go to lunch. Something we tried to do weekly, though with everyone's schedules sometimes it was every other week. A few months ago we'd all gone home to help Mandy move into her dorm for her freshman year in college. Hard to believe Tara was already a sophomore. Bright side, the girls were both at UCLA.

"We were here not even a month ago and none of this was here," I said in slight disbelief because it was like it sprung up overnight.

"Check this out," Dominic said as he hit a button on the wall and Sophia appeared carrying a tray of drinks.

"We have a robot who folds our laundry. Do you remember when we were younger, we tried to figure that out?" Dylan asked.

I couldn't hide my interest. I loathed doing laundry. "I want a robot to fold my laundry."

Dylan flashed me a grin, "Done."

"It's not the robots you sell, it's the programming behind the robots?" Greyson would ask about the logistics, me I was just floored seeing robots moving around Dylan and Dominic's place. They reminded me of R2D2. I wondered if they could make me an R2D2.

"Exactly, we sell the technology behind the robotics."

And sell they did. They were worth a small fortune. You wouldn't know to look at them. They still had beanbags for furniture, still wore the same clothes they had in college. All their money went back into research and development they called it. They'd had girlfriends over the years, but none of them stuck. I understood; their first love was their work. They didn't seem to care about girlfriends or marriage. They were happy and that was all that mattered.

"Hey, can my laundry robot look like R2D2?"

Dylan's eyes went wide. "Yeah, we can do that or similar because of copyright."

Greyson was looking at me, really he was laughing at me. He thought he was hiding it with his hand over his mouth. "What? I hate doing laundry."

"Let's go, I'm hungry," Dominic announced.

Greyson reached for the door when he asked, "You don't have a robot that cooks for you?"

They answered together, "Not yet."

Laundry. I really did hate it. Not the sorting and washing, but folding and putting away sucked. At least we had a laundry room in our apartment. If I had to go to the basement to do laundry, I swear I'd be like that Emperor and his new clothes.

That burn moved down my spine and I turned to see Greyson in the doorway, leaning against the doorjamb. "Your favorite," he said in way of greeting.

"It really isn't."

"Maybe you just need to think about it in a different way," he suggested. And I appreciated him trying to be helpful, but it was laundry. There was no other way to look at it.

"Any way you fold it, it sucks. See what I did there? I'm a poet."

He moved into the room in that stride that never grew old watching. His fingers tightened on my hips as he pulled me back against him. Chills danced down my arms feeling him hard, pressing between my ass cheeks. He kissed my neck and ground his hips into me. I fisted the shirt I was folding even as I tilted my head for him. One hand moved up my body, under my shirt to my breast. He yanked the cotton down, cupping my breast, teasing my nipple with his fingers. His other hand went south, under my sweats and panties until he found the heart of me and sank two fingers in. I was clay and he was molding me, working my body into the shape he wanted and that shape was so freaking turned on. He wasn't immune, his cock was rock hard as he rubbed himself against my ass. He turned me; hot eyes met mine. I was freed of my tee and bra, then my sweats and panties. I was standing naked in our laundry room. I gasped when my ass hit the cold metal of the washer. He pulled his cock free, grabbed my hips and pulled me onto him. My legs went around his waist. He reached behind me. I didn't know what he was doing until I felt the washer shaking under me.

The spin cycle.

He looked wicked. He pulled out then slammed into me again. My hands went behind me so I could get leverage to lift my hips into his thrusts. He took the opportunity to suck on my breasts, first one then the other. My heels dug into his ass when I came, his control slipped, lifting my ass and pounding into me until he came on a growl. He threaded one hand into my hair and kissed me, sweet and hungry. Against my lips he whispered, "You'll never look at laundry the same way again."

"When do you want to start a family?" Greyson asked me later that night. We'd left the laundry room, went to our bedroom and stayed there the rest of the night. He was wishing he had a robot to retrieve us food. Buggers was curled at the bottom of the bed, having joined us when the noises stopped.

We'd been married for five years. It didn't feel that long and I loved having him all to myself, but I also loved the idea of a little Greyson walking around.

"I'm ready now." I rolled to him, and rested my head on my hand. One of his arms was tucked under his head, his tattoo visible. I traced it. "What about you?"

"I'm thirty-four. I'd like to have kids while we're still youngish."

"Agreed. I want a boy who looks like you."

"A girl who looks like you."

"You need a son to continue the line." Greyson was the last direct descendant unless we had a boy who could carry on the name. Of course it was the twenty-first century. A girl could do that now too.

"We'll need portraits done." I was thinking ahead to when we had children. I suppose one needed to be done of me too.

"We have time for that." Greyson rolled and pinned me under him, his hips grinding into me. "We have to make the babies first."

Paige and Grant were visiting. Every anniversary, they took off for a few days to celebrate. This year I convinced them to come to New York. I insisted they stay with us. Heather was with Mel and Dee. We were staying in tonight. Last night we did the town, but today we were all tired.

We were lounging in the living room on the awesome sectional that Buggers was having a good time kneading, it was looking a little ratty, but I loved it. Greyson and I could each take a couch if we wanted, but we never did.

I reached for my glass of wine and curled my legs under me. "How are you adjusting to not having Mandy and Tara home?"

Paige was circling the rim of her glass with her finger, thinking of her girls I was sure. "It was an adjustment and we miss them fiercely, but I have to say I'm liking that we have more time for us. We had our kids so young and I'm glad because I like being young parents. I wouldn't change that, but now that Heather is fourteen, she's off with her friends a lot so we have the house to ourselves. It's like we're newlyweds all over again."

Twenty-one years of marriage and they still preferred each other's company to anyone else's.

"What about you? When are you going to start a family?" Paige asked.

"We've already started."

A huge grin cracked over Grant's face. It took Paige a minute longer then she moved so fast, she scared poor Buggers off the sofa. "Are you serious?"

"We're ready and very dedicated to the cause."

Grant laughed, Greyson chuckled. "It's a good cause," Paige said. Then she jumped up and grabbed me, pulling me into a hug. "We can clothes shop and setup the nursery. I get to be an aunt. I'm so excited."

"You're putting the cart before the horse, Paige," Grant teased.

She dismissed his comment with a wave. "It'll happen. When it's right, it will happen."

19

ALEXIS 2013

It hadn't happened. Greyson and I had been trying for a baby for a year. We'd been to the doctors, had the tests to make sure all was well. We were healthy and able, but little boy or girl Ratcliffe was not ready.

I'd finished what I was hoping to get done for the weekly shows, so pulled out the novel I'd been writing for years. It was more an elaborate journal of my life with Greyson. I spent more time re-reading passages than I did writing new ones. Greyson had been putting in particularly long hours lately. I assumed it was a commission piece. I couldn't wait to see it. The man continued to surprise me with his endless talent.

Buggers curled around my leg. It was time for dinner. He purred and waited for me to pick him up. That was our routine; he was the one to remind Greyson and me to eat. In the kitchen, I fed him first and freshened his water before I looked in the fridge for what to make. I still wasn't much of a cook, but I was adding to my pitiful repertoire slowly but surely.

Heat tingled my spine. "Good timing. You can cook dinner." I turned to see Greyson leaning against the counter. He had been looking at my ass and wasn't shy about it. His hair was back in a bandana, as it always was when he worked.

"I want to show you something."

I closed the fridge at his tone. Intense, like he had a secret. "Is everything okay?"

He didn't answer, just held out his hand. He walked me to his studio and waited for me to precede him but my focus was on the painting in the middle of it, a painting of me. It was the one he'd started on our honeymoon. I was dressed in my wedding gown but it was the size of the portrait. My eyes watered and my breath caught. It wasn't just his sculpture he'd been keeping from me.

"Is that for the portrait gallery?"

His focus was on the painting. "Yes."

I loved how he saw me, how beautiful I was to him. Just like when we were kids, he made me look radiant and ethereal.

"It's exquisite."

His hand moved up my back and curled around my neck, applying gentle pressure to bring my mouth to his. Turning into him, I kissed him deeper. He fisted my tee and pulled it over my head. My bra followed. I yanked at his tee; he grabbed the back of it and pulled it forward over his head. He dragged my sweats and panties down my legs. I returned the favor. He backed me up against the wall, his fingers digging into my ass as he lifted me into his arms. My feet linked at his back, one of his hands slammed against the wall as he jerked his hips and surged into me. Grabbing his face, I kissed him, sweeping his mouth, tasting every part of him I could. It was fast, hard and so freaking beautiful. I came on a scream, he was right there with me. He touched his forehead to my shoulder, his breathing labored.

"That was incredible," I whispered then added, "But that doesn't get you out of making dinner."

He didn't move, but I felt his body shaking from his laughter.

"Greyson!"

"What!"

L.A. FIORE

He was in his studio, but the door was open so he wasn't working on anything I couldn't see. I should just walk to him, but I was comfortable on the sofa.

"What are the chances of getting the blueprints to your home in Ireland?"

His head popped out of his studio. "Why?"

"First, I have to say whoever kept these records was amazing. Everything is detailed, down to the price of napkins for balls."

He walked from his studio, wiping his hands on a rag.

"With the internet, have I mentioned I really LOVE the internet, it's amazing how much easier it is to track this stuff."

He settled next to me. "What stuff?"

"Inventory of assets. Apparently taxes back in the day were based on assets, so it wasn't unheard of for prominent families to hide some of their assets to reduce their tax burden. After the fire, the inventory of assets for your household changed. Among the things missing was the diamond. I've been researching some of the pieces that no longer show up on your household inventory; items similar by manufacturer and date are priceless. If these were sold, they'd be documented somewhere if nothing more than by the auction house that handled the sale. But hard-core collectors would kill to get some of the pieces your family has, which means there would be bragging. I'm finding nothing."

He took one of the pages listing out the assets. "Like the diamond."

"Exactly."

"So you think these pieces and the diamond are still in Taisce Manor."

"I do. What if when they rebuilt the castle they added a room?"

"A concealed room. That's not likely to show up on the blueprints if they want to keep it a secret."

"True, but we could see if the footprint for the rebuild matches the blueprints."

He brushed the hair from my shoulder, his thumb rubbing along my jaw. "You're enjoying this."

"I really am. It's fascinating and it will make one hell of a book."

He reached for his phone and called Callum.

"Hey, Grandfather. I'm good and you? She's fine. She's right here researching the diamond…yeah. She wants to get her hands on the blueprints for the rebuild…yeah after the fire. Thanks, have Nigel mail them to the house. Thanks. Yep, talk soon."

He dropped his phone on the coffee table then swiped everything I had on the sofa to the floor. I was about to protest until I saw the heat in his gaze that was fixed on my mouth. I went boneless. He grabbed my legs and pulled me to my back; he wasted no time covering my body with his.

"We should eat." He looked wicked when he said that. He moved slowly down my body. I closed my eyes. I loved this plan.

GREYSON

Alexis and I were cleaning the apartment, she was singing to her favorite tunes. I loved her, but fucking hell she really did sound like Buggers would if he got his paw caught in a door. She looked cute though, shaking her ass to the beat.

With the amount of times we had sex, I was surprised and a little disappointed that we hadn't conceived. It would come, I was hopeful, but I really wanted to see Alexis in our children. I was looking at plans for a cradle. I'd never worked with wood, but I wanted to make something for our baby. Baby, we needed to make her. That was one way to stop Alexis from singing; my cock twitched in agreement.

The house phone rang, before I could call to her to let it ring, she was answering it. A second or two later, she called to me, "Colin's on the phone."

She held out the phone. I kissed her before I took it.

"Hi, Colin."

"Are you sitting down?"

It wasn't like Colin to be dramatic. The man was reserved, much like William but not as stiff. "Should I be?"

"I think so for this news. Guess who I just got off the phone with, who wants an exhibit of your work?"

It was like a sledgehammer, how hard my heart was pounding. "You're kidding."

"No. Early 2016 The Met will be featuring Greyson Ratcliffe. I know it's close to three years away, but that is how far in advance they book their exhibits."

"Holy shit."

"My thoughts exactly."

Alexis was eyeing me, eager to hear the news. I pulled her close.

"Tell them yes."

"I already did."

"This is incredible. Thank you, Colin."

"You've earned it. I've got to go. I've got paintings to assemble. Let's meet next week so you can approve what I've selected."

"Text me when and where. I'll get a flight. Thank you."

I hung up, Alexis was smiling even though she didn't even know what the news was. She was just happy for me because I was happy. I kissed her. I didn't throw her off the scent though; she looked expectant. "So what happened?"

"The Met is doing an exhibit of my work."

She looked like a guppy. Her mouth opened, but words evaded her so she closed it again. It took about a minute before she replied, "The Met?"

I grinned.

"That was your dream, like your all time dream was to get into The Met."

It shouldn't have surprised me she remembered and still my chest got all tight knowing that she had. "Yes."

She threw her arms around me. "This is incredible, monumental. We have to do something to commemorate this moment."

I had an idea that required no clothing.

"We should go out and celebrate."

I dropped her ass on the counter and kissed her, tasting that mouth, every fucking inch. "We should stay in and celebrate."

Her legs curled around my waist. "You make a persuasive argument."

20

ALEXIS 2016

I didn't understand how he was so calm. I wanted to throw up. It was the premiere of his exhibit; we were hosting a small cocktail party before we made our way to The Met. Our family was here, everyone but Mr. and Mrs. Cantenelli. Mr. C. had the flu. Poor man was bedridden. Paige joined me in the kitchen as I plated finger foods.

"How is he so calm?" Paige asked.

"I don't know. I'm freaking out."

"You look beautiful though. I love that dress."

I did too. It was an extravagance, the beaded cowl-back gown in pale blue, but one Greyson insisted on when he saw me in it. "It's decadent, but it feels like a dream on. And you all sexy in peacock blue." A form fitting sheath, which on Paige with her figure was seriously sexy.

"Grant loves this dress."

"I can see why. Tara and Mandy are growing up so fast. And Heather, I hardly recognized her. The twins love that she's following in their footsteps and going to Berkley next year."

Paige shuddered teasingly, "Seriously, they rubbed off on her big time."

"Is Tara still loving her work at the publishing house?" I asked.

Tara moved to San Francisco after she graduated, got an entry-level position at one of the big publishing houses, but she was a workhorse like her dad so she climbed quickly.

"She has ten full-time clients, edits on the side. She loves it." Paige knocked her shoulder into mine. "She takes after you."

I guess she kind of did. That felt good.

"Mandy has got feelers out for teaching positions. She'd like to stay on the West Coast, but it depends on what's available. What about you? No news on the baby front?" Mandy was finishing her undergraduate degree in early child development. Where the hell had the time gone?

Baby, it was the only shadow in the brightness of my life. As much as Greyson and I tried, and we tried a lot, we hadn't gotten pregnant. I was thirty-six. We were running out of time. That hurt, and there was the added guilt of not continuing the Ratcliffe name, that it would end with us. I hated thinking that, so I tried to stay hopeful.

"No, but we're still trying."

"It'll happen. I really do believe that. And women are having healthy babies later in life. You still have time."

"I hope so."

"Okay." Paige took one platter; I took the other. "Let's feed these people and then get to this shindig."

GREYSON

It was a little surreal, being here, walking through the exhibit that featured my work. The greatest of the greats had graced the walls of these prestigious halls. That I was now amongst them was humbling. Alexis hadn't let go of my hand, her face beaming with pride. It wasn't the fanfare or the beautiful people. She was a bundle of restless happy energy for me. That was even more humbling, deserving the love of this woman.

Callum and Colin joined us as Alexis studied one of my favorite paintings. It was of the moor where Mom used to ride. Lady was off center, grazing on the grass as mist rolled over the hills. Most didn't see it, but the mist took shape in the negative space. I didn't even realize I'd done it, those ghosts the housemaids were always whispering about.

"Your parents would be so proud, Greyson. They knew it, from when you were just a little kid, they knew one day you would be here." Callum couldn't hide his own pride. That was humbling too.

Alexis pressed her face into my arm to hide her tears. I had them burning the back of my eyes too. "I wouldn't be here if not for both of you. This is as much a tribute to you as it is for me."

"Nonsense, but kind of you to say." So like Colin to be humble. "I think a whiskey is in order," Colin added, turning to Grandfather who never declined a good Irish whiskey.

Grandfather kissed Alexis on the cheek then turned to me and winked. "We'll see you later. Enjoy your moment."

Alexis pressed closer, one hand linked with mine, the other curled around my bicep. I wanted a moment with her so I led her to a quiet corner.

"This is incredible. The best day of your life I bet," she offered, her focus on the people crowding the exhibit room.

Her hair was up; a few strands fell from the knot and that beauty mark that drove me crazy teased me. "No, not the best day of my life."

Smiling eyes turned from the scene to me then warmed because my girl could read me too. I played with the few loose strands then met her gaze. "Our wedding day was the best day of my life."

Her expression softened. "For me too."

"The day we played hooky ranks up there." I leaned in and caught her bottom lip between my teeth. "The day I showed you a new way to appreciate laundry is also high on my list."

Her cheeks heated at the memory. "That was a really good day."

"What do you say we get out of here and find a diner that makes hot fudge sundaes?"

Her smile was answer enough.

Reaching for my phone I called Grant. "Meet us at the door. We're going for sundaes."

"You really want to leave this," Alexis asked as she gestured to the sight, and it was a pretty spectacular sight. One I was deeply honored by, but I wanted to be around family because that would make this near perfect night, perfect.

"Yeah. The girls have to catch us up on what's new."

She pressed a kiss on my mouth. "I love you."

"I know."

Ten minutes later we were leaving the gala, I glanced back and felt lucky to call these people my family. Callum and the twins were laughing about something. Paige and Colin were walking together, heads close. Grant was with his girls, all talking at once and Alexis; she was holding my hand tightly in hers. Life was good. Life was really fucking good.

It sounded like a car backfiring; Alexis' hand pulled from mine. I turned to her; her expression was one of confusion and pain, her hands moving to her stomach where red was blooming over the pale blue. It all happened in slow motion and then it all sped up. Grant appeared, his arms going around someone. I saw a gun drop to the concrete. Paige was screaming, the girls were crying and Alexis was on the ground, blood pooling around her. It didn't seem real.

"Alexis!" I didn't know I was screaming her name until the crowd formed. I knew what it felt like when your heart and soul died because that was how I felt. Her beautiful eyes were closed; the hand that had just been holding mine was covered in blood.

"NO!" I roared and dropped down next to her and took her hand. "Call a fucking ambulance." I couldn't see her chest moving. I felt for a pulse, it was so weak. I offered my own life for hers in that moment.

"I'm here, beautiful. Please don't leave me. Come back; come back to me. Open those eyes. I need to see you. Please..." Tears streamed down my face. She was so still. My Alexis wasn't here. I dropped my head and begged, "Let me see you."

The sirens came. I stepped back only far enough to let them work, my focus on her hand that wore my rings, the symbol of our lives together, unmoving, lifeless. I willed her to live. I would give anything, absolutely anything for her to open her eyes.

"We've got a pulse. It's weak but we've got one."

I cried harder. "That's it, beautiful. Fucking fight, fight baby, please."

I didn't let them say no, pushing into the ambulance, taking her hand as the paramedic tried to stabilize her. There was so much blood.

"She's coding." He pushed me out of the way and started chest compressions. I wanted to wake up because this had to be fucking nightmare, it couldn't be real. My girl was not in this fucking ambulance fighting for her life. He got a pulse just as we were pulling into the ER. I never let go of her hand until I had to. I stood, covered in her blood and watched as they wheeled the best part of me away.

Our family poured into the ER minutes later. Paige ran right into me and grabbed my face as tears ran down hers. "She's going to live through this."

I yanked her into my arms. I needed to hold onto something because I was cracking apart.

The cops appeared, Grant with them. It came then, the rage. Who the fuck shot Alexis?

"I'm sorry, Mr. Ratcliffe, but we need to ask you some questions." My hands unconsciously curled into fists. I couldn't focus; I didn't want to answer fucking questions I wanted to be with Alexis.

"I know this is difficult but the more we know," the cop urged.

I fucking didn't know anything except that my wife was fighting for her fucking life. Colin approached, I'm glad he did because I was close to punching the officer. Not his fault, but bad fucking timing. I walked away, thinking of nothing but Alexis. Her beautiful smiling face, holding my hand one minute and the next...

I dropped into a chair, holding my head in my hands because it took too much effort to keep it upright. I hadn't cried since my parents died, but I cried and prayed and offered everything and anything that my girl would pull through.

The wait was killing me, the soft mumbling of voices in the waiting room, the swing of the emergency room doors, one catching in the slide and grinding open then closed. The smell of stale coffee, sweat and tears. You could smell fucking tears. I had them all over me—mine, Paige's, the girls, even Grant and the twins. Seeing her lying there, the blood, so still, so lifeless. I didn't know what I would do if she didn't live. How did you come back from that? I had to be positive, but I was fucking human and I saw her code in the ambulance. I watched her die right in front of me. I dropped my head in my hands; those fucking tears started again.

It felt like fucking eternity, but it was probably only about an hour after Alexis was brought in that the emergency doors opened followed by the sound of heavy footsteps. I glanced over to see as four bikers entered. The same leather cut, the same hard glare, and that look in their eyes that said they'd done and seen everything. I recognized the blue glare, the spiky black hair. He was older, harder but it was Alexis' father. He *had* been watching her. My eyes burned. She would love to know that. His gaze hit me like a fucking punch in the gut before he prowled into the waiting room.

"Where is she?" he demanded.

Grant and the twins rose from their seats and flanked me. I appreciated the gesture, but if things got ugly we didn't stand a chance.

"Surgery."

"What the fuck happened?"

It was the unspoken accusation that I was in any way responsible; that my beautiful Alexis was fighting for her life and I had somehow played a part that had rage overruling common sense. I got right in his face. "Be very careful."

The biker with a tattoo curling around his neck, moved in. "Or what?"

It was in my eyes; if Alexis died, I had nothing left to lose.

Her dad lifted his hand, the signal for his bulldog to back off. "Maybe we should take this somewhere else."

We walked to the chapel. I didn't know why I went there and not the cafeteria. I wasn't a religious person, but it kind of felt like Alexis' fate rested with a higher power. The wooden pews were empty as I walked deeper into the room.

"What happened?"

"I'm Greyson. Alexis' husband."

"I know."

"I met her at sixteen. I was sitting on her jetty..." I chuckled remembering that day. "It was a public beach, the rocks fair game, but it was her spot. I was drawn to those rocks. I thought at first it was the view, but I think now it was her. I felt her first. You know that sixth sense you get? It was like that, but not a brush of awareness. It was a punch. She was holding the handles of the ugliest bike I have ever seen, but she was the most beautiful girl I'd ever seen. I fell in love in that second and I have loved her every second of every day since." I met his gaze then. "My beautiful girl is fighting for her life. Someone shot her. She was so full of life one minute and…" I sat and dropped my head in my hands. "She loves you."

I felt his stare, but I didn't look up. "She even understands why you left, but she has missed you. Has felt the loss of you every day since you left. You need to make that right."

"It's not that easy." He sat down next to me, like the weight of the world was forcing him to his knees. "I wish it were, but it's not that easy. She's going to pull through this and she'll have you to help her find her way back."

"Yeah she will."

He offered his hand, he wasn't the biker now, he was a father. "I'm Finn." He didn't release my hand, waiting for my attention. "I've been able to stay away because she's in good hands."

"You aren't staying." I already knew the answer.

"Only until she's out of surgery. She has a long road ahead of her, throwing me into the mix would be selfish."

"I do understand why you've stayed away, but she's your daughter and you only live life once. You're missing so much."

His eyes turned away and a vulnerability settled over him, something I was sure his club members never saw. "It's been thirty-four years and still I feel the loss of Sade like it was yesterday. She's gone. I met her at sixteen too, the most beautiful girl I'd ever seen. I lost her at twenty. I got four years with the love of my life before she was taken from me and still I love her, miss her, mourn her." His blue gaze shifted and I saw his pain. "I won't be responsible for the death of the only other person I love." And yet as we sat there he was thinking as I was. Was he responsible for Alexis getting shot?

We sat in that chapel for hours. What we needed to say had been said and when the doctor found us to share that Alexis had pulled through the surgery, Finn left. Alexis' father was a ghost of a man living on the outside of his own life and yet it was his own choices that put him there. I wasn't sure I planned on telling her of his visit because the news would only bring her more pain.

The machines were the only noise in the room. The twins were sleeping in the chairs; Paige and Grant were asleep too on a sofa the nurses let us bring in. The girls were taking shifts, getting people food and coffee. I sat at Alexis' bedside holding her hand. She lived through the surgery, but she hadn't woken up. The bullet nicked her stomach and destroyed her spleen, but it missed her spinal cord. There were also neurology problems, at a minimum a concussion. They wouldn't know the extent until she woke. The fact that she lived through the surgery was nothing short of a miracle. She needed to rest; she needed to gather her strength, her body needed to heal. She'd wake up, my girl would wake up, and I would sit here until she did.

I pressed a kiss on her hand. "Take all the time you need, beautiful. I'm not going anywhere."

ALEXIS

I felt like I was swimming in a vat of oil, struggling to keep my head afloat but losing the battle. My body ached and still I struggled. I managed to open my eyes. The light hurt them. Confusion brought panic until I felt Greyson right before he appeared in my line of sight.

"Alexis?"

I couldn't talk and I struggled to see him. He looked broken.

He was gone, but I heard his voice. "She's awake."

It all felt like a dream, unfocused and elusive. A man appeared, the doctor. "You gave us quite the scare. I'm going to take the tube out, okay?"

I nodded. It hurt coming out.

"Don't try to talk just yet."

I motioned for a glass of water. Greyson immediately filled one and helped me drink it.

I tried to stay with Greyson, needed to assure him I was okay, but the darkness took me again. It was two weeks later that I was finally able to stay awake for any duration.

My family stood in my hospital room; bright flower arrangements were on every horizontal surface. Balloons and chocolates filled in the spaces, but it was a mask concealing the gloom with an attempt at cheer. I hurt and I didn't understand what had happened. One minute everything was beautiful and the next it felt like a curtain had been dropped onto my life. I couldn't remember. Maybe I didn't want to remember. The doctor was talking. I had trouble focusing on his words. I heard parts.

"There was extensive internal bleeding when you were brought in. We weren't able to save your spleen. Your stomach was nicked but we were able to stop the bleed and you have a concussion." He took my hand then continued, "The damage was some of the worst I've ever seen and the fact that you've recovered as much as you have in such a short time is nothing short of a medical miracle."

"But?" I whispered.

"Shock to the abdomen can be very destructive. There is so much soft tissue that gets shredded, especially in the case of a gunshot."

"What are you saying?"

"Your uterus suffered trauma. It's possible..." He paused for a moment before he corrected himself. "It's highly unlikely you'll be able to carry a child to term."

I didn't understand him at first, couldn't process those words. When I did, that I would never carry Greyson's children and that our love would never result in the children we both so desperately wanted, I couldn't hold back the sob. I turned my head into my pillow and cried, for the babies I would never have and for the dream of a life that would never be.

Two months after the shooting I was home, but I wasn't healing. There were scars. I hadn't looked, but I felt them. Walking was hard, the muscles of the abdomen played such a part in the body's function and mine were weak from disuse. I needed physical therapy to build up those muscles so I could walk without struggling. But it wasn't just the physical problems; I couldn't find my words. The doctor had said it was natural after a concussion, but being someone whose life was centered on words, not being able to find mine scared me. What if I never could? A depression settled over me. Greyson was trying, but not even he was able to pull me from my funk.

He entered my room carrying my lunch. Instead of the upbeat man who had been trying with no success to get me out of this bed, he looked defeated. "You should have started therapy weeks ago."

I turned from him, couldn't bear to see his disappointment. "I don't want to."

"You need to move, get some fresh air, see your friends, eat something."

"No."

"I know you're hurting, but this isn't the way to handle it."

He was right. It still pissed me off. "What the hell do you know about what I'm feeling? You weren't the one who was almost killed, the one they couldn't make whole again."

He got right into my face. Even depressed, I saw his unfathomable pain. "Every time I close my eyes I see you on the ground, your blood pouring from you, your eyes closed, your breathing so shallow." He turned from me and walked across the room pulling his hand through his hair in frustration. When he glanced back, there were tears in his eyes.

"I thought you were dead and I realized that I didn't want to go on if you weren't here, but you lived, Alexis."

I couldn't stop the tears that rolled down my cheek.

His own eyes were bright. "I need you to come back to me, beautiful. You've been through hell, but I need you to fight, to find your way back."

"I have scars, so many, inside and out."

He closed the distance. "And I wish to fuck I could take them from you, that it was me not you, but..." He touched my chin, "You lived, you're here and that's all that matters."

"I'm having trouble remembering things, words. I can't find my words, Greyson."

His eyes grew bright because he knew what they meant to me. "We'll find them. Together."

GREYSON

It was hard watching Alexis struggling. Something we take for granted, walking, it was a chore for her. It took her four times as long as it should and when she reached her destination she was exhausted. We set up one room as a therapy room. Three times a week a therapist worked with her. She'd eventually get her body back. It was her mind though that was the hardest to witness. Words on her tongue, words she knew but couldn't find, the frustration and fear that she never would. She was working with a cognitive therapist, one who specialized in concussion patients. She was very confident Alexis would get back her words, but it was going to take time.

I was making dinner, Alexis was peeling the potatoes. "I can't give you children."

I stopped slicing the onion and let the pain move through me. We hadn't discussed it. I wanted children with her, but I wanted her more.

"There are other options for us."

"I wanted your children," she said softly.

I didn't want a pregnancy that could put her at risk, but she seemed to need to hear it so I said, "The doctor said it was unlikely, not impossible."

Her voice grew bright. "Do you really believe that?"

I turned to her; her eyes that had been dull had a light in them. It tore me up to see her putting so much stock into something that was likely never going to happen, but she needed to heal and if this helped her then I'd lie.

"Yes."

"Maybe we could do a…" Her nose scrunched up. I'd seen that look more times than I wanted in the last few months. She was struggling to find the word. "The um…in our bedroom. The…"

"Mural?"

"Yes, mural. Maybe we could do one for the baby's room."

My hand tightened on the handle of the knife as rage for the fucker who shot Alexis burned through me.

Silenced followed before she offered softly, "I'll be right back."

She didn't come back, so I went in search of her. She was in our room, sitting on the bed. Her head was down and she was weeping. Instinct was to go to her, but she needed to let it out. If I approached, she'd suck it back up. I fucking wanted to weep seeing her in so much pain and knowing there was nothing I could do to take it away.

2017 ALEXIS

For months and months I lived rehab. I was bone tired, physically and mentally, but every day I pushed myself. I was walking again without getting winded, had even gone for a few walks with Greyson around our neighborhood. The words were harder, it was slow going and I got frustrated a lot and scared, but my therapist was determined to get me all the way back. And Greyson was as good as his word. He was with me every second. I wouldn't have gotten through it without him.

I stood in front of the mirror looking at myself in the black sheath gown. It had been a long road, but physically I was back. I had scars, a reminder of how quickly life can be taken…like my mom's, a reminder to cherish every day. My words weren't quite there yet, but every day I saw improvement. The family was here; we were going out to celebrate life. I felt Greyson and turned to see him leaning against the doorjamb. "You look beautiful."

I walked to him and he smiled at the sight before he closed me in his arms. "I wouldn't be here if you didn't push me."

"You would have found your way."

I touched his face. "It took me a while, but I've realized something."

He touched my lower lip with his thumb. "What?"

"I'm here and whole, for the most part; our dream is different, but we're still living it."

"Yes we are." He pulled his hands through my hair and just stared then he stepped back and took my hand. "Everyone is downstairs."

We hadn't had sex since the incident. It had been far too many months. I ached for him, knew he had to be aching too. "When we get home…" I traced his mouth with my tongue.

He looked heartbreakingly beautiful in that moment. Even his eyes seemed to brighten. "When we get home," he promised then led me downstairs.

There wasn't a dry eye in the room when I walked into it. With tears in his eyes Grant said, "There's our girl."

I couldn't taste him enough, my mouth dragging over his shoulder and up his neck. He was pounding into me, my hips lifting to take him deeper.

"Don't stop, please don't stop."

His mouth found mine, his tongue sweeping and tasting before stroking my own. My fingers dug into his ass when I hit the edge and tumbled off. He pulled from me, seconds before his head was between my legs. He hadn't come yet and he was working me back up again. His tongue teased my clit, licking my opening, slipping into me. Desire coiled in my gut as I started the rise again. He brought me to the brink before he moved back up my body and slammed into me, his cock going so deep I came on a scream. He followed shortly after.

I wrapped my legs around him. I didn't want him to move. "I've missed you."

He brushed my hair from my face. "I was always here."

"I'm sorry."

His jaw went tight. "You have nothing to apologize for."

"I retreated."

"You had a reason." He touched my cheek but I couldn't read him. "What are you thinking?"

"Just so fucking grateful you're here."

"Thank you for never leaving my side."

"I'll never leave your side." He sealed that vow with a kiss.

GREYSON

I stood in Captain Samuel's office, my focus out the window at the birds fighting over a piece of pretzel. Alexis was with the twins. She wasn't ready to hear the details of her attack. As it happens, neither was I. Samuel's words were circling around in my head, words that when I let them penetrate were going to change everything.

"Her name is Millie Ward. She had a wall in her apartment, pictures of you. She said she was your biggest fan. Clearly she needs help. Her attorney is arguing not guilty by reason of mental defect. The DA has requested a competency hearing and will push for institutionalization over imprisonment if needed. Bottom line, Millie Ward will be locked up for a very long time."

My hands curled into fists in my pockets. Sick or not, that woman almost killed my wife. And as horrifying as that thought was, there was another that damn near gutted me. "And you're sure she isn't the same woman from San Francisco?"

"No. Candace Miller is living in a halfway house. Her doctors have found the right meds for her and she's living a productive life. I don't need to tell you. Celebrities are often targets for disturbed people, a way for them to live vicariously. Most know where the line is, some don't."

Standing in that office, the numbness started, creeping over me like a cancer. It hadn't been a random act of violence like I had thought, or linked to her father. Alexis had been targeted, singled out and all because of me.

I left the police station, but instead of going for Alexis, I went home, to our bedroom and stood looking at her painting. It was my favorite because it was Alexis. Not just the girl I saw that first day, but the one formed by the story of us, every road, every path, every choice, every high and every low. She was vulnerable and strong, sweet and sassy. She made me laugh, she made me burn; she could make me angry and at times she brought tears.

I walked to my studio and it was there, surrounded by what I thought was the dream, but was really what led me to the dream that it hit hard and fast. My girl had been shot, she almost died; she'd lost her words, her confidence and her humor because of me. The rage came then. One easel went flying to splinter against the wall. Some random nut almost took her life. Seeing her lying in her own blood, a canvas followed the easel. It wasn't just one disturbed woman. How many others were out there? When would the next one show up? And would Alexis live through it? That thought broke something inside me. I trashed my studio, roaring my anguish with tears of rage streaming down my face. I had spent my life trying to take the pain from her eyes and because of me she not only had that pain, but now she had scars inside and out. I dropped to my knees, my chest heaved in and out. I understood then, in that moment, I understood why her father had left. What he was feeling because I was feeling it too. I had to let her go and just the thought left me dead inside.

It had been a week since learning the part I played in Alexis' shooting, a week to get things in order. I stepped from my studio; Alexis was playing with Buggers. I felt the hit we'd felt so long ago. I loved her; I would always love her. I reached her in two strides, grabbing her to me, my mouth closing over hers as I tore at her clothes, needing to touch her, memorize her, savor her. Surprise turned to hunger as she kissed me back. We didn't get to the bedroom, I dropped her on the stairs, lifted her hips and slammed into her and then I stilled, committing the moment to memory, how she felt, how she smelled, how she looked with love and longing in her eyes. I pulled my hands through her hair. I'd always loved her hair, the silky strands that were a palette of colors. Her eyes, so expressive and always with that hint of sadness, sadness I was now responsible for, her lips, the curve of her cheek, the beautiful line of her throat.

She touched my face as concern clouded her expression. "Are you okay?"

"I love you. I have from the first moment I saw you."

She smiled as she remembered too. "Despite my unfortunate means of transportation."

"I even love that fucking bike."

"What's going on?"

I moved my hips, slowly, drawing out the pleasure. Concern turned to passion. She was my only focus. I brought her to that peak, and then I pushed her over it and even as her body hummed with pleasure I started all over again. I loved her all night; I had to get in a lifetime's worth.

ALEXIS

Something was going on with Greyson. There was a shadow in his eyes since he visited the detective. Whatever he learned he didn't like. I had hoped he would have talked to me, but he was being unusually quiet. Last night he had loved me like he had a time limit, a desperation about him that both scared and worried me. We were supposed to be heading to Paige's, some downtime with our family, but Greyson and I needed to talk.

"What's going on with you?" He was in the kitchen when I hunted him down. "And don't say nothing because even though I can't read you as well as you read me, I know something is wrong."

He turned and leaned back against the counter. The pain in his eyes was palpable. I stepped closer, he said, "The woman who shot you…"

I stopped moving. Instinct was to tune out. I didn't want to be reminded of that night.

"She was a fan."

It took me a minute to follow his logic. "Not a fan, a disturbed woman."

Pain switched to anger in a blink. "Whatever the fuck the semantics, she shot you because of me."

"Is that what this is about? You feel responsible for some random woman shooting me?"

"I am responsible."

"How the hell are you responsible? Did you give her the gun?"

"What the fuck, Alexis?"

"Unless you handed her the gun and told her to shoot me, how the hell are you in any way involved?"

"Why are you being intentionally obtuse?" he growled.

"I'm being obtuse? You're the one taking responsibility for something you had nothing to do with."

He moved into my face. I'd never seen him like this. We rarely fought and when we did it was over in minutes. Not now, he was livid, his anger was eating him alive. "If it weren't for me, you wouldn't have been shot. Don't you get that?"

The first thread of fear moved through me.

"I don't."

He pulled his hand through his hair in frustration and put the distance of the room between us. "She isn't the first one. She won't be the last."

That fear grew stronger. "What are you saying?"

"Being with me puts you in danger."

"So what's the alternative?"

He looked at me and though he said nothing, I read him loud and clear. That fear made me weak in the knees.

I could hardly get the words out; they were words I never ever thought would apply to us. "You're leaving me?"

His shoulders tensed and he dropped his head. "You almost died."

"I lived."

There were tears in his eyes when he lifted his gaze. "Next time you might not be so lucky."

"What next time?"

It was like a switch, fury rolled over his face. "Exactly. There won't be one because I'm removing myself from the equation."

My own temper stirred. "Removing yourself from the equation? It's that simple for you, to just walk out."

"Simple!" He grabbed my hand and pressed it to his chest where his heart was beating hard and fast. "Every fucking beat is for you, but I will not sit in another hospital room watching as machines breathe for you."

I tried to reason with him. "Listen to me. Leaving isn't the answer. Life without you isn't a life. We can figure this out without you being so rash."

"Rash? Every time I close my eyes I see you lying in a pool of your own blood. To know I was in any fucking way responsible for that… it's killing me."

"It was horrific, but it should bring us closer not pull us apart."

"Easy for you to say. It wasn't because of you it happened. Reverse it, Alexis; I was the one shot by someone targeting you. Tell me how you'd handle it."

I wanted to say I wouldn't fucking leave, but I got it. Like my father, he was determined to protect me even if that meant hurting me.

"My dad did this. You know how I struggled, still struggle, with his choice. You're making me live that again, but this is far worse because you are my life. Every moment since I was sixteen you have been part of me and now you're removing yourself from the equation, but that equation is our life."

"Yes."

"No! I won't let you."

He was resigned. Here was the fucking stubbornness his mother had warned about. I understood now why she wanted to rip out all of her hair. Fucking hell, but this was madness.

"Cheshire cat really did have it right," I muttered. Ride out the storm. I shook my head, how the fuck long would this storm last?

"You are prepared to walk away from our life."

"To keep you safe, yes."

"And forcing me to live half a life, to face the years ahead alone knowing the man I love, and who loves me, is out there cowering because of what might happen."

Anger sparked in those eyes. "Guarantee me no one will take a shot at you, tell me there won't be another woman who breaks into my hotel room, or sends me disturbing letters or decides my wife is in the way and shoots her. You know my past history. Fuck, even Stephanie bordered on stalker. Tell me it all ends."

"You know I can't."

"I can't accept even a half percent chance that someone will hurt you because of me."

"So your fear for me outweighs your love. Just like my dad."

All the anger drained from him and a broken man stood before me. "Easy for you to say, but you weren't the one who was almost left behind. A lifetime of knowing the one person I want most in the world was dead because of me. I understand what your father did. It wasn't cowardice. It was strength. And it isn't fear that outweighs love; it's the opposite. Loving someone means you are ready to make the hard decisions, willing to put your own happiness aside for theirs. I love you; you know how much I do. You're the best part of me and it is because you are that I'm letting you go."

"And my happiness?"

"Whatever lies ahead for you, you'll be alive to live it."

"Bullshit."

Startled, he reared back a bit.

"You want to walk, fucking walk, but know this. YOU ARE MAKING A MISTAKE! You promised you'd never leave my side. You promised until death do us part. I'm not dead! Every fucking breath... another lie."

"Alexis."

"No. You've already made up your mind. You've already made a decision that will irrevocably change my life and you didn't even give me a say in the matter. I thought we were partners, we fucking decided together what sofa to purchase, what plates and what color to paint our fucking bathroom, but for the biggest decision, the one that ends the life that I know, that takes away the fucking dream, you made that call all on your own." I wiped at my eyes and headed to the stairs. "I'm going to Paige's. Maybe you should take some time, visit your Grandfather and think about what you're doing." I looked back at him. "Really think about it because if you go through with this, one day you will realize you've made the biggest fucking mistake of your life, but by then I might not feel inclined to take you back. And that will be my decision."

"No. He loves you. The man is crazy out of his head in love with you." Paige was emphatic and she was right, but did he love me enough.

"The woman that shot me, there's a link to him and he's afraid for me."

Grant was pacing the living room.

Restless energy and worry had me on the edge of the sofa. I felt an ulcer forming. "He wouldn't really leave me right? I mean he knows how much it hurt dealing with the loss of my father. He wouldn't do that, right? He wouldn't leave me?"

"No! Of course not." Paige looked horrified at the suggestion. "Where is he now?"

"He's leaving for Ireland in a few days. I encouraged him to go, to recharge, clear his head and think things through." I dropped back against the sofa. "But you didn't see him, the look in his eyes. And what kills me is if the roles were reversed, my first instinct would be to push him away. I don't know that time would change that."

"He's upset. He reacted to horrible news; he didn't give himself time to process. That is human nature, but what you two have is special and to put it aside because of a possible 'what if' is bullshit; he will figure that out. He'll cool off and think logically and then he'll beg your forgiveness for being an idiot. That's what Grant would do. Right, Grant?"

Grant had stopped pacing, but his expression increased my fear not lessened it.

"Grant?"

Paige's head whipped around to her husband. "Grant? What?"

"Had it been you, the girls, Alexis, if I was in Greyson's shoes…" Sad eyes turned to me. "I can't say I wouldn't have done the same."

I jumped from the sofa. "I need to go home." My eyes found Paige's, "I have to go home before he leaves."

The flight was the longest six hours of my life. A car was waiting for me when I arrived at JFK. It took almost an hour to get to the apartment. I hurried inside. I was shaking in the elevator, shaking so badly it took me four tries to punch in our code.

I pushed open the door calling, "Greyson!"

It was eerily quiet in the apartment. I hurried to his studio and yanked open the door. It was empty, every canvas, every tube of paint, the sketches, the brushes, even the sculpture that I hadn't been allow to see. It was all gone. There was nothing left of him, not even his scent lingered. I ran upstairs, into our room. His closet was empty, his clothes were gone, his toiletries. My eyes moved to the bed and my painting. It was gone. That was when it hit me, when the pain was too much and I dropped to my knees. The sob tore from my throat; I stared at the mural that had one time brought so much joy and now it mocked me. He left me. He walked out of my life. Pain exploded in my chest, far worse than when I was shot. It was then I saw the note on the bedside table.

I understand now why your father did what he did. And I know what my leaving is going to do to you. I've spent every day since that day on the beach trying to remove the sadness in your eyes and now I'm responsible for it, but I almost lost you. Knowing it was because of me you almost died, that you lost your words, that you struggled to find yourself breaks me. The fear that it could happen again, that another Mille is out there just waiting. I love you, I will always love you, but I have to let you go. I didn't keep my promise and I broke my vows, but believe that every breath, Alexis, every fucking breath I breathe is for you.

I curled up his note, folded into myself, and cried until I was as empty as our home.

GREYSON

A car pulled up in front of our apartment building and Alexis climbed out. She'd only just left for Paige's and she was back. I knew she'd be

287

back because my girl could read my mind too. I needed to see her one last time. The hope on her face that was clear even from my distance had my hands curling into fists in the pockets of my hoodie. Everything in me wanted to cross the street, pull her close and never let her go. Then I saw her lying in a pool of her own blood. I'd never get that image out of my head. Or the months and months that she struggled to find herself again. She ran inside. My chest ached, like someone was driving stakes into it, but then it should hurt like hell when a dream dies. I waited, knew what she was seeing, knew how it was going to break her. I was breaking right along with her.

Night had settled when I pulled my hoodie lower over my head and walked away from the dream of life that had been all too fleeting. I knew the pain I was causing, knew I had done the one thing I never wanted to do. Hurt her, but she'd be alive to feel the pain.

ALEXIS

He left. Two days I'd been home in an apartment that had no traces of him and I still didn't believe he'd walked out on us. Heartache turned to anger, I was so fucking angry and he wasn't close so I went to someone who was.

I stood outside Lucifer's Warriors clubhouse. Anger fueled me and still there was fear because the place definitely had a scary vibe.

"Hey, babe, you looking to party?" one of the biker's called. Shaved head, muscled, a tattoo climbing up his neck. He was wearing a leather vest, his name over his heart. Gunner.

He walked toward me not at all hiding his thorough inspection. A smile spread over his face when he stopped just in front of me. "I'm here to play, babe." He looked at my breasts. "I'd love to play."

"I want to see Finn."

He cocked his hip. "You're feisty and a sweet piece of ass, but Finn is very picky."

"Yeah, well tell Finn his daughter is here."

His expression changed instantly. The gate opened and he yanked me through it, dragging me across the compound to the clubhouse door.

I was scared; terrified was a better word. Maybe this hadn't been such a good idea. "Let me go."

He ignored me, stopping within inches of the door.

"Shit," he rubbed a hand over his shaved head. "He'll cut my dick off if I bring you through there."

Some of the fear faded seeing his uncertainty. And his comment, talk about graphic. "Why would he remove your…?" I gestured rather than said.

His eyes danced with mischief. "The club whores are working the room."

I didn't know what that meant, but I had an idea.

"There's no other way in and you can't stay outside." His head lowered; penetrating blue eyes with specks of brown stared through me. "Keep your head down," he ordered.

On that warning, he dragged me into the club. I didn't keep my head down, too curious, and boy did I get an eyeful. A woman was kneeling in front of a sofa where three bikers sat, their legs spread and cocks out. She was servicing all three of them right down the line. It reminded me of when I was a kid, hell even now, filling up my cup with each flavor of soda from the soda fountain. It always ended up tasting like Sprite. Watching her, yeah, I didn't think I'd be doing that anymore. In another corner, a woman was on the lap of another biker. No question they were having sex, but it was the man behind her, fucking her ass at the same time that had my eyes dropping. Holy shit, it was like a den of sin.

"Told you to keep your head down," Gunner reprimanded.

"I can't unsee that," I muttered.

We reached an office. Nothing fancy, a desk covered in papers, a chair, filing cabinets against one wall and the Lucifer's Warriors image painted on the wall behind the desk.

"I'll get Finn," Gunner said then added, "Don't leave this room."

Yeah, because that was my first thought, escape the room so I could be mistaken for one of those women. I needed a shower. On second thought, did they autoclave people? "I won't."

I stared at the door, trying not to see the images in the other room. How did one become a club whore and why would you want to be?

A few minutes later, the door slammed open on my dad. His expression was not one of loving father or even mildly happy to see me. He was pissed and still my heart skipped a beat because I had imagined this moment so many times over the years. I had never once imagined his opening words being what they were though. "Are you fucking out of your mind?"

It was becoming clearer that I might in fact be out of my mind.

His anger shifted as he pivoted and slammed Gunner up against the wall by his throat. "You fucking brought her inside?"

"Better than outside."

Finn released Gunner, so clearly that meant something. Angry eyes turned on me. "You can't be here."

Fascination, even love, all took a backseat to temper. "I am well aware of your pathological need to keep me as far from you as possible."

Dad's eyes widened; Gunner chuckled. Dad glared, he shut up. A softness entered his expression when he saw the locket.

"I just wanted to inform you that my husband has walked out on me."

I barely heard him, but a chill moved down my spine in warning. "He what?"

"Yes, he walked out on me and did so following your lead."

"What the fuck does that mean?"

"I was shot."

His expression changed again. Pain burned in his eyes. "I know. I was at the hospital."

That show of fatherly concern deflated some of my anger, even my voice softened. "You were? Never mind." I twisted my fingers together and tallied on. "Greyson has gotten it into his thick and very stubborn head that the shooting was his fault." I started to pace as the anger rolled through me again. "He didn't know her, never met her, and yet it was his fault that she shot me. It's the most ridiculous logic I've ever heard and yet you applied the same fucking logic when you left."

Finn Levy would make an excellent poker player.

"Like you, he made the decision for me, so let me share with you my choice had I been given one. I would have preferred a life with you. I would have chosen the danger, and the possibility of death, to have a chance to know the man in this fucking picture." I slammed the picture of us on his desk. "I have looked at this every day. My whole life wondering what you were like, where you were, why you left me. You walked out for my best interests, but my best interests would have been served better by having my dad in my life. By learning who I was and where I came from. You took that away, you forced me to find my way in the world on my own rather than being the guiding light you should have been. And I am here to tell you that you were fucking wrong to do that. I would have chosen you regardless of how many years I would have had with you."

I wiped at my tears. My hand shaking as I retrieved the picture. "And now my husband has done the same. He's left me alone, to find my way without him all because of some stupid, bullshit caveman mentality of protecting his woman. But a life without love isn't a life worth protecting." My eyes met his. "I'm so fucking tired of the men in my life killing me with their good intentions. I'm stronger than either of you give me credit for. So I'll tell you what I should have told him. Fuck you for leaving me and fuck you for staying away."

I walked out. I wasn't alone, knew Gunner was behind me. He reached for the door of the cab, held it for me. Tears were running down my face when I glanced at him. "You're so much like him." He held out his hand. "It was nice to fucking meet you."

He squeezed my hand then let it go. The door of the cab closed as soon as I climbed in. I didn't look back.

PART
THREE

We come to love not by finding the perfect person, but by learning to see an imperfect person perfectly.

–Sam Keen

21

ALEXIS PRESENT DAY

It felt good; the shock up my arm as my fist made contact with the bag. My muscles felt the burn, my heart pounded hard and strong in my chest. My iPod blared "Now That It's Over" by Everclear. I hit the bag again, felt the connection, and grinned. My feet knew the dance, step in, step out. My sports bra was drenched as sweat dripped down my back.

After an hour of beating the bag my trainer helped me with my gloves. He handed me a canteen; I chugged the water in one long swallow.

"See you tomorrow, Alexis?"

I'd been working with Jensen for a few months. He gave me a way to channel the hurt, because I did hurt, a pain I had gotten used to feeling.

"Yes, same time, if that works."

"You bet. Nice workout today."

I didn't go right home. I walked to my jetty and took my favorite seat on the rocks. I came here every day. In the beginning, I was waiting for him. Fear made him leave, but I believed love would bring him back. I was wrong. Like my father, he was staying away for me. His defection nearly killed me because for twenty-two years we had been an us and now I was back to being just me. I struggled with wanting to hunt him down, but he left. He had to be the one to come back.

Four months I stayed in the apartment with Buggers and buried myself in work. I didn't talk to my friends or family. I worked and I cried. I talked to his ghost, yelled at times. I grieved and I mourned and I struggled to understand how he could have walked away from us. Even knowing his intentions, what we had was rare and beautiful and something you fought for not walked away from.

Anger followed despair, a raging anger. I hated him for leaving me, for not holding on with both hands. I was so angry I almost painted over our bedroom wall. But as I stood there, with brush in hand, I couldn't do it. There were so many memories I couldn't bare to erase.

During that time I rescued Benny and Joon, two German shepherd puppies. Watching as Buggers and the puppies bonded was very therapeutic. As the four of us became a family, my heart started to mend.

Six months after he left me, I moved back to Mendocino. The twins moved with me because family stuck together. I couldn't bring myself to sell the apartment. I hadn't known until I looked into it that he had bought our home under my name only, but I couldn't let go of that last piece of him largely due to the mural he had painted. It was a part of our story, so though it made no sense to have the apartment sitting empty I would never sell it.

I remembered coming home and thought how painful it was going to be because this was where it had all started for us, but I found comfort in those memories instead of pain.

My house, the one Callum had rented, had sold not long after I returned, but that was just as well because that was where I had seen my life when it included Greyson. He was gone, that life was no longer. Instead, I purchased a small bungalow on the beach. Dylan and Dominic lived next door.

The one-year anniversary of him leaving was approaching and here I was. Through it all I had my family. They saved me; when my feet were kicked out from under me, they were there to hold me until I was able to stand on my own two feet again. And I was standing. I was a little wobbly and I still fell sometimes, but I was learning to move on and I was trying to find happy. My hope was one day it wouldn't be so hard.

I took another minute to appreciate the view that never grew old before I headed back up the beach. I needed to feed my babies. Halfway up the beach I heard, "Well, if it isn't Alexis."

The breeze kept me from smelling the warning. Debbie stood behind me. We were middle-aged women and still she acted like a queen bee. She had no minions or kingdom. It was very possible she was overcompensating because as I had predicted, high school really was as good as it got for her. And still she gave me shit whenever she saw me.

"Debbie."

"No Greyson?"

I had no intention of letting Debbie pick at the scab. I walked around her.

"I'm not surprised you couldn't hold onto him."

My feet stopped and my hands fisted. Maybe she knew what happened, maybe she didn't, but I was done with her bullshit.

Turning to her, she still played regal like she was born to it. "What the fuck is your problem? You've had a hard-on for me since we were kids."

"I just don't understand why everyone gives such a shit about you. What's so fucking special about you?"

"Nothing, Debbie. There's nothing special about me but when someone is in my company they don't leave it feeling like shit because I don't bring them down to make myself feel better. That is all you do. Your insecurity and jealousy eat you alive and you are an even bigger fool than I thought if you think for one second people don't see that."

The screenplay for the movie I'd been working on before the accident had been given to another writer because I couldn't meet the deadlines. I couldn't blame them; time was money. Adele recently worked a deal for me on another movie project that she thought was a good fit and she was right. It was a heartbreaking story; I certainly had a pool of pain to draw from. The phone pulled me from the scene.

"Hello."

"Mrs. Ratcliffe?"

I took that hit to my heart in stride. "Yes."

"I'm Marge Jones of State Street Reality. We have a new family for the house on Green Street, but during the inspection we discovered that the furnace has a crack so I wanted to get the okay to replace it. Normally, I work through Mr. Ratcliffe, but I'm having trouble getting in touch with him."

I went numb at the memory. Green Street was where the foster monsters had lived.

"What's the address of the house?"

"24 Green Street."

It was a good thing I was sitting down because my legs went weak. Greyson was the one who bought the foster monsters' house out from under them and forced them to move away.

"Mrs. Ratcliffe?"

"Yes, I'm sorry. This is the first I'm hearing about the house on Green Street. Could you explain to me what arrangements Mr. Ratcliffe has made for that house?"

"Oh, sure. For about ten years the house has been available for families struggling to make ends meet. It's offered to any family who meets the criteria for a year free of charge, though they are responsible for the utilities, maintaining the yard, that sort of thing. Mr. Ratcliffe isn't offering a free ride, he doesn't want to attract sponges, but he wants a place for families to feel they have a home base, to give them that security until they can get themselves back on their feet. His ultimate goal is to help keep families together, to prevent children from being taken from their parents just because their parents have stumbled onto hard times. It's very important to him and I've only ever worked with him directly, but like I said, I can't seem to get in touch with him. We have a family waiting to move in."

I didn't know at what point the tears started. They rolled down my cheeks because I knew it was Greyson's way of preventing another little kid from having foster parents like I had.

I wiped at my eyes. "Please, yes, replace the furnace. Would it be possible to tour the house before the new people move in?"

"Sure. Mr. Ratcliffe bought the property in your maiden name, so it's technically your property."

I swallowed the sob. "Could I stop by today?"

"I can meet you whenever you'd like."

"Is ten minutes too soon?"

"I'll meet you there."

I arrived before Marge and looked at the house that had been my home for sixteen years. I hadn't been down this street since the Cantenellis moved. Greyson had been busy. The place when I lived here was falling apart and now it was the picture of charm. Gray siding had been added, black shutters and a stone facade to match the stone of the chimney. There was a new flagstone front walk and gardens everywhere.

The memory of Greyson walking up the old path brought a smile, the memory of him walking away from me after The Cure concert, climbing onto his bike and riding off into the sunset brought pain.

The old tree in the front was still thriving, and now it boasted a tree house and a tire swing. It was the perfect place for a family. He had done this because of me, because he wanted to make a difference, and he never told me. Even now, with all we'd been through, he was still that boy on the jetty, the one I loved to distraction.

Marge arrived and hurried up the path. She offered her hand. "Mrs. Ratcliffe, Marge. It's nice to meet you in person."

"Likewise. Thanks for coming so quickly."

"Certainly." She looked around the yard. "It's lovely, isn't it?"

"Yes."

"Come, I'll show you inside."

The inside had been completely redone as well, hardwood floors, new bathrooms, a gourmet kitchen, fresh paint and moldings. Greyson's artwork was scattered throughout the rooms. He had made a home here, a cozy and welcoming home.

Marge joined me. "He told me that there was once a girl who lived here and he wished that he could have given to her then what he has been able to give to these families now."

"He did, just in a different way," I whispered. My eyes found Marge's. "I was that girl."

She smiled and reached for my hand. "I know."

22

GREYSON

My phone buzzed, some upbeat tune that Maggie had programmed. It made me want to commit murder. I hurled the thing across the room. That didn't help because it was still chiming, but now it sounded like a deranged android. I rolled over, looked up at the ceiling. I'd counted the gold leaf work. Knew which ones were in need of a touchup, which ones were slightly larger than the others. Daylight was trying to penetrate the thick drapes covering the windows, a few golden rays reflected off the old wood floors.

I missed her, missed…what a fucking joke. I couldn't function. I hadn't painted a fucking thing since I walked out. I'd called her my muse during that interview from so long ago and how true those words were. I had nothing. I was fucking empty, no inspiration and no desire to find any. The days passed and I waited. For what? I didn't know. Maybe the sky would fall and put me out of my misery or I'd fall down a rabbit hole. I wasn't living. I was existing and I'd done it to myself. What brought the self-loathing was I'd forced this fucking existence on Alexis too.

The number of times I almost gave in, prepared to get on my knees and beg her to take me back, yeah that was practically every fucking day. Then I'd see her that night. The look on her face as the bullet tore through her, the blood. I always found the strength to continue on in this pathetic excuse of a life because my girl *had* a life. I didn't have to mourn her, weeping at another grave of an angel resting over a stone heart.

I climbed from bed and retrieved my phone then slammed it into the wall until it shattered. That was my eighth phone in as many months. Fuck it. I headed to the shower; stripped on my way, and set the temperature to scalding because it was the only time I felt anything. I rested my hand against the wall, my head lowered as my nerve endings screamed at the blistering heat. Thoughts of Alexis kept me sane, remembering her wiggling her ass when she cleaned the dishes. She sang when she cleaned, even knowing how she sounded she belted those songs out like she was Celine Dion. And after an afternoon of cleaning, getting her wet and naked, moving my hands over her beautiful body. Fucking her in the shower, out of the shower, against the wall. I slid my hand down my body to my cock, stroked it. Her mouth, her taste and the way she moaned in the back of her throat. I tugged harder, hitting my balls on the up stroke. Watching her ride my cock, the way she drew her lower lip between her teeth, how she whispered she loved me. I slammed my hand against the wall when I came, but instead of finding release I only felt emptier.

I dressed and headed downstairs for a cup of coffee and then research. I was looking into the Ratcliffe history. I couldn't paint a damn thing, so I decided to learn more about those who came before me. Maggie was behind the stove when I entered. I saw the look; they each had their own version of it, a cross between pity and irritation. They didn't agree with me, none of them. They thought I was a fool for walking away. I was a fool for walking away, but I was right to.

"Good morning. How are you this fine morning?" Maggie was particularly cheerful.

"I broke another phone."

She shook her head. "It's becoming a problem."

"They should make them stronger."

"I doubt very much they can make them strong enough to withstand repeated slams into a stone wall."

I shrugged.

"You should stop by the portrait gallery. I just had all the paintings cleaned. It's lovely."

I swear she had a twinkle in her eyes, far too bright for the conversation. "What's going on with you? Why are you so cheerful?"

She feigned annoyance. "I'm like this every morning."

That wasn't true. Pouring my coffee, I leaned against the counter and watched her. She was practically dancing in place. Grandfather entered, saw me and beamed.

"Greyson, good morning."

"All right. What the hell is going on?"

It was uncanny how his expression mirrored Maggie's, that same feigned annoyance. "Were you two abducted and replaced with cyborgs?"

He laughed, like a belly laugh. It wasn't that funny.

"That's funny."

It really wasn't. I had research to do.

I felt their eyes on me when I walked out and know I heard laughter following shortly after. What the fuck?

I'd check out the gallery later. I headed to the library. For the last few months I'd been researching my family. If I was being honest, it wasn't my family that motivated me but the link to Alexis. She'd been working on our family's book, and even with me walking out, I knew she'd finish what she started.

I settled at the desk, took another gulp of coffee before I got to it. It was fascinating reading the thoughts of my ancestors that had lived so long ago. I was focusing my research on Caitlin and Rafer Ratcliffe because it was during their time that the stone disappeared. They were hurting, financially. Theirs was one of the very few love matches in our history, but one that didn't put money in the coffers. Alexis' theory about the fire and hiding the assets seemed spot on. So where the hell did they hide it?

"Simone Ratcliffe almost died of poison. Targeted by an enemy of her husband's." Grandfather stood just inside the library. "Elizabeth Ratcliffe was stabbed in the street, payback for a debt unpaid by her husband. My own sweet Colleen was mistaken for me once driving in my car. She was run off the road. I'll never forget how she looked, the memory is burned on my brain."

"You never told me that. Why would someone come at you?"

"I don't know. Jealousy or just disturbed, but it was a dark time in my life. I too, believing I was doing what was best, left her."

"You left Grandmother?"

"For six months, two days and twelve hours."

"Where did you go?"

"One of the many outbuildings on the property."

"I can't imagine Grandmother was very happy about that."

"She wasn't. She was livid. It took me nearly as long to get back into her good graces. My intentions were in the right place, but you know what they say about the best of intentions."

"You think I was wrong to leave."

"I know you were wrong to leave. I want to show you something."

It was a maze of passages, cold and damp. The dungeons used to be down here, but my great grandfather removed the cells. It was while we moved in the deepest recesses of the castle that it dawned why we were down here.

"You found it?"

He said nothing, but I felt his excitement.

We reached a section of the basement, like all the other sections, but this one had a hole in the wall, a manmade and rather hastily done hole. My blood was zipping through my veins. "How did you know?"

"The room specs didn't match the blueprints. Alexis was right. The fire had been set so Caitlin and Rafer could hide assets, partly to ease their burden, but partly to preserve a piece of our history."

"Why didn't you show me sooner?"

"You weren't ready to listen then. I think you are now. Come see."

We walked through the wall, work lamps were set up but it was the stash that held my complete attention.

"Holy shit."

"My exact words," Grandfather teased.

There were old weapons and armor, silver in the form of candlesticks and trays, chests opened revealing clothes and books and jewels. Big pieces covered in cloth, antique furniture. Alexis had been right.

"This is incredible."

"It really is. We've started an inventory and from what we've researched so far, millions worth of loot."

"Have you found the diamond?"

Grandfather's shoulders slumped a bit. "Not yet."

It wasn't monetary for him, like Alexis, it was the story.

"If it's here, we'll find it."

"That wasn't my point in showing you this. Look around, Greyson." He walked to a dust-covered chair that was massive with a thick ornate wood frame. "These items were set aside to protect them and yet look at them. Dusty, tarnished, forgotten. What was the point? No one got to enjoy them. Stories weren't shared about them. They were hidden away and forgotten." He turned to me and it was one of a very few times I saw not just anger, but disappointment in his expression, disappointment in me. "You did this to Alexis. You hid her away to protect her. She doesn't belong in this room. There's one more thing I need you to see."

We walked to the gallery and as soon as we stepped inside I understood Maggie's encouragement to visit. My heart twisted in my chest. She was so fucking beautiful. Alexis' painting hung next to mine.

"This is where Alexis belongs, at your side. And I know you know that."

"You didn't see her," my throat closed with emotion.

His voice softened. "I didn't and you'll never get that image from your mind, but she's alive. She lived. I got ten more years with Colleen before cancer killed her. Ten years and I lost six months of those because I thought I was doing what was best for her. But it wasn't her I was protecting. I was protecting myself, from the pain, from the loss, from being the one left behind. You can't know the future. You could walk outside and get trampled by wild horses, or get hit by a bus, or you could die of cancer or a heart attack. Nothing is certain in life but birth and death, and believe it or not, that is part of what makes the journey so sweet."

I hated hearing the words that had been gnawing in my gut, but he was right. If I was being completely honest with myself, I left her to protect myself. *She* was right; I was a coward. I walked away from the best fucking thing in my life and I wanted her back so damn much. I almost chuckled because Mom had been right too. I was a stubborn ass, but I finally saw the light. I had been wrong, so fucking wrong to leave. "It's been eight months."

"You'll have some groveling to do."

I'd grovel, beg, and plead, whatever I had to. Looking around at the gallery Alexis loved an idea came to me. "Do you think the diamond is down there?"

"If it is anywhere in the castle, I think it would be there."

"I'll help you go through the stuff," I offered.

"And not return to Alexis?"

"Like you said. I've got some groveling to do. I need to come prepared."

He smiled in approval. "You want to give her the diamond."

"If we can't find it I'll have one made."

"Good thinking."

I glanced around the room. "She can't have children."

He palmed my cheek, something he hadn't done since I was little. "Family is more than blood. Your lovely Alexis must have taught you that. Times are changing and the Ratcliffes will change right along with them. Our name will continue on."

I did something I hadn't done since I was a kid; I hugged him. "Thank you."

His voice broke a little when he said, "Let's go find that diamond."

We didn't find the diamond. We'd searched every chest, every drawer. I'd just gotten off the phone with a jeweler to discuss recreating it; the look would be different but not the intent. I walked to the French doors in the study and looked out. I was going home to Alexis. I hoped like hell she took me back.

It was while I stood thinking about the diamond and Alexis that I noticed the mist in the distance. It looked green. What kind of odd anomaly would cause that? Before my eyes it took shape into two figures much like in my painting. I rubbed my eyes and looked again but it was gone. I then heard the distinct sound of laughter coming from behind me. Turning for the door, I expected to see the housemaids with their heads together, but the room was empty. A chill passed through me, goosebumps rose on my arms. Was it possible I had inhaled too many paint fumes over the years?

A shadow moved just outside the door. My heart slammed into my ribs. Maybe the rumors about ghosts weren't rumors. Was it my mom or dad? I almost called out to them when William entered. I exhaled then pulled a hand through my hair. Holy shit I was losing my fucking mind.

"There's a gentleman outside for you."

For me? Who the hell would be here for me?

"Did he give his name?"

"No." William turned his nose up in distaste. "He simply informed me to get you."

I suspected whoever it was hadn't been that nice about it. "Did he now. Let's not keep him waiting."

We reached the door. There was no one there. William answered my question. "He's outside."

Yanking open the door, the words on my tongue died. Leaning against a black car, wearing his leather cut and looking just the same as he had the last time I saw him was Finn Levy.

"I think you took a serious wrong turn somewhere."

"Is there somewhere we can talk?"

I'd been expecting the visit. I nearly got his daughter killed. I had thought it would have been back in New York, in a dirty room with brass knuckles not half way across the world. His dime. I glanced at my watch, nine in the morning. Not too early for a drink. "Yeah, there's a pub in the village."

I studied the man across the table from me and saw Alexis in his features, but then with how much I was missing her I'd see her features in the fucking bartender. The man had a presence and not just me sensed it. People gave him a wide berth. If I had an ounce of sense, I'd be uneasy but I just didn't feel much of anything these days.

We finished a pint and started on the second before he got to the reason he flew across the Atlantic to see me.

"I had thought you'd come to your senses."

Not how I saw this going. "Excuse me?"

"You left my daughter."

I didn't mean to laugh, but fucking talk about the pot and the kettle. "That's funny coming from you."

He barely moved, just the slightest shifting forward and yet he had my attention. His blue eyes were dark and yet looking into them I felt a chill. The photo Alexis had, Finn was hardened but there was light in him. Looking at him now, he was dark and empty.

"That gnawing hole in your gut. That will only get worse. Time won't heal it, you won't move on. Slowly, every day, you'll lose another part of yourself. You'll get to the point that you'll do anything to feel." His eyes drilled into me. "Absolutely anything to feel something, and before you know it you won't recognize the man looking back at you in the mirror."

I'd already come to that conclusion, but I said nothing. I listened because the man seemed ready to purge.

His focus shifted outside. "I lost Sade and fear for Alexis had me pushing her out of my life." He focus shifted back to me, but he looked fucking tired—tired of hurting, tired of living. "I was wrong to do that."

Anger stirred, for him or myself I didn't know because I knew I'd been wrong to walk away from Alexis. And still I argued because he didn't have the image of her that night in his head, the one that haunted me, that woke me up in the middle of the night soaking the sheets from horror and devastation and a bone deep fear that it could have ended so very differently...tragically different. "Were you? You didn't see Alexis that night, the look on her face, the blood. She was shot because of me, because some unstable woman had a fixation on me. She wasn't the first, she's not likely to be the last."

"And you're afraid it will happen again."

"Fuck yeah. And the next time maybe she won't…" I leaned back in the booth and blew out a breath. "She's alive. I want to make sure she stays that way."

Finn held my stare, direct and no nonsense. "What you're feeling. She is too."

Those words hit me hard because I knew how true they were.

His next words were softly spoken. "I fucked up."

"What does that mean?"

"Her whole life I've been there. In the shadows but watching."

I had an ah-ha moment. "It was you who paid for her schooling."

"Yeah. My baby girl came home. The least I could do was pay her tuition. I kept eyes on her, young, alone and in the city. That bitch that shot her, she sneaked through my crew too. It was fucked up and random and not something you could have planned for. And yeah, she almost died. That fucks with you, especially when you're linked however remotely to that shit, but to walk away. All you had, the big stuff and the little stuff. Happiness, you had it in your hands and you walked away from it. I get it, but now that I'm older and wiser I can tell you with absolute certainty. That's fucking stupid."

I studied the man in front of me. Maybe he wasn't so dark and empty because he boarded a plane with the sole purpose of kicking me in the ass.

"So am I correct to assume you are giving me your blessing."

"I saw my daughter with you. You're her home and she's yours. It's time you went home."

I couldn't help playing devil's advocate even knowing I was going home to her. "And put a target on her back?"

"We can't predict the future. If you knew Alexis would be harmed before you married her, would you not have married her?"

That wasn't a fair question. The moments and memories I clung to, to not have experienced them. How could I say no to them and yet how could I willingly put her in harm's way?

"Denying happiness because of what might happen, I did that too and it is not just stupid, but selfish because you made that decision for her. She came to see me."

"What?"

"Showed up at the clubhouse."

"Alone." When I see her…

"She let me have it. Told me you left to keep her safe, following my lead. She was angry and under that anger she was hurt…so fucking hurt. But do you know what else was there, Greyson?"

My fucking eyes were burning knowing what I had put her through. "What?"

"Strength. She told me that we didn't give her enough credit for being strong. She was right. We left her. Both of us. Took the choice away from her, left her to pick up the pieces and fucking hell if she didn't. Even heartbroken, she picked herself up and she moved on. I've been idle since I walked away from her. You are too, but Alexis is still moving forward. Slower, with less steps or interest, but she's making it work despite the pain."

I looked down at the table. It blurred. I had thought that of her. The pain in her eyes and yet she still had it in her to be funny, to be happy, to look for the bright side.

"I already knew I fucked up." I met his stare. "I've booked my flight."

"I'm relieved to hear my daughter didn't marry a moron."

"The jury is still out," I chuckled.

"Don't waste a single day, Greyson. Take it from someone who is filled with regret, who lost the love of his life. I'd do it all over again with Sade, even knowing I'd lose her, I would do it all over again. The love of your life is waiting for you. Stop making her wait." He then reached into his vest and pulled out a stack of letters. His knuckles were white with how hard he held them. "These are letters to me from Sade. I thought Alexis would like them, to learn a little bit about her mother from her own words."

My fucking eyes burned, but Alexis was going to love them. I handled them like the treasures they were. "I'll make sure she gets them."

He reached for his pint; his hand shook from emotion that he battled back. "And be prepared to get on your knees because you so fucking have that coming."

I was packed. I stood in the portrait gallery. It's funny, I never really appreciated my heritage until Alexis. I'd seen this room, been in it a few times, but I didn't truly get it. All those who came before me, the history that saturated these walls, their lives, their love...she opened my eyes to all of that.

I stood in front of our paintings. Her looking down at me like she had on the day of our wedding. My chest grew tight. "Hers will be the last to hang on these walls. This all ends with me because I choose Alexis. I choose love."

I realized I was talking to the empty room. I probably needed my head examined and still I smiled because Alexis talked to herself all the time. Fuck, I missed her. I headed for the door when I heard the laughter again. Turning toward it, I froze seeing what I could only imagine was the ghost the housemaids always whispered about. It was no more than mist, but why the fuck was their mist inside. It moved, floating right into Aenfinn's portrait. I moved closer to his portrait, half expecting it to pop its head out and scare the shit out of me. It didn't, but as I stood there staring at his painting I saw something I never had before. I moved closer.

"Son of a bitch."

I reached for my cell and called my grandfather. "You need to come to the portrait gallery and bring a ladder."

23

ALEXIS

Benny and Joon were playing, tugging on the same rope. Benny was bigger, he could easily pull it from his sister, but he didn't. The twins were over; we'd been hanging in the back enjoying our view of the beach.

"It still looks a lot like it did when we were kids," Dylan said what I was thinking.

"I'm glad to be home," Dominic said then added, "Mom and Dad are moving back."

I hadn't heard that. "When?"

"As soon as they sell their apartment."

"They've gotten their fill of Paris?" I asked.

"Yeah, and with everyone home they want to be here too."

I smiled as I looked back out at the horizon. "I can't wait to see them."

Nostalgia swept through me, some good, some sad, but life went on. I jumped up from my spot.

"Where are you going?"

I didn't say, returning with my bike, the same bike from my youth. Dylan joined me; Dominic went to play with my dogs. "It really is ugly." Laughing eyes turned to me. "I'll buy you a new one."

It was ugly. Hideous. I loved it. "No, too many memories."

His smile faded as he pushed his hands into his pockets. "I get why he left, I do, but if I see him again I'm punching him in the face."

"No you won't, but thank you for the thought."

"He hurt you."

"He did and he's hurting too."

"That's fucking stupid."

I couldn't argue that point because he was right. It was fucking stupid.

"Change of subject. I saw Debbie the other day," Dylan announced.

"I did too. Still a bitch."

She worked at the salon in town, though it didn't sound like she'd be working there much longer. Apparently, she burned one customer's hair and dyed another's the wrong color.

"She hasn't changed." Dylan wasn't wrong.

"Nope."

"It's sad."

"Yep. Speaking of her, why did she stop hanging out with us?"

He shifted on his feet, looking a bit guilty. "She didn't stop hanging with us, we stopped hanging with her."

"Wait. What now?"

"She didn't want us hanging with you, gave us an ultimatum. Her or you."

"Ah, well that explains her torture of me."

"Yeah, sorry."

"Why? I got you two."

He grinned. I climbed onto my bike. "Where are you going?" he asked.

"For a ride. Watch my babies."

"Yeah, but don't fall off you might break a hip."

I gave him the finger then peddled away. The expression, it's like riding a bike, was so true. The ride was like going back in time. I was that sixteen-year-old girl again. The wonderful salty air brushed across my face and the wind in my hair. It was like I had returned to a simpler time. It was instinct the ride I took through town, just like all those times before, marveling that though decades had passed home was still very much like it had been.

I made my way along the road toward my jetty. Déjà vu hit hard when I reached it because there was someone standing on my spot. I recognized him, knew his body better than my own. We'd been here before, but so much had happened in the space between and still I felt that hit of attraction, the same one that had reached across the beach to me all those years ago. We weren't kids anymore, we had a long story, a beautiful one, not without its ups and downs, but he walked away. I had wished every day for the last ten months for this moment, so the anger surprised me. I was so fucking angry that he took it all away. His body tensed before his head jerked around. Even with the distance of the beach between us, I saw the pain, the hope...the love. He started toward me; I turned from him.

"Alexis!"

My eyes closed hearing my name as only he could say it. He touched my arm and my body remembered his touch. I bit my lip to keep the emotions in. "Please." It was all he said, one simple word and yet there was nothing simple about what he wanted. I loved him, I waited for him to come back, every damn day, but he left. He walked away and stayed away. For almost a year he forced me into a life that was a shell of the one I knew.

I couldn't look at him because I didn't trust myself being so close to the person I wanted, always had, always would, but he didn't get to just walk back into my life.

"You left. You took away my happily ever after."

"Forgive me."

I couldn't keep the pain or the anger from my voice because I was drowning in it. "Ten months, Greyson. Ten months walking around empty." I looked then because I needed him to understand how much he hurt me. It gutted seeing the same pain in his eyes. I loved him, but we were different now, his actions made us different. "I don't know that I can forgive you for that."

I walked away so he wouldn't see the tears rolling down my cheeks.

"He's back?" Paige paced my backyard, chewing on her nail. "This is good, isn't it?"

"Why? He left. Strolling back almost a year later and thinking he can take up where he left off. Fuck that," Grant snarled. The twins agreed. A part of me did too.

"But you know why he left." Her eyes speared Grant. "Hell, you even said you'd have done the same." Paige wanted me to have the dream. I loved her for it. And yes, I wasn't living so much as existing but the anger was suffocating. I appreciated more that fine line between love and hate. "Before you make any decisions, remember the last year. Put yourself in his shoes and how you would have reacted. He's back, which means he knows he was wrong to leave. It's a second chance, Alexis. You would be a fool to walk away from that."

"You're right, deep down I know that, but I apparently still have some lingering anger I need to work through. If Greyson wants me back it has to be on my terms."

Her smile took up her whole face. "Nothing wrong with that."

My agent was in a bit of a tizzy when she sat across from me at the coffee bar. When I moved home, she moved to LA. She'd wanted to make the move, but she stayed in New York for me. It had been a few days since Greyson's return. The town was abuzz that he was back. Rumors were flying around about reconciliation. Even the town hoped to see that happen. I'd be lying if I said I didn't want that too, but I wanted him to experience how powerless it made you feel to have a decision made for you that changed your life irrevocably. Adele studied me with that knowing look of hers.

"Do you want something to drink?" I asked.

"No, I can't stay long. Do you have the pages?"

Just like her, Adele Mansfield was extremely efficient but she lacked social skills outside of her work. She wasn't married because she couldn't afford to be; she was married to her job. I was thankful to have her, but I wondered if she ever found her life lonely. I reached for my portfolio and pulled out the sheets for her.

"We need the rest of the screenplay in three weeks. Can you do that?"

"Yeah, no problem. I'm not leaving my cottage," I muttered. Avoidance was my priority. I desperately wanted to avoid Greyson because I hadn't let myself feel the anger, I'd been numb to it, but I felt it now. It curled in my gut and my instinct was to unleash it on him, but hurting him would only hurt me too because under the anger was love.

"Alexis!"

"Sorry."

"I heard your husband is back."

My eyes widened then narrowed. "How did you hear that? What did he do take out a two-page ad in the *LA Times*? Moving back to Mendocino to drive my estranged wife mad."

Adele chuckled, "No, but you did make the gossip columns. You and Greyson were always a favorite with the gossip papers especially when the seemingly perfect couple split. That was news."

"For me too," I whispered, but Adele didn't hear me. She stood and gathered her things.

"I'll see you soon." She left. I remembered the stories that came out right after the shooting, the photos of Greyson at the hospital. It was hard to believe that man, the one who looked as if his entire world had come to an end, could be the same one to voluntarily walk away a year later. I was so lost in thought I didn't realize I was no longer alone until I heard that deep voice.

"Alexis."

So much for avoidance. I should walk out, but I was a glutton for punishment and hungry for the sight of him. My gaze moved up his body taking in his faded jeans, tee, his beautiful hair pulled back into a ponytail and those fucking eyes. I was in hell. That gunshot had killed me and these past ten months had been purgatory, but I must have pissed someone off because my ass was kicked right into hell. And my hell would be this, haunted by and forced to be near this man. I was looking right at him so I saw the grin that pulled at the corner of his mouth. He always could read me. The thought brought pain not pleasure.

"Greyson."

"Can I join you?"

Hell, no. At my silence his dark brow rose in a questioning arch. I *was* in hell so resolved myself to my fate.

I gestured to the chair and watched as he gracefully folded his large frame into it. We sat staring at each other.

"How have you been, Alexis?"

My eyes narrowed. "Small talk, Greyson, seriously." Almost a year he was gone and now he wants to chat. Fuck him. I stood. "The next time you see me and get the urge to ply me with bullshit small talk, don't. Now that it's over, Greyson, I just don't give a fuck." See? So totally pissed.

Grabbing my stuff, I walked out. My body was shaking, my heart was pounding and tears were threatening. I didn't get far before I felt his hand on my arm. He pulled me into the alley and before I knew his intentions, he kissed me. It was like coming home. My lips moved with his, my eyes closed, my body swayed into him. Like a junkie after a long fast, I wanted to lose myself in him, in what we were together. Instead, I pushed him away. My hand trembled as I brought it to my lips. Love stared back from those pale eyes.

"You decided our fate. And now you're back. I have loved you my whole life, but you hurt me. I know your intentions were in the right place, but my heart and my head are not on the same page."

A tear rolled down his cheek. Instinct was to wipe it away. I fisted my hand instead. "That day on the jetty when I looked up and saw you, your hair flying in the breeze, clutching that beat-up bike of yours, it damn near knocked the breath from me. My life changed that day. And the night you were shot, my world tilted again. I can still see it, every time I close my eyes. The pain, when I thought you were gone, it haunts me. Leaving you, tearing us apart, that haunts me too. I've loved you from the very first moment I saw you."

I hated seeing him hurt, hated that more than the anger I held onto. And I loved him; that trumped everything else. "You broke us. You have to fix it."

Tenderness moved into his expression. "That I can do."

"Is it true?" Dylan said the following morning, slamming into my bedroom like he owned it. "You took Greyson back?"

News traveled fast.

"I didn't take him back…" Yet. "We're working it out."

"Where is he? I'd like to talk to him," Dominic added.

"You're smiling," Dylan accused.

"That should be a good thing. You know as well as I do why he left."

Dylan got in my face. "He left you, moved out of your apartment and your life."

"I know. And I also know he loves me and was afraid for me. Dylan, some crazy stalker shot me."

"I'm not feeling as generous."

"And I get it, but we've all known each other too long to not give him a second chance."

"Grant is going to flip the fuck out."

Yes he was, but when he got over the anger I was sure we'd all find our way back. I hoped.

"I'm with Dylan and Dominic. I'm not feeling as generous." Grant paced his living room. Paige and the girls didn't share the sentiment. Like me, they were ready to move forward.

"I understand why he left, but he fucking left," Grant hissed.

"You would have to."

He had no argument for that.

"He acted poorly, Grant, but his intentions have always been in Alexis' best interest," Paige argued. "He had his reasons."

"Fuck his reason."

"I need you to try, Grant. You're my family, but so is he. Please."

Grant turned to me, the emotions that chased each other, one after another, was hard to watch. "He hurt you, he broke you. I'll listen to him, but I can't promise I'll forgive him."

It hurt to hear, but I nodded my head. What else could I do?

It had been two days since I'd seen Greyson and for a man who wanted me back he was taking his time making it right. And I wanted him to make it right and quickly. It was a new kind of torture being so close to him and not getting to touch him, kiss him…it had been almost a year.

I had to get back to work, but I was running errands. Passing the diner, I thought to pop in and say hi when I heard the sound of a motorcycle coming down the street.

Greyson. The last time I saw his motorcycle was in New York, his bike from when we were kids. He still had it; kept it in perfect condition. He rarely rode it in the city; so seeing him on the back of it again was a really nice sight. He was older, but I still saw the Greyson of our youth, the boy who had stolen my heart. It wasn't hard to see why. He pulled over, his bike idling, his focus on me.

"Take a ride with me?"

My heart twisted in my chest because we hadn't been on a ride in so long. I didn't need to think about it. He handed me the helmet. I climbed on. Like when we were kids, I wrapped him tightly in my arms. It all came back, the feelings, the memories and the dreams. I rested my cheek on his back and we rode. We had no destination in mind; we just rode. I wanted to know where he'd been, what he'd been doing for the last year and why he'd come back now. We'd get there. For now, I just enjoyed the ride.

GREYSON

My girl was on the back of my bike, holding me tight like she used to. The emptiness was gone, the numbness. She breathed life back into me with nothing more than being. I had taken a year from us, a year we'll never get back. I needed to atone for that but right now my girl was on the back of my bike, the wind in our faces and nothing but blue skies ahead. So we rode and remembered.

ALEXIS

It was cleaning day and for the first time in almost a year, I was blaring my music and singing along. I could be offended because my animals were burying their heads in the sofa. Did I really sound like an animal dying? The memory brought a smile.

They looked pathetic, so I let the dogs out. Buggers would have to deal. I opened the back door to find the spiral ring of Greyson's on the stoop. The one he was never without in our youth, the one he used as leverage to get me to marry him.

I sat down and ran my hand over the cover as memories drifted in and out. Inside, the sketches were each more beautiful than the last. He had sketches of the beach, of the locals going about their days; sketches of the town, concept buildings and cars but the last dozen or so were all sketches of me as a teenager. The one I remembered he did the night we walked to the jetty that first time. There were a few others of me working, one I was at my locker and in writing club. There was a sketch of me sleeping after The Cure concert. He hadn't slept; he had drawn me even as tired as he had been. There was also a sketch of me standing on the front path of my house watching as Greyson left for the last time. But it was the last sketch that brought the tears. It was our wedding day. Greyson had sketched me as we spoke our vows. But what had the tears streaming down my cheeks, what had my heart swelling with love, was the date. He had captured every detail of that beautiful memory from eleven years earlier just yesterday. Underneath the sketch were five words, the same five words I had engraved on his wedding band.

My heart is within you

320

I pressed the notebook to my chest, holding it like the gift it was, and acknowledged what I'd always known. He hadn't broken us; he'd just bent us.

GREYSON

I'd called Alexis earlier, wanted to take her somewhere, anywhere, but she was working. I loved that she was. Like her dad had said, she was moving on. Despite the pain, she kept moving forward. Strength, yeah, she had it in spades. I had some things to do, part of my campaign to win her back though she was making that very easy on me. She didn't have to, but I was so fucking glad she was. I told her I'd call her later. I actually watched the clock and felt a bit like my younger self, wondering if it was too early to call. At nine, I couldn't wait anymore. She answered on the first ring.

"Greyson."

"Hey, beautiful. How did the writing go?"

"I wrote three chapters, over ten thousand words. I'm thrilled."

"You found your words."

Softly she said, "I did."

Hearing the tenderness in her voice had the words just tumbling out. "I was scared. So fucking scared of losing you. I couldn't see straight, just saw you that night. Watching you struggling to find your way back and then to learn I was somehow connected to it. I fucked up, Alexis."

Silence followed. My heart was slamming in my chest. What was she thinking?

"That Ratcliffe stubbornness," she finally said and I practically wept. My girl. I didn't fucking deserve her.

"I'm a stubborn asshole."

"I thought you were accommodating."

I chuckled.

"I went to see my dad."

I knew this and still I tensed because that had been a risk.

"I know."

"How do you know?"

"Your father paid me a visit in Ireland."

Silence again and when she did speak, I could hear the tears in her voice. "He did?"

"Told me I was wrong to leave. That he was wrong to leave."

"He said that?"

"Yes." As soon as we made it right, I'd give her his letters. They were going to hurt her before they brought her comfort. She was dealing with enough pain from me.

She chuckled, "Maybe I got through."

"What did you say to him?"

"I told him to go fuck himself for leaving."

"You did not."

"I did."

"What did he say?"

"I didn't stick around long enough to hear his thoughts. It was very cathartic. Do you think he'll try to reconcile?"

"I think your dad is a very complicated man, but yes I think a time is coming when you won't have to look at that picture to see him."

I heard her weeping softly and I wanted to drop the fucking phone and go to her, but I hadn't earned that right yet. This was on her terms.

"I imagine you have some choice words for me too."

"You hurt me, Greyson. I understand, I truly do understand where your head was at, but you hurt me."

"However you need me to make this right, I'll do it."

Silence again.

"What are you wearing?"

Fuck, I loved this woman. Our brand of phone sex, I got comfortable on the bed. "Leather chaps and a cowboy hat."

She yawned before asking, "Do you have a lasso?"

"Yes, but it's all tangled around my ankles and my ass is fucking freezing. What are you wearing?"

"My flannel pajamas and my grannie panties since I need to do laundry."

"What color are your grannie panties?"

"White cotton, tight elastic around the waist, but a bit saggy at the legs and it covers past my belly button. And my pjs cover me from neck to toe, long sleeves. I'm very proper. Oh, I suppose I should tell you I've another man sleeping in my bed, two actually."

"What, now?"

"Buggers has taken your side of the bed. And I have two dogs. Benny and Joon. You'll have to meet them."

My heart ached. Even broken she had love in her to bring dogs into her life.

She added, "You'll have to sleep in Buggers' bed."

She didn't know what those words meant to me, but I felt on top of the fucking world because she was already talking about me being back in her home and her heart. To her I teased, "Fuck no."

"See, there's that accommodating nature of yours."

"Alexis."

"Yeah."

"I love you."

She didn't miss a beat. "I know."

ALEXIS

The following day while I was doing the dreaded laundry there was a knock at the door. Thinking it was Greyson had the butterflies flapping around in my stomach. I was two years shy of forty and yet I moved like a teenager to the door, stopping myself before opening it so I could calm down and not look like I'd just run to the door.

I was disappointed to find it wasn't Greyson on the other side of it, but that didn't last long when the courier handed me a note on stationery I remembered.

Join me for the evening? If yes, tell the courier. I'll pick you up at seven. If no, that's the wrong answer.

I smiled; I had missed his humor.

"Please tell him yes."

I closed the door and leaned back against it. I couldn't stop the smile. I had a date with Greyson. I had to shower and shave and lotion. I ran to my room feeling much like I had at sixteen.

At seven there was a knock at the door. We'd been married, lived together, knew each other better than any two people could and still my hands went damp and my stomach flipped with nerves.

I pulled the door open on Greyson looking as nervous as I felt. He was actually rubbing his hands on his jeans. He turned to me and those eyes took their time moving down my body. On cue, goosebumps rose.

"You're beautiful."

As many times as I've heard that, it never got old. I looked past him to the limo sitting in the street.

"We're taking that?"

He glanced over his shoulder then looked at me from the corner of his eye. Sexy as sin, made more so when he grinned. "I'm trying to woo my girl."

His girl. My eyes burned. I was his girl. Always had been.

He didn't take my hand, but touched my elbow as he led us to the car. I missed holding his hand.

"I thought we'd do dinner first," he suggested.

"Okay." I assumed he meant at the diner. I was wrong. Sitting on the bar in the limo was a hot fudge sundae and two spoons. He settled next to me and like he had done once before, he spooned up some whipped cream and offered it. And like then, he removed the excess with his thumb.

Chills danced down my arms and not because of the ice cream.

"Where are we going?"

"Dancing."

Lust took a backseat to suspicion. "A plastic bag caught in a tree has more control than I have when dancing."

He chuckled at the memory. "I think dancing is much like laundry. You just don't have the right experience."

Damn, it got hot in here all of a sudden remembering his lesson on doing laundry.

He knew what I was thinking when he smiled and called to the driver. "Could you put the air on?"

The club was packed with bodies pressed together and the music so loud the bass throbbed through you. Greyson led me through the bodies, his hand on the small of my back, which was causing my insides to go haywire. He didn't search out a table; he led us right to the dance floor. He turned into me, his hands found my hips and he drew me close, so close we were touching. I bit my lip to stifle the moan. The beat was a fast one, but Greyson took his time, looking me right in the eyes as he moved in a way that could only be described as making love, fully dressed, but he was seducing me right there on the dance floor. Having been denied him for so long, I let myself be seduced. His hands moved over my body, relearning, remembering. I touched him too, starting at his shoulders and slowly moving down his muscled arms. My fingers dug into his biceps when he palmed my back and drew me even closer. His hips moved, mine moved with him. I felt him against my stomach as heat pooled between my legs. Edgy and needy I ran my hands around his back and down over the curve of his ass. I wanted to kiss him, wanted his mouth on mine and his taste on my tongue. I wanted to drink him in until I was sated. We didn't kiss; we didn't talk, not with words. Our bodies were saying plenty. We spent the night in that spot, no one else existed. It was just he and I. The ride home was so wrought with sexual tension, the driver had to feel it. I wanted to crawl into Greyson's lap, wanted to straddle him, wanted to rub myself against him, wanted his hands and mouth on me; I wanted his cock inside me. He felt it too; his fingers were curled into fists but he kept his distance.

At my door, he gave in to the need to touch me and ran his finger along my jaw.

"I'd like you to meet Benny and Joon." Dylan had taken them for a walk when Greyson arrived earlier, but they'd be home now.

"I'd like that."

I unlocked the door and they were waiting. Usually, they were well behaved with visitors, but as soon as I opened the door they were jumping up on Greyson and with enough force it knocked him back a few feet. It wasn't aggression. Like me, it was love at first sight.

"Benny, Joon come."

"They're beautiful," Greyson said.

"Benny is the bigger one, my big boy, and Joon is his sister."

Greyson was rubbing their heads when his focus shifted to something behind us. Buggers came strolling into the room as only a cat could. He assessed the situation and recognizing Greyson he beelined to him and rubbed up against his leg.

"It looks like even Buggers is welcoming you home."

He looked over at me. "Am I welcomed home?"

I held his gaze. "I never wanted you to leave."

He reached for me in the same move he slammed the front door closed with his foot. His mouth came down on mine. His taste saturated my tongue. My hands moved up his arms and over his shoulders, into his hair pulling him closer so I could kiss him deeper. Teeth, lips and tongues devoured. I couldn't taste him enough. He yanked off my shirt. His hand moved over my body then stilled when he touched my scar. He broke the kiss, his fingers tracing it. They were shaking. He curled his spine and pressed a kiss on it, his lips lingered before he turned me around so he could kiss the one on my back. I felt his tears on my skin. I turned to him, took his face in my hands.

"I lived," I whispered the words he had said once to me.

He kissed me, sweetly at first but all the passion that had been banked demanded release. My bra followed my shirt. His mouth closed over my breast. Chills shot down my arms as I pulled at his shirt. I needed to feel him. He yanked his shirt off. I pressed hot kisses over his chest, his hand curled in my hair as I kissed down his body. We moved into the bedroom never breaking contact. My fingers shook as I worked on his jeans, pulling the denim and briefs down his legs. Slowly, I moved my hands back up his legs, across his hips. Wrapping my hand around his cock, I fisted. He moaned. I took just the tip into my mouth, swirling around the slit, tasting the saltiness. He lifted me, my back hit the mattress and he followed me down. He kissed me, not crazed like the first kiss, deeper, slower, like he was savoring the moment, savoring me. His hand moved down my body, touching and claiming. It all came back. Not just the sex, but the connection. The bond that formed when we were kids and only grew stronger in the years that followed. I didn't realize I was crying because I wasn't sad. I was overwhelmed with being here again; every kiss, every touch breathing life back into the dream I thought had died.

"Alexis?"

"It isn't just love."

He brushed his thumb over my cheek.

"You're in my blood and bones. Losing you, it wasn't just losing the dream. It was losing a piece of me. All the times I reached for the phone to call you. You are my husband, but you're my best friend too. I've been empty; so desperately empty without you."

A tear rolled down his cheek. I pulled his mouth to mine and kissed him with everything I was feeling. His fingers dug into my thighs to lift my hips. I broke the kiss when he pulled me onto his cock, filling me so completely. More tears, I had missed this. Our eyes locked as we moved, it had been a long time but our bodies remembered. We moved in sync reaching for that peak and when we came, it was together.

24

GREYSON

Alexis held my hand tightly in hers. I felt like a dead man walking as we made our way up the front path of the Atzer home. I needed to atone to more than just her.

The door opened without us knocking, Paige stood there. Her expression wasn't one I could discern. She looked from Alexis to me then to our joined hands.

Those blue eyes lifted. "So have you pulled your head from your ass?"

"I'm working on it."

Her expression changed, softened seconds before she had me in her arms. I thought it would have been harder. I hugged her back. "We've missed you."

Grant appeared. Paige stepped back and wiped her eyes. "Look who's here?" She reached for Grant's hand, but he was too busy glaring at me.

"Greyson and I need a minute," he announced.

"I'll stay," Alexis volunteered.

I touched her cheek. Loved that she was willing to, but this I had to do alone. "We'll be right out."

"Are you sure?"

"Yes."

"Okay." She turned to Grant. "Don't you hurt him."

"No promises."

He took me to the garage, his office so to speak.

He turned to me and it was only then that I appreciated how pissed he was. His muscles flexed and he was shaking with rage. His voice was soft, deceivingly so. "I walked her down the aisle to you. I witnessed as you promised to love her in sickness and in health and I was there when you walked out on that promise. We, my family and I, were left to pick up the pieces. Do you know what it's like to look into the eyes of a woman you've known most of your life and not see her looking back?"

Hearing what I'd put Alexis through had my eyes burning. Fucking hell. I lived it too, but fucking hell.

"Why come back now?"

"My grandfather knocked some sense into me then her dad paid me a visit in Ireland. He didn't want to see me make the same mistake he did."

Grant pulled a hand though his hair. "Does she know?"

"Yeah. He was the one who paid for her schooling."

"I wondered." As a father he would have. "Leaving her, whatever your intentions, was a dick move."

"I know, but I reacted out of love and fear. Had it been Paige, can you say you would have done it differently?"

"No."

He studied me for a few minutes then offered his hand. "It's good to see you again." He didn't release my hand and added, "You hurt her again and I'll fucking kill you."

"Fair enough."

We stepped onto the deck to find Paige and her girls sitting with Alexis. The girls all came home when they heard I had. Even pissed at me, they came home. That felt really fucking good. Grant was willing to forgive me, but his generosity apparently only went so far. "Sorry, man." He gestured to his girls. "You're in for it."

He walked away, but my focus was on the girls. No longer did they look at me with wide-eyed innocence. There was censure in their gazes. I took that hit. I deserved it.

Tara was the one to break the silence. "You hurt her. You hurt all of us."

Tears burned my eyes and I let them fall. "I know."

"You were hurting too, weren't you?" she whispered.

"Yes."

"Well, maybe we could start again."

I stepped toward her and like I had done when she was four, I kissed the back of her hand. "I'm Greyson."

Her eyes filled before she threw her arms around me. "Welcome home, Greyson."

ALEXIS

Watching Greyson reconnect with the girls was beautiful. Paige reached for my hand. We were both crying. The twins arrived.

Dylan marched right up to Greyson. "A year of her life you took. And I get it, but taking that year was fucking selfish."

I stood; Dylan raised his hand to me. "I've known her since she was six. She's my sister in every way that counts. You..." He pointed at Greyson. "I thought of you as a brother," Dylan's voice broke. "Don't fucking hurt her again."

Greyson nodded, giving the moment the respect it deserved.

Dominic, in an attempt to lighten the mood added, "What he said."

It had been too long since we were all together like this and yet it felt as if it were only yesterday. Grant and Greyson must have reached an understanding because the easiness that always existed between them was back. The twins weren't as easy to slide back into it, but I caught them both talking with Greyson throughout the day. They would get there.

Greyson must have felt me staring, because he looked my way, then started over to me. Those long legs clad in denim. His hair was down, tucked behind his ears and those pale eyes that had haunted my dreams. He brushed his lips over mine before he took the seat Paige vacated.

"What are you thinking about?"

"The first time I saw you, sitting on my jetty, looking so perfect there. I thought you were an intruder."

His mouth twitched into a grin. "You did?"

"Yup, it was my first thought but I was wrong. You do belong and you are so wanted."

He reached for my hand that wore his rings. "I love you."

"I know." Leaning closer to him, I brushed my lips over his. "Come home with me tonight."

"Hell, yeah."

"Hey, you." We both looked over to see Dylan, Dominic was right behind him. They were looking at Greyson. They said nothing for so long it got a little awkward. Then Dylan said, "We're picking teams for volleyball. Do you want to play?"

Love for the twins brought a smile. Greyson stood, kissed my head then joined them. "Yeah, I'd like that."

The following morning, Greyson dragged me from bed. There was somewhere he wanted to take me. I wanted to stay in bed. We had a year to make up for. He didn't say where we were going, didn't even talk on our way there.

He pulled up the familiar drive and I didn't understand. He shut off his bike and waited for me to climb off.

"Surprise."

I'm sure I looked dimwitted because I just stared at him. "I don't understand."

"Welcome home."

"This house isn't for sale."

He held up a key. "Welcome home, Alexis."

"You bought it? How the hell did you do that?"

"The owner is a huge art collector."

I looked around. "Are you serious. This is ours."

"Yes."

"Home?"

He pressed a kiss in my palm. "You're my home."

I threw my arms around his neck and kissed him. He was my home too.

"It hasn't changed much," he said as we strolled around the back yard. He was right; it looked as it had when we were kids.

"Shall we go inside?" He led me to the front of the house and unlocked it, but before I could step inside he lifted me into his arms. We'd been here before too.

Inside on the floor was a black box with a red bow.

"What's that?" I was already moving to the box, removing the ribbon and lifting the lid. It was a wedding band like the one I wore. Confused I looked at Greyson.

Reaching for my hand, he stared me right in the eyes. "I broke my promise and my vow." He slipped the ring onto my finger. "I promise to never break my vows again."

I needed to invest in Kleenex.

I looked down at my hand, his rings winking up at me. "You are very good at apologies."

"I'm not done."

He led me into the living room. It was empty, but for a sculpture on a pedestal. "What is that?"

"Why don't you go see?"

I glanced over at him; his voice matched his expression. Tender. Curious, about not only the sculpture that was clearly one of his, but also his reaction, I walked over to it. Nothing could have prepared me. It was my parents and me. The picture I had. Greyson had lovingly recreated it in stone. He'd captured their expressions; somehow he had captured all that emotion in stone. He joined me.

"This is what I wasn't allowed to see. The sculpture in your studio."

"It took me a while to get it right."

I grabbed his hand while battling tears. "It's perfect."

He kissed my temple. "Wait here."

He left me in the living room, returning shortly after with another black leather box. He handed it to me and pushed his hands into his pockets.

"Open it."

I lifted the lid and my knees went weak. My eyes jerked to his face. "Is this…"

"There's a tradition in my family that if a man marries for love, he gives his wife…" He lifted the diamond from the box, it had been changed once again and was now just the stone, that incredible stone.

"It's too big to wear so I thought we could build a case for it that was on motion sensor so every time you walk into the room it lights up and one of your Celine Dion songs plays. I'm even hoping you'll sing along—"

I kissed him; I wrapped him tightly in my arms and kissed him with everything I was feeling. He didn't hesitate to kiss me back, his tongue sweeping my mouth. I broke the kiss and grabbed his face. "I forgive you."

He moved with superhuman speed, putting the diamond back in its box and resting it on the floor next to the sculpture. His eyes were on fire when he kissed me and started for his old bedroom. He worked on my blouse and I worked on his jeans.

"Please tell me you bought a bed," I asked between kisses.

"King-size."

Two weeks later I came down with a stomach bug. I couldn't keep anything down but when it lasted for over a week Greyson insisted on taking me to the doctor. I wasn't really sure what a doctor could do since it was more than likely a virus and just needed to run its course.

We were sitting in the examination room, Greyson holding my hand, as we waited for the doctor who was reviewing the results of the tests he had run. After what seemed like forever he looked up from the chart and smiled, "Congratulations, you're pregnant."

Greyson said what I was thinking and it was directed more to me than it was to the doctor. "That's not possible."

The doctor, clueless to the undercurrent, sought to assure Greyson. "I know about Alexis' injuries and the diagnosis, but she is definitely pregnant."

It felt like a hive of bees was buzzing around my head and as I tried to come to terms with the fact that I was pregnant a thought had me going cold. The diagnosis wasn't that I couldn't conceive. It was I wouldn't be able to carry a baby to term.

"Can I carry the baby to term?"

Greyson's eyes found mine at that question and I saw fear in his gaze before he looked back at the doctor.

"Yes, this is a high-risk pregnancy but we'll monitor you every month with ultrasounds and modify the frequency as you progress. But seeing your uterus in the ultrasound and the fact that the egg even attached, if we work together, and you understand your limitations, there is no reason you can't bring this child to term."

Greyson looked as dumbfounded as I felt, and like me, we both were thinking the same thing. The diamond.

"You don't think…" He started to say.

Yes, I did. "I do."

With the doctor standing right there, he tangled his fingers into my hair and kissed me.

"You will have your feet up all the time. No arguments," Paige said then started to cry again. Grant held her, his eyes shining. It had been two weeks and still we marveled that something we thought couldn't happen had.

"She's right. No heavy lifting," Grant agreed.

"No lifting at all," Tara chimed in.

Paige pointed at her eldest. "Yes, no lifting."

"I have blankets to knit," Mrs. C. said.

Dee and she shared a look, "And booties."

Greyson sat next to me in the living room of our home, his arm around my shoulders. The dogs were sleeping by the fire. Buggers was on my lap.

"Dylan is a name that works for both a boy and a girl."

Dominic threw a pillow at his head.

Callum strolled into the room. After learning we were pregnant, he moved to Mendocino for the pregnancy and the birth. Lived in my cottage, neighbor to the twins. If he was hoping to slow down, he was in for a rude awakening.

"I found a journal in the room, one kept by Caitlin Ratcliffe. She and Rafer were the ones to hide the diamond, not to ease their monetary responsibilities, but from theft. Whispers were circulating. She had something else in her journal." He had the attention of the room. "Aenfinn was duty bound to continue the line so he had to forsake his love to fulfill his obligations, something that many who followed him elected to do. In the end though it was love that prevailed, according to Caitlin 'tis said that on the night Aenfinn passed from the mortal world a strange green glow was seen in the woods beyond his great estate and the sound of lovers' laughter was heard to echo throughout the forest."

Greyson stiffened at my side and he looked pale. "What's wrong?"

He tried to shake it off, but he was unnerved.

"What?"

"I saw that green mist, heard the laughter too."

"You did?"

"Yeah. The housemaids always talked about ghosts, I never believed them then I heard the laughter. It was as real as my own voice."

"That's incredible," Paige whispered.

My attention was on Greyson because there was more he wasn't saying. "What else did you see?"

His head jerked to me, and even being off balance he smiled and touched my cheek. "Looks like I'm not the only one who can read minds."

It just took me a little longer.

"It sounds kind of weird, but in the portrait gallery I announced that I was choosing love." Those damn tears hit my eyes again. "I saw that mist right after I made that declaration. It was what drew my attention to Aenfinn's portrait. To the diamond."

The painter of Aenfinn's portrait hadn't been phenomenal after all. A fake back and some clever painting and the most sought after Ratcliffe treasure had been hiding in plain sight. It was fitting too. Where best to hide the symbol of their love than with the one to whom it was bestowed.

It was so quiet you could have heard a pin drop.

"His goddess," I whispered in awe.

"I think so. I chose love, so she showed me where the diamond was." Greyson's eyes were bright when he kissed my temple.

"I have learned in my eighty-two years on this Earth that there are some things we can not explain, but it's in the blind acceptance that the real gifts lie. Love is the greatest of those gifts. You both learned that on your own and perhaps your pregnancy is their way of rewarding you for seeing what it took them a lifetime to learn."

Greyson and I sat at that booth in the diner where he used to always sit. Paige approached us. She had the weirdest look on her face.

"I just hired a new employee."

"Why do you look like the Cheshire cat?"

"You'll see," she said cryptically and walked away.

Two minutes later, Debbie Demato stepped out of the kitchen, an apron wrapped around her waist and carrying a notepad.

The door opened and the twins strolled in. I didn't think there was a chance in hell it was a coincidence.

"Yo," Dylan greeted, taking the seat next to me. Dominic slipped into the booth next to Greyson.

"I heard the diner has a new employee." Dylan was already looking in Debbie's direction. His arm shot up. "Oh, waitress. We're ready to order."

She looked over as the emotions moved one after another over her face—insecurity, jealousy, annoyance and resignation. She swayed her hips as she approached.

"She's going to spit in our food," Dominic said.

"Likely," I agreed.

"What do you want?" she asked as soon as she reached our table.

"Did you go to training for that because that is just some of the best customer service I've ever heard," Dylan said.

She glared.

"I'll have a salad, dressing on the side." Her eyes darted to me. I smiled sweetly.

After the others ordered, she left returning first with my salad. She dropped it down so loudly I thought the plate might break. It was childish and immature and I was too old for such behavior and still I looked her right in the eye when I poured the dressing on the salad.

"I asked for the dressing on the side, Debbie."

Her jaw dropped.

I tilted my head like she had once done to me. "It's really not that complicated."

She lasted all of three days at the diner before Paige fired her. We were hanging at their place when I asked, "Why did you hire her in the first place?"

"I thought that maybe under the insecurity there was actually a good person." She took a sip of her wine. "I stand corrected."

Greyson and I went to the ultrasounds, every month as scheduled. At the third month ultrasound the tech got quiet. Fear hit that something was wrong.

Greyson felt it too when he demanded, "What's wrong?"

"Excuse me for a second." She hurried from the room.

"Greyson." Worry had my voice a little too high.

He took my hand as we waited. They were the longest few minutes. The doctor entered, the tech behind him.

"What's wrong doctor?" I asked.

"Just give me a minute." He moved the thing around my stomach, pressing into me in a few places before he looked over and smiled.

"She's right."

"About what?"

"You're having twins."

By eight months pregnant, sitting was impossible; standing was impossible, walking, sleeping, all impossible. The only things that I could still do, and did often, were eating and peeing.

One night, Greyson and I were sitting outside on the deck. I pointed my ice cream covered spoon at him. "Do you suppose they're already six feet tall because they sure feel like it."

Greyson was sitting back, his legs stretched out in front of him, his hands behind his head, but his attention was completely on me. He still looked at me like I was the sexiest woman alive even when I ate my body weight in ice cream.

He smiled at my question. "That'll make for an interesting delivery."

I just gaped at him as he threw me a wink. "Do you need something else?"

Did I need, no, did I want, yes. A pound of bacon, a side of beef, a mile-high turkey sandwich with pickles and beets, cake, chips. He grinned reading my thoughts perfectly. "No, I think this half gallon of ice cream is enough."

"All right, beautiful, I'll be right back."

I waited until he disappeared inside before shoveling an enormous spoonful of ice cream into my mouth. I was just hungry all the time. I reached the bottom of the carton and decided I'd better move around a bit. I mean I did just consume a disgusting about of ice cream. I stood and my water broke.

"Greyson!"

He appeared a heartbeat later. "What's wrong?"

"It's time."

It took him a minute before his eyes grew wide with panic. "It's too early."

"I think they'll be just fine, but there's a little thing called an epidural and if I don't get one of those it isn't going to be pretty."

Greyson effortlessly lifted me, though that was probably only possible because he was experiencing an adrenaline rush, and started for the car.

"Hey, guys, where are you going? You promised us food." I looked behind us to see Dylan and Dominic.

Greyson continued toward the driveway. "We need to get to the hospital," he called from over his shoulder.

They both looked confused so I clarified, "The babies are coming."

It took them a minute but they were shouting with joy as they ran up next to us.

"What can we do? Call the others? What about your bag, aren't you supposed to have a bag?" Dylan was panicking.

I laughed, "I didn't pack it yet."

"I'll call Paige. Okay, well go and do the, you know have those babies. We'll be in the waiting room with champagne and cigars."

Greyson reached our car and gently settled me on the seat, pulling and clicking the seat belt himself. He dropped a kiss on my head before he closed the door and walked around to his side. Dylan was opening the door for him.

"Take care of our girl, Greyson."

He didn't miss a beat when he replied, "With my life."

Ten hours and countless pushes later the next generation was born, Finn Callum and Cara Sade Ratcliffe.

EPILOGUE

ALEXIS

Finn and Cara were turning one soon. Greyson had always wanted a little girl who looked just like me and he got his wish. Little Finn, he was all Ratcliffe just like all those who came before him.

Greyson was taking me somewhere for a surprise and it was our first time away from the twins since they were born. Paige had won the drawing. We had to have a drawing because everyone wanted them. Dylan and Dominic offered to take our animals. Heather worked with them now, an official employee. Vice President of Research and Development. They were still rolling in the dough, more and more as the world shifted to one of automation, and Heather came to them with fresh new ideas.

Tara and Mandy moved to New York, Tara to take a job at one of the top publishing houses in the country, and Mandy for a teaching job at a private school in Westchester. They were living in our apartment. The only restriction we put on them was to leave the mural, but it was a touch of home that they both needed. It had been hard on Paige and Grant having the girls living so far away, but the twins had a private plane so they could visit as often as they wanted.

After the twins were born, Greyson gave me a stack of letters from my mom to my dad. He had to read them to me because I couldn't stop crying. Hearing her words, getting that insight into her when I never thought I would, it still made me choke up. There was a lot of my mom in me and that made me really happy.

The book on the Ratcliffe family was done. It was in fact a coffee table book, a best seller. The diamond was in a case, but not one in the living room. It was an invaluable family heirloom so the case was alarmed with sensors, but in our bedroom so we could see it and remember the magic that had touched us too. Greyson and I couldn't wait to share the story with our children about the long line of incredible people who had come before them. But it was the menagerie of people we had picked up along the way that were our true family, as real and strong as any family could be. We'd been blessed.

The screenplay I'd been working on was in post-production with an award-winning lead actor and director. Nomination rumors were beginning to circulate. Maybe there'd be another case, this one in the living room, for a handsome golden bald man.

I was sitting outside. Greyson had run out. He didn't say where. I heard his car and moved from the deck to greet him. I rounded the house then stopped. Greyson was coming up the drive and with him was my dad. I was a forty-year-old woman, but when I saw my daddy I ran to him like a little kid. He caught me as I threw my arms around his neck.

He buried his face in my hair. "I'm sorry, baby girl."

I said through my tears. "You're here now."

GREYSON

I watched Alexis and her dad walking along the cliff, heads close as they got caught up on a lifetime of memories. He'd surprised me when he called to say he was coming. When he hadn't come for the birth of the twins, I assumed he never would. I was happy for Alexis that I'd been wrong about him.

Everyone was coming over later, a chance to meet Finn and a chance for him to meet the twins. Watching father and daughter, all that he had missed out on, I would be forever grateful that he'd given me the kick in the ass I needed. Our story wasn't without its ups and downs but when you fell asleep every night next to a woman who still made your body hum and your blood burn, when you still noticed new things about her, still felt that jump when she stepped in a room and still laughed at her jokes, that's a story of a life lived and loved. I didn't know what the future held, but I did know I would be at her side through all of it because there was nowhere else I wanted to be.

ALEXIS

My surprise was a trip to London, but it wasn't until we parked at the O2 arena that I learned the real surprise. Greyson brought me to London to see The Cure. Our seats were far better seats than our first concert. His hand was wrapped around mine the whole night and like our first concert, when I glanced over he was watching me not the concert. The first notes of "Just Like Heaven" echoed around the arena.

Greyson touched his lips to my ear. "Every time I hear this song I think of you. At sixteen when you changed my life and twenty-one when you walked back into it. On our wedding day, I've never seen you looking more beautiful. Cleaning the house, doing laundry and dancing." He grinned. "Carrying our children, watching you with your dad. Just like heaven. The lyrics couldn't be more accurate."

Unlike in our youth, it was me who kissed him. At sixteen I thought I understood what heaven was, but Greyson was right. It wasn't a moment, or even a feeling, it was a lifetime with the one person who saw all of you, the good and the bad, and who loved you because of your scars and baggage not despite them. With Greyson, we had found our own version of heaven.

Several weeks after the concert, I sat in the living room reading the book I had written about Greyson and me. I had it bound, the first part, but knew there would be other books because we were still a work in progress. I loved going back and remembering. I flipped the page, but it turned farther ahead to the place that was marked by a folded piece of paper. It was worn and yellow but I remembered vividly the day I got it. Carefully, I opened the worn page to read the single line written so long ago. Everything that had happened with us from then until now and still I got gooey-eyed looking at his note; I still felt the rush of nerves in my belly. I felt sixteen again.

I knew Greyson had joined me by the heat that sizzled along my nerves. He sat right next to me and brushed his lips over my cheek.

"The twins are napping, finally. The social worker called too, left a message, making sure we're ready for Jamie and Alex."

Greyson and I were going to foster two young boys. Our family was growing, but there was enough love to go around.

His smiling eyes looked down and saw what I held. He reached for it. "You kept it? That was so long ago." His gaze moved to me. "That first day in biology, what were you thinking?"

I grinned at the memory. "I had our lives planned, a romance to rival the greatest in history."

Tenderness moved into his expression. "How did we compare to your imagination?"

"Real life is so much better."

He took the book from me and placed it on the coffee table along with the note. "We've lived enough to fill two lifetimes."

Yes we had.

"We know each other as well as any two people ever could."

He wasn't wrong.

He brushed his thumb over my lips. "So why is it that even now when I kiss you it's like the first time?"

"Love."

He threaded his fingers through my hair. Everything we'd been through and still he looked at me like he couldn't get enough. Life wasn't like the fiction I wrote. It didn't follow a script; it didn't have a formula. Our story was still being written, unscripted, real, he kissed me, and so unbelievably beautiful.

343

The Beautifully series...
Beautifully Damaged
Beautifully Forgotten
Beautifully Decadent
Beautifully Played: Coming 2019

The Harrington Maine series...
Waiting for the One
Just Me

Lost Boys Series...
Devil You Know
Demon You Love: Coming 2018

AUTHOR

Shipwreck Series...
Elusive
Title to be announced: Coming 2018

Standalones
Our Unscripted Story
Savage: The Awakening of Lizzie Danton
His Light in the Dark
A Glimpse of the Dream
Always and Forever
Collecting the Pieces

Anthologies
Incognito
Ten Things I Love About You, A Love in the 90s Anthology

To learn more about what's coming, follow
L.A. Fiore…

https://www.facebook.com/l.a.fiore.publishing

https://www.facebook.com/groups/lafemmefabulousreaders

https://twitter.com/lafioreauthor

https://www.instagram.com/lafiore.publishing

Contact me through email at:
lafiore.publishing@gmail.com

CPSIA information can be obtained
at www.ICGtesting.com
Printed in the USA
LVOW13s0007060618
579763LV00008B/448/P